I Knew You

D1456914

Marianne Kane

ISBN 978-1-64003-962-9 (Paperback)
ISBN 978-1-64003-963-6 (Digital)

Copyright © 2018 Marianne Kane
All rights reserved
First Edition

All rights reserved. No part of this publication may be reproduced, distributed, or transmitted in any form or by any means, including photocopying, recording, or other electronic or mechanical methods without the prior written permission of the publisher. For permission requests, solicit the publisher via the address below.

Covenant Books, Inc.
11661 Hwy 707
Murrells Inlet, SC 29576
www.covenantbooks.com

Acknowledgments

I AM MOST THANKFUL TO GOD the Father, God the Son, and God the Holy Spirit for His many blessings and the gift of faith, which I pray for daily.

I also thank my husband, Howard Jenkinson, for his love, support, and patience; Father Carmen Perry, pastor of the Church of Saint Luke in Stroudsburg, Pennsylvania, for his service and his counsel on the abortion issue; the women (a special thank-you to Beverly) whom I spoke with who bore a child out of rape—those who gave the child up for adoption and those who kept and reared the child; and the children, now adults, who were conceived via rape and were either reared by their birth mother or by their adoptive family.

Chapter 1

THE WORLD OUTSIDE VITA'S BEDROOM window was alive. The pastel lavender sheers billowed like ripples in a pond with each breath of the spring breeze. The excitement of the children across the street could be heard as they took part in their Saturday ritual of skateboard competitions. The drone of the neighborhood lawn mowers meant the spring grass was growing at a fine clip. Birds abound chirped their melodies. One bird in particular, a small sparrow, made frequent visits nearby Vita's window. Vita named the sparrow Bebe. Bebe sang the same blissful song each morning. On this day, Bebe's notes blended nicely with those blitheful sounds of spring outside of Vita's window. Only Vita hadn't taken notice of Bebe. Inside of Vita's room was another world. She sat alone and felt alienated in a room filled with rays of sunshine. Vita's heart had sunk down into a dark hole of despair. She should have been out with her girlfriends doing what they did just about every Saturday, which usually included making up baton twirling and dancing routines. Her energy and will had been sucked out of her. Numbness, sadness, and confusion had taken residence in her heart. And yes, anger, let's not forget about the anger. The only sustained connection Vita had at the moment was with her buddy, Chaz, a three-year-old male pug, who had just entered into Vita's room. Chaz hopped up onto Vita's bed, sprawled himself out, and stretched his legs. He looked more like a cat. Sensing her sadness, he sprung up from his sprawled-out position and crawled over to where Vita sat, placed his head on her knees, and peered up with his huge protruding soulful black eyes so that the whites of his eyes shone underneath. He looked as melancholy as Vita felt.

Carmen was heavy-footed as she approached the almost-closed bedroom door. She gave two swift knocks on the door molding with the knuckles of her right hand. Before Vita could respond, Carmen stood in her daughter's room. Carmen tried to make eye contact with Vita, whose head hung down as she stroked Chaz. "I don't know where to start!" Carmen said hastily. She placed on the bed remnants of the pregnancy test packaging she had found in the trash. "I am just gonna come right out and say it. We are the only two females in the house, and this certainly does not belong to me. Vita, what is going on here? Have you been with boys?" Carmen continued with the rant, "You are hardly home by yourself. I'm almost always here . . . When have you had the chance to be with any boy? I don't understand why you wouldn't . . ." Carmen was rattling off words, not giving Vita a chance to speak.

"It's not mine!" Vita exclaimed. "I didn't want to have to tell you anything. One of my friends, she needed a place to take this pregnancy test, so I told her it would be okay for her to come here and do it."

"When, when was this, Vita? I have been home. And who? What friend? What friend of yours thinks she is pregnant?" responded Carmen.

Vita continued to fabricate her lie as quick as it could come into her head. "When I came home from school last Wednesday, you weren't here."

"Vita, I can't remember last Wednesday." Carmen paced and pondered as she tried to recount the past week. She consulted her calendar, which confirmed the fact that she had an oil change that day and then recalled having returned home that day about one hour after Vita's school dismissal. "How could you have possibly gotten home from school with your friend and taken the test before I had gotten home? Besides, I'm pretty sure those tests have to be done in the morning." Vita squirmed. "There was no one here with you when I had gotten home. Who was it? Who was here?" pressed Carmen.

"No one you know. Besides, I can't tell you. I promised her. That is her private business!" responded Vita.

"Vita, you are thirteen years old. Your friends and what your friends do in this house are my business! Now tell me who!"

"Mom, I can't . . . I just don't want to talk about it right now." Vita's body tightened as she continued to weave her web of lies. Chaz sensed the tenseness and decided to distance himself from the uncomfortable vibes. Animals always seem to seek out the more tranquil parts of their environment, and this was far from being "Tranquility Base."

Carmen persevered. "Vita, we need to talk. You girls are way too young to be concerning yourselves with sex. I know what you see on TV and in the movies and what you hear on the radio. You all think that it is okay to be 'doing it' 'cause you all really believe everyone else your age is. You think to be accepted and to be cool, you have to be having sex." Vita sat motionless as her mother tried to read her. "Sex is meant to be used between a man and a woman who share something special. One needs to be mature and grounded because once sex becomes part of the equation, you know, enters the relationship, all kinds of emotions and feelings become attached to that."

"Mom, you act like I am having sex, and I already told—"

"Well, are you, Vita?" Carmen abruptly interrupted.

"No!" Vita responded emphatically as she suddenly felt her insides drop and realized she had backed herself into a corner.

"As a relationship develops over time," Carmen continued as she emphasized the word "time," "and you get to know one another and it becomes apparent that you may be feeling something special for that person and vice versa, and then the relationship takes the turn for the serious. A sexual relationship, which is a commitment, may then begin. And you know, Vita, ideally, sex should wait until marriage." Vita rolled her eyes and sighed in boredom, having heard parts of this spiel before. "And the consequences, let's talk about the consequences of sex outside of marriage, like pregnancy, disease, and—" Carmen interrupted her train of thought with another thought. She shook her head and said, "Oh, and your friend, what about the test? Is she pregnant, Vita?"

"No. But like you said, Mom, we did that test in the afternoon, so maybe she will have to do it again," answered Vita.

"Well, Vita, I would like to speak to the mother because she has got to know what is going on so she can help her daughter," said Carmen.

"Mom, stay out of it! I can't say anything more, okay! Please leave me alone!"

Several seconds of silence transpired before Carmen gently laid her hand on her daughter's lap. In a quiet and relaxed voice, she told Vita how much she loved her and just wanted the best for her. "I'm sorry that sometimes I seem to come on strong. Maybe now is not the time to discuss things, but, Vita, I want you to be able to come to me," Carmen paused and then added, "with anything." Carmen suggested that perhaps they would try to sit down and talk about such girl matters tomorrow. "We need to do this, Vita." Carmen slipped out of Vita's room, and before she could close the door a bit so as to give Vita the privacy she desired, Chaz scooted back into Vita's room. Then Carmen slowly closed the door so that it was slightly ajar, enough to let a slit of sunshine fall onto the hallway floor.

Dinnertime was mellow and subdued. Brendan, the master griller that he was, had thrown some marinated steaks onto the grill and a couple of hotdogs on for Vita. Vita did not as yet appreciate the fine taste of a steak grilled to perfection—the medium rare melt-in-your-mouth-type steak. Carmen was working on one of her creative salads, never seeming to replicate the same salad twice. Needless to say, Vita had not as yet developed an appreciation for salads or anything green for that matter either.

Nettie—Vita's grandmother and Carmen's mother—busied herself with the slicing of the watermelon as she monitored the time that the tater tots were baking in the oven. Tater tots and watermelon were the kinds of food up Vita's alley. All four gathered at the picnic table in the screened-in porch to eat. Make that five as Chaz managed to show himself for dinnertime as usual. After they filled their plates from the array of food on the table, Carmen and Nettie said grace aloud. Brendan usually bowed his head and rested it on his clasped hands as the ladies prayed. Vita usually chimed in, but this evening as she had been doing lately, she prayed in the same manner as her father. As usual, Chaz would use his soulful black protruding eyes to coax a tidbit from one of the diners. Chaz knew just how to move his eyes as he would ardently follow a piece of meat on the tip of the fork from the plate to the diner's mouth. As Chaz was an integral part of the family, he ate his hard dog food from his personalized ceramic bowl not far from the table. Of course, he did get a treat or two of a steak tidbit of which he felt entitled to. Vita had picked out that heavy clay ceramic dog food bowl while on a vacation to Arizona. The bowl was beautifully handcrafted by the Navajo Indians. Vita felt Chaz had been deserving of it. She even had his name painted on the bowl. Chaz had stayed with Brendan's brother, Vita's Uncle Corbin, who Chaz was not particularly fond of. Brendan, Carmen, and Nettie could not understand why Chaz was never comfortable with Corbin, but Vita knew exactly why.

Conversation was not at a premium. Brendan, Carmen, and Nettie each tried their hand at making small talk. It was apparent that Vita was in a melancholy way, putting a damper on dinner that evening. Neither her parents nor her grandmother wanted to provoke her into talking, knowing how precocious a thirteen-year-old could be. "Mom, can I go over to Chelsea's house for a sleepover tonight?"

"Brendan, would that be all right?" Carmen said as she peered over at Brendan.

"Dad, paleeeze . . ." pleaded Vita.

"Sure, honey. Is it okay with Mrs. Hartman?"

Vita nodded. Carmen was somewhat relieved that Vita was out of her funk enough to want to do anything at all. It was a good idea if Vita took her mind off whatever was ailing her. Carmen certainly had her own ideas about what might be troubling Vita, and those ideas brought Carmen waves of great apprehension.

"Brendan, I can take Vita over to Chelsea's house on the way to dropping Mom off," said Carmen.

"Oh, Carmen, would you mind popping in with me? I just need a hand getting my curtain rod up in the living room," Nettie asked.

"Sure, Mom."

Brendan suggested that Carmen spend some time over her mother's house as he had wanted to work on his painting. "I was in the office all day trying to tie up the loose ends and would just love to sit down and paint a bit," he added. Brendan enjoyed dabbling in watercolors with his forte being water landscapes. He found this to be a way to offload some of the stress that came with being a partner in a busy law practice with his brother Corbin.

"Sounds like a plan to me," Carmen said as she realized that she would likely be spending the evening with her mother, engaged in a serious conversation about a serious matter that could not wait.

Vita stuffed some clothes into a backpack and pulled her lavender slumber bag down from the top shelf of her closet. "What's the matter, Chazzy?" Vita questioned softly. Chaz sat on Vita's bed and watched as she packed haphazardly. He cocked his head from side to side as his little quizzical dog face seemed to say, "Leaving me? Whoever will I sleep with then?"

"Love ya, Chazzy," said Vita as she planted a kiss atop of Chaz's rounded pug head and quickly sidestepped past the bed with slumber bag and backpack in hand.

Carmen had just gotten off the phone with Mrs. Hartman to confirm the sleepover plans as Vita bounded down the stairs with sleeping bag and backpack in tow. "Got your toothbrush, Veet?" reminded Carmen.

"Yup. And, Mom, can I take a box of brownie mix with me? Maybe Chelsea and I could make some brownies tonight." Carmen okayed the brownie mix with the stipulation that the two girls ask permission from Chelsea's mom before commencing with the baking.

The three generations of girls piled into Carmen's BMW sedan with the first stop being the Hartman house. "Have a good time, sweet pea," Nettie said as Vita exited from the passenger side back door of the car. "I will, Gram."

"Enjoy, Vita. Love you! And call me in the morning when you need me to pick you up. We'll have to allow enough time to get ready for church tomorrow," Carmen added.

"Do I have to go?" chided Vita.

"Yes, Vita. You have to go. We will plan to make noon Mass tomorrow, okay? See ya." Carmen waved bye to her daughter.

"See ya!" Vita yelled back as she was already halfway up the driveway.

Carmen waited until the door of the Hartman home opened. Karen Hartman waved her hand, signaling that Vita was safe inside.

Chapter 2

NETTIE'S SMALL HOUSE WAS IDEAL for her. She had downsized and moved into an over-fifty-five adult community two years earlier. It had been difficult for Nettie to move out of the house that she had reared her three children in. Her beloved husband of thirty-five years, Anthony, had died unexpectedly five years ago. Nettie desperately missed Tony. Their house with all its memories had been a constant reminder to Nettie of times gone by. She hardly had left the house that first year after Tony had passed. After much thought, Nettie and her three children—Carmen, Tony, and Frank—decided it best for Nettie to move into a smaller home with new surroundings. This community had an uplifting effect when one drove through it. Like Nettie's, most of the homes were two attached units forming one residence. Each unit had two bedrooms and two baths. The small yards were always neatly manicured. The talented landscaper hired by the homeowners' association left his trademark imprint tastefully on all the outside areas. The homes were all a pastel color with white trim. The two units that made up Nettie's building were painted an airy lemon yellow.

Carmen and Nettie entered through the front door into a splash of pink and olive green, two colors that Italians love to put together. On the living room mantle were her true treasures—pictures of her husband, children, and grandchildren through various stages of life. Over the mantle hung a large oval-shaped frame that held a lovely portrait of Tony and Nettie taken at their thirty-year wedding anniversary.

Vita looked strikingly similar to her grandfather, Anthony DiAngelo. The blue eyes, a trait of many a Sicilian, had been passed down to Vita. Vita's eye shape and her smile were no doubt that of Grandpa Tony. Every time Nettie looked at Vita, she felt a sort of comfort. It would be unfair to say that Vita was the favorite of her six grandchildren, but nonetheless, Vita held a special place in her grandmother's heart.

The spare bedroom closet held Nettie's most valued treasures from her life with Tony and her children. Boxes were stacked neatly for easy access. The room had a twin bed, which had been frequently used by Vita when she was eleven and twelve years of age. Vita would spend the night at her grandmothers on occasion when Brendan and Carmen went out. A favorite pastime would be to go through all the memorabilia.

Nettie and Carmen had the curtain rod up in no time. Carmen was quite adept at window treatments and had a good eye for placement of curtains and dealing with the hardware that comes with such things. "I'll make us some tea. How about some biscotti, Carmen? What do you want to watch?"

Carmen didn't even hear her mother. Her mind was off somewhere else as this was the first time that she had allowed her mind to wander since dinnertime.

"Carmen, is tea okay?" Nettie repeated.

"Yeah, Ma, that's fine."

Nettie sensed the distant Carmen. "Are you okay? You know we don't have to watch anything if you don't feel—"

Carmen interrupted Nettie, "Mom . . . Mom," Carmen hesitated, not sure how to begin this particular conversation.

"Carmen, what's going on? I could sense that something was not right at dinner. Are you and Brendan arguing?"

"No, Mom. It's Vita. I have to talk to you about Vita," responded Carmen.

"Well, I have noticed that Vita has been keeping to herself the past few months, but I figured it was the age. You know, the hormones going overboard," assumed Nettie.

They were interrupted by a screaming teapot. Nettie poured the hot water into two tea cups, each with a tea bag inside.

"Mom, I think Vita is pregnant." Those words that Carmen found so difficult to utter just seemed to spill out of her mouth as if there were no holding them back any longer. That statement cut the air like a knife.

Nettie looked confused. "What? What do you mean?" Carmen looked at her mother and shook her head. "What are you saying?" Nettie questioned as she put her hand to her mouth in disbelief. She then laid her hand on Carmen's wrist.

"I think she is pregnant, Mom. I am almost sure of it." Carmen proceeded to describe to Nettie what had transpired earlier that day, following the discovery of the remnants of the pregnancy test kit in the garbage.

"How do you know that what Vita is telling you isn't the truth? She could be dealing with this knowledge of her friend's situation. She may be her friend's only confidant, and that is a lot to hold in. Who do you suspect it is?"

"That's just it, Ma—I can't think of any of Vita's friends to whom this could have happened to, and Vita absolutely refuses to open up to me about who it is," Carmen said. "Besides," continued Carmen as she held the tea cup between her two hands, drawing the cup slowly to her lips to sip, "I have noticed that Vita is getting, you know, chestier." She quickly put the cup down on its matching saucer and motioned with her hands, placing them about four inches in front of her own chest.

"Carmen, girls are developing sooner these days. You know she could just be uncomfortable with all the body changes and mood swings that are going on. Don't you remember that you used to lock yourself up in your bedroom for hours when you were in your early teens?" Carmen gave a slight nod and a half smile. "Look, Carmen, have you discussed your concerns with Brendan?"

"You mean my suspicions? No, I have not. I don't even know how I would even approach the subject with him. I think he would just fly off the handle and come down hard on Vita." Carmen took a deep breath in and let it out in one big sigh. She then asked her mother,

"Mom, do you think you could be there with me when I approach Vita on this matter? She won't be apt to be so confrontational."

Nettie assured her daughter that she would do whatever it took to help out and asked Carmen when she planned on approaching Vita on the matter. Carmen suggested after church tomorrow. Carmen and Nettie could pick Vita up from the Hartmans' and swing by the house for Vita to change into appropriate clothes for church. The four of them could make the noontime Mass if Brendan decided to come. Brendan was not in the habit of going to Mass on Sunday, which had become a sore point between Carmen and her husband. Vita would often try to get out of going to church, stating the fact that her dad did not attend most Sundays. So tomorrow it would be the three females and possibly Brendan. No matter what, the plan was for Carmen and Nettie to have a sit-down discussion with Vita sometime tomorrow after they got home from church. The two women did not plan for Brendan to be part of this initial discussion.

Chapter 3

OVER AT THE HARTMAN HOUSE, Vita and Chelsea savored what was left of the brownie batter as the aroma of chocolate permeated the kitchen. They set the timer for fifty minutes, cleaned the utensils, and then went upstairs to Chelsea's bedroom to try on some clothes while the brownies baked.

The girls had the whole evening planned. The brownies with milk would go deliciously well with the movie Chelsea's mom had rented for them. Before that though, the girls would raid Chelsea's older sister's room to try on some of Danielle's cool clothes. Danielle was seventeen and out with her friends. Chelsea and Vita, as they had done on many occasions, invaded Danielle's closet and dresser for a quick shopping spree. The borrowed items were swiftly carried out of Danielle's room and piled on top of the bed in Chelsea's bedroom. Chelsea was a bit taller than her older sister minus the curves. Vita was slightly shorter than Danielle but now had the curves. With Chelsea's bedroom door shut and locked and Janet Jackson music blaring loudly, the girls had a blast trying on various articles of clothing from Danielle's wardrobe and modeling it for each other.

It didn't take long for Chelsea to notice what Carmen had noticed about her daughter. "Oh my god, Vita . . . You look so good in that!" referring to a form-fitting camisole top Vita had tried on. Chelsea continued, "Like when did you get those boobs, girl? I can't walk next to you . . . Look at me . . . I have nothing."

"What do you mean?" Vita questioned naively, truly not realizing herself how much her bust size had indeed increased.

"C'mon, Veet, you look better than Danielle does in that top," chided Chelsea.

"Ya think?" Vita responded somewhat proudly. Vita had temporarily shelved her emotions. She had become very good at repressing her feelings. For the time being, Vita was having a good time, caught up in the moment with her best friend. They squealed with delight as each girl took a turn modeling a new outfit as they grooved to the beat of the music on the Janet Jackson CD.

All of a sudden, there was a loud rap on the door. "Chelsea, the timer's gone off!" yelled Mrs. Hartman.

"Sorry, Mom. I'll be right out," blurted Chelsea.

Mrs. Hartman went downstairs to turn the oven off. The girls quickly got into their own clothes and stuffed all of Danielle's clothes under the bed to be dealt with later. They had done the fashion thing many times before and had it down to a science when it came to returning Danielle's clothes back to their proper resting places.

Chelsea and Vita bounded down the stairs and into the kitchen to get the brownies out of the oven.

"You two have to be more responsible when you are baking. I don't mind you girls baking, but the next time, I want you to remain in the kitchen until the brownies are done. Okay?" reprimanded Chelsea's mother.

Chelsea used a small steak knife to test the doneness of the brownies. "Done to perfection!"

Vita began to open the can of frosting. Mrs. Hartman advised them to wait at least an hour before icing the brownies.

"Oh, man!" declared Chelsea. "They smell sooo good! Can't we have a taste?"

Mrs. Hartman cut off a long one-inch thick edge along the side of the pan and cut it into smaller pieces, allowing the girls to each take a half of teaspoon of the frosting to top the morsels. There is nothing more satisfying than a deluge of rich chocolate to coat the palette. Coupled with a small glass of cold milk and the girls were in heaven. And as with most women who cannot resist anything chocolate, Mrs. Hartman popped one of those delightful bits into her mouth. It is a given that the female gender and chocolate are a natural combo. Mrs.

Hartman motioned the girls over to her as she savored the delicacy. "Would you mind if Denny watched the movie with you?"

"Mom, do you really think that he's gonna like it?" Chelsea questioned.

"Chels, it's okay. Why not?" Vita quickly said.

"You know Denny is just happy to hang out with the two of you," added Karen Hartman.

Denny, a Down syndrome child with the face and disposition of a cherub, was content to just be among family and friends. He was such a sweet and social little fellow. Denny was mainstreamed into the third-grade elementary class. A teacher's aide assisted Denny with his schoolwork, and his classmates treated him as one of them because he was one of them. Denny at that moment, as if on cue, ran into the kitchen. With his straight strawberry blond bangs poking into his bright blue eyes and his always rosy red cheeks aglow, he squealed, "Brownies goody. Brownies! I want one. Okay? Now." So Mrs. Hartman made Denny another one of those delightful chocolate brownie morsels. He snatched it out of her hand before she could place it on a plate. Mrs. Hartman gently scolded Denny and reminded him of his manners. "I sorry, Mom. More. More please," said Denny as he devoured the treat.

"We're going to let the brownies cool so we can put icing on them a little later, Denny. How about watching a movie with Chelsea and Vita? And I have popcorn coming."

Denny did his little dance as he wiggled from side to side and then skipped off into the family room and asked, "Chels and Vita gonna have some too, right, Mom?" Little Denny always seemed to be concerned about others. Vita always noticed this about this sweet little boy who seemed to endear her.

Vita popped the movie *Honey, I Shrunk the Kids* into the VCR and readied it for showing as Denny looked on. He bounced his excited self up and down on the couch in anticipation. Chelsea brought in a large bowl of popcorn and filled the four smaller bowls with popcorn, making sure that each bowl was spilling over with what she thought was a decent portion. Mrs. Hartman had decided to watch the movie too. Mr. Hartman was away on a business trip and would not be back until the middle of the next week. Danielle would be home by her eleven-thirty curfew for Saturday night. And so it was the four of them having a comfy family night of sorts. The plan was to ice the brownies during an intermission halfway through the movie.

Before the movie began, Chelsea ran upstairs. "I'll be right back." She ran into her room and quickly, neatly, and methodically returned Danielle's clothes to where they belonged. She returned downstairs wearing her favorite pair of slippers, the ones with a huge Tweety Bird head mounted atop of each slipper.

"Honestly, Chelsea, your gonna break your neck with those things," warned her mother as Chelsea bounded back down the stairs into the family room.

And as planned, the four of them watched the movie with a break midway to frost the brownies and indulge themselves with one of the best combinations in the world—freshly baked rich chocolate brownies and ice-cold milk as they sat and watched the second half of the film. The kids were allowed two brownies each with as much milk needed to wash them down with. Two frosted brownies were placed on a plate covered with Saran Wrap so Danielle could have a midnight snack when she got home.

After the movie, Mrs. Hartman readied Denny for bed. The girls gathered up the bowls, dishes, and glasses from the family room, rinsed them off, and placed them in the dishwasher. They got ready to retire into Chelsea's bedroom for gossip time. Chelsea's mother would stay up until she knew Danielle was home safe and sound. One of Danielle's friend's older sisters was going to drop Danielle home.

The girls lay on Chelsea's queen-sized bed, each in their own slumber bag. After spending much time rating the boys in their classes from zero to five, with five being absolute perfection and zero being a dud not worthy of a rating, the conversation shifted quite abruptly. Vita had already had her mind on questioning Chelsea about little Denny. "Chels, can I ask you something and you promise not to get mad?"

"Yeah—I guess. What is it?" Chelsea responded.

"Well, your brother, Denny"—Vita paused as she tried to choose the right words—"Denny . . . Did your parents know how Denny would be? I mean, you know, like did they know he would be . . ." Vita paused once more.

"Different?" Chelsea said, filling in the gap.

"Yeah—different," said Vita.

"You mean when my mom was pregnant with Denny, did my parents know that the baby was going to have Down syndrome?"

"Yes. Did they know?" Vita pushed for the answer.

"I was six when Denny was born, so to me, he was just my baby brother. My mom and my dad told me later on when I was about nine or ten that Denny had certain problems and that some things, I mean many things, would be hard for him. Then when I started learning more about Down syndrome and Down syndrome children, I found out about those tests that pregnant women can have and asked my mom if she had one. She did. My mom and dad did know that Denny would have it—Down syndrome I mean."

Vita wanted to pursue with the next question. As she pondered on how to ask the question, Chelsea sensed where Vita was going with this and added, "And you want to know what? Why my parents decided not to have an abortion?"

"How'd you know that was what I wanted to know? I feel strange asking you about that," Vita said to her friend.

"My mom and dad said it was never an option. That Denny was a present from God . . . that we all are. To me, he is my baby brother, and I just can't imagine him not being here in our family," answered Chelsea.

"Well. I do love your brother Denny. He is just so sweet," said Vita.

"I know," Chelsea said as she tilted her head and smiled. "You know, he is so lovable. I just can't ever get that mad at him, but sometimes he really does annoy me. But that's because I think that is what little brothers are supposed to do."

Chelsea was curious at what sparked these questions from Vita. Vita recounted to Chelsea some of her experiences at a prolife rally that she had accompanied her mom to. Carmen had participated in the March for Life the past four years, and Vita and Nettie had gone with her for the past two years. Vita told Chelsea of a sign that a girl their age had held. It had two big photos on the sign. One was an ultrasound picture of a baby in the womb, and the other was of a little girl with Down syndrome about three years old with blond curls. In big letters, the sign had said, "Meet my little sister, Arielle. We loved her from day one."

Chelsea asked, "Can I come with you and your mom next year if you go?"

Vita, sounding unsure, said, "Sure. I guess if we go . . ." Vita felt her emotions begin to swirl.

It was too dark in the room for Chelsea to see Vita's worrisome expression. She broke the silence with a concerned tone in her voice, "Vita, what is the matter?"

Vita tried to shake herself free of the sinking feelings of desperation and said, "I guess I'm just real tired. Anyway, yeah, of course, you can come if your mom says it's okay. Maybe she would like to come too. It is always in January."

"That would be cool. Why is it always in January?" asked Chelsea.

Vita explained to her that, as far as she knew, the March for Life in Washington DC was always on January 22 as that was the day abortion became legal in the United States in the early seventies.

Vita waited until she was able to tell that Chelsea had drifted off to sleep. When Chelsea's breathing had become loud, deep, and rhythmic, Vita figured that her friend was in a deep slumber. Vita quietly unzipped her sleeping bag and gingerly wriggled out of it and off the bed. There was a small night-light on in the room in the far corner. She crawled on the floor and groped her way along to where she had put her backpack. Vita stuck her arm down into her backpack and felt the familiar form of her diary. She had decided to take it with her, not wanting to leave it behind in her bedroom just in case her mom decided to go snooping. Vita nuzzled herself into the corner by the night-light and listened to make sure that her best friend was still sound asleep. Once she had assured herself that Chelsea's continued deep and rhythmic breathing meant just that, she brought

Chapter 4

Vita, Chelsea, Danielle, and Denny had been playing hide-and-seek at the insistence of Denny when the familiar honk of the Bimmer horn was heard outside.

"My mom's here. Sorry, Denny, I've got to come out of my spot," Vita said as she emerged from behind the long drapes that hung from the dining room window. She ran into the kitchen to thank Mrs. Hartman and then gathered her backpack and sleeping bag in the foyer by the front door. "Thanks, Chels . . . I'll call ya later. See ya, Danielle. Bye-bye, Denny," and she patted Denny's strawberry blond head before she headed out the door.

Carmen was already dressed for church. Vita slung her backpack and sleeping bag in the back seat and then got in the front seat with her mother.

"Did you have a good time, Veet?"

"Oh yeah," said Vita, "and we actually got some sleep too. I'm stuffed. Mrs. Hartman made these to-kill-for pancakes. She made some with chocolate chips in them and some with blueberries in them. And we had whipped cream too!" exclaimed Vita.

"Sounds like my kind of breakfast," joked Carmen. Carmen told Vita how Chaz would not settle down. Apparently, he went to sleep on Vita's empty bed but, somewhere during the night, decided he needed some human companionship. He had gone into Brendan and Carmen's bedroom and slept on the floor at the foot of their bed. Carmen had not seen Chaz lying there and tripped over him early that morning but managed to stay on her feet.

When they had gotten home, Vita had about fifteen minutes to change into some nicer clothes for church. Her mother did not permit her to wear blue jeans to church. She put on a pair of white denim pants, which were deemed acceptable by her mom, and a dark pink lightweight pullover sweater. Vita noticed how much harder zipping the pants had become and had to lie down to get the zipper up. She sat up feeling very uncomfortable and decided to leave the snap atop the zipper open as her pink top was long enough to cover it. Vita slipped her feet into her white Candies as she declared that she was ready to go.

Brendan decided he was going to go to church today, which made Carmen a happy lady. Carmen seemed content when her husband, daughter, and mother were with her for Sunday Mass. The Malloys got into Carmen's car with Brendan doing the driving. Brendan had a sports car, a brand-new black Nissan 300ZX, which would be too tight of a fit for the four of them, even though there was a shelf of a back seat in the coupe.

Nettie was already outside her house waiting when the Malloy car pulled up. Carmen moved to the back seat with Vita so that her mom could sit up front. Nettie always thought of Brendan as a third son. And Brendan was quite fond of his mother-in-law. He felt closer to her than he did to his own mother. Brendan felt comforted by Nettie's nurturing ways. Brendan and Corbin had lost their dad when Brendan was fifteen and Corbin was eighteen. Their father, Corbin Michael Malloy Sr., was an attorney. He had died at the young age of forty-six after suffering for a short time with lung cancer. He had smoked entirely too much for too long. The boys had been close to their father and missed him desperately. They were heartbroken to have him leave them so early in their lives but were thankful that he did not have to suffer very long with the debilitating illness. Especially sad was that their dad had passed away a month before Corbin graduated from high school. Corbin's high school graduation was bittersweet as the thing he wanted most was for his father to be there. Corbin would be entering Rutgers University that fall to start his freshman year as a prelaw student. Immediately after Corbin started at the university, Mrs. Malloy—the boys' mother—

had started going out more with friends and dating. Their parents' marriage had not been a particularly strong one.

Right after their father passed away, Brendan and Corbin spent that summer with each other as much as possible as Corbin would be going away to college in the fall. Corbin allowed Brendan to join him and his friends on camping trips and to the beach at the Jersey shore. In fact, once Corbin went away to college, he came home every other weekend so that he could be with his brother and tried to attend many of the basketball games and tennis matches Brendan had played in on those weekends. Brendan never forgot that. Corbin looked after him as their mom seemed to indulge herself in her selfish wants.

Mrs. Malloy eventually married a man three years later, whom both Corbin and Brendan despised. He had moved into the Malloy house, making it his own. Both boys had felt betrayed by their mother's decision to allow this man to move in. Brendan luckily had already graduated high school when the stepfather had moved in. He and Corbin, who had been home during summer break, had only to get through that summer before both would be away at college. Brendan would be starting as a freshman at Seton Hall University, and Corbin, a college senior, was planning on attending Fordham Law School.

Brendan had started dating Carmen DiAngelo while they were both students at Seton Hall University. He used to love going back home with Carmen, who happened to be from the same part of New Jersey, with their homes only being a few miles away from each other. Carmen's parents, Anthony and Antoinette DiAngelo, always made him feel at home.

Vita, Nettie, Carmen, and Brendan filed into the third row of the center section of pews. This was where Carmen and Nettie chose to sit for every Mass given that space was available. They had claimed unspoken ownership of that particular spot over the years. It was funny to see how certain churchgoers sat in the same spot in the same pew, week after week. If someone else was in the predeclared spot, that intruder would most certainly get an unwelcome glance, never quite understanding their infraction. Usually, these were folks who did not attend Mass regularly or never took notice of where some of the regular attendees sat. The white-haired elderly ladies, whose hair was so white that it was blue, held primary ownership as they were the daily Mass attendees, praying the Rosary fervently before each Mass.

The celebrant for the Sunday noon Mass was Father John O'Brien, the pastor of the Church of Our Lady. Father John was a merry but stern red-faced man in his middle fifties. His homilies were quite meaningful, short, and to the point, many times moving Carmen to tears. One of the older priests, Father Sledinski, near retirement, gave long barely audible homilies. Brendan referred to Father Sledinski as Father Windbag. The readings included Jeremiah: chapter 1 and Psalm 139:13–16. Carmen's heart panged at the words from Jeremiah: "Before I formed you in the womb, I knew you. Before you were born, I dedicated you." The burning pain within Carmen continued as Father John read the words of Psalm 139: "You formed my inmost being; you knit me in my mother's womb. I praise you, so wonderfully you made me; wonderful are your works! My very self you knew; my bones were not hidden from you, When I was being made in secret, fashioned as in the depths of the earth. Your eyes foresaw my actions; in your book all are written down; my days were shaped, before one came to be."

Carmen felt a pained sadness in her heart. She wondered if these words somehow penetrated Vita but knew most likely they would just sail over Vita's head. Carmen became distracted with thoughts of how she was going to have "the talk" with Vita. Somehow, she would have to be able to get Vita to come along with her and Nettie out of earshot of Brendan. Perhaps, Carmen thought, it would be better to bring Vita over to Nettie's house only because if there was going to be a crying and yelling scene, who knew how Brendan would react if Carmen's suspicions were correct.

In her mind, Carmen already had Vita pregnant, and if that was the reality, this would be something that would have to be dealt with ever so carefully with Brendan. Carmen's thoughts had taken her from the gospel reading and homily. She was brought back out of her daydreaming with the Nicene Creed: "We believe in one God, the Father the Almighty, maker of heaven and earth . . ."

After she returned to the pew following Holy Communion, Carmen buried her face in her hands as she customarily did after receiving the Holy Eucharist and prayed to the Lord to give her the right words in speaking with her daughter later on that day.

Mass was dismissed at one o'clock in the afternoon. Brendan suggested that the family go out to eat at Hamilton's Steakhouse, a favorite of the Malloy clan. They would sometimes go for an early afternoon Sunday dinner once a month or so.

Vita couldn't believe how hungry she was, especially after the filling breakfast she had only a few hours before at the Hartman house. "Dad, remind me to get a doggie bag for Chaz."

"We always do, Veet."

As they rode in the car on the way to the restaurant, Carmen, in the back seat with Vita, patted her daughter's lap and then kept her hand on her daughter's knee. Nettie would probably spend part of the afternoon at the Malloy household after dinner, so Carmen thought she would have Vita accompany her when she dropped Nettie back home. Nettie's house would be the opportune place to talk without having the worry of Brendan being in the vicinity. As Carmen sat in the back seat with Vita, her hand still on Vita's knee, she came to the realization that this day could potentially be the last normal day this family would have for some time—the calm before the storm.

Hamilton's was a restaurant specializing in American fare. The best Italian food was made at home, especially when Nettie was at the helm. Everyone seemed to go for their favorites that afternoon, not venturing to try something new. This meant that Chaz would dine like a king tonight as there would be some prime rib specifically set aside for him from Carmen's and Nettie's platters. Vita's usual was a cheeseburger with onion rings. The prime rib at Hamilton's was the melt-in-your-mouth-like-butter prime rib. Brendan went for his usual surf and turf, and as always, a double order of portobello mushrooms stuffed with crabmeat appetizer was ordered.

Brendan reminded all that it was the beginning of May, and it was time to think about where the family would go on summer vacation. They always liked trying new destinations. Nettie had been going along too for the past three years. Beginning of May, Carmen thought to herself that meant next Sunday will be Mother's Day already. Brendan threw out some suggestions for summer vacation, including an Alaskan cruise. Brendan wondered why Carmen was not fired up like she would usually get when it came to vacation talk.

In the recent years, Vita was allowed to bring a friend along, especially if the trip was only a week long. Vita suggested a dude ranch vacation with horseback riding, not giving a thought about her present predicament. "Gram, would you ever get up on a horse?"

"Maybe I would, Vita . . . just maybe I would." Everyone chuckled.

Carmen tried to push her negative thoughts out of her head for the time being. Her family was gathered together, and they were enjoying quality time. That was all that mattered. "So," Carmen chimed in, "Veet, who would you want to ask to come along this summer?"

"Depends on where we go, Mom, but probably I would ask Chelsea first."

They left the restaurant in a jovial mood, each claiming to have had eaten entirely too much and ready for a nap. Vita made sure she kept the white bag with the Styrofoam containers that held the leftovers straight on her lap during the drive home. She couldn't wait to surprise Chaz with such delectable treats. As the car pulled into the driveway, Chaz—upon recognizing the familiar hum of the car's motor—jumped up onto the couch to peer out the window. He began to bark with anticipation as he saw Vita exit the car with the very familiar white bag. Chaz was at the front door before Brendan had even gotten out of the car.

It was already three thirty in the afternoon, which meant that the New York Yankee game was likely to be in the middle innings. Brendan, as full as he was, grabbed a beer out of the refrigerator and parked himself on the sofa to watch the rest of the game.

Vita had one happy pug trailing on her heels, making little circles at her feet. Once in the kitchen, Vita commanded Chaz to sit nicely. He promptly obeyed. Chaz cocked his head from side to side as his little curled tail wagged as best as that little curled tail could wag. He kept lifting both front paws off the floor as he let out yelps of excitement. "Here ya go, Chazzy! Good boy!" Vita exclaimed as she emptied the contents of one of the containers into his Navajo ceramic bowl, which sat atop of a large plastic placemat decorated with colorful paw prints and bones.

"Chazzy, slow down. You want to enjoy that, don't you?" Carmen said when she looked over upon hearing the loud slurping sounds.

"All done?" Vita exclaimed as Chaz looked up with his large protruding dark brown eyes. His tongue smacked his lips, and he wore an expression that seemed to say, "I'm ready for more!"

Vita was in good spirits as denial had sprung back into action. She wanted to get the rest of her homework done so she could call Chelsea and maybe Michelle later. Vita preferred to do most of her homework while sitting on her bed. That was how she felt most comfortable, and that was where much of the schoolwork was efficiently done. Chaz, of course, would plop himself down on the bed out of range of the books and papers. He made like he was Vita's right-hand man executive assistant Chaz Malloy.

In the meantime, Nettie and Carmen had sat down at the kitchen table. Not a word had been spoken yet concerning the talk that was to take place later. The look between Carmen and Nettie confirmed that each other knew what was forthcoming. Carmen opened her rather large handbag. She held the top of the handbag wide open to show her mother the contents inside. "Take a look." Nettie's eyes honed in on the scraps of a blue-and-white small cardboard box with the letters "P R E G N" clearly visible on one of the pieces. The word "TEST" could easily be seen on an adjacent piece.

"Mom, how am I going to talk to Vita? Where do I begin? I want her to be able to be honest with me."

Nettie replied, "The right words will come, Carmen. You will see. I know you prayed on it at church." Carmen nodded. Nettie continued, "God will provide you with the proper words. You have to trust in that. I will be there right next to you."

"Thanks, Mom. Maybe we will head to your house around six thirty. I figure I'll make a light salad at five thirty for anyone who wants it," said Carmen. Italians were always thinking about the next meal, even after just having eaten. Brendan would likely be hunting around the kitchen for something to gnaw on in a little while.

It was six twenty in the evening by the kitchen clock when Carmen announced to Vita by yelling at the bottom of the stairs that led up to the bedrooms, "Vita, we're going to drop Grandma off. You can take Chazzy along if you'd like." Carmen knew that, by suggesting that Chaz go along for the ride, Vita surely would not hesitate to go. More important, Carmen knew the emotional support that Chaz would provide to Vita. Chaz lifted his head and perked his ears up when he heard his name.

"Chaz, you want to go for a ride in the car?" Vita said, raising the intonation of her voice at the end of her sentence. The two buzz words being "ride" and "car" set Chaz into a circling frenzy on the bed. "Okay, Mom. I'll be right down!" yelled Vita. Communicating in the two-story Malloy house was usually done via the shouting method when each of the speakers was on a different level of the house, including from the basement to the second floor.

Vita snatched Chaz's leash off the hook on the foyer wall, confirmation to the pug that indeed he had heard those two buzz words correctly. Carmen left Brendan a note on the kitchen table as to where they were going. Brendan had fallen asleep on the couch after finishing the salad. A note, however, was not necessary as Brendan was familiar with the Sunday evening routine of taking Nettie back to her house with Carmen and Vita staying awhile, but Carmen knew they might be at Nettie's longer than usual.

Vita walked Chaz on the front lawn so that he could do his business before getting into the car. Nettie got into the front seat of the Bimmer with Carmen while Vita and a happy Chaz sat in the back seat.

Chapter 5

NETTIE BUSIED HERSELF BY MAKING a pitcher of ice tea the old-fashioned way. She already had the brewed tea refrigerated from that morning and proceeded to add and stir in the sugar, honey, lemon, and her secret ingredient, the peppermint leaves. She had peppermint plants growing in one of her window flower boxes, and it was those peppermint leaves that gave Nettie's ice tea its uniqueness. She even used a touch of peppermint leaves in her gravy. Gravy is what Italians like to call their tomato sauce. If you were not part of the immediate family, you were not privy to know of that one special ingredient that flavored Nettie's gravy just so.

Nettie could see Carmen out of the corner of her eye who sat at the kitchen table with her forehead leaning on her index and middle finger of her right hand. She knew Carmen was contemplating on how to approach the subject of the pregnancy test kit.

Vita had plopped herself on Nettie's living room couch. She surfed the channels and finally settled on MTV. Chaz was in investigation mode as he scurried from one place to another, sniffing this and sniffing that, basically wherever his nose would take him.

Carmen looked over at Nettie. She sensed her mother's watchful eye. "Mom, I am not knowing what to do here. Maybe Vita was telling me the truth."

"Having second thoughts?" questioned Nettie.

"I suppose not. I wish I were. I just have a feeling that something *is* going on. And if my suspicions are right, I cannot afford not to have this discussion with her." Nettie was in agreement. "It's just that," Carmen continued, "it's just that I thought Vita just got over her period a week or so ago. You know. I had seen the rolled-up sanitary pads wrapped in toilet paper in the bathroom garbage. Plus the fact that she was complaining of cramps." Carmen tapped her foot and sighed as she looked up at Nettie for some input.

"Well, Carmen, you are right about not putting this off any longer. I can tell it has been eating at you, and if your suspicions are right, we do not have time on our side," said Nettie as she placed her hand on Carmen's shoulder and gave a gentle squeeze. "We will be gentle and honest with her," added Nettie. Carmen reached up to her shoulder and touched Nettie's hand.

Carmen stood up and glanced at Vita in the living room. She saw her thirteen-year-old daughter and wondered where the next hour would take them. "Vita, can you come in here. Gram made some ice tea, and we, uh, we would like to talk to you about things." Carmen sat back down and rummaged through her pocketbook as Vita slowly got up with a sinking feeling in her stomach and a sobering look on her face. Nettie had already placed three tall glasses of ice tea on the table and then pulled out the kitchen chair. She patted the chair pad with her hand for Vita to have a seat. Nettie then sat down next to her and put her hand on Vita's knee. Carmen by now had placed the remnants of the pregnancy test kit box on the table.

Vita started to say, "Mom, why are you showing me this again? I told—"

Carmen held her hand up like a traffic cop and said, "Vita, hold on. Just listen to me here. That is all I am asking. I am not going to lecture you like I did yesterday . . . okay?" Vita stared down at the table. "Look, I love you. Dad loves you. Gram loves you. You know that. I am concerned for you. We only want what is the best for you. No matter what, we love you . . . always." Carmen spoke calmly but with a matter-of-fact tone, "I am not going to be angry with you, but I need you to be honest with me, and I know that sometimes the truth hurts."

Nettie then spoke, "Vita, we are here for you," as she kept her hand on her granddaughter's knee. Vita gave a quick glance up to meet her grandmother's loving eyes and then quickly back down to her lap as she made like she was inspecting her nails. She continued to listen.

Carmen continued, "Vita, I have to say that I did not believe what you said about a friend coming over the house to take a pregnancy test. I have to ask you again, and you need to tell me the truth here. I won't be mad. We will deal with whatever we have to deal with, no matter how difficult the situation is. Did you take the pregnancy test?"

There was silence. The seconds of silence were broken by the clicking of Chaz's nails on the kitchen floor. "C'm' 'ere, Chaz," Vita said softly and lifted her pug onto her lap. He sat on Vita's lap, straight-backed as if he were a military sergeant. It became quiet again.

"Vita, did you take that test?" repeated Carmen in a concerned voice.

Vita took a long deep breath in and let it out slowly, "Yeah. I did." Her eyes met her mother's eyes for the first time since they were seated.

"And?" Carmen questioned softly as she raised her eyebrows.

"And, and I don't know," Vita said worriedly. Her voice quivered, "I think it said I was, but I don't know for sure." Vita knew the test strip had indeed turned to a blue color.

Carmen tried her best to acknowledge to Vita that this meant Vita was indeed having sex. "How long have you been seeing this boy?" No response. "Have you been having sex for some time, or was it just one time?" Carmen didn't want to push her daughter.

Nettie had removed her hand from Vita's knee when Vita had placed Chaz on her lap. Nettie gently touched her granddaughter's forearm. "Vita, is there just one boy?"

Vita was feeling trapped. She wanted her mother and grandmother to know the truth, the whole truth because she wanted the weight of the burden lightened, but she was a frightened little girl with a deep dark secret. As she distanced herself subconsciously from reality, she was not sure what she wanted her family to know. She just wished with desperation that she could go and hide and all of this would go away. As distant as she felt, Vita was still aware enough to know that her mother and grandmother were waiting for a response. She uttered, "It's just one person."

Carmen wanted to cry. It took all her strength to fight back the tears. She knew in that moment that life would take on a very drastic change in direction if Vita was indeed with child.

Carmen suggested the need to repeat the test. "But you know, you do need to tell us the name of the boy you have been with. You know you have to do that."

"Mom, I can't. I can't do that. If I am not pregnant, then let's drop it, and I promise I won't ever be with him anymore, okay?" Vita felt sick to her stomach the more she continued with half truths.

Nettie felt the need to get off that line of questioning. "Vita, we can see that your body has changed recently, honey. You know it just may be you growing up, or it can also be from changes your body goes through when one is pregnant."

"What looks so different?" Vita asked as if she were clueless. Chelsea last night had brought up the fact that she looked bigger on top.

"Well," said Nettie, "you look chestier."

Carmen mentioned to Vita that she had seen the wrapped sanitary napkins in the bathroom garbage a week or so ago. "I realize that some do get their periods during the first few months of pregnancy," stated Carmen. "So what is going on here?" Vita felt her insides sink. Her surroundings closed in on her. No room or air to breathe. Vita began to cry. She could no longer hold in her confused emotions. Her grandmother picked Chaz up off Vita's lap as Carmen held Vita's hands. She looked into her daughter's very blue eyes, made bluer by the tears and the contrast with reddening of the whites of the eyes. "We love you, Vita, and we will do whatever we need to do to help you, but *you* have to let us help you." Nettie placed her hand on Carmen's shoulder, signaling Carmen to give Vita some time to sort out what just happened.

After several minutes, Vita managed to tell her mother and her grandmother how she pretended to have her period. Carmen gently told Vita she knew how difficult this must be for her but that they needed to continue to talk. She questioned Vita as to when her last period was. Vita had started getting her period irregularly when she was eleven. She seemed to be getting it every twenty-eight to forty-five days or so. "I don't remember, Mom. I will have to look it up." Vita usually kept track of her period in a little calendar as her mother had taught her to do. She also made note of it in her diary. "I think it was about three months ago. That's why I bought the pregnancy kit."

"Vita, we need to have you see a doctor, a gynecologist," Carmen said.

"No! No!" yelled Vita.

Carmen was in such a tizzy that she never questioned Vita on how and where she bought the pregnancy kit. The fact was that Vita had stolen for the first time in her life. She was too embarrassed to bring the pregnancy kit to the drugstore counter.

Nettie stood behind Vita. She put her hands on the girl's shoulders and nuzzled her cheek next to Vita's. "Your mom is right. Girls your age should start seeing this type of doctor and not wait until their late teens anyway."

Vita was emphatic as she responded, "I do not want some man down there! Please, Mom. I don't want to go!" Carmen tried to calm Vita down and suggested that they would find a female gynecologist.

Carmen and Nettie tried in vain as gently as they could to get Vita to tell them the name of her boyfriend. She would only tell them that it was only a few times that she had sex. "You know, honey, that you are way too young for all of this. I have tried to talk to you about such . . ." And Carmen caught a quick stern glance from Nettie. Carmen realized she was going into her lecture mode and quickly changed her tone and her words. "I'm sorry, Vita. I don't want to lecture you. That is not what I want to do. I just want to help you, support you, and guide you; and I feel as if I somehow have failed you. You must realize, Vita, that if you are pregnant, life as you know it will be very, very different. You have to let us help you. We will need to know who this boy is."

Vita cried, "I can't, Mom! I can't! Please not now! I told you enough." Between sobs, she asked, "Are you going to tell Dad?"

"Honey, Dad has to know. You know I can't keep this from him."

"Nothing need be said tonight to Brendan," Nettie said to Carmen.

Carmen and Nettie both hugged Vita with Vita in between the two of them. Nettie told Vita that they would get through these difficult times together.

"What if I am, then what? I go with you to the March for Life, and I know what I saw, and I know how I felt if it happened to someone else. Am I going to have this baby?" Vita worried aloud.

Carmen continued to hug her daughter. "Vita, I think we three here know that if there is a baby inside of you, we do not have the right to decide if that baby should not live. I know you know that." She made that comment softly as she stroked Vita's hair.

The three generations of women huddled together with tears in their eyes as nothing else was said. For those few minutes, Vita felt the warmth and the security. For those few minutes, she wasn't scared. For those few minutes, she was able to feel the envelopment of the unconditional love that emanated from her mother and her grandmother. It was a bonding moment. She felt safe in the cocoon of this maternal embrace.

The feeling was fleeting and gone all too soon. Vita knew in her deepest depths that she would have to rely on being able to get back into her safe little cocoon in order to survive the coming trials and tribulations. They sat quietly for the next few minutes and sipped slowly from the tall ice tea glasses. Each wondered what was running through the minds of the others. Carmen broke the silence by saying how late it was getting and that she and Vita should be heading home. The plan was to pick up the home pregnancy test kit from the twenty-four-hour CVS pharmacy on the way home. Carmen herself planned to administer the test the next morning to assure that the test would be done properly.

Chapter 6

O N THE WAY HOME, CARMEN drove to a drugstore that she normally did not frequent. Vita waited in the front seat of the car with Chaz while her mother shopped for the pregnancy test kit. The ride home was silent, except for the few utterances of "I love you, Chaz" Vita said as she kissed the top of the rounded pug's head as Chaz sat on her lap.

"Oh, I see Uncle Corbin decided to stop by," noted Carmen as she pulled up the driveway next to Corbin's shiny black brand-new Corvette.

Vita clipped on Chaz's leash, set him down on the driveway pavement, and walked him toward the house. Chaz sniffed the tires on Corbin's car and emitted a low-level growl. He continued to sniff the front and rear tires on the driver's side. He lifted his leg and tinkled on the tires as Vita tugged at the leash, having to drag Chaz away from the tires.

"Mom, is it okay if I go straight upstairs to bed? I'm kind of tired."

"Sure, but don't you want to say hello to Uncle Corbin first?" asked Carmen.

"Not really. Not tonight. I just want to go upstairs."

Carmen knew Vita had a trying evening and did not want to push her further. "Okay, I will poke my head in later to say good night to you." And she kissed her daughter on the forehead. They walked through the front door, and Vita headed straight to her bedroom with Chaz in her arms. Carmen was grateful for the soothing effect that Chaz had on Vita. They were buddies. No doubt about that.

Brendan had woken up shortly after the women had left and was working on his painting when Corbin had stopped by. It was a watercolor of a seascape sunset in a small harbor of sailboats in New England that the family had been to on one of their long weekend getaways some time ago. Brendan's easel was set up in a corner of the family room. Both men were sitting with a beer when Carmen entered the room with a much-forced smile as she greeted Corbin.

Brendan called out to Vita, "Aren't ya going to say hello to Uncle Corbin?"

Carmen hastily chimed in that Vita had gone straight upstairs to her room and stated that Vita was feeling out of sorts.

Corbin, three years Brendan's senior, could pass for Brendan's twin, except that Corbin wore his sandy-colored blonde hair longer than Brendan's more cropped look. Corbin also put something in his hair to make it a few shades lighter than Brendan's hair, giving Corbin more of a surfer dude look. One would never look at him thinking he was a suit-and-tie lawyer. Both brothers had athletic frames and stood around six feet two inches. Both shared the twinkling blue eyes of the Irish, not to mention the Irish temperament with both parents being of Irish descent.

Carmen kept her handbag tightly against her body as it contained the concealed pregnancy kit in the small paper bag with the CVS logo. Brendan had just gotten his paints set up when Corbin had stopped by. Corbin had retrieved the beers from the refrigerator. The two Malloy brothers had conversed as Brendan painted. Brendan was one of those people who was not distracted by conversation. "We were just talking about vacation," Brendan mentioned, trying to involve Carmen in the conversation. Brendan could see that Carmen's mind was elsewhere as it had been when they were out for dinner. "Come up with any ideas for our summer, hon?" he added, trying to get Carmen's attention.

"Uh . . . no, I'm sorry . . . I guess my mind went drifting . . . again," Carmen joked halfheartedly.

Brendan, remembering Mother's Day was next week, said, "Never mind plans for vacation. What would you like to do for Mother's Day next weekend? Think about it . . . okay?" Brendan loved his wife and would do anything and everything for her. He could see that she was tired.

She was physically and emotionally spent with thoughts of how all their lives could potentially be very different by tomorrow at this time. Carmen tried in vain to make fun of herself, saying, "Well, for Mother's Day, maybe I need a new brain and a recharged body!"

"Think ya need a beer, or can I get you a glass of wine?" Corbin asked.

"What . . . and kill off more of my brain cells," Carmen quipped. "Thanks anyway, Corbin, but I think I am just going to make myself a cup of tea." She went into the kitchen and heard Brendan and Corbin continue with their ideas for their prospective summer plans.

Vita decided she would shower in the morning. All she wanted to do now was to get into her comfy pajamas, which consisted of a light flannel set of lavender shorts and a matching long-sleeve T-shirt. She sat on top of her bed after retrieving her diary from its newly concealed spot. With key in hand that was kept in her jewelry box, she unlocked the lock, undid the clasp, and wrote in her diary. Never did Vita mention her uncle Corbin by name when writing about the horrible experiences nor did she ever describe the assaults in detail as she would rather forget about them. She wrote more about her feelings, and she referred to the person who had committed these atrocities as "him," "he," or "the monster." There were, however, many references in her diary log about Uncle Corbin. It would not take a rocket scientist to know who the perpetrator was. Vita only wrote for a few minutes, locked her diary, and returned it back to its most recent hiding place. She placed the key back into the jewelry box. Vita turned her night-light on and turned off the lamp on her night table before she crawled back into bed and under the covers. She drew the covers up tightly under her chin and held them there with clenched fists. Chaz had hopped on the bed and positioned himself near Vita's feet, circling like a cat, until he found just the perfect spot to settle down and curl up in. Vita had the covers held so snug around the tops of her shoulders as if covered in Saran Wrap. She felt safe like this. No one could touch her. She envisioned the sheets and the light blanket to be an impenetrable shield—a magic shield that would protect her. Still, Vita felt vulnerable. She was scared. She was confused. She felt disgust as she tried to block out the images seared into her mind of her uncle Corbin coming toward her. Vita pulled the covers even more taunt and turned her body onto her left side, curled up in a fetal position as she buried her face into the pillow and trembled with the awful memories of her uncle's hands pawing all over her body. She could still feel them. She couldn't even cry herself to sleep. All she could think about now was the pregnancy test her mother would administer to her early tomorrow morning. Vita tried in earnest to convince herself that perhaps the test she had taken was in error. Maybe she didn't interpret the test correctly. Maybe she had read the directions wrong and had done the test incorrectly causing a false result. *How could this be happening to me? Why did Uncle Corbin do such things to me? Why? No one would ever believe me. I know it. They would say it was my fault.* Vita spoke her thoughts, "Maybe Grandma, yes, Chaz, Grandma will believe me."

Chaz lifted his head and perked up his ears. Chaz slowly got up and inched his way into the C-shape of Vita's curled body. Thoughts continued to swirl in Vita's mind. *This baby should not be born. This should not have happened to me, but why did God let it happen? Why? How could He? I wish Uncle Corbin would just die. I don't care if he is Dad's brother. I wish he would have died a long time ago. I hate him, and I hate this baby . . . if there is really one inside of me.*

All these thoughts continued to bombard Vita's consciousness. Her mental whirlwind was interrupted with a knock on the bedroom door. Carmen poked her head in. "Still awake?" She bent over to kiss Vita good night and whispered, "We will be all right." She reminded Vita to wait for her before going to the bathroom in the morning as the urine collection had to be done first thing.

Chapter 7

VITA'S ALARM WENT OFF AT the usual six fifteen in the morning, signaling the start of another school week. Somehow, Vita had been blessed with a good night's sleep despite the turmoil of her emotional state. Chaz had maintained his position in the C-shape of Vita's fetal position. Neither one had moved much during the night, but when Vita bolted out of her bed to shut off the alarm on the clock radio on her dresser, Chaz too bolted off the bed. Vita had her morning routine, and Chaz had his. He knew he would find Carmen and sometimes Brendan in the kitchen (depending if Brendan went for a morning jog or not). Sure enough, Carmen was ready to greet the amiable pug who was anxious to get into the backyard to relieve himself. After Carmen had let Chaz out into the fenced-in yard, she ran upstairs to get Vita set up for the pregnancy test. Fortunately this morning, Brendan had decided to go out for a run. The crisp air and the clear sky, illuminated by the rising sun, was perfect jogging weather.

Carmen met Vita in the hallway in front of the main bathroom. The master bedroom had its own bathroom, so Brendan would always use that bathroom to shower after his run. Carmen explained to Vita the process of collecting the urine sample. Carmen had read the instructions carefully the night before as time was of the essence. Brendan usually would run for thirty minutes or so, just enough to get him pumped up and primed for the day. He had been working on a complicated case and was to represent a wealthy, prominent client tomorrow in court. Carmen estimated that Brendan had left about ten minutes before she had let Chaz out.

Vita went into the bathroom and meticulously collected the urine sample into the paper cup just as her mother had instructed her to do so. When Vita opened the bathroom door, Carmen placed the test strip into the cup and placed the cup on a shelf in the medicine cabinet. So much of their world could be in that small cup. Brendan never used that bathroom in the morning. All of his shaving and showering paraphernalia were housed in the master bedroom bath. Carmen daintily closed the medicine cabinet door until she felt the click to confirm it was securely shut. Mother and daughter gazed at each other in silence with the realization of what would be next time the cabinet door was opened. The silence was broken by Vita begging to stay home so that she could see the results. Thirty minutes was all it would take. Carmen had to convince Vita that it would be better all the way around to stick to the usual routine. "Dad is going to question why you are not leaving for school, and besides, Vita, you cannot afford to miss school. I know your mind is elsewhere, but I do think you are better off in school today."

Vita nodded. "I guess so." She then showered and went into her bedroom to get dressed. Carmen returned downstairs to finish setting up breakfast. During the week, breakfast usually consisted of a bowl of cereal with fresh fruit, a waffle with fruit or a bagel with cream cheese, and fresh fruit on the side. Carmen always insisted on there being fresh fruit as part of the breakfast meal.

Brendan returned from his run. He let the bounding pug back into the house. Brendan continued his jog upstairs into the master bedroom bath for his shower. Then the Malloy family sat down together for breakfast with Brendan having a bowl of cornflakes with fresh blueberries and a cup of coffee. Vita opted for some waffles with Cool Whip and blueberries on top and a glass of milk. She had a bit of an appetite this morning regardless of being apprehensive. Carmen, as she had done often, sat and sipped coffee from her mega-sized mug from Maine. The mug had a comical picture of a cartoon moose that looked a bit like Bullwinkle from the old *The Adventures of Rocky and Bullwinkle and Friends* cartoons. After Brendan would be off to work and Vita off to school, Carmen would usually eat her breakfast after a quick twenty-to-thirty-minute workout. This morning, Carmen's stomach was churning. She was surprised that Vita was chowing down her food. Carmen was fidgety, knowing that the test results would be known shortly. She couldn't wait for Brendan and Vita to be out of the house this morning.

Vita would take the school bus most days, but once in a while, if Brendan planned on going into the law office early, he would drop her off at school. This morning, Brendan decided he would like to get an early start, so he offered Vita a ride to school. She accepted because that meant she could linger in the house a bit longer rather than rushing out to the bus stop.

Brendan took notice that Carmen was again preoccupied. When Vita went upstairs to get her backpack, Brendan put his arm around his wife and in a concerned tone asked what was bothering her and why did she seem distant. "You just seem like your mind has been elsewhere. I noticed that yesterday and especially last night." Carmen tried brushing it off with the excuse that she was just tired, but Brendan sensed that there was more to it than that. He reasoned to himself that she would bring it up to him with whatever was troubling her when she was ready to do so.

Vita came downstairs with Chaz following closely at her heels. He had followed her upstairs. She picked up Chaz's favorite tug-of-war toy, which was a heavily knotted rope with a rubber ball at one end. A quick game of tug-of war ensued with Chaz getting the knotted rope end and Vita holding on tight to end with the ball. It was comical to watch how Chaz would plant his back end firmly pressed to the floor, leaning back with all his might. He would push off with his two front paws meanwhile jerking his neck back. Then he would violently shake his head from side to side to try to wrestle the ball end out of Vita's hands, all the while letting out his ferocious growl. Chaz was strong for a small fellow and could easily shake his pug head with such force while maintaining a vice grip with his mouth on the rope, that one's wrist could snap. Vita, however, was prepared and would hold the ball using both hands. She could even lift Chaz up off the ground as he dangled, not daring to let go. He was determined to win. They both enjoyed this little game, and this morning, the laughs that it generated from Carmen, Brendan, and Vita were well needed.

"Sweet pea, are ya ready to go?"

"Yup . . . Okay, Chazzy, I'll see ya later. Bye, Mom," said Vita as she kissed her mother on the cheek.

Carmen kissed Vita. Their eyes locked. Carmen said softly, "You have a good day at school. Love you."

Vita had on a pair of jeans, which were getting to be a bit snug, and a lime green T-shirt. She wore her long brown hair back into a ponytail, which danced from side to side as she ran out to Brendan's car, backpack in hand.

Brendan kissed Carmen goodbye with his hands on her shoulders. "Call me later, okay, hon . . . Love you."

"Okay, Bren . . . Love you," responded Carmen with a forced smile.

Carmen watched Brendan's sports car as it went down the block, and then she took off up the stairs. Carmen forced herself to take several deep breaths, psyching herself before walking into the main bathroom.

She stared at the medicine cabinet, her hand on the mirrored cabinet door. Carmen hesitated and thought of phoning her mother. She decided that she would check the results first and then call Nettie no matter what the outcome. Again, she placed her hand on the door of the medicine cabinet and looked at herself in the mirror. "Dear Lord," she muttered as her fingers curled around the top edge of the door. She slowly pulled on the door to hear the latch unlock and proceeded to swing the door open. There stood the cup with the top of the test strip visible. With both hands, she carefully picked up the cup and set it on the marbled vanity in between the two sinks. She took the strip out of the cup. Without a doubt, it had changed to the distinct blue color indicative of pregnancy.

Carmen felt her insides sink as she sat down at the edge of the tub, her elbows on her knees and her forehead resting on her clasped hands. Suspicions and what-ifs no longer existed. The reality that Vita was with child was setting in, and it was overbearing. Carmen seemed to transcend into another level of consciousness for a moment where she somehow had a sense of peace. She quickly came out of that mindset, and a deep sadness overcame her. She walked out of the bathroom and into her bedroom to call Nettie. "Mom, I need you to come over," Carmen said in a melancholy voice. "Now, if you can . . . please," she added and hung up the phone.

Chaz had followed Carmen into the bedroom. Carmen lay on the bed and cried till there were no more tears. She then sat by the edge of the bed and tried to organize her thoughts. She couldn't think. Carmen felt numb and sat there motionless with a concerned Chaz looking up at her. Chaz pawed at her feet, and Carmen awoke out of her spell. How would she break the news to Brendan that Vita was pregnant? What would happen to Vita now? She's too young to go through this, but this child, this baby . . . It's not right to take that life. Carmen volunteered often at her church and had organized and coordinated many of the prolife activities. She was one of the organizers of the annual bus trip to the March for Life held every January in Washington DC. Vita had accompanied her mother many a time to the various prolife events. Now what? What will happen? How is this situation any different? She got out her rosary beads and began to pray the Rosary.

She was on the fourth decade of the Rosary when Chaz's barking indicated the arrival of Nettie. Carmen rushed down the stairs to the foyer, rosary beads in hand, where Chaz was already waiting by the door to let Nettie in. Carmen ran outside to greet Nettie as she was coming up the walkway and gave her a tight embrace.

Nettie knew. "Dear God."

"Should I get Vita out of school?" wondered Carmen.

"No. Why don't you let her finish the school day? I think that would be best," suggested Nettie.

"Mom, what do we do? Does Vita go through a pregnancy because of what we believe about life? I mean, what will this do to her?" sounded a desperate Carmen. She continued, "We have to find out who the boy is, and we, we . . ." Carmen's words came racing out of her mouth.

Nettie took her daughter's hand and led her into the kitchen. "I'll make us some tea, and we will get our thoughts together."

"How am I gonna tell Brendan? I have to find a doctor!" Carmen's words continued to spill out.

Nettie pulled out the phone book from a hutch shelf in the kitchen. "I'll find a female gynecologist, and we will set up an appointment first thing. See if we can get one for tomorrow, and"—paused Nettie—"you are going to have to tell Brendan tonight."

"Mom, could you please be there when I tell him? Please."

"Are you sure you don't want to tell him just you two yourselves?"

"I don't know. I don't know. Mom, perhaps you're right."

Nettie brought the teacups over to the kitchen table where Carmen sat and then set out the milk and sugar. "Mom, we are no different than other families in this situation, ya know, where abortion is the easy option. We know that the baby Vita is carrying is a creation of God . . . just like every other baby in the mother's womb. Does the fact that Vita is only thirteen give us the right to kill that child?" Nettie just listened. She knew what Carmen was going to say next. A tear slipped out of the outer corner of Carmen's eye as she said in a barely audible voice, "I can never forgive myself for the child I aborted. I will always regret that for the rest of my life."

Nettie tried to console her daughter, "Back then, we didn't fully realize that the fetus was indeed a human life. You know, women were fed lines like 'it is just a blob of tissue' and such."

"Doesn't matter, Mom," Carmen said defiantly. "We, Bren and I, we did it because it was too damn inconvenient for us to have a child while we were both in college. I gotta face the truth, and that is the truth. Deep down, I knew that was a baby, a life, and now . . . and now . . . I have to live with the fact that I murdered my child." Nettie put her hand on Carmen's forearm. Carmen continued, "Yes, that I murdered Vita's brother in a most horrendous way. And, Mom, I do not want Vita to have to go through that either."

"Then you are thinking that Vita will need to go through with this pregnancy," said Nettie.

"What do you think, Mom? We know that life begins at conception. What do you think we should do?"

"I think you and Brendan and Vita will have to decide, but yes, that child is your grandchild and my great-grandchild, and our faith tells us that God knew that child ever before he or she was formed in the womb."

Carmen nodded. "I know Vita knows in her heart what a baby in the womb is." Carmen lamented to Nettie how she had not as of yet brought herself to tell the truth about her abortion. She spoke to Nettie about how she wished she was courageous enough to stand with those other women at the March for Life who bravely held their signs with the words "I Regret My Abortion." She told Nettie how she hoped that one day she would have the courage to do so.

Nettie questioned Carmen as to how she thought Brendan would react.

"Well, Mom, you know Brendan. After it sinks in, he will be saddened and numb and question how did this happen, but you know his first response will be to kill the kid, the boy, I mean and come down hard on Vita. He'll make her have an abortion. Just don't know what he'll do first." Although Brendan was a cradle Catholic, his parents had not been regular churchgoers. He never really learned his Catholic faith and what it represented. To get him to church on Sundays could be an effort at times. This was a sore spot between Carmen and Brendan. Brendan's not going to church did not set a good example for Vita. Carmen would never openly argue with Brendan about going to Sunday Mass in front of Vita because that would just add more fuel to the fire, arming Vita with reasons why she shouldn't have to go to church.

Vita received her Confirmation seven months earlier and continued to attend CCD classes, which had ended two weeks ago and would resume in the fall. Carmen was intent on Vita finishing her religious education to grade 12 as was deemed necessary by the pastor, Father John O'Brien. Nettie had taught Vita to say the Rosary, and many times, Vita would accompany her mother and grandmother in praying the Rosary.

"You absolutely think he would push for Vita to have an abortion?" Nettie questioned.

"Oh, I know for sure without hesitation. He will take her there himself. Mom, you know I don't want Vita to go through this either . . . carrying this child, giving birth, people talking behind her back . . . The stories, the gossip . . . Don't you think I want to spare her that? And the baby . . . Vita herself is a baby . . . Who would take care of the baby? You know I would, Mom, if I had to. I would. I will."

Nettie interjected, "There are loving families out there desperate to have a child."

"I know, Mom, and that would probably be the best answer for us." Carmen shook her head in disbelief and commented on how she couldn't fathom that this conversation was taking place.

"I think that after we make the doctor's appointment, we need to call Father John. You should speak with him; or have you, Brendan, and Vita all go to talk with him," suggested Nettie.

Carmen was certainly for the idea. At least, she by herself could go and speak with Father John first and then perhaps set up another time for the whole family to confer with him. Carmen was thankful to have her mother there. From the Yellow Pages, they located a female gynecologist. Carmen phoned the office of Dr. Martina Santiago. She found out there would be a two-week wait. Carmen painstakingly explained the situation to the receptionist, something that she did not want to have to do. The receptionist was fortunately a kind-sounding woman. She told Carmen to hold on, and she would see what she could do about getting Vita in earlier. She returned back on the phone within minutes with the good news that the doctor could see Vita on Wednesday at two fifteen in the afternoon. A relieved Carmen then gave the necessary information requested by the woman on the other end of the line. She thanked the receptionist for her understanding and patience and then hung up the phone.

Nettie picked up the phone and held it up so that Carmen could make the next call. Carmen was not ready to tackle the next step just yet. "Mom, that was really difficult. I don't think I can call the church just yet."

Nettie offered, "Would you like if I call and make the appointment for you?"

A hesitant Carmen replied, "No . . . I'll do it, but I can't just yet. I'll call later or maybe tomorrow." She felt her mind doing somersaults, her thoughts tumbling from one thought to another. The wave of being overwhelmed was once again consuming her. Occupying her mind were superfluous thoughts, which she spoke out loud, "Have to take Vita out of school early on Wednesday. Hate for her to miss school, but after tonight, I don't think she'll be going to school tomorrow." There were about four weeks left in the school year with the last week being all half days.

Carmen and Nettie wondered how far along Vita was in her pregnancy. They talked about how difficult it was going to be to have this discussion with Vita as to when and how frequent her sexual encounters were. Carmen and Nettie pondered on how Vita could have or even why she would have wanted to become so sexually active at such a young age. And with whom? Who was this boyfriend who she managed to conceal?

"Look," Nettie said, "let me call the church office and at least get something set up for you. You really can't afford the luxury of time here, Carmen."

Carmen nodded in agreement and, with a broken-up voice, said, "I know you are right."

Nettie took that as a go-ahead signal and immediately proceeded to pick up the phone and dial information for the telephone number of the church.

When Nettie got off the phone, she informed Carmen it was a good thing she called. Father John had one opening for this coming Friday at twelve thirty in the afternoon. The other alternative was to have seen Father Sladinski, who would be available today, tomorrow, Wednesday, and Thursday. Nettie knew that Carmen would much rather speak with Father John O'Brien. She was much more at ease with him and had worked with him in running the prolife events. Nettie booked the twelve-thirty slot on Friday for Carmen to see Father John. She had told the church office secretary that it was a personal issue that needed the guidance of Father John as soon as possible.

Carmen felt thankful that her mother had taken the initiative. At least now, they had the doctor's appointment set up along with the much-needed meeting with Father O'Brien. Nettie thought it a good idea while the two of them had the time to do research and make some calls regarding adoption agencies. Nettie saw how uncomfortable this was for Carmen. It hurt her to know her daughter was in such distress as Carmen tried to hold it together for the eventual confrontation with Vita and Brendan.

The two women spent the next hour perusing the Yellow Pages with Nettie making the inquiry calls.

Nettie insisted they take a break and pulled out the leftover salad from the night before, which was still fresh. She cut up some deli turkey meat and added some black olives and freshly cut tomatoes. Nettie fixed a salad plate for Carmen and one for herself. "You have to get something in you." To an Italian mother, food was the fix all for most every situation.

They discussed whether or not to pick Vita up from school early or let her come home the regular time on the school bus. Carmen could not remember if Vita had baton-twirling tryouts after school for next year's team. She excused herself from the table and went upstairs into Vita's bedroom. In the corner stood the baton. She returned moments later to the kitchen table. "Her baton is in her room, and she has no other after-school activity that I can think of. I think I will just let her come back on the bus." Carmen was just about to bring up the subject of how to tell Brendan when the phone rang. Carmen answered the phone, pointed to the phone, and mouthed "Brendan" to her mother. Brendan told Carmen he would have to stay later and not to have dinner wait on him. He had an important case in the morning and needed to meet with his client for last-minute details.

Carmen sat back down at the table. "Brendan won't be home until later in the evening. He has a case in court tomorrow morning that he has been working on for some time now and has to meet with his client later. I just don't think it would be a good idea to tell him tonight."

"Carmen, he is a big boy. You need to let him know. I'm sure he can handle his business matters just fine," Nettie said.

"Mom, no . . . I can't have him be totally distracted and emotionally distraught while trying to plead a case in court. And I know well enough to know that he will not be able to function after he hears the news. I will tell him tomorrow as soon as he comes home from work."

Nettie reassured Carmen that she would support her in whatever she decided. "Look," Nettie said, "Vita can stay with me tomorrow evening. This way, you can be alone with Brendan."

Carmen agreed that that would probably be the best way. Carmen picked up the plates after they were done eating, rinsed them off, and placed them in the dishwasher and then put on some coffee. While the coffee was brewing, mother and daughter decided to get some fresh air by taking a short walk with the dog. "Mom, Vita will be home only a few hours from now, and it will all be different. Her life is about to go in a completely different direction—one that we would have never anticipated. Oh dear Lord, please help us."

The crisp, dry air and sunshine from the morning had continued into the afternoon. The warm pleasant breeze ruffled the leaves in the trees. Carmen wished she could appreciate the lovely weather, but her senses were numbed. Nettie felt the same way—as if a great tragedy had befallen them. The short walk turned into a long walk with several interludes of silence, except for the clanging of Chaz's dog tags. When the women returned back to the house; the clock read two forty-seven. Vita's school dismissed two minutes ago, and she would be coming through the front door shortly. Nettie and Carmen sat to have their coffee; each nervously cradled the mugs in their hands. Carmen had asked Nettie to stay so that Vita would have her grandmother there when Vita would know that she was with child.

Chaz bounded through the living room and hopped onto the top of the couch to peer out the window. As dogs do, he had an uncanny sense of time of day. Perhaps he felt the vibrations of the school bus, even though the bus stop was over a block from the house. Remnant smudges from Chaz's last greeting were still evident on the window pane. Chaz wined excitedly as his tightly coiled pug tail wagged incessantly when he caught sight of his beloved Vita. Chaz intently watched Vita walk toward the house until she reached the foot of the driveway, at which point he made a beeline to the front door.

Carmen unlocked and opened the door and then swung open the screen door. Chaz bolted out to greet his Vita, almost jumping into her arms. She picked up the wriggling and squirming dog who couldn't lavish her with enough doggie kisses. Carmen managed a half smile. Vita stepped into the foyer as her mom held the door ajar. Their eyes met. Carmen's expression quickly transformed into a sobering look, and with the nod of the head, Vita knew. Vita gently placed Chaz on the floor. He circled around Vita's feet, just wanting her to play with him. Nettie grabbed one of Chaz's toys and threw it into the kitchen for Chaz to go after. One could hear his nails as they made contact with the tiles of the kitchen floor. Vita dropped her backpack right there in the foyer.

"Can I see it?" asked Vita. Her mother led her by the hand up the stairs and into the bathroom where she had left the test strip in the cup. Nettie followed them but stood at the bathroom doorway. Chaz followed with the toy dangling from his mouth. Carmen lifted the strip out of the cup and held it so that Vita could see that the strip had turned to the blue color. Vita felt sickened. She made her way to her bedroom and sat on the edge of her bed and stared at the floor. Her mother and grandmother sat down alongside Vita, and each placed a hand on Vita's thigh. "Does Dad know?"

"No, not yet," replied Carmen. "But you know that we will have to tell him. And, Vita, you know that we now have to know who you have been seeing."

"Why, Mom? Why? Why can't I just have an abortion and then no one will have to know anything?" pleaded Vita.

Nettie squeezed Vita's thigh gently. "Is that what you really want to do, Vita?" Nettie rubbed Vita's thigh as she said, "You know sometimes the easy way is not the right way."

Vita, with her elbow on her knees, buried her face in her hands.

Carmen spoke, "I know we have talked many times of the consequences of sex. You are only thirteen. I don't know, Vita, if you have had sex only once with this boy or if you have been having sex with him regularly, but you are going to have to talk to Dad and me about what's been going on. You know you have to. We are going to have to know who this boy is. He needs to know. His parents need to know."

Vita continued her plea, "Why, Mom? No one needs to know! I don't want Dad to know! Why can't I just get it out?"

Carmen walked out of the room because she had to.

Nettie pulled Vita to her. She held Vita and rocked her. "Vita, I think you know deep down inside the answer to your own question." Vita sobbed in her grandmother's arms.

After several minutes, Vita told her grandmother that she wanted to be by herself. Nettie understood. She rubbed Vita's shoulder and whispered to her that things would work out. As Nettie left, she asked Vita if she wanted Chaz, who was also in the bedroom, to stay. Vita nodded. Nettie slipped out of Vita's room and quietly closed the door behind her as she did so. Nettie hand motioned to Carmen, who was still in the hallway, to follow her downstairs. "Let's give her some time to herself. When she is ready to talk, she will. She has a lot to absorb right now."

Vita felt ready to burst—so full of emotions, so full of conflicting thoughts, so full of anger, so full of desperation, and no one to talk to—except her diary and Chaz. She got off her bed and went to the door to lock it before getting her diary out from its most recent hiding place. She located the diary key in her jewelry box and then lifted Chaz onto the bed to sit with her. Unlocking her diary, she whispered to Chaz, "Chaz, only you and my diary really know." Vita opened her book of secrets and began to write "Dear Diary . . ."

The women had gone into the kitchen, and Nettie decided that she would start dinner. Carmen was able to pitch in with the small tasks. Nettie could almost hear Carmen's wheels spinning. "Maybe it's a blessing that Brendan is working late tonight," Nettie said.

Nettie busied herself preparing broccoli and cavatelli. She also decided to make some chicken cutlets. Carmen managed to put together a simple salad. "I certainly don't feel like I can eat tonight," commented Carmen as she tossed the salad with the salad tongs. "Try to have something. You will need your strength, Carmen." Carmen knew her mother's exact words even before she had said them. To Italian mothers, food would always make things better—*mancia, mancia* . . . "you'll feel better" kind of thing.

"Mom, why make all of this? Vita is not going to want to eat much either," said Carmen.

"Look, Carmen," Nettie responded, "better to have it made. Vita needs the nutrition now, and we'll leave Brendan a nice plate. And you will have plenty left over for tomorrow when I am sure cooking will be the last thing on your mind." Italian mothers, especially the older generation, were of the mindset to have the meals planned out ahead of time—an inherent characteristic of sorts.

"Yeah . . . tomorrow," said Carmen sadly, "I think cooking and eating will be at the bottom of the list."

Carmen thought that perhaps a walk would clear her head. Nettie told Carmen to go on ahead as she would finish cooking dinner and would be here if Vita needed her. Chaz needed his exercise too, but Carmen was hesitant to go up to Vita's room to get Chaz. She knew that Chaz was Vita's soul buddy and thought it best that Chaz remain in the room with Vita. Chaz was such a source of comfort to Vita, and his presence would always give Vita a calmness. "Thanks, Mom. I'll be back in a bit. I'm only going to walk up the block and around the park. I won't be long. Half an hour, maybe forty-five minutes," said Carmen as she headed for the front door.

"Take as long as you need. Be careful, dear," said Nettie.

Carmen always walked at a brisk pace. She desperately tried to get her thoughts in line; however, her mind was still in a state of chaos. She decided to pray as she walked. Oblivious to her surroundings, she prayed the Rosary, using her fingers to keep track of the Hail Marys. She prayed for guidance and for strength for her family and that somehow the good Lord would see them through this. And she prayed for Brendan. How would he take all of this? Thoughts of Brendan and how she would tell him distracted her from her prayers. Carmen prayed for the right words to use on Brendan tomorrow. Her plan was to talk to him tomorrow after he would get home from the case, hopefully by early afternoon.

When Carmen returned, Nettie had already finished cooking. The table was set. Vita had not as yet come out of her bedroom. Carmen tiptoed up to the second floor and stood a few moments outside Vita's door before putting her ear to the door. She then gave two light knocks. "Vita?" She tried to turn the doorknob. It was locked. Carmen instantly panicked and repeated, "Vita?"

A few seconds later, a voice responded from behind the closed door, "I'm not hungry, Mom."

"May I come in? Would you like some company?" asked Carmen softly.

"No. No, thanks, Mom. Not right now," said the voice from behind the door.

Carmen went downstairs and relayed to Nettie that Vita would not be eating as of yet. Neither Carmen nor Nettie desired to eat, so Nettie covered the pot of the broccoli and cavatelli and put foil over the plate with the chicken cutlets. They then went into the family room to watch the five o'clock news, which was more of a distraction than anything else.

Chaz's internal clock had gone off. He hopped off the bed from where he had been parked next to Vita and whined by the door. Vita finished writing in her diary, clasped it shut, and locked it. "Okay, Chazzy boy, c'mon."

Carmen got up as she heard Chaz's dog tags approaching and let him out into the backyard before feeding him.

Nettie went toward Vita and held out her hands to meet her. "Vita, come and I will make you a little something to eat. You need to eat something." Nettie prepared three plates, each with small portions of chicken cutlet, broccoli and cavatelli, and salad while Carmen readied Chaz's dinner for him. She set Chaz's Navajo bowl onto the floor as Vita went to call for Chaz to come in from the backyard, but no need to call him. He knew the routine. Having done his business, he was at the back door ready to charge his bowl.

The three generations of women sat down to eat. There was no conversation to be had at first. All three of them chased the food around the plate with their forks. Carmen broke the silence, "Thanks, Mom . . . It really is delicious."

"Yeah, Gram . . . thanks," Vita echoed quietly as she lifted her eyes to meet those of her mother and grandmother. "Soooo," said Vita, dragging out the word, "where's Dad?"

Carmen explained to Vita that her father had to work late. Vita was somewhat relieved and even more so after her mother told her that she wasn't going to be able to talk to her father about the pregnancy until tomorrow afternoon. The conversation switched to the doctor's appointment Vita would have on Wednesday afternoon. Vita was again somewhat relieved to learn that she would be seeing a female gynecologist. This would be her first visit ever to such a doctor. While most girls her age were having their first female exam to learn about and examine the changes the pubescent body was experiencing, her first female exam would be a prenatal exam. "Soooo," said Vita, "am I gonna go to school tomorrow? And what's gonna happen to me when all the kids find out?"

"Vita, let's take one day at a time. I think it best if you do go to school tomorrow. You may be having to miss some school in the coming days, so I just think you need to go." Carmen found her thoughts jumping ahead. Nettie supported the idea.

The phone rang. Carmen answered. It was Brendan saying he and Corbin were just leaving the office and would be stopping at the bar for a beer or two and some eats. "No problem at all, Bren. We're just finishing eating supper, but I'll make a plate up for ya just in case you get hungry again later." This worked out well for Carmen. She had told Brendan on the phone how tired she was and that she planned on calling it an early night and would likely be asleep by the time he came home. She knew that when Brendan and his brother Corbin went out to unwind at their favorite watering hole, a pub that doubled as a sports bar, they would be there for several hours. As much as Vita looked forward to seeing her dad, as she was most definitely a daddy's girl, she was once again feeling a sense of relief, as temporary as it might be.

Carmen, Nettie, and even Vita realized there was much to discuss, but this day had had its full of emotional roller coasters. Nettie and Carmen cleared the table and loaded the dishwasher. They cleaned and straightened up the kitchen and left a Saran Wrapped dish with a nice-sized portion of broccoli and cavatelli and a large chicken cutlet for Brendan along with a bowl of salad. Vita had gone upstairs to get her homework done as for the time being she felt that she could focus on it. The relief from knowing that she would be in bed asleep by the time her father came home had something to do with it.

Nettie decided she should get home to get a good night sleep herself. The coming days would be trying ones for all. Nettie poked her head into Vita's room. "Can I come in for a moment?"

"Sure, Gram."

Nettie kissed Vita on the forehead. "Everything will eventually work out. Stay strong, my child. Life is not always easy. This is something you will learn. You go to school tomorrow, and then we will deal with things as they come."

Vita gave her grandmother a half smile and nodded. As Nettie let herself out of Vita's bedroom, Vita said, "Love you, Gram."

Both Carmen and Vita were in bed by eight thirty, knowing that Brendan would likely be home within the hour or so. Vita actually did fall asleep soon after her head hit the pillow. She had felt good about being able to finish her homework. She had felt somewhat cleansed of her emotional turmoil after writing page after page into her diary and after knowing that she did not have to face her father tonight. Carmen, however, lay awake, trying to organize her thoughts about how to tell her husband tomorrow. She again prayed to be given the strength to do so.

When Brendan came home around nine forty-five p.m., he walked into a quiet house. He went upstairs and softly knocked on Vita's door, which was partially open. Brendan daintily opened the door enough so that he could slip into Vita's room to kiss her good night. He heard Chaz's tags rattle and saw the silhouette of the pug's rounded head with perked alert ears in the dim light that emanated from the night-light. Brendan stooped down to kiss Vita lightly on her head and gave Chaz an affectionate pat on his head. Brendan didn't say a word to his daughter but only smiled contently as he left Vita's room. Vita was in a deep sleep, never knowing her father had been in. Chaz put his head back down to settle in for the night.

Carmen lay on her side of the bed and pretended to be asleep when Brendan quietly strolled into their bedroom. By the time Brendan actually got into bed, Carmen was fast asleep.

Chapter 8

THE NEXT MORNING WAS ALMOST a repeat of the previous morning, even weather-wise. Brendan felt refreshed after showering following his morning run and was ready to face the day in court. At breakfast, Carmen as usual cradled her moose coffee mug while Brendan and Vita ate. Brendan attempted to make conversation with Vita as she dug into her waffles topped with Cool Whip and fresh blueberries. She was nervous about making eye contact with her father lest he sense that something was awry. She realized that the mood at tomorrow's breakfast table would be vastly different. Vita distracted her thoughts with Chaz, calling him over to go fetch his tug-of-war toy. "Dad, are you going in early again?" Vita asked as she threw the ball with the rope that Chaz had just brought over.

"Yep. I'm gonna leave in about twenty minutes. Why? Would you like a ride to school?"

"Yeah," said Vita. That meant that she had some extra time instead of having to leave in a few minutes to get to the bus stop. Chaz was right there at Vita's feet, toy dangling from his mouth, ready to have a go of tug-of-war to which Vita aptly accepted the challenge.

Carmen took in the scene and knew that the morning routine would no longer be routine. She and Brendan spoke briefly about the relief of getting on with this litigation. The preparation and paperwork for this case had seemed endless. The proceedings would most likely take several hours in court today. Carmen told Brendan how handsome he looked, straightened out his tie, and adjusted the tie knot. She kissed her husband and daughter goodbye. Watching Brendan's car disappear down the street, she took a deep breath in and let out a long sigh.

Carmen decided to take Chaz out for a walk. She again needed to go over in her head the possible scenarios of confronting Brendan with the news that their thirteen-year-old daughter was pregnant. Chaz led the way. It was no surprise that his desired destination was the park in hopes of smelling his way through all the doggie stops so as to know what the other neighborhood canines had been up to. Carmen planned on following through on Nettie's offer to have Vita stay with her after school for as long as was necessary. It was also her hope that Nettie could get Vita to open up to her grandmother as to who the boyfriend was. It seemed oftentimes that Vita would confide in her grandmother first.

Carmen and Chaz returned from their walk. As they entered the house, Carmen unclasped his leash. As soon as Chaz heard that familiar click, he headed straight for his water bowl. Carmen thought the walk would have rejuvenated her; however, she felt even more fatigued. Perhaps a shower would get her going. But even after showering, Carmen still felt exhausted. She chose to lie down and thought that a quick half-an-hour nap would do the trick.

The phone rang. Carmen sat up, startled. She peered at the clock and was shocked to see it was four hours later. Nettie had become concerned. She had anticipated hearing from Carmen in the morning. "Your body is letting you know how desperately you need the rest" came the voice out from the phone. Plans were confirmed for Nettie to be at the bus stop to pick Vita up. Even though the bus stop was only a block and a half from the house, Carmen and Nettie both thought it best that Nettie take Vita directly from the bus stop rather than chancing Brendan being home and have him wonder why Nettie was there to get Vita.

"Mom, if you can get Vita to talk somehow, someway, about who she has been seeing and how long and—" Carmen was interrupted by Nettie.

Nettie reassured Carmen, "I'll try my best. I will try to give her the opportunity to talk, but she is quite fragile, and I don't want to pressure her."

Carmen told her mother how Vita seemed most at ease with telling her grandmother almost anything and added, "It would be the gentlest way of handling the situation because I am afraid of Brendan doing the pressuring. You know how his temper can be."

"You have enough to handle once Brendan gets home. Don't worry. I will take care of Vita. I will talk with her and try to get her to open up a bit," Nettie calmingly said to Carmen. Nettie offered to stop by, but Carmen had not heard from Brendan, and for all she knew, he could walk in at any moment if the case was done with.

"Maybe I'll call the office and find out from Corbin if he has heard from Brendan yet." Before she got off the phone, Nettie let Carmen know that she would spend the rest of the afternoon before she had to get Vita, making more phone calls to adoption agencies.

No sooner did Carmen hang up the phone when it rang again. Carmen jumped. Her hand had been on the phone ready to make the call to the office. Carmen fully expected to hear Nettie at the other end of the line, perhaps remembering to tell Carmen a last-minute something.

"Done deal, honey!" came Brendan's booming voice through the phone.

"Brendan? . . . Oh"—Carmen paused—"you mean you're finished?"

Brendan, still at the courthouse, replied, "Things seemed to be going smoothly all morning long, so we decided to go through lunch rather than break. Yup! Done! Do you believe it?"

"That's wonderful!" Carmen said, trying her best to sound upbeat.

"Look, being I've been working late and going in early lately, I'm gonna just stop off at the office for about fifteen minutes or so and then head home. Listen, it's only one o'clock, so why don't we go out for a late lunch?"

Carmen was thrown off guard. "Um . . . yeah . . . okay . . . I guess so . . . sure. I just have to freshen up. That would be really nice, Bren."

Carmen quickly went into the bathroom to throw some cold water on her face and then hastily applied some makeup, brushed her hair into a ponytail, and changed into a pair of dark denim designer jeans. She chose a dark pink and crème-colored striped shirt and crème-colored sandals. Carmen then phoned Nettie in a panic to let her know what was happening.

"Carmen, Carmen, dear . . . listen to me," Nettie spoke firmly but with a kind tone. "You have to get hold of yourself. Take some deep breaths now and ask God to help you get through this. Go ahead out with Brendan."

"Mom!" exclaimed Carmen. "Do you really think I can fake it? How can I sit there at the restaurant and celebrate his case knowing that what I am about to tell him later will bring his whole world crashing down around him!"

Nettie thought for a second. "Maybe you're right. You will know what to do when he comes through that door. Maybe it's best to have a little something ready for him to eat. I don't know."

Carmen responded to her mother, "Pray for us, Mom. And thank you for taking care of Vita. You know I will call you as soon as I can. Love you."

Somehow, Carmen was able to gear herself up. She took several deep breaths in and out and took one of her rosaries off her dresser. She began to pray. She asked for strength. Carmen felt some sense of confidence and was determined to focus on the task at hand. She knew how difficult this was going to be, and she knew she had to tell Brendan as soon as he came home.

It was almost two o'clock when Brendan walked through the door. Carmen had already been alerted by Chaz's barking when he heard Brendan's car pull into the driveway. Carmen set her rosary beads down on the dresser and looked at herself in the mirror. "I can do this!"

She heard Brendan call, "Honey?"

As she came down the stairs into the living room, Brendan commented on how lovely his wife looked. Seeing Brendan's open collar, Carmen reached for Brendan's black leather attaché case to retrieve his tie. She knew that was where the tie always ended up if he remembered to bring it home. She imagined that he must have some sizable tie collection in his office somewhere. "Thanks, Bren," responded Carmen to his compliment.

"Ready to go?" asked Brendan. As he looked into Carmen's face, he could read from her saddened expression that she was unable to hide that there was something drastically wrong.

With tears welling up in her eyes, she grabbed hold of Brendan's hands. Walking backward, Carmen led him into the kitchen, still not saying a word.

The silence and the tears scared Brendan. "What happened? Is it Vita? Is Vita all right? Something happened at school?" asked Brendan anxiously.

"Vita is fine," Carmen heard herself say. "I mean she is not hurt."

"What's going on?" said Brendan who was starting to panic.

Carmen still held on to one of Brendan's hands. "Brendan, I . . ." And as a tear fell out of the corner of Carmen's eye and tracked down the side of her face, she blurted out those words she did not think she would be able to say, "Our little girl is pregnant."

Brendan, as if he didn't hear a word, sat there in silence for several seconds and stood up. "What did you say?"

How painful it was for Carmen to have to repeat those words, but she did. Her eyes met Brendan's.

Brendan felt weak. He planted his hands onto the kitchen table, carefully lowered himself onto the kitchen chair. He shook his head slowly in disbelief and said, "What are you talking about? Vita pregnant? When did all this happen? Where is she?"

Carmen tried her best not to lose it. She painstakingly explained to Brendan how she had found a disposed home pregnancy test kit on Saturday, the stories Vita had told her about it, and how Nettie and she finally confronted Vita again on Sunday night. Brendan hung his head low in shock and in disbelief. Carmen told Brendan that she had Vita take another home pregnancy test yesterday, which confirmed that Vita was pregnant.

"How come I didn't know yesterday?" said Brendan as his voice broke up.

"Because I knew you had this case that you had been working so hard and long at, and I thought it would be better not to distract you. I knew you wouldn't be able to function in court today if I had told you," said Carmen, trying to justify her actions.

Brendan nodded his head. He understood that his wife did what she thought was best. Brendan's eyes reddened. He tried holding back his tears but could no longer do so. Burying his face in his hands, he sobbed for several minutes, muttering, "Can't be. Can't be. Just can't be."

Carmen rubbed his shoulders and was ready to hand him a tissue when he lifted his face from his hands. "Who is the boy she's been with? How? Why? I don't understand. She's never even brought a boy over here or talked about one; at least to me, she hasn't said anything." Brendan continued, "Where is Vita? She should be getting home soon, right?" Brendan took the tissue still dangling from Carmen's fingers and wiped his eyes and nose.

"My mom is going to pick her up from the bus stop, Bren, and take her over to her house for a while."

"What was she thinking, Car? Where did we go wrong?"

"Brendan, I have been asking myself that same question. You and I both know we have been nothing but loving, nurturing, and responsible parents. Perhaps we overdid things, gave her too much . . . doted on her . . . I don't know," Carmen said, trying to reason.

"How far along is she? Do you know?" asked Brendan in desperation.

Carmen then let Brendan know of the doctor's appointment for tomorrow. They would know then how far into the pregnancy Vita was. Carmen talked to Brendan about how tight-lipped Vita was as to who the father was and about anything to do at all with this relationship.

"I'm going to get it out of her, Car, and then I am gonna kill the son of a bitch! What in the hell were they thinking!" Brendan's temper flared as Carmen tried in vain to calm him down.

"Bren, we don't know who he is. And you want to kill this kid? It takes two to tango. He probably doesn't even know."

"I'm telling you, Carmen, I am going to get it out of her!" insisted Brendan again.

"Bren, you know how Vita is with Mom. She is going to try to talk with Vita this afternoon. They have that special bond, you know. If anyone can, she will be the one to whom Vita opens up to. You can't pressure Vita like that."

"Carmen, don't tell me what to do. I am going to tell you one thing—I will be going with you to the doctor's office tomorrow, and I am going to insist on an abortion."

Carmen's face turned pale. "Do you really think that is a good idea for you to go to the doctor's office and push for an abortion right then and there?" argued Carmen.

"Like hell it is! I am her father!"

"Brendan, I'm sorry, but we are not going to talk about abortion right now. We need to be concerned about her health—her mental and physical health and what condition she and the baby are in."

"Oh please, Carmen," said Brendan in disgust.

Carmen did not want to rile up Brendan any further, but she felt the need to add, "And the father of this child, the boy . . . whoever he is, and that boy's family . . . they have the right to know before any decision is made!"

Brendan got up from the kitchen table and went over to the kitchen cabinet that housed a bottle of whiskey. He poured himself a tall shot glass full and downed it as Carmen watched. "She is thirteen! Of course, she is going to get an abortion!" ranted Brendan. Carmen began to say something and was hastily cut off by Brendan, "And don't go there, Carmen. It is not the same thing as, you know . . . what happened to us."

Carmen badly wanted to voice her convictions to Brendan, but she held them in. She thought now was not the time to bring up their past. He was already agitated, and she decided it best that she not escalate his temper further. Brendan continued his rant. She allowed him to go on uninterrupted. *If he can get past some of the anger, perhaps he'll settle down enough to where we can actually have a serious conversation later*, thought Carmen to herself.

When Brendan went to pour himself another shot of whiskey, Carmen left the room and went upstairs to change out of her outfit. When she returned, Brendan was still sitting at the kitchen table, staring ahead, his mind elsewhere. "Would you like a sandwich or something?" Carmen asked.

"Huh . . . uh, no, no, thanks."

"C'mon, Bren. Let me make you a little something. You need to eat something. You haven't eaten since breakfast." Brendan agreed to half a sandwich, so Carmen fixed him half a tuna and cheese sandwich on rye bread and a glass of ice tea. Carmen glanced at the kitchen clock and figured that Nettie should have picked up Vita by now.

Brendan mechanically ate his sandwich, not even stopping to drink the ice tea. As he got up from the kitchen table, he picked up the glass and downed the ice tea before he headed upstairs to change into his running clothes. "I gotta get out and run," declared Brendan. A few minutes later, he was out the front door. Carmen was drained. All she wanted to do was to lie back down on the bed. She was hoping that her mother was getting through to Vita.

Brendan jogged to the park and ran around the running track like a teenager doing sprints for the track team. He ran as fast as he could. He was forced to stop and stooped over with hands on his thighs to catch his breath. He then walked several laps just trying to make some semblance of what was happening in his family's life. He knew he needed to get his head around this and make some decisions. First and foremost was the concern for his daughter. Despite being supportive of Carmen's and Nettie's prolife stance and activities, there was no way Brendan would ever allow his little girl to go through this pregnancy. She was a child herself. And that was that. This was his decision, period. Brendan wanted to see Vita but was unsure if he could control his emotions enough to be able to speak to her as the loving father he was. He was aware that he had an anger issue that he shared with his brother Corbin, and it was that angry side of him that he did not want to attack Vita with. Brendan strolled home with the plan of attempting to handle Vita as gently and lovingly as possible. He was her dad—her big strong dad, and he would do what it took to protect his only child.

Brendan walked into a quiet house. He caught a glimpse of Carmen as she sat on the recently purchased patio set in the backyard. Chaz was at her feet. *She's doing what she needs to do*, Brendan thought. He went upstairs to take a quick shower, and by the time he returned downstairs, Carmen was back in the kitchen feeding Chaz. Carmen noticed that Brendan seemed to have calmed down and was shocked when she heard Brendan on the phone as he said, "Mom, I know. We are on our way over."

Chapter 9

MEANWHILE, VITA KNEW EXACTLY WHY her grandmother was waiting for her at the bus stop. She was relieved to be going to Nettie's house. As soon as Vita went through Nettie's front door, she went straight over to the television and proceeded to watch MTV. Her grandmother allowed her to watch for about half an hour. She knew Vita needed to distract herself from the inevitable. Nettie made Vita a grilled cheese sandwich and placed the plate in front of her.

"Dad knows by now, doesn't he, Gram?"

Nettie nodded. "I believe he knows by now. Your parents have much to talk about." Nettie went over to the television and turned it off as she added, "It's something you need to do, sweetheart . . . to talk. Vita, we love you more than anything. You know that. And we only want what's best for you."

"I know that, Gram."

"Would you like to talk with me?" Nettie asked. "About how you and this boy met?" Nettie paused and waited for a response. "It's okay to let it out, Vita. You need to. You know, this boy and his parents have the right to know." Nettie could see Vita's jaw muscles move as she clenched her teeth. Vita was determined not to say a word about it. "Why do you not want to tell us, sweetheart?" Vita sat motionless and stared at the plate with half of the sandwich on it. Nettie sat down next to her. She placed her hand on Vita's knee. "Does the boy already know? Has he threatened you?"

Vita put her head down to her knees and, after several seconds, muttered, "No. No one knows."

Nettie tried to speak in the gentlest of tones. "Vita, you know your father . . . how angry he can get. Wouldn't it just be best if you just start talking? Talk to me, Vita. You can talk to me. I would never judge you. You know I am here for you."

Vita picked up her head off her knees and could not look at her grandmother. "I can't tell you who the boy is, Gram. I just can't. I'm too . . . I'm too . . . embarrassed."

Just then the phone rang. Vita could tell by Nettie's expression that the phone call was her mother. Nettie got off the phone and went over to hug Vita. "They are on their way over. That was your father on the phone."

"Gram . . . I'm scared. I'm scared . . . if I tell. 'Cause if I tell, there will be a lot of trouble in his family, you know . . . a lot of trouble in the boy's family. I just know it."

The ride over to Nettie's house was quick and quiet. Chaz sat soldier like atop Carmen's lap as Brendan drove Carmen's car. It was Brendan who decided that Chaz should come along. He knew that Chaz would give Vita something to hold on to. Brendan parked on the street in front of Nettie's house. Brendan got out of his side of the car and went around to the other side to open the door for Carmen. He picked Chaz up and looked at Carmen and then down at Chaz in his arms. "C'mon, buddy, you have a job to do." Brendan recalled in his mind the scene when he and Carmen took a ten-year-old Vita to pick out a pug puppy. It was the runt of the litter who picked out Vita.

Nettie had opened her front door upon hearing the car doors shut. She kissed Carmen and Brendan each on the cheek. Brendan, with Chaz still in his arms, walked over to where Vita sat on the couch. She lifted her head enough to see Chaz in her father's arms and was so overcome with emotion that her dad would think to bring Chaz that she wrapped her arms around her father and Chaz and began to cry. Brendan managed to free one hand and held his daughter's head close to his chest as he kissed the top of her head. Both Carmen and Nettie were thankful and proud of Brendan for being able to approach Vita with such tenderness. They also both knew that his mood could change rather quickly given any uncertain impetus.

Brendan set Chaz down onto the floor. As Brendan rocked Vita, Carmen motioned with her fingers for her mother to move closer to her. She whispered, "Any luck talking to Vita?"

Nettie shook her head from side to side. "Just that she said she was very frightened and afraid that if she says anything at all . . . she seems to think that this will cause real turmoil in the boy's family." Nettie and Carmen stood watching Brendan with Vita, both curious as to how he was going to handle these moments.

In between sobs, Vita sputtered out the words, "Please, Daddy, don't be mad. Please don't hate me. This wasn't supposed to happen."

Brendan hugged his daughter tighter. "I know, I know," he said, comforting Vita. "Vita, you know we will need to talk." Brendan loosened his embrace and pried Vita's arms gently off. He placed his hands on her shoulders, looked her square in the eye, and repeated softly, "We will need to talk. You know we will, honey."

Carmen and Nettie had not given Brendan enough credit. They assumed he would fly off the handle in a rage and were relieved to see him being so nurturing. It was obvious he wasn't going to pressure Vita for the time being. Vita nodded her head in acknowledgment that she had heard her father. She picked Chaz up and placed him on her lap as she sat back down on the couch. She stroked and cuddled Chaz, afraid to lift her eyes to see if all three sets of eyes were on her. Nettie offered Brendan and Carmen some coffee or tea. Coffee for both, so Nettie went off into the kitchen to put a pot of coffee on.

The conversation among the three adults was all about Vita. She felt as if she did not have a say in anything. Here it was her life that was being discussed. Brendan planned on going with Carmen and Vita to the doctor's office for the afternoon appointment tomorrow. He would have his secretary reschedule his afternoon commitments. They had decided that it would be best if Vita went to school for half the day.

"Dad, you can't come in when—" Vita began to say.

Carmen interrupted, "Don't worry, it will just be you and the doctor and a nurse during the examination, and if you would like, I will go in with you. But Dad will want to be there to talk with the doctor after she has seen you."

Vita, all of a sudden, became concerned with the embarrassment of such an exam and began to fire question after question to Nettie about what to expect. Vita's constant response to Nettie's explanations was either "Ewww" or "I'm not doing that . . . no way!"

Nettie went back into the kitchen to bring out the mugs of coffee, one for Brendan and one for Carmen, each made to their liking—both light and sweet.

"Vita, I know this is difficult for you to talk about, but can you at least tell us how long you have been seeing this boy?" questioned Brendan.

Vita did not respond. She was unsure of how to respond. "I don't know . . . a while, I guess" was the best answer Vita could come up with.

"Did he pressure you into having sex? I mean, you're too young . . . When did all this start?" asked Brendan, still trying to maintain a calm and nurturing tone.

"We only did it two times. It, it just happened," claimed Vita.

"Well," Brendan said, "we will find out tomorrow how far along you are, Vita."

"I don't want to be pregnant, Daddy. I don't want to be."

Brendan responded, "Don't you worry. We will speak to the doctor about having an abortion." And as soon as the word "abortion" came out of Brendan's mouth, Nettie could see Carmen's horrified expression. Brendan looked at both women and said, "What do you think? That I'm gonna let my daughter go through this trauma . . . 'cause that is what it would be . . . traumatic for her to go through with this pregnancy and have this kid! And then . . . and then . . . I will have a word or two with this young man and his family, period."

There was real tenseness in the room now. Nettie knew that Carmen would not be able to hold her thoughts. Carmen started with "And you don't think the guilt of killing a baby would be traumatic?"

Brendan raised his voice in anger, the first time since arriving at Nettie's, "She is only thirteen! I will not put my daughter through this pregnancy."

Chaz jumped off Vita's lap and ran into the kitchen.

"Brendan . . . that child . . . that baby is an innocent in all of this, and you know it!" said Carmen firmly. "That baby is still God's creation no matter what, and who are we to decide if he or she should die?"

"Cut this Catholic shit out right now, Carmen!" screamed Brendan.

Nettie sat down next to Vita and huddled Vita into her arms as if to shield her. She wished she could spare Vita what she knew was coming next.

"Being a faithful Catholic has nothing to do with it, Brendan. Do you know the pain, the guilt that I feel every day of my life for having murdered my child, our child? Yes, Brendan, we killed our son!" yelled Carmen. Carmen was out of control as she looked her husband directly in the eyes. "Yes, Vita. I have to live every day knowing that I said yes to taking the life of your brother." Carmen walked over to where Nettie and Vita were huddled together.

Brendan sat down and held his lowered head in both hands. He kept muttering, "I don't believe this. I don't believe this."

Carmen knelt in front of Vita, and with tears streaming down her face, she held both of Vita's hands. "I am so sorry. I am so sorry, Vita, that you had to find out this way." Vita sat in shock as Nettie tried to hold in her own tears. Carmen continued, "It was my hope that one day I would have the courage to tell you, Vita, about your older brother. It was my hope that one day at the March for Life that I would have the courage to hold that sign that we see so many women holding that says, 'I Regret My Abortion.'"

"I have . . . I mean I had a brother?" asked Vita, still wearing the look of shock. Vita then continued with a barrage of questions. "And this was Daddy's too? And when? And why? Why would you do that?" Vita looked at both her parents. The silence was unforgiving, only to be broken seconds later by the clicking of Chaz's nails on Nettie's kitchen floor. The curious dog had come to poke his head out of the kitchen seemingly to check on the quietness in the adjoining room. "Mom? Dad? Why?"

Carmen tried her best to answer. "I had just graduated college, and Dad was already in law school. We were planning on getting married. We had just gotten engaged when we found out I was pregnant."

"So you weren't even married yet?" Vita asked emphatically in a condescending tone implicating the fact that she had been preached to about not having sex before marriage. Vita felt her grandmother give her a squeeze, which was Nettie's way of letting her know that it was time to let up.

Carmen continued as she held Vita's hands. "I, I mean, we, Dad and I . . . we were . . . selfish. We thought we couldn't deal with having a child at that point . . . It was too inconvenient. And this is not meant to be an excuse, but back then in the seventies and even into the early eighties, we were told that *it*—you know, the newly formed fetus—was just a blob of fetal tissue." There again was another silence, and Carmen continued as Vita listened intently, "But, Vita, I knew in my heart and by what my faith had taught me that a life starts right there at conception. I knew what I was doing. A part of me wanted to believe the blob of fetal tissue thing. But, Vita, deep inside my own heart and soul and especially the moment the abortion was performed . . . I felt my heart tear."

Vita, with tears running out of her eyes, held tightly on to her mother's hands. "Mom. Mom, Mom?"

And as Carmen sputtered the words, "I knew I had killed my baby, our baby." Carmen looked at her husband. "And I live with that guilt every single day of my life."

Brendan had buried his face into his hands and looked up only when he heard Vita call out, "Daddy!"

Nettie, Carmen, and Vita could see Brendan's reddened eyes. Carmen never knew how this had ever affected Brendan. They had rarely spoken of the abortion. It had been a taboo and forgotten matter. Carmen and Nettie gazed in sadness at Brendan as they realized that Brendan had held his feelings in about the abortion for all this time too.

Brendan began to speak, hesitantly at first, "Your brother would have been about two years older than you, Vita. I do think about our decision . . . I do." Brendan stood up as if none of this scene had transpired and changed his tone. "But this, this is different," he demanded. "Vita is a child! Thirteen years old! We were engaged, and we were in our early twenties."

Carmen shook her head. "How, Brendan . . . tell me how is this different? There is still the life of a child at the center of all this. It doesn't matter how old the womb is!"

Vita had honed in upon hearing the word "brother" again. She temporarily forgot about her own predicament. Still in awe and disbelief, she asked again, "I had a brother? I always wished I had a brother or a sister."

Nettie, still with her arms around Vita, gave her another little squeeze, this time a comforting squeeze, and said, "We know. You always would wish for a brother or sister as your birthday wish when you were blowing out your candles when you were younger."

"How come you didn't have another baby after me?" questioned Vita. Carmen looked at Brendan and Brendan at Carmen.

"We were lucky to have you, Vita," Brendan said. "It was difficult for Mom to get pregnant. We did try for another baby, but—"

Carmen interrupted Brendan, "But the doctor said there was likely to be too much scar tissue as a result of the abortion." Carmen began to sob, "And sometimes I feel that God has punished me in this way . . . not being able to have a brother or sister for you."

Nettie got up from the couch and gave her daughter a comforting hug. "Please don't ever think that . . . ever."

Vita, still sitting on the couch, wheels spinning in her head, was trying to absorb these new revelations. Brendan's eyes welled up with tears as he tilted his head back, but not a drop fell out.

Out of Vita's mouth came the words "Mrs. Hartman, I mean Mrs. and Mr. Hartman . . . they decided to have Denny." And after pausing, she added, "And they knew he was going to have what he has . . . you know . . . Down's syndrome. They didn't think Denny was too inconvenient." Those words pierced through Carmen's heart. She looked over at Brendan and could tell those words had the very same effect on him. The silence that ensued was again broken by Vita. "And I think Denny is the most lovable boy ever. I do! I just love him!" she declared.

"And we love your brother. Vita, you don't know how badly I want to undo what I have done. We were so selfish, so selfish . . . just trying to get by. We didn't think we could afford a child at that time," cried Carmen.

"Then how come you didn't have the baby and just give the baby up for adoption?" questioned Vita. There was no immediate answer from her parents. Vita continued, "I mean then you wouldn't be feeling bad and sad about to having to kill . . ." Vita caught herself and quickly changed her wording, "About having the abortion."

Brendan shook his head. He looked at Carmen and said with sorrow, "We never even discussed doing that. Your mom had just finished college and was working, and I was still in law school. A baby just did not fit into our plans. Even to have your mom go through a pregnancy . . . it didn't fit into our plans. Vita, it was as the word you just used . . . 'inconvenient.'"

"Dad, the priest tells us in church that our plans might not be God's plan," added Vita.

Brendan nodded. "That sounds about right, Vita."

Both Carmen and Nettie were surprised to hear Vita make that comment. Perhaps Vita did pay mind to the Mass.

Vita, seeing the pain her parents felt fifteen years after the abortion, could begin to feel that maybe she should give the baby in her womb a chance at life. After all, that baby had no say in how it was conceived. The violent acts committed toward her had been done. And how much more harm would be done if she didn't allow this life to continue in her? On the other hand, a part of her still hated this baby. This baby was not created by two people in love but was the result of repeated rape by her uncle, her father's brother. She thought to herself, *If I could only find a small bit of love for this baby . . . maybe . . . I don't know . . . Why would God do this to me and then expect me to have this baby?* Such thoughts ran rampant through Vita's head, and she could not wait to get back home to lock herself in her bedroom to write in her diary about all that had transpired.

Brendan did not push the abortion issue any further. In fact, he said that he would not request that an abortion be scheduled while at tomorrow's visit to the doctor but that he would still want to hold it as an option to discuss along with the option of adoption. Carmen knew that this was a big step for Brendan to take. She felt some progress, some hope.

The emotional and mental anguish had taken its toll on all. As the Malloys gathered themselves to leave Nettie's home, Carmen pulled Nettie aside and asked her not to mention a word of this to her brothers, Frankie and Tony. Vita was not pressured into revealing the identity of the father anymore that evening with the understanding that she would have to come forth with the truth very shortly.

When Brendan, Carmen, Vita, and Chaz arrived back home, everyone needed to be in their own space. Carmen insisted that Vita at least have a glass of chocolate milk before retreating upstairs. Vita was thankful that she had completed her homework while in study hall as there was no way that her present state of mind could deal with John Steinbeck. She decided to take a long hot shower, and then it was off to her room to seclude herself to reflect in her diary. Vita dimmed the lights in her room and then sat Indian style on her bed with Chaz nuzzled up against her. With diary open and pen in hand, she began with her usual salutation of "Dear Diary" and proceeded to write for almost an entire hour about this day in her life. She recorded in her diary her feelings about the child inside her, about her aborted brother and her parent's decision to withhold this information from her. She wrote again about her feelings toward her uncle and her fears about what would happen if her parents found out the truth about who the father was. Would they even believe her? She even told her diary about the possibility of somehow being able to find an ounce of love for this baby but still could not find it in her heart to pray to God for help in being able to do so.

Vita was exhausted but felt somewhat cleansed after having revealed much to her diary. She slipped the diary under her pillow for the night as she was too tired to place it back into its new hiding place. She crawled under the covers and reached over to her night table lamp to turn the light out. She thought of her brother as her head sank into the soft, thick comforting pillow. Vita drifted off to sleep rather quickly as did Chaz.

Chapter 10

BRENDAN DROVE. CARMEN SAT NERVOUSLY in the passenger seat and contemplated what to say to the doctor. She figured that the doctor had seen many a pregnant young teen during her years in practice. Carmen had written a note for the teacher to excuse Vita at 12:45 p.m. for a doctor's appointment. Brendan pulled up to the front entrance of the school and parked while Carmen went inside to the main office to sign Vita out. She returned about ten minutes later with Vita walking alongside, both solemn-faced as they got into the car. Brendan started the car and pulled away after he heard the click of the seatbelt from the back seat. No words were spoken for the first few minutes of the ride. Brendan and Carmen could hear Vita almost hyperventilating.

Carmen turned around to speak to Vita as Brendan gazed into the rearview mirror to see the panicked expression on his daughter's face. "We are right here for you. We will just take it one moment at a time at the doctor's office," said Carmen in a comforting voice.

"I don't want to go! I really don't want to go!" insisted Vita.

"We know. We know, sweet pea, but it's something that we have to do," said Brendan lovingly.

After Brendan had made it clear yesterday that he wanted to be present for the office visit, it was decided that it would be too much if Nettie were to come along also. Carmen tried to prepare Vita once more on what she might expect so far as the exam was concerned and as to what the doctor might ask. It was apparent that Vita was not at all comfortable with this discussion while her father was in the car.

The Malloys pulled into the parking lot of a large modern-looking mostly glass building that housed several medical practices, one being that of the private practice of Dr. Martina Santiago, an obstetrician/gynecologist who had been in practice for almost twenty-five years.

When the Malloys entered Dr. Santiago's waiting room, they were impressed with the homey and comfortable feeling that the décor imparted as opposed to the typical sterile and institutionalized décor of many a physician's office. Vita's attention was immediately drawn to a large uniquely shaped fish aquarium in the corner of the room filled with colorful creatures, plants, rocks, and things that people put into their aquariums to make a realistic home for its inhabitants.

"Can I help you?" came a voice from behind the tall countertop. Carmen and Brendan walked over to the receptionist to let her know that the patient was their daughter Vita. The kind-faced woman made copies of the insurance cards and handed Carmen a pen and a clipboard with several pages of paperwork that new patients were required to fill out. "You can bring this back to me when you are finished. Take your time."

Brendan and Carmen took a seat. Carmen began the arduous task of filling out necessary forms. They lifted their heads to survey the clientele in the room. There were two ladies waiting, one in her fifties and the other one perhaps in her thirties and well into her pregnancy. Both women had their faces buried into gossip magazines getting caught up on the news of the A-listers. Generic mellow office music played continuously through hidden speakers. Vita had become absorbed with the fish and was not aware of being in a waiting room with other patients until she heard the door close after another patient entered the room. She then noticed the others in the room and decided to walk over to where her parents were seated. Brendan tried to make conversation with Vita about the fish. He followed Vita back to the aquarium so Carmen could finish the paperwork.

Carmen returned the completed forms to the kindly receptionist and thought to herself that this must be the very woman that took care of her on the phone the other day. "Was it you with whom I spoke with when I made this appointment for my daughter?" When the receptionist confirmed it was she, Carmen thanked her for her help and her kindness. When Brendan and Vita saw Carmen return to her seat, they both came over and joined her.

A blond woman, likely in her late twenties and dressed in a brightly colored floral scrub top, peered her head out from the door she had opened and called out, "Sheila . . . Sheila, we are ready for you." Sheila, the woman in her fifties, closed the magazine she was immersed in and took it with her as she followed the nurse into one of the exam rooms. As a seasoned patient, she knew it was more than likely there would be another wait for her once in the exam room.

Brendan, Carmen, and Vita pretended to watch the talk show on the television. They each gazed indiscriminately in the direction of the TV. Each had his or her own scenario playing within. Patients came and went.

It was close to twenty minutes later that another woman, probably in her midforties and dressed in the same brightly colored floral scrub top, came out into the waiting room and announced, "Vita?" And again, "Vita?"

Carmen, Brendan, and Vita all looked as deer caught in headlights. Carmen turned to Vita. "Would you like me to come with you?"

Vita nodded nervously. Brendan, suddenly feeling overwhelmed and out of place, sputtered out the obvious words, "I'll just wait here, but please get me when it is time to speak with the doctor."

Both Carmen and Vita got up and headed toward the door leading into the office where the nurse waited with the door held open.

"Hi, Vita. How are you today? My name is Mindy, and I am one of Dr. Santiago's nurses. I will be taking care of you today," said the attractive dark-haired nurse as she extended her hand to Vita. Vita could only muster up a barely audible hi. "And you are . . ."

"I'm Vita's mother, Carmen."

"Nice to meet you both," said Mindy. "Just follow me to the back here." The nurse motioned Carmen and Vita down the hallway and into the doctor's office. "Being you are a new patient with us,

Vita, we will have the doctor come talk to you first before we have you go into one of our exam rooms."

Carmen looked back down the hallway toward the door from which they had come through. "Oh, I didn't know we were going to speak with the doctor in her office first. Would you mind if I get my husband?"

"I'll be happy to show him in. Just have a seat and make yourselves comfortable." And with that, nurse Mindy headed back toward the waiting room. Not a minute later, Brendan was escorted into Dr. Santiago's office to join his wife and daughter. "Dr. Santiago will be with you in a few minutes. She will speak with you now and again after the exam."

Vita felt at ease for the moment, partly due to the warm and cozy feeling of the décor. Both the waiting room and the doctor's office had a modern flair but yet maintained a homey feel to it. The three Malloys did not say a word to one another as they gazed at the plaques, the paintings, and the photographs on the walls. Dr. Santiago was apparently quite credentialed, including specializing in many of the latest techniques and procedures in the obstetric and gynecological field. Lovely frames that held presumably family photos were strategically positioned on the large oval-shaped dark cherrywood desk. One would assume that was Dr. Martina Santiago in the pictures with her husband and three children. There were photos of the same three children through various stages of their lives. Dr. Santiago, if that was indeed her in the photos, appeared to be a short stocky woman with short curly brown hair. Brendan noticed and silently admired a painting on the wall, a somewhat abstract and Picasso like painting of a mother and infant. He wondered if a former patient had painted this or if the doctor found this work in some gallery. Carmen wanted to get up to take a better look at some of the photos on the wall but decided that for now she would best stay seated.

Vita's eye caught hold of a small ceramic pug on the doctor's cherrywood desk. "Look, Mom, Dad . . . it's a little Chaz! That's so cute!"

Brendan and Carmen smiled at Vita. "Maybe she has a pug. She must certainly like them. You can ask her about that, Vita," suggested Brendan.

Carmen was already taking a liking to Dr. Martina Santiago, and she hadn't even met her yet. Before Vita could even respond to her dad's comment, in strolled the doctor herself, Dr. Martina Santiago.

Dr. Santiago appeared much the same as she did in the more recent photos. She certainly was short and stocky in stature with a jovial face framed by short brown curly hair with few strands of gray. She smiled as she carried the makings of Vita's medical chart. With an extended hand and a kind natural smile on her face, she said, "Hello. I am Dr. Santiago. You must be Vita." Vita nodded and shook the doctor's hand.

Carmen and Brendan both stood up. "Hi, Dr. Santiago. Thank you for seeing us. I am Vita's father, Brendan Malloy, and this is my wife, Vita's mother, Carmen."

Handshaking and salutations went on for the next several moments. Carmen's eyes were drawn to a lovely delicate and ornate gold crucifix the doctor wore on a gold chain around her neck.

Dr. Santiago spoke directly to Vita, "I see this is your first time seeing a gynecologist." Vita nodded. "And do you know what kind of a doctor a gynecologist is?"

Carmen was tempted to speak for her daughter but allowed Vita to answer. "Well, sort of. You take care of things that only girls and women have, and you deliver babies."

"That's right," said the doctor as she glanced down at the paper-work Carmen had filled out. "I'm reading here that you took a pregnancy test at home and that it showed that you are pregnant." And as Dr. Santiago gazed up from the chart, she could see Carmen and Vita nodding.

Carmen interjected, "We took it two days ago."

The doctor now directed her attention to all three of the Malloy family. "First, we have to make sure you are indeed pregnant, and secondly if you are, we need to find out how far along you are. Then we will go on from there. Okay?" She paused and then continued,

"Vita, Mom, and Dad, I am going to have to ask some questions that are going to be very private, very personal, but because we are dealing with a young girl here who may be pregnant . . . I have to do so."

The doctor saw that her statement did not sit well with Vita. A paleness swept over Vita's face. She became agitated and looked to her parents and indicated to them by shaking her head slightly side to side that she did not want to answer any questions. Carmen placed her hand on her daughter's knee as the doctor pressed on in a gentle manner. "I need to know, Vita, if you have been involved with a boy or if you were forced by a boy or even an adult to do something that—"

The doctor was abruptly interrupted by Brendan, "What are you insinuating here, Doctor?"

"I am sorry, but these are questions that I have to ask. It is my moral obligation to do so," counteracted Dr. Santiago diplomatically.

"Don't you think we would know if that was the case? I think we would!" exclaimed Brendan, implying that he was insulted by that question to Vita.

"I'm sorry, but I need you, Vita, to tell me the truth—if you have been sexually active by your choice."

Vita looked at her mother and then at her father and then down at her lap. She just was not ready, not at this moment, to divulge the truth. She shrugged her shoulders and blurted out, "I guess me and my boyfriend went too far. It . . . it just happened. We only did it a few times."

Carmen addressed the doctor, "Doctor, we have never met this boy or have ever heard mention of his name. Vita will not tell us his name. Please, please you must understand that we are good parents. We are strict with Vita. We are still in shock." Vita looked down at her lap.

"Look, I don't want to make this harder than it already is. Let's do this. I'll have you go into the exam room. I will explain everything to you, Vita, as I am doing the exam. We are also going to get a urine sample and draw some blood to start with. Okay?" Dr. Santiago tried to lower her head down to Vita's eye level so as to catch a glimpse of Vita's eyes. "Mom, you may go in with her if Vita would like you to do so." Vita looked at Carmen. "We will talk more after the exam," said the doctor to Brendan.

Dr. Santiago got up and set out into the hallway to track down nurse Mindy. Together, they returned to the office.

Nurse Mindy placed her hand on Vita's shoulder. "C'mon with me. I'll take you and your mom into the exam room, and Dad . . . I'll have you wait back in the waiting room. Okay? When we are finished with the exam, I will have you come back into the office."

"Fair enough," answered Brendan. He kissed his daughter and went back to the waiting room.

Nurse Mindy ushered Vita and her mother into a small alcove off the main hallway and had Vita sit on what nurse Mindy termed "the throne." Vita sat on the large padded chair with the wide padded armrests. The nurse explained to Vita and Carmen that she would be drawing some blood for the necessary tests. Vita remembered having her blood taken one time before, so she had an idea of what to expect but nevertheless was anxious. Her anxiety level was upped a few notches about now being confronted on who had fathered the baby. Vita immediately tensed up. Her body became rigid.

"Try to take deep breaths. I need you to relax, sweetie," said the nurse. She added, "Not to worry, they all tell me I'm the best at this." Vita obliged and took several deep breaths in and out. She tried to divert herself with thoughts of her Chaz. With the tourniquet on her arm, nurse Mindy had Vita make a fist. "Just relax, Vita . . . You are doing fine . . . just fine." The nurse palpated a nice vein, in went the needle, and into the tube flowed the blood. "Now open your fist for me. See, we are just about done." She took three vials of blood. Vita looked up at her mother with a half smile and a proud expression. While still on the throne, the nurse took Vita's blood pressure and then had her stand on the scale for height and weight measurements.

Vita and Carmen then followed nurse Mindy to an exam room like goslings toddling behind their mother goose. The nurse handed Vita a paper cup and gave her instructions on collecting her urine as she directed her to a nearby bathroom. Vita was familiar enough with this procedure by now. The nurse took the cup from Vita as the girl emerged from the bathroom. Once back in the exam room, Vita was handed a clean gown wrapped in a plastic bag and told to remove all her clothes and to put the gown on with the opening to the front. Vita was horrified.

Carmen stepped out of the room momentarily as Vita hurriedly shed her clothes and slipped the gown on. She wrapped the gown around her snuggly and secured the ties. "Okay, Mom. You can come in" came the voice from exam room 2.

When nurse Mindy and Dr. Santiago entered the room, Vita was sitting cross-legged atop the exam table as Carmen sat in a chair she had pulled aside the exam table. Vita quickly uncrossed her legs and moved herself up to the front edge of the table with her legs dangling down. She was apprehensive and had ambivalent feelings about having her mother in the room. Vita motioned her mom close to her face. "Mom, I think I can do this myself. I kinda feel funny about you, ya know . . . seeing me."

"Are you sure, sweet pea?" Carmen asked.

"Yeah."

Dr. Santiago understood Vita's shyness typical of a teen's first gynecological exam. "We can have you wait just outside the door or in my office while I examine Vita. And, Vita, at any time, you can let us know when you want your mom to come in."

Carmen nodded and kissed her daughter. "I'll find my way back to the office and wait there."

Vita gripped the sides of the exam table as she was positioned for the internal exam. She repeated the mantra to herself, "It will be over soon. It will be over soon." Her heart pounded against her chest wall. She felt light-headed and faint.

Nurse Mindy gently pried Vita's hand from the table and sandwiched it in between her own hands. "It'll be all right, honey. Take some deep breaths . . . in and out . . . That's it . . . in and out . . . You're doing fine."

Dr. Santiago reassured Vita, "I will let you know everything I am doing beforehand."

Several minutes later, nurse Mindy appeared in the doorway of Dr. Santiago's office and summoned Carmen.

Carmen was preoccupied in a daydream. Somewhat startled, she asked, "How did she do? Is she—"

"She's a trooper. She did fine," assured nurse Mindy with her hand on Carmen's shoulder. "The internal was a bit difficult for her. She was very tense, but we were able to get through it." The nurse paused and then added, "Yes, by the internal exam, Dr. Santiago could tell that your daughter is indeed pregnant. The doctor plans on doing an ultrasound now."

Carmen and Mindy entered the room as the doctor positioned the ultrasound equipment next to the exam table. She prepared to apply the water-based gel onto Vita's abdomen. "We warmed the gel up for you, Vita. You are going to feel something warm and wet on your tummy, and then you will feel me moving a probe over your tummy . . . okay?" Dr. Santiago then held up the probe so Vita could see it.

With the room darkened, the doctor began to scan Vita's womb. Nurse Mindy and Carmen stood by Vita's feet, staring at the ultrasound monitor. Vita tried to pick her head up to get a glimpse of the screen to try to make heads or tails of the strange images on the screen. Vita held her breath automatically as she was transfixed and frozen.

"It's okay, Vita, you can just breathe normally," urged the doctor. "Ah," said Dr. Santiago, "here is the baby. Can you see the head? See here," as she pointed to the image on the screen. "And this flickering you see here is the heart beating. Now you are going to hear something . . . and that will be the heartbeat." With that, the doctor turned on the Doppler control so that the rapid heartbeat was audible.

"That's inside of me?" Vita questioned in awe.

"Yes, Vita. That little person is inside of you," responded nurse Mindy with a smile.

"Nice, strong heartbeat," commented Dr. Santiago. Carmen placed her hand on Vita's lower leg. She stroked it gently and tried to hold back her emotions. "I'm going to take some measurements, and from that, I can give you an idea of how old this baby is," said the doctor.

Carmen wept softly. She knew in her heart that she would never get the chance to know her grandchild. Dr. Santiago continued on with the exam, freezing the images and taking measurements. "Do you think that Dad might want to come in and see the baby?" Carmen asked in a loud whisper. Vita though was adamant about being uncomfortable with the idea of her father coming into the exam room.

Nurse Mindy who was used to looking at such images said to Vita, "I think you have a gymnast there. Look at that . . . Flips . . . Can you feel that, Vita?"

"Sort of. Sometimes I get these feelings as if there was a butterfly flying around inside of me."

"Well, that is the lil' fella or lil' girl just a movin' about," added the nurse.

"Wow," said Vita as she stared trancelike at the monitor. Carmen kept her hand on Vita's calf the whole time.

Dr. Santiago turned the ultrasound equipment off and collected the pictures she had taken. "I have some calculations to make from these measurements I have taken." She told Vita to get dressed and to have them return to her office for a discussion.

Nurse Mindy cleaned off the equipment and returned it to its original spot in the exam room. She repeated the instructions to Carmen and Vita to meet Dr. Santiago back in her office once Vita was dressed. As Mindy exited the exam room, she poked her head back in. "I will get your husband and have him meet you and Vita in the doctor's office. He will be able to see the pictures there too."

When nurse Mindy entered the waiting room to fetch Brendan, he had been trying to distract himself by being engrossed into *Auto Magazine*. Dr. Santiago's office had subscribed to two men's magazines to give prospective dads something to occupy themselves with. Brendan was the only male in the waiting room at the time. In fact, he was the only male in the entire office, but that did not seem to faze him as that mirrored his home life with Carmen, Vita, and Nettie. He immediately saw nurse Mindy out of the corner of his eye. She motioned him to come in. "How's my daughter?" asked a concerned Brendan.

"She did fine. I know it was difficult for her, but she was able to get herself through it. She's a trooper. Dr. Santiago will speak with you, your wife, and Vita in a few minutes." She had Brendan follow her into the doctor's office. "Your wife and daughter will meet . . . Oh, here they come now."

All three Malloys sat in the same chairs they had previously sat in at the beginning of the appointment. Vita and Carmen and Brendan were each feeling their own sense of being overwhelmed. Carmen nodded to Brendan.

Vita's eyes were drawn again to the ceramic pug on the doctor's desk. "Darn. I forgot to ask Dr. Santiago if she had a pug!"

"It's definite?" Brendan asked Carmen, interpreting her nod.

"We saw the baby on ultrasound, Brendan. She is much further along than I would have thought," whispered Carmen, out of earshot from Vita.

Dr. Santiago entered the office with medical chart and pictures in hand. She sat behind her large oval cherrywood desk, which did not match her short stature. A desk like that would seem befitting for a tall statuesque man and not a short chubby woman. Nevertheless, the doctor strategically positioned her reading glasses on her nose and held the pictures close to her face and then placed them down onto the desk. Carmen, Brendan, and Vita anticipated the doctor's words. She then daintily removed her glasses and said, "I can calculate from the measurements I have taken that the fetus is approximately sixteen to eighteen weeks gestation. In other words, Vita is almost halfway through her pregnancy. I will know more when I get the results of the blood tests, but in the meantime, I would like to start you, Vita, on some special vitamins to help you and the baby inside of you stay healthy." The doctor outlined a plan regarding Vita's prenatal care and future visits.

Brendan asked to see the pictures, and although the ultrasound images were something he obviously was not used to looking at, he could definitely make out the shape of a tiny person.

"Daddy, it was doing flips!" exclaimed Vita.

"You can even see in this one picture here that the baby is sucking its thumb," Dr. Santiago pointed out.

"Where? Where? Can I see?" asked an excited Vita. Brendan did not know quite how to respond.

"I have to ask . . . What is the plan for this child? Will the child be raised in your home, or will the baby be given up for adoption?" questioned Dr. Santiago. The doctor immediately sensed that there was no definite plan in place, at least not one that had been agreed upon.

"Uh, adoption is the likely choice," Carmen quickly responded.

"Well, I would like to see you, Vita, next week. I also think it a good idea to have Vita get some counseling. This is a lot for a young girl to handle. I can suggest some very good and well-credentialed psychologists, yes, females"—as the doctor looked at Vita with an understanding smile—"that have experience with helping a young lady such as yourself, Vita."

"Thank you, Doctor. That is something I think we need to do very soon," said Brendan as he and Carmen nodded in agreement.

Dr. Santiago fingered through her Rolodex and jotted some names and telephone numbers on a pad with her letterhead. She tore off the sheet of paper and handed it to Brendan. "Anyone of these people is excellent. When I get the results from the blood tests, I will call you with them." She looked at Vita. "Vita, I would like to speak with you privately before you leave." Dr. Santiago looked at Carmen and Brendan as she definitively said, "Okay, Mom and Dad?"

"Any questions or concerns, please, please call me. And, Vita, I know how difficult this has got to be for you, but we will need to know about the father. You know, the father of this child does have a right to know, so when you come in next week, we can talk about that."

Dr. Santiago got up from behind her desk, opened the door, and motioned to Vita's parents to step out. "I'll just be a few minutes with Vita, and I will have her meet you back in the waiting room." Dr. Santiago stood against the door while Carmen and Brendan walked into the hallway. She stepped out into the hallway and poked her head back through the doorway. "I'll be right back with you, Vita," then closed the door to her office leaving Vita in there by herself. The doctor put one hand on Carmen's shoulder and the other hand on

Brendan's shoulder. "She has had enough for today. I wouldn't push the father issue tonight."

Carmen and Brendan nodded in agreement. "Oh, Dr. Santiago, I am sorry for raising my voice regarding your line of questioning. I was out of place, and I apologize," Brendan said with sincerity.

"It is understandable. I didn't take offense to it, but thank you," said the kindly doctor.

"Oh, one more thing," added Brendan "uh, do you perform abortions? Not that this is an option but . . ." Carmen shot Brendan a look of astonishment and disappointment.

The doctor herself was somewhat taken aback by the question. "No, Mr. Malloy. I do not believe in abortion. I do not perform them. I'm sorry."

"I see," said Brendan.

Carmen had been pleased with how the appointment had progressed up to this moment until Brendan had put a damper on things with that question. "Thank you very much, Doctor. We will make the next appointment for Vita and will wait to hear from you in the meantime," Carmen said as she hooked her arm into Brendan's to lead him back into the waiting room. She did not dare make a comment about his abortion inquiry as that would no doubt instigate an argument. Brendan did not bring it up either. He could tell from Carmen's reaction that she was not at all happy with him bringing up the abortion option.

Dr. Santiago knocked on her own office door as it was her way to show respect and courtesy for her patients. She slowly opened the door and closed it behind her in the same fashion. Vita watched the doctor with the kind smile maneuver her way back behind her grand desk. "Vita, there is something called patient confidentiality, which means that no matter what . . . if you tell me something and you tell me in confidence, I cannot repeat it to anyone. Now when you start seeing a counselor, it will be the same. So whatever you say to the counselor in confidence, she cannot divulge or tell anyone what was said. Are you following me?" Vita nodded. "Vita, is there anything . . . anything at all you feel you need to talk about?"

Vita was feeling the crunch but was not ready to begin to talk about her nightmare. She knew the good doctor was just doing her job. "Not really," said Vita, and then her eyes once again caught hold of the ceramic pug on the large shiny cherrywood desktop. "Oh yeah . . ."

"Yes?" questioned Dr. Santiago.

Vita continued, "Do you have a pug?"

"Yes, I do, Vita. She's about five years old now," said the doctor proudly.

"I have one too!" exclaimed Vita. "His name is Chaz, and he's the best! What's the name of your dog?"

"We call her Stella."

"That's a cute name," said Vita with a smile.

"Well, Vita, if you have any questions or concerns, here is my card with my telephone number, okay?"

"Okay," said Vita, and she tucked the card into the back pocket of her jeans.

"Now you take care of that Chaz . . . It's Chaz, right?" Vita nodded. "I will see you next week, Vita." And with that, Dr. Santiago got up and maneuvered herself back to the door to let Vita out. Vita smiled as she filed past the doctor and headed out to the waiting room to join her parents.

On the drive home, they talked about how nice the doctor was and how friendly and kind the nurses and the receptionist were. Vita thought she needed to distract from the father issue. She suddenly asked, "Can I invite Chelsea over for dinner tonight . . . please?"

Brendan and Carmen glanced at each other. Brendan nodded his head. "It's okay with me if it's okay with your mom."

Carmen turned to Vita in the back seat. "I suppose it would be okay. You can call Chelsea when we get back home, but don't forget it is a school night, so it will just be dinner and then a quick visit, okay?"

"Thanks, Mom . . . and Dad," said a relieved Vita. At least, she was able to buy some time for the inevitable. She did not know that the doctor had suggested to her parents not to push the paternity issue for that evening.

As soon as Vita stepped into her house, she ran over to the phone to call her friend. Carmen got on the phone with Mrs. Hartman. Plans were made for Chelsea to be dropped off in thirty minutes. Carmen told Chelsea's mom that Chelsea could certainly stay awhile after dinner and that she would be more than happy to drive Chelsea home around seven thirty in the evening. It was already four thirty, so Brendan suggested takeout.

"What will it be, sweet pea? It's your pick," Brendan asked his daughter.

"How about Chinese, Dad? I know Chelsea likes that too."

"Okay with you, Mom?" Brendan asked his wife.

"Deal," said Carmen.

And Brendan was out the door to get their usual family order. Meanwhile, Chaz who was ecstatic to have his people back, couldn't wait to take a run in the backyard, and then come in for his meal.

Carmen reminded her daughter, "Vita, not a word about this to anyone yet. Okay?"

"I know that, Mom!"

Vita and even Carmen and Brendan needed the distraction of having Vita's girlfriend over for takeout dinner. It was an oasis moment for those few hours and would certainly help diffuse some of the tension.

After dinner, Vita and Chelsea retreated to Vita's bedroom where they listened to music and talked. There was no time to watch a video.

Chelsea noticed the edge of what appeared to be a diary, a lavender one, under the headboard end of the bed. "Is that your diary, Veet? You never told me you kept a diary," chided Chelsea.

"What? Where?" Vita asked, surprised. Chelsea pointed. Vita pounced on the diary as a football player would pounce on a fumbled football. She held it tight to her chest and wondered how it got there. "Yeah . . . uh, it's personal."

"Oh, c'mon, Veet . . . show me," pushed Chelsea.

"No, Chels . . . it's just for me . . . Maybe one day, okay, but not now." And with that, she quickly shoved the diary in between the mattress and the box spring. Vita suggested that they go downstairs and practice some of their baton routines. The two girls did just that. They reviewed and performed the routines minus the batons.

While the girls were in the family room, Carmen decided to give Nettie a quick call. "Hi, Ma,'" said Carmen. She proceeded to give Nettie a quick overview of Vita's visit with Dr. Santiago. She told Nettie she would stop by tomorrow and fill her in with the details.

When it was time for Carmen to take Chelsea back to her house, Vita thought of bringing something special over for Denny. "Mom, can I put a little baggy together with some of the cookies Grandma made and take them to little Denny? I know he would really love them!"

"Sure." Carmen smiled.

Carmen pulled out of the driveway with the two girls in the back seat of the Bimmer. She could see Brendan down by the corner with Chaz for an evening walk. Carmen gave a honk as they passed Brendan and Chaz.

Vita stuck her head halfway out the open window and yelled, "Hey, Chazzy!"

When the car pulled into the Hartman's driveway, Chelsea thanked Carmen for having her over for dinner and for driving her home. Vita told her mom that she would go with Chelsea inside to give Denny the cookies. As the two girls walked into the Hartman household, Chelsea called for her brother in a loud voice, "Denny, someone is here to see you, and she has a special surprise!"

"Surprise" being the buzz word, little Denny came bounding to the foyer repeating "Surprise, surprise, surprise" with a beaming smile and cheeks so round and rosy that they were aglow.

"Here ya go, Denny," and Vita handed the bubbly boy the bag with her grandmother's homemade cookies.

After a big hug, Denny ran into the kitchen to show his mother. The girls could hear Mrs. Hartman say, "That was very nice of Vita, wasn't it, Denny? You may pick one cookie to have now." The cherub-faced child skipped around the kitchen and the living room as he munched on the cookie.

Karen Hartman came out to where the girls stood. "Thank you and thank your parents for me for having Chelsea over and for getting her back home."

Vita turned to go back to the car as Mrs. Hartman gave a wave and a mouthed thank you to Carmen. "I just love Denny," said Vita as she sat herself in the front passenger seat.

When Vita got home, she immediately went to her room to retrieve her diary out from under the mattress. She tried hard to retrace her steps about where she had last left the diary as she knew she did not put it under the bed where Chelsea had spotted the edge of the book. As she rubbed her thumb over the diary cover, her fingertips sensed tiny holes in the leather. Careful examination of the front and back cover of the diary revealed several pierced spots. Vita instantly recognized that Chaz had likely gotten hold of the diary. She remembered that she had haphazardly slipped the diary under the pillow last night and that Chaz must have gotten it out from there.

After doing her homework, Vita showered and got into her pajamas. She then sat on her bed with the bedroom door closed and made a lengthy entry into her diary. When she finished, she made certain to put it in a better hiding place for the night. Vita went downstairs to kiss her parents good night. They didn't discuss the day's happenings. It seemed best to leave things on an up note. She collected Chaz on her way back to her room. Tomorrow was another day. Vita was ready for a good night's sleep.

Chapter 11

I T WAS THURSDAY MORNING AND Vita's alarm sounded at its usual school day time. Vita awoke and was immediately anxious. She had had such a peaceful night's sleep, but now the anxiety hit her like a hammer in the chest. Not wanting to look her parents in the eye with the fear that the inevitable question about who the baby's father was would resurface, Vita scampered from bedroom to bathroom to kitchen. Being she had showered the night before, she just threw on her clothes, washed her face, brushed her hair into a ponytail, and bounded down the steps and headed into the kitchen.

Carmen and Brendan sat at the breakfast table. Vita sensed the awkwardness of the silence as Carmen got up and opened the back door to let Chaz back into the house. Chaz was delighted to be back in from the yard, knowing his meal was soon to follow. His dancing paws with nails clicking on the kitchen floor broke the unsettling quiet. Brendan had been out for his run earlier and was already dressed in his shirt and tie for the day at the Law Offices of Malloy and Malloy. Both Brendan and Vita had cornflakes with blueberries as Carmen sat with her mug of coffee. She preferred to eat her light breakfast after the morning rush was over.

This was one morning that Vita did not want to linger around the house to play with Chaz. "Dad, I think I'll just take the bus this morning."

"You sure?" Brendan asked.

"Yeah." Vita picked up her cereal bowl and tilted it to her mouth to get the remainder of the milk, blueberries, and cornflakes.

She hopped off the kitchen chair and ran back upstairs to brush her teeth. Before slinging on her book bag that sat on the bedroom floor, Vita double-checked to ensure that she had indeed hidden her diary where she had strategically placed it between two books on a shelf the night before.

Vita bolted back down the stairs. Carmen barely had a chance to drop Vita's lunch into her book bag. "Gotta go!" Vita kissed her parents goodbye and patted Chaz atop his rounded pug head. Out the door and down the block toward the bus stop went Vita.

"You know we are going to have to get answers from her . . . soon . . . very soon," said Brendan.

"And she knows it," answered Carmen.

"I think today when I get home from work, we should sit down and have this conversation, don't you? She is more than just a few weeks pregnant."

Carmen agreed. Carmen mentioned to Brendan that she was going to use an out-of-town pharmacy to get the prenatal vitamin prescription filled. "We don't need people knowing our business. Are you going to talk to Corbin about our situation?"

"Oh, I don't know if I am ready to discuss this with anyone yet. I am still trying to wrap my own head around everything that has happened, you know." And with that, Brendan let out a loud sigh.

Brendan wanted to get to the office early this morning to catch up on some work. "Corbin and I have a lunch meeting with some corporate clients of ours, so maybe I will get a chance to talk with Corbin afterward. I'll see how I feel." Brendan finished his second bowl of cereal while Carmen topped off his coffee.

"After I run my errands, I'll stop by Mom's house to let her know how everything went at the doctor's yesterday," said Carmen.

"Oh, speaking of moms . . . that reminds me—you never did mention what you wanted to do for Mother's Day," said Brendan.

Carmen looked solemnly at her husband. "I don't know, Bren. In light of all that has happened . . . I don't know if I really feel like going out to, ya know, celebrate Mother's Day this year." Carmen made the finger motion for quotation marks as she spoke the word "celebrate."

"Well," Brendan said, "you shouldn't have to cook, and neither should your mother, *and* we still have to eat. Why don't we do what we did last night and get takeout? We could order from a restaurant of your choice. Your mom can come over here if she doesn't already have plans with one of your brothers."

"Bren, that sounds like a plan." Carmen smiled. Brendan finished his coffee and put his suit jacket on. As he turned to kiss Carmen, she stepped back to look at his tie and gave it a quick adjustment and then pulled in close to him for their goodbye hug and kiss. Carmen felt some comfort and relief in that she no longer had to keep any secrets from her husband. Together, they would get through this.

With Brendan and Vita out of the house, Carmen sat with another mug of coffee, yogurt, and a sliced apple as she began to plot her day out. She hoped to get some house cleaning done and walk Chaz. She rationalized this would fill her exercise quota for the day. She could then shower and run her errands.

Before Carmen left to run her errands, which included the out-of-town pharmacy, she phoned Nettie to let her know she would be stopping by around one o'clock. Nettie, being the Italian mother that she was, said she would have a nice lunch made for the both of them. Italians always seemed to like to use the word "nice" as an adjective describing just about any type of food they deemed worthy, for example, "I'll put on a nice steak for you" or "I'll make some nice gravy and meatballs" or "have a chunk of this nice cheese," and so on.

Sure enough, when Carmen arrived at Nettie's house a few minutes after one, there was a nice lunch laid out on the table. "How about a nice glass of ice tea?" Nettie asked her daughter as they sat down at the kitchen table.

"Sure, Mom. Sounds great. I could use something quenching . . . been running around all morning. Thanks."

"So?" asked Nettie.

"Mom, did I mention on the phone to you last night how far along Vita was into her pregnancy?"

"No. You just said that she was indeed pregnant . . . very much so and that she was able to tolerate the exam."

"Mom, Vita is just about halfway through her pregnancy. The doctor estimated that the baby is sixteen to eighteen weeks old."

Nettie placed her hands together as if in prayer and lowered her head to her hands. "Oh dear God. I wouldn't have known it."

Carmen proceeded to tell her mother the details of the afternoon at the doctor's office from the office décor to the doctor herself, the drawing of the blood, and what the nurse told her of how Vita was able to get through the internal exam. She told Nettie of the lovely gold crucifix that Dr. Santiago wore around her neck.

"A good sign," commented Nettie.

Carmen told Nettie how Brendan almost jumped down the nice doctor's throat when she began questioning Vita about having sex willfully or was she being forced perhaps by an adult. Carmen explained that Brendan was upset because he felt that the doctor was insinuating they were bad parents and that they would certainly know if there was an adult involved who was pressuring Vita.

"Well, I certainly understand both the doctor's and Brendan's views," said Nettie.

"He did apologize for his tone later on. He felt badly about how he spoke to Dr. Santiago," replied Carmen.

As they finished the platter of nice fresh mozzarella balls with slices of nice fresh tomatoes and basil and open-faced prosciutto sandwiches, Carmen reached down into her pocketbook and pulled out a large envelope. She wiped her fingers with the pretty blue-and-white checkered cloth napkin and slid the pictures out from the envelope. "Look at these, Ma," said Carmen as she handed them to Nettie.

Nettie did the same thing with the blue-and-white checkered napkin before gripping the photos. "The baby?"

"Uh huh." Carmen nodded. There was quiet as Nettie stared at the pictures, one by one. "Your great-grandchild, my grandchild. We will never get to know him or her," said a morose Carmen.

"I know dear. This is very sad. Very sad, but we must pray to the Lord that this child will have a good life with a loving family," said Nettie, trying to comfort her daughter.

This prompted Carmen to bring up the inappropriate and impromptu question that Brendan put to the doctor just before they had left the doctor's office yesterday. "I couldn't believe that he still had that in his mind as an option after all that we had been through the past two days," Carmen said, shaking her head in confusion. "Well, guess what, Mom? Dr. Santiago said she does not believe in abortions. She does not perform them."

Carmen and Nettie talked a while more, now over some nice hot tea and biscotti. "Ya know, yesterday at the doctor's office . . . it went much smoother than I thought it would. The doctor didn't want us to pressure Vita last night into naming the father. And we didn't. In fact, Vita had her friend Chelsea over last night for dinner and a quick visit. I think that helped things—helped Vita to settle down some."

"She is far along, Carmen. The sooner, the better . . . for everyone's sake," Nettie said firmly.

"I know, Ma. Bren and I are going to have to confront Vita today with the question of who the father is. We will have to be firm and persistent and somehow gentle at the same time. In fact, I had better leave in a few minutes. Vita will be getting home, and hopefully, Brendan will be home soon after." Carmen paused and then continued, "Oh yeah, Mom, Brendan brought up Mother's Day again. I think if we do anything, it is going to be very low key. Would you like to join us Sunday for some takeout after Mass?"

Nettie slipped the ultrasound pictures of the baby back into the envelope and smacked the bottom edge of the envelope on the table to align all the photos to the bottom. "Don't even worry about Sunday. Let's just take one day at a time. There are more important issues to deal with other than a Mother's Day dinner." Nettie held up the envelope and handed it back to Carmen.

"Thanks, Mom." Carmen gave her mother a hug and a kiss.

"I'll be praying and thinking about you, Brendan, and Vita this afternoon. If you need me to be there for support for Vita, please, please call me. Okay?"

Carmen nodded. "I will. Love you and thanks again." And she gave another wave before disappearing into her car.

***

Brendan and Corbin got into Corbin's black convertible Vette. "Workable clients," Corbin commented as he stuck the keys into the ignition, put down the rooftop, and started the engine all in one swift hand motion.

"Very—makes our job easier when they are good listeners like these guys are," replied Brendan.

Corbin tore out of the prime parking spot in front of the Cabaret Restaurant as if he was pulling out of a pit stop at a NASCAR race. The sudden acceleration plastered both their heads against the head-rests. Brendan looked at his brother with a smile and shook his head. "Some things never change." Corbin gave Brendan a wink, a tilt of the head, and a smile.

Brendan gazed at the rapidly passing view and was quickly transported back to reality. He was trying to come up with an approach to their family situation concerning Vita and was caught up in thinking about different scenarios.

"Hey . . . bro . . . what's going on with you? I can tell something is eating at you. You all right?" Corbin asked with concern.

Brendan looked down at his lap and sighed, "Just have some stuff, ya know . . . some major stuff to deal with on the home front," said Brendan.

"Everything okay between you and Carmen? She seemed kind of distant the other night."

Brendan responded quickly with "No . . . no. We're okay."

Corbin was genuinely concerned. "You want to talk with me? I am here for you. You know that. Is Vita okay?" he asked.

"Look, I gotta sort my head out. Maybe tonight I'll stop by your place for a few beers. I'll fill you in then," replied Brendan.

"I'll be there," said Corbin.

The Corvette pulled into a small lot next to the Law Offices of Malloy and Malloy. The men exited the black shiny roadster, both

99

looked dapper and statuesque in their designer suits and ties, as if two gents out of a *GQ* magazine. They entered their office and proceeded to retrieve messages from the secretary. Brendan had some paperwork and calls to make.

Corbin grabbed a folder off the top of his desk, flipped it open, and thumbed through its contents. "All there." He opened his attaché case and placed the folder on top. "I'm off to court. I have a three o'clock DUI case. Linda, if I don't see you when I get back, have a good afternoon." He yelled toward Brendan's office, "Call me later, Bren!"

"Will do!" Brendan shouted back.

Brendan tried calling Carmen, but there was no answer. He left a quick message on the answering machine, "Guess you are at your mom's or still running errands. It's about two thirty now. I should be home around four thirty. Love you. Bye."

***

When Carmen walked into the house, it was almost three o'clock. She tossed the bag from the drugstore and the car keys on the counter and noticed the red light blinking on the answering machine. Chaz tried his best to get Carmen's attention as she listened to her husband's message. Carmen grabbed Chaz's leash that hung in the foyer and snapped it onto the dog's collar. "C'mon, Chaz. You want to go meet Vita at the bus stop?" Chaz danced impatiently on the foyer floor as Carmen ran back into the kitchen to get her keys. She took hold again of Chaz's leash and the two of them walked around the block before heading to the bus stop.

School bus number 26 pulled up to the curb. Several young teens bounded off. A few of them walked to where Carmen stood. "Hi, Mrs. Malloy . . . Hey, Chaz . . . Oh, cool . . . Can we pet him?"

"Sure thing." Carmen laughed.

Chaz ate up the attention and the affection. The kids knew who he was, and he knew who they were. He was such an ambassador.

"Hey, Mom! Hey there, Chazzy boy!" squealed Vita as she squatted down to plant a kiss on Chaz's head.

Carmen took in the whole scene and thought this little bit of normalcy was what she needed.

"I'll walk him, Mom." Vita took the leash from Carmen's hands.

One of Vita's classmates walked part of the way with Vita and Carmen before turning down her block. "See ya, Veet! Bye, Mrs. Malloy." She bent down to pet Chaz. "You be a good boy, Chazzy!"

"Mom, can I go over Chelsea's house for a little while?" Carmen hesitated as they walked into the foyer. "Pleassssse, Mom," pleaded Vita as she unleashed Chaz.

"Not today, Vita. Not today. Your father will be home around four thirty, and you know . . ." And after a deep breath, Carmen continued, "We all have to have this talk." Carmen tried her best to sound firm yet empathetic.

"Why can't that wait!" argued Vita.

"You know it can't. Vita, you are nearly halfway through the pregnancy. We will work it out. We will. Your father, your grandmother, and I . . . we will get through this with you." Vita stormed up the stairs. "Where are you going? I am trying to talk to you, Vita!"

"To my room! Is that okay with you?" Vita said with a sarcastic snip. "C'mon, Chazzy." And then Vita slammed her bedroom door shut and slung her book bag into the corner of her room. Chaz huddled close to the floor with his ears down and against his head.

Vita curled herself into a fetal position on the bed with shoes and all and pulled the lavender comforter around her. Chaz jumped up and got as close as he could to her. He managed to crawl underneath the comforter so as to be right up against her.

The phone rang. Carmen answered, thinking it would be Brendan.

"Hi, Mrs. Malloy. Is Vita home?" said the voice on the other end.

"Is this Chelsea?"

"Yes."

"Hold on, Chelsea," said Carmen as she walked to the foot of the stairs and called for Vita. "Vita, Chelsea is on the phone for you." No answer. Carmen asked Chelsea once more if she would hold on. Carmen went up the steps and knocked on Vita's door. Still, no answer. "Vita! I said Chelsea is on the phone!"

"I just want to be left alone," said a muffled voice from inside the bedroom.

Carmen returned to the kitchen and picked up the phone. "I'm sorry about that, Chelsea. She is doing homework right now. Is this about her coming over?"

"Yeah. I just wanted to know if she could come over . . . and my mom said she could pick Vita up," said Chelsea with great hope.

Carmen responded with "That is very nice of your mom to offer, but Vita won't be able to come tonight. Maybe another night. Thanks, Chelsea. Bye-bye."

Carmen hadn't started supper yet and decided that there was plenty of Chinese food from the night before to reheat. *I'll just make a nice salad*, she thought. She heard the sound of Brendan's car door shut. Apparently, Chaz also heard the familiar sound and let out a meek bark. Vita did not want to have to face her parents right now. She pulled the comforter tighter like a cocoon around her and Chaz.

Carmen greeted her husband at the door. She kissed Brendan and took his attaché case from him to set down on the floor while he removed his jacket. His tie was already off and likely to be in the car, in the office, or in the attaché case. Dinner first or talk first? Both Brendan and Carmen decided that the inevitable should not be put off any longer.

"It's been on my mind all day, Carmen."

"Were you able to confide in Corbin at all?" questioned Carmen.

"No. He could tell I wasn't right. I told him I may stop by later to hang out with him to get things off my chest. Where is she? Isn't Vita home?" Brendan asked.

"She locked herself in her bedroom Bren. She wanted to go to Chelsea's, and I told her no . . . that we had to have our family talk."

"Let's do this. We have to do this." And Brendan took Carmen's hand. They headed up the stairs and stood in front of Vita's bedroom door. Brendan knocked lightly on the door. "Vita. Vita. We need to talk with you. Please come out." He paused and then continued, "Or I and your mom can come in and talk in your room." Brendan spoke in a deliberate but compassionate voice. There was no response.

"Vita? Vita! I am talking to you and asking you to open your door," said Brendan, this time sterner and somewhat louder.

Vita begrudgingly unwrapped herself and Chaz from their lavender cocoon. "Vita!" yelled Brendan.

"I'm coming. I'm coming," responded Vita. The door opened slowly. Carmen and Brendan saw the tears welled up in Vita's eyes.

"We can sit right here on your bed and talk," suggested Carmen.

"I want to go downstairs," declared Vita.

"Okay. Then let's go downstairs," said Brendan, holding out his hand for Vita.

She looked at his hand and then took it as he led her to the living room. She wanted to sit on the big lounge chair. Carmen and Brendan sat next to each other on the couch facing Vita.

And so *the inquisition* began with Brendan cutting right to the chase. Maybe that was a lawyer thing. "Vita, you need to tell us who your boyfriend is. Who fathered this baby?"

Vita buried her face in her hands. "I can't! I can't! It will cause too much trouble. You'll see. It will! I know it will!"

"Sweet pea," said Carmen, "the boy and his family have a right to know too. They need to know."

Vita pleaded, "Please don't make me! Why do I have to tell? Why?"

"Because someone else besides you is responsible for you being pregnant," said Brendan. "How long has it been going on, Vita?" And then Brendan said something he shouldn't have said, "Your mother and I did not raise you to go sleeping around. You are only thirteen for God's sake!" Brendan was losing his patience. His temper was beginning to flare.

"Please," Carmen said to Brendan as she touched his shoulder in an attempt to calm him down.

"Please what!" yelled Brendan.

"Vita," Carmen interjected before Brendan had a chance to get off another rant, "listen, we have to know. If you don't tell us, I am going to have to start making phone calls."

"Who are you going to call, Mom? Who?" asked a sobbing Vita.

"To the parents of your girlfriends. Maybe one of your friends will fess up as to who your boyfriend is because we can't seem to get that information out of you. I don't want to have to do that, Vita."

Vita suddenly stood up. She screamed and cried at the top of her lungs, "Okay! Okay! You want to know? Here . . . I'll . . . I'll be right back!" She ran to her room and pulled out her lavender leather-bound diary, the beautiful-looking book that held the ugly dark secret. Her parents had gotten off the couch to follow her and were partway up the steps when she appeared out of her room. Crying hysterically, Vita hurled the diary downstairs across the foyer and into the living room. "Here! Are you happy now? You can read all about it!" And she ran back into her bedroom, pulled the comforter off the bed, and huddled under it in the corner of her room.

Carmen and Brendan looked at each other in astonishment. Carmen went over to where the diary lie and picked it up. It was still locked, so she brought the diary with her into the kitchen and used a pair of scissors to cut the leather tab loose.

Brendan was torn between going upstairs to his distressed child or read what was in the diary. He went back up the stairs and into Vita's room toward the trembling girl. He coddled and held his daughter with his muscular arms wrapped around Vita and the comforter that held her. He rocked her gently. "I'm right here. It will be all right."

From the kitchen came a bloodcurdling scream that sounded as a fox in the woods in the dead of night. It was a horrific sound that Brendan had never heard come out of Carmen. "Dear God! No! Dear God! No!" were the words formed by Carmen's hysterical and cracked voice.

Brendan released Vita and flew out of the bedroom and down the steps to find Carmen hyperventilating on her way to the bathroom in the hallway. She proceeded to vomit into the toilet as Brendan placed his arm on top her wrenching back. She tried desperately to get the words out, but she could not. Finally, the audible but unbelievable words that would destroy Brendan came out. "It's Corbin! Corbin! Corbin has been raping our child."

Those words rung and echoed in Brendan's mind. It was as if he was frozen in those moments, unable to discern reality from the bad dream that unfortunately was the reality. He could not move. He was paralyzed with disbelief. Then he screamed, "Noooooo! Nooooo! Where is it? Where is it? Where is the damn diary?"

Carmen got herself up off her knees. She threw cold water on her face. And then she pointed to the diary that sat on the floor outside the bathroom door. She hadn't read much but had read enough to know the dark truth. Carmen scampered upstairs to find her daughter shaking and sobbing while still wrapped in the comforter in the corner of the bedroom. She fell on top of Vita and covered her like a mother bird covers and shields her young. "Why did you not come to us? I am so sorry. I am so sorry. When? How? Please, Jesus, please, Mother Mary . . . help us . . . help us now." She held Vita as tightly as she could and rocked her. She did not know what else to do.

A loud thundering boom came from the living room downstairs. Brendan had put his fist through the wall and at the same time let out a loud inhuman growl. He cried uncontrollably and fell onto his knees. He then got up and lunged toward the cabinet that contained the whiskey bottle. Brendan downed one quarter of the bottle and then wiped his lips with his sleeve. He then went to Vita's bedroom in a wild frenzy, unable to control his sobbing. Carmen and Vita were still huddled in the corner. Brendan went over to them and wrapped his arms around them both. He tried to talk . . . to have some consoling words, but none would come out.

"Why didn't you come to us?" repeated Carmen.

"I couldn't. I couldn't tell you. Now he will do something bad 'cause I told," cried Vita.

Brendan stood up; his trembling hand wiped his eyes. "I'm going to kill that son of a bitch. He calls himself my brother. My big brother . . . the brother that took care of me . . . the brother I always looked up to!" screamed a devastated and crazed Brendan. "I'll be back later!"

"Brendan, where are you going?" Carmen knew but asked anyway. "Please be . . ." Carmen's voice trailed off as she tried to comfort her daughter. Carmen and Vita heard the front door slam shut and then the sound of Brendan's car tires screeching in the distance.

Carmen pulled Vita's head close to her own chest under her neck and held her there for a long while. No words were spoken. Carmen gently helped Vita to stand up. "C'mon, Vita, let me help you onto the bed. We're going to Grandma's for the night. You sit here a bit, and I will pack an overnight bag. Chazzy can come too."

Nettie always kept a bag of the dog food Chaz ate as he was a regular visitor. Carmen phoned her mother from her bedroom phone. Nettie answered and could immediately tell something was drastically wrong by the tone of Carmen's voice. "Mom, we are having a crisis here. I need to come over with Vita for the night. I'll tell you when we get there."

Chapter 12

S HOCK, NUMBNESS, ANGER, AND RAGE alternated with great waves of sadness for the unimaginable atrocities of what his daughter had been through at the hands of his own flesh and blood consumed Brendan as he floored the acceleration peddle. As he hyperventilated, his heart pounded so hard as it felt as if it was slamming up against his chest wall. Brendan was light-headed and nauseous as his car somehow sped along the shortest route to Corbin's townhouse. Brendan felt his emotions spiraling out of control. The pressure inside of his head made his eyes feel as if they were going to explode out of their sockets. The car came to an abrupt halt after it haphazardly entered into the first available parking spot in the lot for the townhomes.

Brendan shut the engine off. He gripped the steering wheel with both hands clenched. His fingers were wrapped tightly, and his nails dug into the leather wheel cover. Brendan allowed his head to rest atop of the steering wheel momentarily as he tried to arrest the panic attack and rage that had engulfed him. He had no clue how he was going to handle this. He yanked the key out of the ignition and exited the car. He walked briskly to the second third-story building of the newly built townhomes. Brendan headed straight for the door with the numbers 2022. He rang the bell once, stood a brief second, and followed it with four hard knocks on the door. He had seen Corbin's car in the lot, so he knew Corbin was around. What if Corbin had a friend over or some woman? Four more hard knocks this time pounding with the side of his fist. "Corbin, Corbin . . .

C'mon man . . . It's Brendan! Will ya . . ." He could hear the door being unlocked from the inside as the knob turned.

"What the hell is wrong, Bren?" Corbin questioned as he swung the door open enough for Brendan to forcefully step inside. Corbin was in his sweat clothes and had been lifting weights in his make-shift workout room. Brendan's chest was heaving. He held his arms straight down by his sides with his fists still clenched as he scowled at Corbin. His piercing eyes were daggers that penetrated into Corbin's psyche.

"You tell me, brother of mine!" Brendan rammed Corbin up against the wall before Corbin had a chance to allow things to click. "But before I let you tell me, my dear brother, I am going to beat the living shit out of you . . . you—my big brother, my buddy, my best friend . . . you lousy piece of shit." Brendan was in a full-blown rage. He pummeled Corbin as Corbin sank down unto his heels, trying to shield himself from the onslaught of relentless punches. Corbin could not hold steady. Brendan pushed him down onto the floor. Corbin lay on his side. Blood oozed out from his nose and lip. Brendan grabbed his brother's T-shirt by the neck and the back of his sweatpants and yanked Corbin up. He screamed, "Why? You tell me why!" He threw Corbin down on the couch. Corbin's face was visibly swollen. He rolled onto his side with his back facing Brendan. He buried his bloodied face into the couch cushion. Brendan went over to the bar Corbin had set up in the living room and pulled out a mostly full bottle of Dewar's whiskey. He grabbed two glasses from under the bar and placed them on top of the bar. His hands shook as he proceeded to pour the whiskey into each glass.

Brendan brought the two glasses over to the coffee table in front of the couch and slammed them down onto the dark mahogany wood tabletop. Corbin did not flinch as he lay on the couch in a fetal position with his back still to his brother. Corbin felt his brother's hand on his left shoulder as Brendan tried to turn him on his back. Brendan could see the dazed expression on Corbin's already bruised and puffed face as the blood still oozed out from his nose and lips. Brendan was a wild man. He sat Corbin up as if he were a rag doll. "Now drink up! C'mon, drink this!" as he pointed to the glasses on the table. Brendan picked up a glass and downed all its contents with the tilt of his head. Corbin could not make eye contact with his brother. His head hung low as he tried to get his bearings. "I said drink up! Now!" Without lifting his head, Corbin raised his eyes to meet Brendan's fiery stare, and he quickly shifted his gaze back to the whiskey glass still on the table. Corbin reached for the glass with an unsteady right hand and somehow managed to draw it up to his lips. Between his unsteadiness and the immense stinging of the alcohol on his cut lips, Corbin spilled about a third of the whiskey out of the glass onto his already bloodstained T-shirt. Brendan, seeing this, assisted his brother with steadying his hand and getting the rest of the whiskey down into Corbin's mouth. Corbin winced.

Every ounce of Brendan wanted to rip his brother to shreds, but a part of him already realized the injuries he had already inflicted. As he cupped Corbin's head with a hand on each side of Corbin's bloodied face, Brendan had a flinching thought of crushing his brother's face. But he did not. Brendan sobbed and sputtered out the words, "Why . . . why . . . I don't understand . . . How . . . Why would you do this to my little girl? Goddamn you! Goddamn you, Corbin!" Brendan spoke brokenly through his tears. "You are my big brother. I have always looked up to you. I love you, and since Dad died, we have been it, man . . . you and me." Corbin's eyes were nearly swollen shut. He stared straight ahead, numb in pain in more ways than one.

Brendan placed his hands on his brother's shoulders and shook him. "Talk to me! Goddamn it! Talk to me!" Corbin continued to stare through Brendan. He finally shifted his eyes to meet Brendan's eyes and still said nothing. "I should kill you; you know that! You know that!" Brendan ranted. Corbin slowly raised his hands to his head and ran them through his hair. He placed his hands, one on each temple, and held his own head as he looked down at the floor. Brendan stood up and once more filled the two glasses with Dewar's. He stuck the one glass under Corbin's face. "Drink it . . . go ahead and drink it." Brendan downed the other glass. "Talk, Corbin," demanded Brendan.

Stumbling to find words, Corbin managed to mumble a barely audible "I don't know what you are talking about."

Brendan asked him to repeat what he had just said. Corbin did so. "My Vita is pregnant, Corbin." The words penetrated into Corbin's head. He was hurting too much, but somehow those words jarred him enough into continuing on with his defense mode. He knew full well what he had done to Vita. He thought to himself, *How could she be pregnant? It was only four times over the past year and a half.* His mind swirled with the ramifications of all this. Thoughts bounced around in his head. *Why did Vita tell when I had threatened her good? Why did I even start this stuff with Vita? I couldn't help it. Now what? My whole world . . .*

His thoughts were interrupted by a stern-voiced Brendan as he repeated the words, "My Vita, my baby, is pregnant, and you know something about it, don't you?"

Corbin mumbled, "What did she do, Bren? Get knocked up? Well, she didn't confide in me."

Brendan felt the rage take hold once more. With strength that comes from those moments of insanity, he stood Corbin up on is feet and laid a hard punch into the underside of Corbin's right jaw that landed Corbin back onto the couch in a contorted position and out cold. "You mean to tell me that my little girl is a liar. I don't think so!" screamed Brendan.

Brendan downed another two shots of whiskey and then slid down onto the floor as he leaned against the front of the couch where Corbin's right leg hung down. Brendan began to sob. He cried himself to sleep. There, the two Malloy brothers lay.

It was hours later when Brendan was awoken by the ringing of the phone. He could hear a distant phone ringing as if it were in a dream. Brendan, groggy, opened his eyes and realized that the ringing phone was in Corbin's living room. It must have rung ten times because that is when Corbin's answering machine was set to go off. "Hi there. You have reached me, Corbin. Can't come to the phone right now, but if you leave me your name, number, and a quick message, I'll get right back to ya." The caller had hung up. Brendan's brain rapidly assessed the sad scene. He recalled what had transpired before he had nodded off. He felt nauseated as he sensed the reality of what had occurred and the tragedy of the overwhelming dilemma.

His thoughts went immediately to Vita and Carmen. Brendan rose slowly and noticed the red swollen and bloodied knuckles on his right hand. He hoisted himself up onto the couch that held Corbin's limp body and sat beside his brother. Brendan was concerned. He gently lifted and cradled Corbin's head and could see that Corbin was indeed breathing. The blackened eyes, swollen lips and jaw, and the dried blood beneath his brother's nose and lips reminded Brendan of a prizefighter having lost after going through twelve agonizing rounds. Brendan again felt waves of nausea. *Corbin's all right,* he thought to himself. Brendan stumbled over to the phone and dialed his home number. He hung up after the phone rang the fifth time, before Carmen's recorded message would come on the answering machine. *Nettie's number . . . What's Nettie's number? I can't think.* His fingers then pushed the numbered buttons as Nettie's telephone number flooded back into Brendan's mind.

Nettie answered. She held up the receiver while motioning with it to Carmen.

Carmen took hold of the phone and held it tightly against her ear with both hands. "Where are you? What's going on?"

"I'll tell you when I get there. Stay there. I will be right there!" said Brendan and abruptly hung up the phone before Carmen could tell him to be careful. Carmen could tell that Brendan had been drinking.

Corbin stirred, grunted, and flinched in pain as he tried to move. Brendan went over to the couch. He could make out the blue of Corbin's bloodshot eyes through the slits of the swollen eyelids. Brendan could tell that Corbin was still out of it. "You'll be all right, big brother of mine. I'll be back later," Brendan said snidely. And then he hastily left Corbin's townhouse to get to his family.

Chapter 13

NETTIE HUNG UP THE PHONE after Carmen said she would be on her way. Nettie prepared the bed for Vita. She paced the house until she saw Carmen's car pull up to the curb. Nettie opened her front door and swiftly walked down the driveway toward the sidewalk to meet Carmen and Vita. She saw Vita in the front seat wrapped in her lavender comforter. Vita would always be the first one to bound out of the car, but she just sat motionless in the front seat like an expressionless statue as Carmen got out of the car with Chaz. Nettie had never seen her granddaughter like this. Her heart sank.

"Mom, can you hold on to Chaz's leash and grab my pocketbook?" asked Carmen as she handed Nettie the leash.

Tears welled up in Nettie's eyes as she watched her daughter help her paralyzed granddaughter out of the car.

Vita was in shock. Her deepest darkest nightmare that had been held in for so long was now known. The truth being out there for all to know was too much for her to handle. She wore the same blank stare from the time her parents came into her room after the revelation to the present.

"I'll bring the rest of the stuff in later," Carmen said. "I got you, sweet pea. We're at Grandma's now. C'mon, help me get you inside."

Vita's stride was short and stiff. Her mother led her like someone guiding a visually impaired person. Carmen had her arms wrapped around Vita who was still wrapped in her comforter.

Nettie held the front door open for them. "Why don't we go to my room," suggested Nettie after seeing that Vita was in no condition to go into the small bedroom with the lone twin bed. Chaz followed as grandmother, daughter, and granddaughter meandered their way into Nettie's bedroom. Nettie quickly pulled down the bedspread and put new pillow cases on the pillows. Carmen and Nettie helped Vita onto the bed. She immediately curled into a fetal position and closed her eyes as Nettie rewrapped her in the lavender comforter.

Nettie sat beside her granddaughter and stroked her hair. "What happened?" she whispered to Carmen.

Carmen broke down as she heard her own voice speak the words: "The baby's father is Corbin. Brendan's brother has been raping my little girl. And . . . we did not know. How could we not know, Mom?"

Nettie lay with Vita and pulled the bed covers over her and Vita in her comforter with her thin arm wrapped around Vita. "C'm' 'ere, Carmen."

And Carmen slid under the covers. There, the three women lay together. Nettie's and Carmen's arms enveloped Vita who was in the middle.

"I'm so sorry. I'm so sorry. I'm so sorry," whispered Carmen over and over as she stroked Vita's head.

Nettie kissed the top of her granddaughter's head. With her arm still wrapped around Vita, she reached over to grip Carmen's arm. "We will get through this . . . We will . . . Dear Jesus, please give us all the strength and whatever we need to get through this."

There were no further words spoken. Carmen, Vita, and Nettie remained huddled together on the bed, exhausted and drained from the anguish of the pain. Chaz curled himself on the throw rug at the side of the bed where he was able to glance up to check on his people. He nestled his head atop his paws to sleep after he was certain that all on the bed were in a sound slumber. Perhaps God was blessing them with this much-needed tranquility.

No one stirred for nearly two hours with Nettie being the first to awaken. She gingerly wriggled and slipped from under the covers and out of the bed. Chaz's dog tags clinked when he picked up his head.

"Sssh, Chaz," said Nettie softly with her index finger to her mouth as if Chaz could interpret the gesture. Carmen stirred. With one eye open, she saw Nettie standing on the side of the bed. "Carmen, I was just going to make a nice pot of hot tea." Vita apparently was in a sound sleep. Perhaps an overbearing weight had been lifted from her heart and her soul. Carmen got herself out of bed, trying her best not to rouse Vita. She tucked the covers all around Vita, picked up Chaz, and placed him next to the sleeping girl. Chaz nuzzled himself so he could get right into the middle of the fetal position Vita was still curled up in.

The two women tiptoed out of the bedroom and into the kitchen. Carmen parked herself at the kitchen table. She ran her fingers through her hair and then buried her face in her hands for a few seconds. She proceeded to tell Nettie what had happened. She related how Vita reached the point of a meltdown and how, while in a screaming and crying hysteria, ran back to her room, grabbed her diary, and hurled it at her parents.

Carmen got up from the table and found her pocketbook in the living room where Nettie had placed it. She returned back into the kitchen with the pocketbook as Nettie poured them each another cup of tea. Carmen reached into her pocketbook to pull out the lavender leather diary with its severed leather strap. Nettie remembered giving that diary to Vita three years ago. Vita and Nettie were shopping in the mall, and Vita fell in love with this lavender diary with the daisy on the front. Nettie remembered they had gotten it from a Hallmark store.

Carmen held the book up. "I only had read enough to know what I told you. I am afraid to read the rest of what is in here, Mom, but I am going to have to. We have to know."

"You will read it when you and Brendan are ready. You don't have to read it right now. We are all shattered by this. I can't begin to imagine how Vita managed to hold this all in," said Nettie. She pulled her chair next to Carmen's.

"Mom, I have to read what is in here, only because I am supposed to see Father John tomorrow. Remember, I was going to speak with him about dealing with Vita's pregnancy and now . . ." Her voice trailed off, and then she continued, "What do we do with this baby that is the product of an incestual rape?"

The two women talked. They both realized how this didn't change things for Vita. She had been dealing with Corbin's abuse for a long time.

Carmen said, "It must have been a huge relief for Vita . . . the truth be known now of her forbidden secret, and now it is time for healing to take place. I think we both know that to abort this baby would be wrong. It's still a life . . . no matter what, and to have Vita go through the trauma later on in life of having to live with the fact of killing the baby inside of her . . . it would just be too much to bear."

"Carmen, maybe you should take Vita with you tomorrow. I think that would be a good thing for her right now. Father John is so wonderful with the teenagers," suggested Nettie. Nettie quickly went on to another subject and said it as quick as she thought it, "You think you would have heard from Brendan by now."

"I know," Carmen replied. "I'm worried. I don't know if I should call over to Corbin's house. Maybe I'll wait a little longer."

They sipped their tea slowly. They talked about getting immediate help for Vita and how confused and tormented she must have been for all of this time. "Mom, how could Brendan and I have missed this? How could we not have known? We have failed her . . ."

"Dear, you know . . . and I know . . . how good and nurturing and how on top of things you and Brendan are. You cannot blame yourselves," said Nettie, consoling her daughter. She topped off the tea in both mugs with what was left in the teapot.

"Mom, will you read the diary with me? As much as I can't bring myself to read this now, I do need to know more before we are to talk with Father John tomorrow," said a reluctant Carmen.

Nettie nodded and placed her hand on her daughter's knee. They finished their tea and went into the living room. Carmen sat at the end of the couch next to the end table with the ornate white wrought-iron Mediterranean-style lamp on it. Nettie reached over to turn the lamp on and then went back into the kitchen to retrieve her reading glasses.

Mother and daughter huddled together at the end of the couch. Carmen took a deep breath in. Nettie watched as Carmen's long fingers daintily opened the lavender cover of the diary, the book that had been the recipient of Vita's outpourings. How long had Vita been telling her dark secret to this pastel book adorned with the embroidered daisy? Mother and grandmother of the victimized child tried in earnest to support each other as they read Vita's nightmarish truth. Reading Vita's own words made them wonder even more how Vita held in the pain, confusion, and torment for so long. Their hearts were pulled down to the deepest depths of darkness with each line on each page. They understood why Vita dared not say a word or even let on to the ongoing abuse as the threats made by Corbin to her were more than enough to silence her.

Shaken and shattered, they forced themselves to read Vita's diary to completion. To know that one's own child had gone through such horror and at the hands of a trusted family member with no one coming to her rescue would tear at the soul and core of any parent. Both again questioned themselves as to how they could have not known. They would do anything to lift Vita's burden and onto themselves. But what was done was done. The past was the past, and they knew how vitally important it was in moving forward with the healing process. Speaking with Father John would be a good first step. Carmen tried her best to recall each and every time Vita had been left in Corbin's care for the past eighteen months as that was when the abuse started.

"Oh my god! Brendan! I hope he's all right!" Carmen picked up the phone that was on the end table and hesitantly dialed Corbin's number, not knowing what to expect. Nettie could see Carmen's eyes darting back and forth. The phone rang and rang. It rang ten times before Corbin's answering machine kicked in. It disgusted her to hear his voice. Carmen hung up the phone and watched Nettie still paging through parts of the diary.

"No answer? I feel that Brendan may be upset that I read this before he was able to," said Nettie.

"No, Mom. He will understand that I wanted you to read it with me. Please don't worry about that."

Just then the phone rang. Nettie picked up the phone. "Brendan, dear . . . Hold on . . . She's right here." And she handed the phone to Carmen.

Carmen was off the phone in less than a minute. "He wouldn't tell me what was going on. He said he will tell me when he gets here. He's on his way now, and"—Carmen paused—"and I can tell he has been drinking."

Carmen went to Nettie's bedroom to check on Vita. She slowly turned the doorknob and pushed the door open just enough to peek in. All Carmen could make out was the shape of Vita's back curled under the covers and the top of Chaz's head with his bulging eyes peering over Vita to see what the disturbance was all about. Vita had not moved, with her and Chaz in the same position as they had been two hours before. Vita was still in a sound sleep. Carmen wondered if she should awaken her but decided it best to leave her be and closed the bedroom door without shutting it. Chaz lowered his pug head and stayed with the sleeping girl, the loyal sentinel that he was.

Carmen went out to her car to bring in the overnight bags. She and Nettie awaited Brendan's arrival. Nettie put on a fresh pot of extra strong coffee in anticipation of it being a long night. Carmen and Nettie spoke of the drastic mix of emotions that Brendan must be going through. After all, Corbin was not only his older brother to whom he always looked up to but was also his best friend. They were inseparable, especially ever since their father passed away when they were still in their teens. Corbin had always looked out for Brendan. Brendan trusted his brother. He loved his brother. Only God knew what immeasurable, intolerable pain Brendan was being consumed by. How could his beloved brother commit such heinous acts that attacked the very heart of Brendan's core by repeatedly inflicting the most horrendous abuse to Brendan's child? Carmen and Nettie could only imagine what had transpired at Corbin's house.

It was just after ten o'clock in the evening when Brendan knocked on Nettie's front door. The two women never heard the car door shut. Chaz, whose hearing was attuned to such sounds, never barked. Carmen opened the door and glanced up at Brendan's weary and tear-stained face as he stepped through the door. They embraced. The two of them held each other tightly and rocked side to side, not knowing what words to utter. They just held on to each other. The strong smell of whiskey was evident on Brendan's breath. As they loosened their embrace from each other, they stood face-to-face. Carmen could see Brendan's bloodshot and swollen eyes, with the blue of the iris appearing even more brilliant and intense by the contrasting red. She wondered whether the redness was from crying or drinking or both. Carmen then gazed down at Brendan's hands, each lightly gripping her forearms. The knuckles on his right hand were oozing blood.

"Where is she? Where is she?" asked Brendan in a slightly audible voice, his voice broken up.

Carmen described to Brendan how Vita had become withdrawn and how she wore a vacant stare before she fell asleep on Nettie's bed. "She's been asleep now for over four hours."

"I want to just see her," said Brendan with a sense of urgency. Carmen pointed toward Nettie's bedroom. Brendan lightly pushed open the slightly ajar door and poked his head into the room. A night-light was on, so he was able to make out the shape of Vita curled up. She seemed so little and so vulnerable. He could also make out the shape of the rounded top of Chaz's pug head with a perked ear on either side of it as the dog again detected a disturbance in the room. Chaz lowered his head back down and remained next to Vita after determining that the threat level was low. Brendan stared at Vita's motionless form and wanted desperately to hold and protect her. He leaned his head on the edge of the door and sobbed.

Leaving the door as he had found it, Brendan walked into the spare bedroom with the twin bed. He sat down and with his face buried in his hands. He shook his head back and forth, sobbed, and muttered, "I couldn't even protect her. I'm her father, and I couldn't protect her." Nettie and Carmen both appeared in the doorway of the unlit room. Brendan was not aware of their presence as he continued with his woeful mantra. "I couldn't even help her. What kind of a father am I?"

Nettie, who had always been more of a mother to Brendan than a mother-in-law, moved slowly to the bed and sat down next to him.

She placed her arm around his shoulder. She cared, loved, and nurtured Brendan like one of her own sons, something he did not receive from his own mother. As Nettie went to hug Brendan, he collapsed in her arms as if he were a hurt little boy. She held him tight as he sputtered out the same words, "I failed my daughter. I couldn't even protect her. I didn't know . . . I didn't know . . . How could the person close to me do this to my own child?" Brendan's crying was inconsolable as the words continued to spill from his lips. "My own flesh and blood . . . my brother . . . has destroyed my own flesh and blood. He's taken Vita's soul, her heart. He's taken my soul, my heart. I feel like I have done this to her."

Nettie held Brendan tighter. She stroked the back of his head and gently guided his head down onto her small bony shoulder. "Don't do this to yourself, Brendan. None of us could have known. Don't do this to yourself . . . Just let it out. You have to let it out." Brendan kept his head on his mother-in-law's shoulder, his eyes closed. Nettie had what Brendan needed at the moment, and Carmen could see that. It pained her to see her husband this way. Two of the people he loved and cared for the most had brought him the deepest of pain. Knowing that his precious daughter had been through a nightmare that would remain with her forever and that the terror had been inflicted by his beloved brother was more than he could bear. Carmen could find no words to say to Brendan. After several minutes, Nettie gave Brendan's arm a rub. "C'mon to the kitchen. I have coffee on."

Brendan picked his head up off Nettie's shoulder and nodded. "Thanks, Mom."

Carmen, who was still standing in the doorway, walked toward her husband as he got up off the bed, and together, they went hand in hand to the kitchen with Nettie.

Carmen, while still clutching Brendan's right hand, brought it to her eye level. She remembered he had punched a hole in the wall in their living room wall and could see his swollen bloodied knuckles. Their eyes met. Nettie watched. Brendan said nothing.

Nettie prepared the three mugs of coffee to each of their liking. She set them down on the kitchen table where Brendan and Carmen were already seated with their chairs drawn close together. No one spoke. Neither Nettie nor Carmen nor Brendan could find words. They all knew that they were there for one another, and it would be that very love and support that would somehow get them through the pain of this tragedy. Brendan gripped his mug with both his hands, his right hand more noticeably swollen. He brought the mug to his lips. He took a quick sip and had to set the mug back down onto the table as his hands were shaking so badly. Carmen placed her hand on Brendan's wrist, and again, their gazes met.

Brendan took in a deep breath and let out a long sigh. "I beat the hell out of him. I just couldn't stop myself. I don't know how badly I hurt him. I just left him there." He rubbed his forehead and temples with his fingertips. "Tell me this isn't happening!" And he proceeded to pound his fists on the table, declaring again, "Tell me this isn't happening!" causing coffee to splatter out of the mugs and startling the two women. Carmen knew not to press Brendan into talking. She thought it best to let him get it out the way he knew how to. Nettie and Carmen had had the past several hours to allow the situation to begin to sink in. Brendan was only now just coming to grips with the enormity of the tragedy.

"Why? Why, Carmen, did Vita not say anything to us?" sobbed Brendan. He looked away from the two women as if talking to someone else on the other side of the kitchen. "My own blood. My own flesh and blood! What did he want with Vita? How could he?" Brendan turned back to look at Carmen and Nettie as if they could offer him an answer. Tear flowed from their eyes once more. "She won't ever be right! She'll carry this scar forever. How can she ever have a normal life?" He again turned away to talk to the imaginary person on the opposite side of the kitchen and asked, "What is normal anyway?" He continued, "I wanted to just kill the son of a bitch!" Brendan got up from the kitchen table and told his wife and mother-in-law that he was going to step outside to get some fresh air. Carmen and Nettie looked at each other in silence.

Brendan's heart ached. Brendan's heart raged. Such sadness. Such a sinking feeling followed by waves of sheer rage. He began to jog. He was still in his dress shoes, trousers, and dress shirt, never having changed the clothes he had worn to his office that day. Running always seemed to help Brendan calm down. He usually could sort through his thoughts best when he ran. It did not matter to Brendan that his feet were tightly bound and hurting as the leather edging dug into the bottom of his ankle bone on either side of each foot as each stride hit the pavement. He was numb. Numb all over. Brendan ran hard, and a part of him wished he could run to escape from his life. This escape from the moment was what he needed to maintain some semblance of sanity.

It had been a half an hour since Brendan had gone outside for air. Carmen decided to take a look outside to check up on him. There was no sign of Brendan; however, his car was still parked on the street in front of Nettie's house. Carmen walked back into the kitchen. "He's probably walking around the neighborhood and defusing."

Carmen and Nettie checked in on Vita, who remained in a deep sleep in the same fetal position. Carmen bent down close to Vita's face to make sure she was still breathing as there was no apparent rise and fall of her torso. Chaz raised his head and looked at Carmen as if to say, "Don't worry. I am here. I will make sure that she is all right." Vita did not stir. Carmen was able to feel the light current of warm air escaping from Vita's nostrils. Perhaps Vita was now at peace. *Her deep dark secret had been revealed, and her body was getting the rest that it had longed for*, Carmen thought to herself.

The two women returned to the kitchen table. Each nursed another mug of coffee and discussed what Brendan's next action might be. They heard the front door close, and in a matter of seconds, Brendan stood facing them. He was dripping with sweat. He kicked off his shoes and leaned against the kitchen doorframe to peel his socks off. The skin below the ankle bones on the inner and outer part of each foot was red, chaffed, and raw. "I'm going to get Vita to a doctor. She has to have an abortion. Has to be done!" exclaimed Brendan as he wiped his brow. Both Carmen and Nettie knew it best not to contradict him, not at this moment. They just listened. "When I get into the office tomorrow, I am going to make some calls." The women still did not comment. Both gazed into their coffee mugs and then glanced at each other. "Carmen, you know this situation is entirely different than Vita being impregnated by a boy-friend. This warrants immediate action."

Carmen looked at Brendan, her eyes spoke of sadness. She did not dare say what was on her mind. "Brendan, I have an appointment to see Father John tomorrow. I would still like to go, and I would like Vita to come with me. It would be a good thing for her . . . some-place to start."

Brendan again wiped his forehead, scratched the back of his neck, and took a deep breath in and out. "If you think that will help her, go ahead." And then Brendan added, "Let Father John know the whole story, and I'll bet that he will understand why this preg-nancy has to be terminated." Carmen realized that Brendan did not fully comprehend the teachings of the Catholic Church. She let his last comment be and decided to quickly change the subject before Brendan would change his mind about Vita seeing the priest.

"Look at your ankles! Let me clean them and put some ice on them," Carmen offered.

Brendan appeared to be in a rush. He told Carmen not to bother with his ankles. Carmen detected a sense of urgency about Brendan. "I had better get back to Corbin's house. I think I hurt him pretty bad. Oh God! I hate him! First, I need to sit with Vita." He headed back into Nettie's bedroom and tiptoed up to the side of the bed and then sat himself down gently next to Vita's backside. He stroked her hair with the lightest touch and whispered, "I'm so sorry. I'm so sorry, sweet pea." He sat there for several minutes and kissed her. As he got up, he patted Chaz, who was monitoring the situation.

Brendan walked sullenly out of the bedroom. He apologized to Carmen and Nettie for his behavior. Brendan gathered his shoes and socks and sat down on the living room couch. He noticed Vita's lavender diary sitting on the end table next to the couch. Brendan picked up the diary, its broken leather straps dangling. He held it with his swollen, blood-crusted hands. He had not bothered to clean the dried blood off his hands. He stared at the cover with the embroi-dered daisy and the embroidered words "My Diary" on it.

Nettie brought him a dampened hand towel and a dry towel from the kitchen. "You might want to wipe your hands first."

The sound of Nettie's voice jarred Brendan from the fleeting trance he was in. "Oh, thank you, Mom."

"Bren, would you like me to sit next to you as you read Vita's diary? I did read it already with Mom."

Brendan did not appear upset that Carmen had read the diary. In fact, he preferred that she had done so. He expressed that he would like to go off on his own into the spare room and read it there.

"Are you sure, Bren?" asked Carmen. He nodded and disappeared.

Carmen and Nettie wondered if he would be able get through the whole diary. Nettie decided that she would try to get some rest and that she would lie down next to Vita. Carmen opted to wait in the living room for her husband to emerge from the other bedroom. She tried to fathom all that had happened the past week. She tried to recall the past two years, especially the encounters with Corbin. Were there any signs or signals of anything that was remotely suggestive of the abuse that Vita had endured?

Carmen's mind pondered on. She was startled by the sound of the bathroom door being closed. Actually, Brendan had closed the door quietly, but it was the click of the lock snapping into place against the eerie quietness of the house that had startled her. She went into the hallway to see the door to the spare room open, but no Brendan. Carmen stood outside the bathroom door and placed her ear against it. She could hear running water, and she could hear Brendan heaving and trying to catch his breath. She heard the toilet flush and the water still running from the sink faucet.

Brendan cupped and filled his hands with cold water and threw the water on his face. The coolness soothed his hands and his swollen eyes somewhat, but nothing could soothe his heart.

Carmen waited for him outside the door for what seemed like an eternity. Finally, she heard the cessation of the running water. The door opened. Somehow, Brendan knew Carmen would be there waiting for him. He looked pale. He looked drained. Carmen reached out and took his hand as he lifted his eyes to meet hers. "I have to go now. I'm going back to Corbin's. I don't know what I am going to do when I get there, but I have to go," Brendan said in a withdrawn and broken voice.

"I know. I can't stop you. Bren, please, please be careful. Please don't do anything that you will regret," pleaded Carmen.

"I've already done that, Carmen. I trusted my brother with our daughter, and—"

"Bren, you can't blame yourself. I am as much to blame then . . . just please . . ." She paused and then said, "I love you." Carmen kissed Brendan and asked that he call her later. She told him that she was going to try to lie down but that she wanted to hear from him at some point. "Brendan, you know that we will need to sit down and talk."

"Look," said Brendan, his voice fatigued and weak, "I'm going to have to go into the office in the morning and do my work and whatever I can of Corbin's. Linda will have to move his appointments. There is no way he will be in . . . not with the way I left him. And now that I have read the diary . . . Let's just say he won't be . . ." and Brendan's voice trailed off.

Carmen gazed into Brendan's bloodshot eyes. Beads of water coursed their way down Brendan's face. She couldn't tell if they were from sweat or water he had splashed onto his face. His hair was wild from him running his fingers through it. His shirt was stained and disheveled. "I'll walk with you to the door. Call me." Carmen watched Brendan's figure disappear down the driveway into the dark. As she closed the door, she heard Brendan's car pull away, this time in a civil manner. Brendan was on his way to Corbin's townhouse. It was already past midnight. Carmen was worried about her husband and what he was capable of. She decided too that it would be best to get some rest. Before she joined Nettie and Vita on the bed, she managed to coax Chaz up and gently lifted him off the bed so as not to disturb Vita. She took Chaz for a quick walk in front of the house and then returned him to his spot on the comforter, which was still indented and warm.

Chapter 14

BRENDAN KEPT A KEY ON his key ring that Corbin had given him to hold on to for the townhouse. He walked up to the door and noticed how dark the house was except for the dim light that emanated from the living room window, the same light that he had turned on several hours earlier. Brendan attempted to insert the key into the door lock several times, but to no avail. He was emotionally and physically spent. The anxiety, the depression, the guilt, and the anger made him unsteady, plus the fact that he had not eaten since the lunch meeting at the Cabaret Restaurant. His stomach pained him, but not from the hunger. He took a deep breath in and out and used his left hand to steady his right hand as he slipped the key into the keyhole. He hesitated before turning the doorknob to let himself in. Would Corbin still be where he had left him? How badly hurt would he be? Was he alive? Or had he been able to get up and about? Perhaps he was in his bed.

When Brendan entered the living room, he saw Corbin lying on the floor between the couch and the coffee table. He was on his side, and Brendan was able to make out the rhythmic slow rise and fall of Corbin's shoulder with each apparent breath. Brendan surmised that Corbin likely fell while trying to get up or had simply rolled off the couch. The coffee table felt like it weighed a ton as Brendan pushed it farther away from the couch. The two empty glasses, sticky from the whiskey, still on the table, fell but did not break. Brendan placed his hand on Corbin's shoulder to rouse him. Brendan called to Corbin and jostled his shoulder once more. He then rolled Corbin onto his back. Corbin's entire face was swollen and bruised. Dried blood had set in place under his nostrils and the sides of his mouth. His lips were split with the gashes filled with crusted blood. His eyes were mere slits. Corbin opened his eyes just enough for Brendan to make out the blueness of the irises. Corbin kept rolling his eyes up and moaned in pain. Part of Brendan was moved to help his brother, but there was the other part of Brendan that was ready to explode with rage. And it was that part of him that was capable of killing his brother. Somehow, Brendan was able to take a step back. Maybe it was his guardian angel or their father's spirit, but whatever it was, Brendan was able to let the rage subside. He looked at Corbin with pure disgust. "How could you! Why? Why would you want to hurt Vita? Why would you want to hurt my child?" Brendan asked in desperation as he clutched his brother's T-shirt by the collar.

Corbin tried to mumble something, but Brendan kept on with his grief-stricken questioning. He did not realize Corbin was trying to tell him something. Corbin managed to flail his arm a bit before it collapsed back onto the floor. This was enough to garner Brendan's attention. Corbin garbled some words that Brendan was not able to understand. Brendan still had the collar of Corbin's T-shirt tightly clenched in his fist. He yanked on the shirt. "What? What could you possibly have to say to me?" ranted Brendan.

Corbin sputtered the words, "You're wrong. I didn't do . . ." He coughed and choked and continued, "Please. You're wrong."

With that, Brendan flung his hand loose of Corbin's collar. "You are a liar, Corbin. You're a goddamn liar! Look, I will be back to deal with you later. Don't dare come into the office today! Not that you're in any shape to do that!" Brendan grabbed Corbin by his shoulders, picked his torso up off the floor, and shoved him back down onto the floor as hard as he could. "I will do what I have to do to clear your calendar for today, but when I come back, you had better have some answers."

When Brendan arrived back home, it was almost one thirty in the morning. The dark house sat silent. His home felt different to him. It didn't feel like home anymore. Perhaps it was the emptiness of it, or perhaps it was the emptiness of his heart. Not bothering to turn on the lights, Brendan stumbled and groped his way upstairs and into the bedroom, but not before peering into Vita's bedroom and feeling that same emptiness.

Brendan shed his clothes onto the bedroom floor and showered in cold water. The cold water brought momentary relief to his blistered feet, his swollen eyes, and his bruised hand. His heart yearned for such relief. Brendan toyed with the idea of not calling Carmen to let her know he was home. He did not want to wake up Carmen, Nettie, or Vita. However, his wife had asked him to please call her.

Brendan sat naked at the edge of the bed and picked up the phone. "Carmen? Just me. I'm home now—just wanted to let you know. I'll call you later on. I have to lie down. Love you too." Brendan tossed off the freshly laundered comforter and pulled the clean cool cotton sheets over him as he slid under the sheets.

Brendan's mind was running in circles as it felt as if it were disconnected to his fatigued and aching body. He knew he wanted to find an out-of-town abortion center as soon as possible. He would fix this as best he could for his little girl. She would one day thank him for it. And Carmen would come to understand that this was the right decision. He thought about how he could punish his brother. *Corbin will have to answer and pay for what he has done . . . either to me and the law if Vita wants.* He wondered too if all this would affect his law practice. Then came the thoughts about all that had to get done in the office in the morning. He would have his work and what he could handle of Corbin's work. Finally, Brendan's mind succumbed to sleep as these thoughts that incessantly bombarded his mind ceased.

He awoke only a few hours later. Groggy and momentarily confused by the lonesome bed, he rolled his head toward the nightstand. The red illuminated numbers on the digital clock read four thirty-two. Reality then set in like wildfire that jolted him upright. The same thoughts that had flooded his head before he had fallen asleep suddenly took up residence where they had left off. He threw the sheets off in a hurry and bolted out of the bed. Brendan felt his weary body and glanced down at his blistered feet. He decided not to go jogging, and besides, he was anxious to get to his office to clear as much of his and Corbin's work as possible. Thankfully, neither he nor Corbin had court. Brendan did not have to don a suit. He opted for khaki trousers and a mint green dress shirt. He didn't bother with a tie, knowing that he had a collection of them in his desk at the law office.

Brendan was seated in his office by five thirty in the morning, and that included a stop at Dunkin' Donuts. He figured he needed some sustenance even though his stomach felt unsettled. Brendan sat the cup of coffee and the bag with the bran muffin on his desk. He was used to the silence of an empty office as oftentimes he stayed after Corbin and their paralegal/secretary Linda had left. Brendan's goal was to clear the desk of his work and do whatever he could manage of Corbin's. He would have Linda rearrange Corbin's appointments when she came in at eight o'clock. His intention was to get most of this done so that when morning business hours rolled around, he would be able to make the necessary phone calls that included setting up an appointment in an out-of-town abortion center for the next morning. He had one client he had to meet with, but that was not until early afternoon. After that, he would return to Corbin's house. Perhaps by then, Corbin would be coherent enough to face and answer the accusations.

***

Vita, her mother, and her grandmother were awoken by Chaz's barking, with each bark preceded by a growl. He heard the sanitation truck workers throwing the empty trash cans back onto the sidewalk.

Nettie sat up. "Oh, I forget it was trash day. It can wait till next time."

Carmen watched as Vita opened her eyes. Vita was greeted by a flurry of licks from Chaz's small curled tongue as his small coiled tail danced in delight. Vita smiled and put her arms around Chaz before she realized that she wasn't in her own bed. Her expression suddenly changed to a look of confusion as her surroundings began to register and the reality of how she found herself in her grandmother's bed slowly came back to her. She wasn't sure how long she had been there. "What day is it?"

"It's Friday morning about eight thirty, sweet pea," answered her mother as she stroked Vita's forehead with her thumb.

Vita sat up, still dazed. "Oh." Carmen and Nettie watched Vita try to piece together the circumstances that had led her to this moment. Neither could find words to say to Vita. Vita then asked, "I'm not going to school today?"

"No, Vita. I think today you need to rest and relax, and later we can talk when you are ready." Carmen embraced Vita and held her head close to her chest under her chin. She whispered, "I am so sorry. I am so very sorry, sweet pea. Please . . . why didn't you tell us? You could have told Mommy and Daddy, don't you know that?"

Nettie placed her hand atop Vita's head, stroking and gathering her long hair. The recollection of the hysteria of the previous day with the screaming, the crying, the pressuring, and the hurling of the diary at her parents. It all became real again. Carmen felt Vita shake her head. Vita's voice cracked, "I couldn't, Mommy. Please don't be mad. He made me do it. And he said if I told . . ." Vita began to cry.

"I know, honey. I know what he told you. I read it in your diary."

Vita then continued, "He said he would kill Chazzy, and he said he would make it look like an accident but that I would know it really wasn't."

"We know. We know," Carmen said softly as she tried to console Vita.

Vita pulled away abruptly from her mother and looked around in earnest. "Where's Dad? Did Daddy read my diary too?" Carmen replied that her father had indeed read the diary. Vita's face wore the expression of disgust. "I'm so . . . so embarrassed. I don't want anyone to know!"

Nettie, still stroking Vita's hair, said, "Vita, you have nothing to be embarrassed about. You were a victim of something horrible, done by a very sick person." Her grandmother's comment served only to remind Vita that her father might be with her uncle Corbin.

"Where's Daddy? Where is he? Is he with Uncle Corbin?"

Carmen and Nettie looked at one another. "I believe he is at work now, Vita," replied Carmen.

"Oh no! No!" exclaimed a worried Vita. "Uncle Corbin might come looking for me and then Chazzy. What if he has hurt Daddy already?"

Carmen reassured Vita that her father had dealt with Uncle Corbin for the time being. "Dad called when he got home early this morning. He said he was going to try and get some rest and then go to the office." Vita tried to push her mother into telling her how her father had dealt with her uncle. Carmen herself did not know the details of what went on between her husband and brother-in-law. "Uncle Corbin will be punished for what he has done, Vita. Somehow, someway, in the end . . . he will get what he deserves. All I can tell you is that Dad had gone to see him. We will deal with your uncle Corbin, but right now, you need to know that you are safe and Chaz is safe. And Dad is safe."

"I don't want to see Uncle Corbin again . . . ever!" insisted Vita.

"I know. I know, sweet pea. And you won't have to," Carmen said reassuringly.

"We are here for you, Vita," said Nettie. "We love you. You know that. We will do what it takes to get you through this. You know the three of us ladies here are strong ladies."

"Now what do you think, Mom, about this baby?" This question from Vita caught Carmen and Nettie off guard. "Don't you think I should get rid of it? It's bad! It came from a bad thing done to me by a bad person!"

Carmen got up off the bed and walked over to the window to look outside. Vita and Nettie sat on the edge of the bed next to each other with Chaz having crawled partway onto Vita's lap. "What do you think, Vita? Is that what you want to do?" questioned Carmen as she gazed out the window and waited for a response from her daughter.

"I don't love this baby . . . How could I? But after I saw the baby in my stomach when the doctor did the ultrasound, that made me realize that there is a little person who is alive inside of me," Vita paused and then said, "so I don't know what to do. I am so confused now."

This response from Vita was a ray of hope to Carmen. Vita was certainly aware that the fetus was more than just a blob of tissue. Carmen turned away from the window and walked over to where

Vita and Nettie sat on the bed. She placed her hands upon Vita's shoulders and smiled. "I already have an appointment for myself to see Father John at noon today. I arranged it when I first found out you were pregnant. I needed advice from him. I needed to know what to say to you about the life inside of you. I want you to come with me today. He can help us."

"Mommy, I don't want people to know, and he's . . . well, he's a priest!" Vita was hesitant about agreeing to go.

"He helps people like us all the time," Carmen said. "You know how Father John is. You like him. You know how kind and gentle he is and how, yes, sometimes he has to be strict."

Vita nodded in agreement. She looked over at her grandmother. "Can Grandma come too?"

"Absolutely," said Carmen, "if Grandma would like to."

Nettie, her arm still around Vita, said, "Of course, sweetheart."

Chaz jumped onto the floor and started to do his pee-pee dance.

"Can I walk Chaz, Mom? He's got to go. But I want you to come with me outside."

Carmen and Vita walked Chaz while Nettie made a light breakfast of scrambled eggs, toast, and some sliced cantaloupe along with another pot of strong coffee for her and Carmen. Despite having had the super-charged coffee late last night, the two women were somehow able to get some solid sleep.

After breakfast, they got themselves ready to go to the church. "We'll drop Chaz off back home first," Carmen said while she gathered the overnight bags and her pocketbook.

"No, Mom, no!" sounded a frightened Vita. "You can't leave Chazzy home all by himself. Uncle Corbin has a key, and he will hurt him now that he knows I told!"

Nettie quickly interjected, "Chaz can stay here. It's okay with me, Carmen." Chaz was not a chewer, even when he was upset. Carmen agreed to let Chaz remain in Nettie's home, not wanting to agitate Vita more than she already was.

"I'll fluff up my comforter and put it on top of the bed for him," Vita said with a sense of relief, knowing Chaz would be safe while they were gone.

The Bimmer pulled into the parking lot behind the church and the McLaughlin Center, named for a longtime pastor from decades before. The McLaughlin Center housed the rectory, the offices, and the classrooms for the CCD classes. Carmen thought it would be a good idea if she spoke with Father John first. She could relay to him the whole truth of Vita's pregnancy and spare Vita from having to listen to it. Carmen had the diary with her in her pocketbook. As with confession, anything told to a priest remained with the priest. Carmen trusted Father John O'Brien. She had known him ever since he was assigned to that parish fifteen years ago. Nettie also belonged to the same parish even though it was not the closest Catholic church to her home. Both women were active as volunteers for the church.

The two women and Vita entered into the large foyer of the McLaughlin Center. There was a waiting area, an alcove, off to the right with couches and chairs. Nettie and Vita sat there while Carmen went into the office to let the church secretary, Helen, know that she had an appointment with Father O'Brien. Carmen and Helen chatted briefly, and Helen said she would let Father John know she was here and for Carmen to have a seat back in the waiting area until he was available. Carmen returned to the waiting area and sat in a chair next to the couch Nettie and Vita were seated on. "Helen will let us know when Father John is ready to see us." Vita liked the waiting room at the doctor's office much more. There were no fish aquariums to be had here. The plain furniture would certainly be labeled as missionary-style furniture. There was, however, a beautiful large hand-carved wooden crucifix, handcrafted from olive wood from Jerusalem that hung on the wall. The painful expression of the face of the crucified Christ was so real that it was mesmerizing, and it often brought tears to those who gazed upon Him. There were also statues of Mary, the Virgin Mother, and of the Holy Family along with several large framed photographs of Pope John Paul II that hung on the wall.

Father John appeared in the archway of the alcove within ten minutes. He apologized as he had been on a lengthy phone call in his office. His perpetually ruddy cheeks made him look like he had either been in the sun a bit too long or had a few beers too many. His gentle demeanor, genuine smile, and twinkling eyes endeared him to his parishioners. He greeted the three visitors. He held Vita's hand in between his hands when he greeted her. He knew the reason for the appointment had to do with her pregnancy. He would soon find out the morbid facts of Vita's pregnancy. Carmen requested that she speak with him alone first.

Father John led Carmen back through the main office where Helen and another woman sat at the desk and then into his private office. Vita became visibly anxious as she watched her mother leave the waiting area. Nettie tried her best to distract Vita. She asked Vita to tell her about sleeping over Chelsea's house the past Saturday.

Carmen was offered a seat in a comfortable couch across from Father John's desk. The priest sat in his high-backed swivel chair and listened to Carmen's story. As Carmen began to talk about the repeated incest committed upon Vita, Father John got up from his chair and walked over to the front of the desk and sat next to Carmen. He held her right hand in between his hands like he had done with Vita. From time to time, she dabbed her eyes with a tissue she held in her other hand.

Father John was surprised to hear that Carmen herself had aborted a baby before she and Brendan were married. Carmen and the priest discussed how the added trauma of the violence of abortion does indeed cause more harm to the woman. Not only has an innocent been killed via a most violent of means but the mother's soul forever bears that burden of guilt. Carmen knew that firsthand. Carmen also expressed Brendan's desire to save his daughter from this whole ordeal by wanting to set up an appointment for an abortion.

Carmen was with Father John for almost a half an hour before he suggested that it would be a good time to have Vita come in. He opened his office door and poked his head out and then motioned to Helen at the desk to have Vita and Nettie come into his office.

"Vita," said Father John in a compassionate tone, "your mother has told me everything." He took Vita's small hands into his hands. "I know how difficult this must be for you to come here to talk with me, but I want to thank you for your courage in doing so. I am so sorry that this has happened to you." He stood up while still holding

Vita's hands and gently raised her hands as he stood so that she would follow and stand up. He then embraced her and told her, "There is a good that will come out of this evil, my dear child. I want you to believe that."

Vita spontaneously mumbled out some words that the priest was able to discern. "Then why did this have to happen to me?"

The priest guided Vita back toward the couch and helped her sit down in between Carmen and Nettie. "Vita, we do not know why God permits certain things to happen. That is the question that all of us . . . God's children . . . ask. We are given free will here in this world. Believe me, it hurts God, our Father, to see how his children behave . . . to watch as we disobey and how we hurt our fellow brothers and sisters. We will never understand why he allows the tragedies that take place in our world to happen. But one day, we will understand. When we are with Him in heaven, we will understand the course of our individual journeys. Vita, I know that does not take away any of the pain you are in and the suffering you have been going through. Sometimes it helps to offer up our sufferings to God."

Vita stared down at her knees as she listened intently. There was a brief silence. Neither Vita nor Carmen nor Nettie said a word.

Father John then asked Vita, "How do you feel about the baby inside of you?"

Vita did not know how to answer. Truth was she did know how to answer but was afraid to say something that she thought the priest would not want to hear. She had been to several prolife events with her mother through this church. Father John placed his index finger under Vita's chin and lifted it slightly. Her eyes slowly rose to meet the understanding eyes of the kindly priest. Father John O'Brien's bright Irish blue eyes always had a twinkle, even now. *Maybe those are angels*, thought Vita to herself as she focused on the sparkles in his eyes.

With his finger still under her chin, he said, "It's okay, Vita. I want you to be honest with me. You can tell me that you hate the child . . . If that's how you feel, then that's how you feel." He removed his finger from Vita's chin.

An awkward half smile crept across Vita's face. "Well, I don't love this baby . . . not at all," said Vita. "Maybe I even hate it. I don't know."

"And that is okay to feel that, Vita. It's okay," repeated Father John. Nettie, who was sitting on one side of Vita, patted Vita's knee. Father continued, "Your uncle did horrible things to you, and this baby is a result of that, and you are reminded of that all the time now. But let me ask you this. Do you think that getting rid of the baby would help you now?"

Vita gripped the sides of her chair. "Well, yeah, if God could magically make this baby disappear . . . I guess that would help 'cause then I wouldn't have to worry about what people at school and my friends would say." She thought for a moment and then added, "But I would always remember what he did to me. I don't think getting rid of the baby would help that. Nothing can take away how bad I feel inside." Carmen was proud of Vita to hear her being able to express some of what she felt. "Sometimes I feel like the baby is from the devil. Is it? Isn't this a devil child?" This question had gnawed at Vita.

"No. No, sweetheart. No child, no baby comes from the devil . . . no matter how the child was conceived. Only God can create life. That is something the devil cannot do. Why God allowed this child to be conceived this way . . . I do not know. But God does not interfere with the free will that he permits in our imperfect world. And you know that God loves all of us. He loves you, and He loves that child inside of you.

"Your mom told me that you had an ultrasound at the doctor's office, and you saw the baby inside of you. How did you feel when you saw that little person?" asked Father in a compassionate manner.

"I guess I thought it was kind of cool . . . you know. I saw it sucking its thumb, and it was doing somersaults, and I could kind of feel it inside of me when it was doing that . . . you know . . . like butterflies flying around in there," said Vita as she pointed to her stomach.

"That must be an incredible feeling, I bet," said Father John. "Vita, I know you know what abortion is about. You know what happens to the baby. You have been to many of our prolife rallies and prayerful protests with your mom and your grandmom. I know you have seen what abortion looks like." And Father John once again took hold of Vita's hands. He made eye contact with her when she would permit it. He then went into a long explanation about why abortion was the wrong choice. "You know," he said as he looked at Nettie, Carmen, and then back to Vita, "faith comes into effect when we truly have to practice our faith. Terminating this pregnancy will create more problems. It is really not the quick fix the abortion people say it is. Think about it. How will you feel years from now about hurting and ending the life of this innocent child? And this child is innocent. You have already been traumatized and deeply hurt, Vita, by violent acts done to you. Sadly, you cannot have that taken from you. The hurt has already been inflicted upon you. Would you really want to magnify that hurt and trauma even more by deciding to allow more violence to be inflicted upon this child? You have seen the pictures of an aborted baby."

Carmen could no longer contain herself. She began to quietly sob as her own feelings of guilt and remorse came crashing down upon her. "I'm sorry. I didn't mean to . . ." Carmen's voice trailed off.

Carmen sensed Father's questioning expression on his face to mean "Does Vita know about your abortion?" She looked at Vita and then to Father John. "I didn't mean to interrupt. Yes, Vita knows. She just found out about the baby boy I aborted before Brendan and I were married."

The priest put his hand onto Carmen's shoulder. "Carmen, you and I will need to sit down and talk. You have never come to terms with yourself and God. I want to help you with this. You need to ask forgiveness of the child and know you'll see the child. And I think you and Brendan should name the child and put that child in the arms of Our Lady." Father John added, "Vita, do you see your mother's pain? How do you feel about the abortion your parents had?"

Vita did not hesitate with an answer. "I feel sad. Very sad for my mom and sad because I had a brother and I will never get to know him." This comment exacerbated Carmen's misery and caused her to sob even more.

Nettie leaned across Vita to take hold of Carmen's hand while she spoke to Vita, "You will know your brother one day, Vita. You will see him in heaven, and you will recognize each other."

Father John echoed Nettie's statement, "Your grandmother is right.

"Vita, you know that adoption is an option, and through Catholic Social Services, the child within you will have the opportunity to grow up in a loving home. There are many couples out there who are waiting to adopt. The adoptive parents can be from anywhere in the United States, so you don't have to worry about this child living in the same town as yourself. Now, how do you feel about carrying this baby for the remainder of your pregnancy . . . about five months, is it?"

Vita replied that she did not want anyone to know that she was pregnant, especially all the kids at school.

"I know, I know," said the compassionate priest, "but sometimes what looks to be the easy way out really isn't the easy way out. Sometimes we have to be as courageous as we can be and do things the right way. You know you can ask Jesus to help you. You can offer up your suffering to Him. These will be a difficult several months for you, but you know what?" Father John paused and picked up Vita's hand. "Jesus will see you through this as I know Mom, Dad, and Grandmom will. And yes . . . people will talk . . . Let them. That is human nature. But one day, those people may come to realize your sacrifice and your courage in allowing this child to live . . . giving this child his or her life . . . as God intended it to be."

Vita felt a sense of peace for the moment and, with a quizzical look on her face, asked Father, "Is that kind of like when Jesus sacrificed Himself on the cross so that we could have everlasting life?"

Father John patted Vita's shoulder and peered over at Carmen and Nettie. He couldn't help but smile. "I see she has been paying attention in catechism class, that, and she has great teachers at home."

Carmen, Nettie, and even Vita managed a smile too. Nettie mentioned that she had spoken to someone at Catholic Social Services. "They gave me quite a bit of information over the phone and put a packet in the mail for me."

Father offered, "And you can call our parish center office any-time you would like to set up an appointment with one of our social service counselors. If you would like, we can even arrange for that when we are done here."

Carmen, her eyes still watery, looked directly into Vita's eyes. "What do you think, Vita? Should we go ahead and arrange to speak with someone about adoption for this baby?"

Vita felt she was beginning to have a sense of purpose. She thought to herself how it would certainly take much courage and strength to go through this pregnancy and perhaps God would give her the strength if she asked for it. Deep in her own gut, deep in her heart, she knew the right thing to do would be to honor God by sacrificing herself to allow His creation to be. She heard the words flow from her lips, "I think I can do it. You know, I think I can get through the rest of this pregnancy and have the baby so that the baby can have a life with a nice family somewhere. And maybe this baby will grow up to become a really important person, you know, like the president of the United States or something."

Carmen threw her arms around her daughter. She hugged her and rocked her from side to side. "I am so proud of you. You will know in the coming years that this decision was the right one. You will never be haunted by the relentless guilt that burdens the soul of us women who did not know better. I did not want you to have that added pain on top of the pain you are already dealing with."

Father John arose from his chair and laid both hands atop Vita's head. "Bless you, my child." He walked over to a row of filing cabinets and pulled open the bottom drawer of a tall black metal one. "Carmen, I will make you a copy of a study done in 1979 by a Dr. Sandra Mahkorn of rape victims who were impregnated. It is the only study I know of on the topic. You, Vita, Nettie, and Brendan too can look over it. You will find it fascinating that seventy-five to eighty-five percent of these rape victims did not have an abortion." He walked out of his office to make the copies himself at the copy machine in the main office. When he returned to his office, he found the three generations of ladies holding hands with one another. Father John handed Carmen the copy of the study, which she folded and placed in her handbag.

"Thank you, Father."

Father John scribbled something on a notepad. "These two women are psychologists, both PhDs who specialize with teens and work with pregnant teens in particular. I want you to call one of them for counseling for Vita. They are both beautiful people whom I trust and believe can help Vita and you all to deal with all that has happened."

Carmen read the names on the slip of paper the priest had handed her and immediately recognized one of the names as one of the counselors that Dr. Santiago had recommended. She pointed to the name. "Father John . . . this one here, Rachel Vitale, is one of the names that Vita's obstetrician gave us two days ago. The doctor doesn't know the circumstances surrounding Vita's pregnancy . . . Well, you know Brendan and I did not find out until yesterday ourselves."

"Then that is the lady to call," confirmed Father John. "I believe you will like her very much, Vita. And everything you discuss with her is in strict confidence. She has a wonderful way with teens and has helped many young people with all sorts of difficulties." Father John smiled confidently.

"Then calling Dr. Vitale will be at the top of my list," agreed Carmen.

Carmen, Nettie, and Vita sat with the priest for another half hour so that they could get some sort of plan together and begin to implement it. Learning the steps of the adoption process and getting the initial paperwork readied was what Carmen wanted to get a move on. Carmen, Nettie, and Vita thanked the good priest as he gave them a blessing before they exited his office.

The women and the girl were almost out of the building when Carmen handed Nettie the keys. "I'll meet you back at the car. I forgot to ask Father something." And with that, she hurried back into the main office where the priest was chatting with the two women behind the desk. "Excuse me, Father . . . one last thing." The priest escorted Carmen back into his office. Carmen without hesitation asked, "What if this child has a handicap of some sort, you know, because it was conceived through incest, and a bad gene, if there is any, can come through on both sides?"

Father John put his hand on Carmen's shoulder and looked directly into her concerned brown eyes. "However God has created this child is up to Him. Every life, no matter how we humans look upon that life, is precious, sacred, and has a purpose. We ourselves cannot make that judgment. That life, that baby's salvation, or the salvation of those that have a relationship to that child are in play here. You have to trust God."

Carmen smiled and rested her hand atop of the priest's hand still on her shoulder. "Thank you. Thank you."

She joined Nettie and Vita who were already seated in the car. Vita sat contently in the back seat and pondered the thought of having this child and giving the child to a loving family. The idea of adoption sat well with her, and her heart somehow felt settled.

When they arrived back at Nettie's house, Carmen called Dr. Rachel Vitale and was able to get an appointment for Vita for Tuesday afternoon. Nettie and Vita meanwhile had taken Chaz for a quick stroll.

Chapter 15

BRENDAN'S MORNING WENT ALONG AS he had planned. He managed to plow through his work and clear from Corbin's desk what he could. Linda successfully rearranged Corbin's schedule with Corbin to resume work on the following Monday. Brendan told Linda that Corbin had to have necessary minor surgery as he had taken a fall. He left it at that. Linda let Brendan know that she was stepping out for lunch, and she would be switching the phones over to the answering machine. "Can I pick a sandwich up for you at the deli, Brendan?"

At first, Brendan declined. He reconsidered, "You know . . . I think I could go for a little something." He dug into the pockets of his khaki pants, pulled out his wallet, and took out a twenty-dollar bill. "Just pick me up my usual tuna sub and a Gatorade, any flavor. Get yourself lunch. Thanks for going."

"Brendan, are you feeling okay?" asked a concerned Linda. She had noticed the bags under his eyes along with his bruised and swollen hand. "Yeah, I'm just tired. Did some lawn work last night and forgot to take my Benadryl. Thanks for asking."

"Well, okay," Linda responded, "I'll be back in a bit, and oh, thanks for the lunch."

Brendan shut the door to his office after Linda left. He called an out-of-town Planned Parenthood and asked the woman who answered the phone for a recommendation of a reputable abortion clinic.

"We refer our clients only to places that are reputable, sir."

Brendan jotted down the two telephone numbers he was given. He succeeded in getting an appointment with the first place he had called, which was about a forty-minute drive from their home. The receptionist at the clinic briefed Brendan on the proper patient preparation, after Brendan had explained that the patient was his thirteen-year-old daughter who had recently become sexually active. He felt terrible about telling such a lie about Vita. The appointment was set for the next day at ten thirty in the morning. He hung up the phone knowing that this decision would make life more bearable for Vita.

She will thank me. And well, Carmen . . . she will eventually thank me. We need to get back to some normalcy as soon as we can, he thought to himself. Brendan was not sure how he would approach Carmen about taking Vita tomorrow for the abortion. The more he thought about it, the more he thought it best not to say anything to her until tomorrow. One thing he had to make sure of and that was for Vita not to have anything to eat or drink after midnight.

Brendan readied the paperwork he needed to meet with his client due at one thirty in the afternoon. He called both his house phone and Nettie's number and left messages on both answering machines that he hoped to be home by five or six o'clock. He added that he planned on stopping by Corbin's house when he was done with his last appointment. Corbin had not called into the office, so Brendan assumed his brother was still out of it.

Linda knocked on Brendan's door before opening it enough to poke her head in. She dangled the long tubular bag. "Here ya go."

"Oh, thanks, Linda. Thanks." Brendan walked over to the door to meet her and grabbed hold of the lime-flavored Gatorade and the long bag housing his tuna sub.

"Mr. Walker is scheduled to come in about half an hour from now," reminded Linda.

"And thanks for preparing the documents. They are right here," said Brendan as he patted the folder sitting on the corner of his desk.

Brendan unwrapped the sloppy sandwich. As he ate his lunch, his mind pondered on how to handle Corbin later that afternoon and about what he would say to Vita and Carmen in the morning.

He had trouble concentrating as his mind jumped back and forth between scenarios he had concerning these dilemmas.

Linda buzzed Brendan to let him know Mr. Walker had arrived. The meeting lasted only twenty minutes, had been a follow-up to a consultation, and was basically a form-signing session with explanation of the legalities. This worked in Brendan's favor as he knew the way his mind was haphazardly firing distracting thoughts. He was thankful not to have to appear in court as any court performance would have suffered.

Brendan was on the road by two ten in the afternoon. On his way out the door, he had told Linda she could leave an hour earlier to enjoy the afternoon and wished her an enjoyable weekend.

***

Corbin was headed to the bathroom to splash some cold water on his face. He could barely stand up straight and stumbled along the hallway as he held his side with one arm and guided himself along the wall with the other arm. Corbin was not surprised when he saw his swollen, discolored face in the mirror. He felt every bit as bad as it looked. He turned on the cold water as he leaned on the sink vanity for support while he waited for the water to get as cold as it could get. Cupping his hands that noticeably shook, Corbin collected the frigid water and splashed it onto his raw face. Deciding a washcloth would work better, he soaked the washcloth in the ice-cold water coming out of the faucet and spread it over his entire face. The instant coolness against his hot skin gave him a small sense of relief, though accompanied by a tinge of pain from the touch of the cloth fibers against the bruised and cut skin on his face. Corbin thought about showering but felt too weak to do so. He was just coming to grips with what had transpired. He realized that the domino effect would soon be upon him.

Corbin came out of the bathroom. Still bent over like an old man, he meandered his way back toward the living room. There stood Brendan. Corbin had not heard his brother come in while the faucet was running. Brendan took two deliberate steps toward Corbin.

Their eyes met. Corbin took a step toward Brendan, gave him a glaring look, and then stepped away. Brendan clenched Corbin's upper arm and swung him back around so they were facing each other. Their eyes met again in a locked stare the way two aggressive male dogs look at each other before one of them pounces.

Brendan growled, "You are gonna talk, brother. And I will do my best not to destroy you . . . for now."

Brendan let go of Corbin's arm only after he sat him down forcefully onto a chair. Brendan grabbed a chair from the adjoining dining room and set it down across from Corbin. Managing to distance himself from the emotional upheaval, Brendan spoke in a stern, abrupt, almost robotic tone, "Fess up, Cor. I think you have something to say to me."

Out of the two brothers, Corbin was the shrewder and more cunning lawyer, always the one to think quickly on his feet, traits that Brendan was certainly familiar with and well prepared for. Corbin was a convincingly smooth talker and an artful manipulator. "Bren," said Corbin, his voice dry and raspy, "I don't know what you want me to say. Look, bro, I am so sorry Vita is pregnant. I believe that is what I heard you say to me, ya know, when you were beating the shit out of me." Corbin paused. Brendan did not respond but only continued to glare into Corbin's still-bloodshot and swollen eyes. Corbin continued, "Look, I know how angry and upset and hurt you must be, but did you really have to take it out on me?" Still, no response from Brendan. "What? Why? Why do you think I would ever have something to do with Vita being pregnant?"

Finally, firm words from Brendan, "You tell me, bro."

Shaking his head in disgust, Corbin declared, "That is sick, Brendan . . . For you to think that I would ever do anything like that to Vita. I would never do anything to hurt your daughter, my niece, whom I adore. How could you ever, ever think that?"

"I don't think it, Corbin. I know it. I know that you, you . . . you forced my daughter, my child, into having sex with you on four occasions," said Brendan in a matter-of-fact lawyerly way, which was the only manner for him to get those words out without breaking down.

"Is that what Vita told you? I don't understand why she would tell such a—" Corbin stopped midsentence when he saw Brendan put his hand up like a traffic cop.

"Vita didn't have to tell me anything, Corbin. It's all in her diary, dear brother. Would you care to read it? Refresh your memory perhaps?" said a cynical Brendan.

Corbin looked into Brendan's cold-eyed stare. He placed his hand on Brendan's wrist and returned a pseudo-compassionate look, "You have got to believe me. I really don't know what you are talking about. I never laid a hand on Vita. Never." Brendan continued to glare into Corbin's eyes. He said nothing. Corbin continued, "Look, bro, I am shocked and sorry that Vita is pregnant." And then Corbin relayed to Brendan an elaborate scheme that Vita likely concocted so as to keep the identity hidden of the boy who fathered the child. He suggested how Vita and this boyfriend or even the boy himself came up with the plan of blaming her uncle Corbin, and that part of the scheme was to record supposed sexual assault stories into her diary. Corbin had a way with words. He could be quite compelling and manipulative at the same time. He spoke as if he believed what he said was truth. If he managed to plant one small seed of doubt into Brendan's thoughts, his objective was accomplished. That was what made Corbin such a successful trial attorney. And indeed, the slightest shadow of doubt did creep into Brendan's mind.

Brendan continued to stare intently into Corbin's bloodshot eyes, trying to detect any kind of wavering. The thought of either Vita or Corbin lying was too heavy of a burden. He broke his stare to take a few deep breaths and removed Corbin's hand from his forearm. "I always wondered why Chaz never seemed to like to be around you . . . You know how he snarls at you . . . Now I know why. You disgust me. You really disgust me, Corbin!"

"Believe what you want, Brendan. C'mon, man! Think about it! Not only would I ever do anything like that to Vita, but do you really believe that I would do anything to jeopardize our law practice? The practice that Dad so proudly passed onto to us. We worked our asses off in law school, man. This practice is what Dad envisioned for us and for us to carry on the family name. There is pride to be had here, Bren. There is."

Brendan sank his head into his hands. He shook his head, not knowing what to believe. He felt overwhelmed. He felt exhausted. Corbin could see the internal pain his brother was in. He placed his hand on Brendan's shoulder and offered to talk to Brendan about Vita's pregnancy. "Look," said Brendan, "I'm taking her for an abortion tomorrow. She doesn't know it, and Carmen doesn't know that I set up an appointment for tomorrow morning. I just want this nightmare to be over with for Vita."

"And I want this nightmare to be over with for you all too," said Corbin.

"You really expect me to believe you, don't you?" said Brendan. "So you are telling me my daughter is lying. Somehow, Corbin, I am not believing you," said a numb Brendan.

"Look, man," said Corbin, "can't you see it?" Corbin then proceeded to explain why Vita's plan had indeed worked perfectly. By blaming Corbin for the pregnancy, the boy would go unnamed, and Vita herself would not be held responsible for being in this situation. The idea that the child Vita was carrying was from an incestual rape would surely demand an abortion fix to end the pregnancy, and even a prolife advocate such as Carmen would surely not dispute an abortion in a case such as this. "You see, Brendan . . . you played right into Vita's hands. Her plan—and it is a good one—would result in her parents taking her for an abortion. Vita and the boyfriend would be out of trouble."

Brendan listened to Corbin's reasoning of why Vita had accused Corbin of such a thing. He knew that Corbin had a knack for instilling a morsel of doubt. Brendan thought for a moment after Corbin presented his case. "What if I have DNA testing done on the fetus? You know, Corbin, I can get samples of your DNA from anyplace . . . in here, the office. And what if there is a match to you and that fetus? Huh? 'Cause I'm gonna do just that!"

Corbin didn't flinch. He did not display any body language that indicated that he felt threatened. "Listen, Bren, you do what you feel you have to do. I understand that." Corbin paused and then added,

"And I forgive you for this beating you ambushed me with. I feel for you, Bren. I do." And Corbin put his arm around his brother's shoulders.

"I swear to you, Corbin, if I ever find out that what is written in Vita's diary is true . . . you will be sorry. And if Vita chooses to bring you to court, I will back her one hundred percent. I really can't think of Malloy and Malloy right now. And, Corbin, if you are found out and are guilty, our business is destroyed. Yes, it has been our bread and butter. And yes, I am proud of our family name and the honest and good reputation that we carried on from Dad, but my first concern is my child. Vita and Carmen are my life, and everything else is secondary."

Brendan excused himself to use the bathroom. Water was still spattered all over the sink vanity from when Corbin had been in there. Brendan sat on the edge of the tub. Why would Vita lie? How could Corbin, his mentor all the while they were growing up, do this to Vita? One of the two was lying. He felt drained and just wanted to remain seated there on the rim of the tub.

Corbin in the meantime had gotten two clean shot glasses out from under the bar and filled each to the top with tequila. He knew he had managed to defer the situation and was relieved at least for the time being to know that the child Vita was carrying would be aborted by this time tomorrow.

Corbin waited for Brendan to return from the bathroom. After about fifteen minutes, he went over by the bathroom door and listened with his ear to the door. He heard nothing. He knocked. "You okay, Bren?" He went to knock again. The door slowly opened. Brendan's eyes met Corbin's eyes once again as he slid past Corbin and headed back into the living room. Corbin followed. "Here. I poured us some shots of tequila."

Brendan hesitantly picked up one of the shot glasses, brought it to his mouth, and downed it. Corbin watched and then did the same. Brendan came face-to-face with Corbin. "Corbin, I am going to ask you once more. Do you have anything to tell me? Did you force my daughter to have sex with you?"

Corbin appeared irritated. "You have to ask me that again? I already told you. *I did not . . . and* I suggest that you talk with Vita and find out why she is doing this. I'm telling you, Bren, she is trying to hide the identity of this kid and the fact that they have been having a sexual relationship."

Brendan remained steadfast and calm. "So that is it."

"What do you want me to say? There is nothing more I can tell you, Bren . . . other than saying again that I am so sorry for the pain that you are all going through right now."

Brendan nodded. He headed for the door to leave. Corbin followed and managed to place his hand on Brendan's shoulder as he exited through the door. Brendan never turned back to look at his brother. Corbin closed the door. He sat on the couch that he had slept on for the past twenty hours or so. Taking hold of the tequila bottle still on the coffee table, he guzzled straight from the bottle. Corbin sat back on his couch and began to ponder and plot.

Chapter 16

BRENDAN ENTERED THE SAME SILENT house that he had left early in the morning. He thought about changing into his running clothes to take a run, but his ankles were so raw and chafed and still burned from the night before that he decided against it. Brendan wanted peace for his mind, even for only a moment. He tried in desperation to quell any thoughts arising about Corbin, Vita, and Carmen. He decided he would resume the watercolor painting of the seascape he had been working on. Perhaps this would help distract him. Brendan painted with harsh brushstrokes that resulted in a tumultuous and turbulent sea.

It was near five in the late afternoon when Carmen and Vita with Chaz pulled into their driveway behind Brendan's car. Nettie had thought it best not go back with Carmen and Vita, even though Carmen had asked her mother to do so. Nettie had given Carmen one of her frozen lasagnas that she had thawed. As she had left Nettie's house, her brother Tony had called to invite Nettie for Mother's Day dinner. Carmen was happy to know her mother accepted.

Carmen called out to Brendan as she entered the house. He appeared in the living room with the paintbrush in his hand. They kissed with Brendan holding the paintbrush out and away from them. "We can talk later?" whispered Brendan. Carmen could tell by her husband's expression that he didn't want to deal with anything at the moment. She kissed him again, honoring his request.

He met Vita in the kitchen as she was filling Chaz's water bowl with fresh water. Brendan kissed his daughter. "Everything will be all right," he told her before returning to his easel in the family room.

Vita watched her mother turn on the oven. She spotted Carmen's open pocketbook sitting on the kitchen chair and peered in. "Mom? Where is my diary? I want it back." It had gotten buried in the spacious handbag. Carmen dug her hand into the pocketbook, shuffled the contents, and pulled out the lavender diary, with the severed leather straps. "It's broken!" said Vita.

Carmen apologized to Vita as she was to blame for cutting the strap. Vita took the diary from her mother's hand. Carmen reminded Vita that she needed to put the diary in a safe place and not to leave it where a curious friend might get a peek at it. Carmen added, "I know you don't want to think of this now, but that diary needs to be protected. Do you know what I am getting at?" Before a confused Vita could respond, Carmen continued with "If you ever decide you want to have Uncle Corbin put in jail for what he—"

Vita held the diary tightly against her chest. She was upset by her mother's comments. "No one, no one . . . no one else ever needs to read this." Vita turned abruptly and went up to her room with Chaz in tow.

After dinner, Vita asked to go over Chelsea's house. She had wanted to sleep over, but Brendan squashed that notion before Carmen had any thoughts about it. Dinner had gone on as if nothing had happened. Conversation when it occurred had been nothing more than small talk. As Brendan drove Vita to Chelsea's house, he asked his daughter if she was sure she was okay enough to see friends. Vita explained to him that things hadn't changed so much for her the past couple of days. What was done to her was something she had been dealing with all along. In fact, as she told her father, it was somewhat of a relief now that her parents knew the truth. "Your friends know any of this?"

"No, Dad. I do not ever want my friends to know."

Brendan dropped Vita off at the Hartman household. "I'll be back for you around nine thirty, Vita." Brendan kissed Vita on the cheek and watched her enter the house as Chelsea held the door open.

Vita's comment about not wanting her friends to know of her situation was enough confirmation for Brendan to go ahead with tomorrow's appointment for the abortion. The decision to do this now sat well with him. He even felt more strongly that his wife would understand.

Carmen had just finished with loading the dinner dishes into the dishwasher when Brendan returned home. She could read from Brendan's body language that he was not ready to talk. She hooked Chaz up to his leash to take the pug out for a walk. Brendan went back to his easel in the family room. Even though he was more at ease with his decision, there was apprehension about how he was going to tell Carmen. He thought it best to tell her in the morning.

Brendan's gut still gnawed at him. Corbin's side of the story disturbed Brendan to no end. In his heart, he believed his daughter, but that heart was ripped apart by his brother's apparent actions and lies.

Brendan's seascape began to reflect his emotions. What had initially been intended to be a serene painting of the coastal waters of New England somewhere—with the blue sky, billowy clouds, and calm seas—became a canvas of wild brushstrokes with dark stormy ominous clouds hovering over the turbulent ocean waters.

Carmen returned some forty-five minutes later with a worn-out dog. Chaz plopped himself down onto the cool kitchen floor after he noisily lapped up the remaining water in his bowl. Carmen went into the family room and came up behind Brendan. She gently massaged his shoulders and noticed Brendan's dark painting. "You want to talk, Bren?"

Brendan put his brush down. He muttered how alone he felt. "I . . . I . . . can't talk about it right now. I just don't understand how Corbin can be like he is." He took hold of his wife's hands and asked for her patience. He wanted her to know that it was nothing against her and that he needed some time to absorb what had happened at Corbin's house that afternoon.

Carmen understood her husband had to diffuse and organize his thoughts. "Okay, Bren. I understand. We can talk when you are ready." She had ironing and laundry to do, including Vita's lavender comforter.

Brendan lifted up the paintbrush as if it were the weight of a brick. He set it back down on the easel's ledge. Brendan was beyond fatigued. His eyelids were heavy, and his head fell forward and snapped back with a jerk. Brendan lumbered toward the couch in the family room. He collapsed onto the sofa and was in a sound sleep seconds after his head took rest on the arm cushion.

The phone rang at nine forty-five in the evening. Carmen raced up from the basement where she had been ironing in the laundry room to answer the phone in the kitchen. Vita was on the other end, wondering where her father was. Carmen peeked into the family room and saw her husband asleep on the couch. "I'll be over to get you in a few minutes, okay, sweetie. Dad fell asleep on the couch."

Vita took the opportunity once again and tried talking her mother into letting her sleep over Chelsea's. "I can wear Chelsea's pajamas."

Carmen firmly told Vita, "No, your dad wants you home tonight. It has been a tough day for all of us. We've all got to get a good night's rest. I will be leaving in a few minutes." Carmen peeked back into the family room. Brendan was in the same position. He snored lightly. "C'mon, Chazzy. Let's go get Vita. Want a ride in the car?" Chaz tilted his head from side to side upon hearing two of his buzz words—Vita and car. He immediately went to the foyer and danced excitedly as Carmen took the leash from where it hung.

Carmen, Vita, and Chaz were back in the house twenty minutes later. Brendan stirred when he heard his wife's and daughter's voices. He jolted up, his eyes half shut and not sure of his surroundings. It took him a minute or two to get his bearings. He looked over to the easel and realized he had never cleaned his paintbrushes.

Carmen and Vita joined him on the couch. "You were fast asleep, so I picked Vita up."

"I'm sorry. I am just beat. Did you have fun, sweet pea, at your friend's house?" asked Brendan.

"Yup," said Vita.

"I'm glad." He kissed his daughter.

As Vita headed up the stairs to take a shower, she asked loudly, "Dad, can I stay up and watch some TV?"

Brendan looked at Carmen and then yelled back up to his daughter, "Sure, honey! I want you in bed by midnight!"

"Okay . . . thanks, Dad" returned the voice from upstairs.

Brendan kissed Carmen.

"I think we all need to have a family meeting tomorrow," Carmen uttered softly to Brendan. He nodded as he placed his paintbrushes in a jar of water that was already set on a small table by the easel.

"I know we have to do that, and we will. Just right now, I am so out of it. I'm gonna head up to bed. I love you." Brendan kissed his wife again.

"I love you," said Carmen. Carmen could see how drained Brendan was. He had not even asked Carmen about her meeting with Father John.

As Brendan showered, he became more cognizant of the impending situation. He remembered the appointment for tomorrow morning. He made sure to set the alarm clock for seven o'clock in the morning. Vita would not be up any time before then as she liked to sleep late on Saturday mornings. He had to be certain that she would not have anything to eat or drink in the morning. He also had to be sure that Vita would not wake up in the middle of the night for a drink of water.

Brendan lay down and was in and out of a light sleep. As tired as he was, he could not settle down to sleep. He kept replaying Corbin's words to him. Scenarios of what could happen tomorrow ran through his mind.

Carmen decided to head up to bed around eleven thirty. She noticed that Vita, who had come back downstairs to watch TV, had fallen asleep on the living room couch. Carmen gently stirred Vita awake enough to guide her upstairs and into her bed. She covered her with the freshly laundered lavender comforter. Chaz had followed them upstairs and immediately seized the opportunity to lie next to Vita on the fluffed-up comforter.

As Carmen slipped herself under the covers so as not to disturb her husband, she heard "Don't worry, honey. I'm awake." Brendan pulled Carmen over and held her tightly. He started talking. And

Carmen listened. "I feel so alone, Carmen. So alone." He proceeded to tell Carmen about his visit with Corbin that afternoon including Corbin's version. "Dad has been gone a long time now. And well, my mother," Brendan sighed, "well, Mom . . . for all intensive purposes has been gone too. You know that she just has not been a part of my and Corbin's lives. It was Corbin and me. Just Cor and me for such a long time. We were always so close. I loved my brother. I thought I knew him inside and out. I can't fathom that my brother would do anything like this to Vita . . . or to anyone for that matter. I cannot comprehend it. And now he is lying. I know it. I just feel so alone."

"I am here, honey . . . for you . . . always. You know I love you," said Carmen tenderly.

"I know that. I know that. And I know that you and Vita and your mom are my family. But I just feel such a hole inside now." And Brendan placed his hand over his heart. "Sometimes I just want to run home to my dad or mom or my brother . . . but no one is home."

Brendan and Carmen held each other tighter and kissed and then made love. It would be the last time that they would.

Chapter 17

BRENDAN AND CARMEN FELL ASLEEP in each other's arms. Carmen slept solidly, but Brendan awoke an hour later. He went to use the bathroom in their bedroom and then tiptoed to Vita's room. He could see Vita on her side, motionless, and could hear a barely audible snore coming from the foot of the bed. Even the pug was in a deep sleep.

Brendan lay back down next to Carmen. His mind was back on hyperdrive. He wondered how the next twenty-four hours would play out. He also kept an ear out for Vita, should she awake and get up for a drink of water, but she did not.

Hours later, Brendan sat down gently on Vita's bed and put his hand on his sleeping daughter's shoulder. Chaz perked up and snorted. He got up to lick Brendan's hand. Brendan was already dressed. He had decided to turn the alarm off at six thirty when he had gotten out of bed. He had never fallen back to sleep. He was able to dress in the bathroom without disturbing Carmen. Brendan tried to stir Vita awake while Chaz continued to lick Brendan's hand and then Vita's face. "Vita, sweetheart . . . Vita . . . wake up."

Vita turned her head to see her father sitting next to her, dressed to leave the house. Vita had to push Chaz away from her face. "Huh . . . Dad? What time is it? What day is it? Am I late for school?"

Brendan told Vita that it was Saturday morning and that he had made an appointment for her to talk with another doctor. He apologized for not mentioning it the night before, but he was so tired that he had forgotten to do so.

In a groggy voice, Vita said, "Okay." She assumed that it was one of those counseling doctors that Dr. Santiago had spoken about. "Why so early, Dad?"

"Why not?" responded Brendan as he tried to maintain a light mood.

"Does Mom know? 'Cause she didn't say anything to me either," questioned Vita.

"Does Mom know what?" sounded an alarmed Carmen as she stood in the doorway. "Brendan, are you going into the office . . . today, Saturday . . . so early?"

Brendan was at a loss for words. Vita realized her mother had no idea about any appointment but decided to stay mum for the moment. Chaz jumped off the bed and ran downstairs to be let out.

Brendan immediately got up from the bed and slid past Carmen to follow the dog downstairs. "Just a moment. I'll let him out."

Carmen sat on the bed and looked confusingly at her daughter, who now sat up.

"Dad said he was taking me for a doctor's appointment. I guess to talk or something."

Brendan was back up to Vita's room in an instant, lest Vita take the opportunity to get a drink of water. Brendan knew there was no avoiding the unavoidable.

"You didn't tell me that you made an appointment for Vita," said Carmen. "How come you didn't mention it to me last night?"

Brendan got quiet for a moment. He felt his face become flushed. Carmen knew he wasn't being totally truthful. Brendan's demeanor changed. The tone of his voice was firm. "Vita, you need to shower quickly and get dressed. And listen to me . . . you are *not* to drink any water . . . Just brush your teeth but do not swallow any water."

Vita, stunned by the seriousness of her father's no-nonsense voice, did what she was told without questioning why. She was clueless and worried.

Carmen figured out exactly what was going on. With Vita now in the bathroom, she confronted Brendan, "You are taking her for an abortion, aren't you?"

"That is exactly what I am doing. Now that we know the circumstances of Vita's pregnancy, there is no other alternative," said Brendan firmly.

Carmen whispered loudly, "No other alternative? What do you mean? Life is life, Bren . . . no matter what. That child inside Vita does not deserve to be murdered!"

"C'mon, Carmen. Lose the goddamn halo, will ya! Is that what your priest told you yesterday? I would think he would understand that under these circumstances, abortion is the only answer," Brendan snapped back.

Carmen looked at the rage in Brendan's eyes. He just did not get it, and those were the words that slipped out of her mouth. Carmen could feel Brendan's sense of having taken control of the situation. She knew she could not stop him from going through with getting Vita to this appointment, but she was going to try. "What if I told you 'over my dead body' is she going to have this abortion!"

"Don't push me that way, Carmen."

Brendan went over to the bathroom door and rapped on it with his knuckles. "Veet, almost ready?"

Vita was still under the belief that she was going to talk with a counselor or a psychiatrist. She had no idea of the conflict that had gone on in her bedroom. "I'll be out in a few minutes, Dad."

"Remember, no drinking water, Veet."

"Oooookay," Vita said as she did not understand why her father was adamant about making that request. Perhaps there was some kind of medicine that she had to take and was not allowed to have water with it. Or maybe he was going to take her to breakfast and didn't want her filling up with water. *No, that's crazy. He doesn't even want me to swallow a little bit of water when I brush my teeth*, she thought to herself.

Carmen went after Brendan and grabbed hold of his arm with both her hands and pulled him aside. "She has no idea you are taking her for an abortion. How can you do this? I won't let you do this!"

Brendan and Carmen locked elbows and stares. "I will tell her now. Carmen, this is what has to be done. She does not need to go through this hellish nightmare another day. She needs to move on, and this is the best way to do it. You must know that in your heart."

Carmen looked down and sobbed, "She has seen the baby inside of her. She has known who the father is. And I believe she was at the point of being able to go forward and carry this child so that he or she could be adopted."

Brendan then brought up the fact that this child is likely to have problems because its parents have the same gene pool and chances that some unbeknownst condition could come through. Carmen tried in jest to explain to Brendan that whatever life God created in Vita was meant to be as He created it. She so wanted him to understand that this life was sacred and had a purpose and who were they to question it. Brendan did not want to hear any of it. He was convinced that he was solving the problem.

Vita came out of the bathroom, dressed and ready to go. She saw that she had interrupted a heated argument between her parents. They stopped hurling words, and both just looked at Vita.

"We have to leave now, Vita," Brendan said with a sense of urgency. "I don't want to be late for this appointment."

"Tell her where you are taking her!" demanded Carmen.

"Mom, I know. I am just going to talk to one of those counseling doctors," said Vita.

Carmen shook her head. "That's not where you are going." She looked at her husband. "Tell her now of your plans . . . or I will."

Brendan placed his hands on his daughter's shoulders and looked into her wondering eyes. "Vita, listen to me. We need to remedy this situation. I can't let you suffer like this. We are going to a medical facility where you are scheduled to have an abortion."

There was silence. Vita looked to her mother and back to her father. She did not expect to hear this. Vita was confused.

Carmen spoke, "Vita, your father and I are in disagreement. You know what we talked about yesterday with Father John."

Vita wriggled anxiously. She was overwhelmed with internal conflict and went to sit down on the top of the carpeted steps.

Brendan put his hand up to stop any more of Carmen's comments. "Enough of this Catholic shit!"

Carmen angrily responded, "It's not Catholic shit . . . It's a life!"

Brendan was about to lose his temper. "Enough! This is a pregnancy out of an incestual rape! I cannot and will not have my daughter suffer any more than she already has." He turned to his daughter. "Vita, we have to go."

Vita's emotions were so fragile that she could easily be swayed with whatever seemed right at the moment. The idea of returning to life as it was prepregnancy, at least so far as going back to school and hanging out with her friends, was enticing. No one would ever have to know. She also knew in her heart that what had already been done to her could not be undone. "Will it hurt, Daddy?"

"No, sweetheart. I will make sure you get whatever medicine you need so you will not feel anything."

Carmen could not contain herself. "That's not true, Vita! You are not guaranteed that, and you know you saw that baby inside of you."

"That's it, Carmen. We have to go!" declared Brendan. He took Vita by the hand to lead her down the steps.

While in the foyer, Vita frantically asked, "Can Mom come?"

Brendan held the door open and ushered his daughter outside. "Mom's not ready. We have to leave now, or we will be late. We cannot put this off any longer."

Carmen stood in shock. All this had happened so fast. She was unable to react and watched as Brendan and Vita exited out of the house.

There was a part of Vita that had a sense of relief that a decision was being made for her. She thought to herself that maybe this was what was supposed to be, maybe this was the better way.

Carmen heard Brendan's car backing out of the driveway and then motoring down the street. She heard the car stop at the corner stop sign and then heard the engine resume and then fade away. Carmen sat on the top step at the end of the hallway where Vita had sat moments before. Feeling as if the plug was pulled, the life force drained out of her, she was in a sense paralyzed. In disbelief, she sat motionless with a blank stare.

***

"I'm scared, Daddy. I'm afraid."

Brendan ran his hands down Vita's ponytail. "Trust me, sweet pea. I won't let anything bad happen to you."

"And what about Mom?" Vita was concerned.

"Mom will be all right. You'll see. She will come to realize that this is the best choice for you . . . for all of us."

"What are they going to do to me? Do you know, Dad?" queried Vita. Worried and anxious, she knew at least part of the answer to that question. Visions ran through her head of the horrific abortion posters of mutilated babies she had seen at the March for Life in Washington DC.

"I wish I could answer that for you, Vita, but these people are health professionals. They perform this procedure all the time. You'll be okay." Brendan was not well versed with what went on at these abortion centers. Carmen knew all too well what went on in such places, and Vita herself had a better idea than her father had.

As she gazed out the window, the rapidly passing scenery reminded Vita of how her life was evolving. Brendan's mind was too occupied to make conversation. The car drove itself as he envisioned various scenarios of what Vita would be going through, of what Carmen was doing at the moment, and of how he would confront his brother again. Vita leaned her head against the cool glass, slouched down, and turned onto her right side to get more comfortable. She closed her eyes and pretended to be asleep. She tried in vain to erase the ultrasound images of the child, which were seared in her psyche, but the film clip of the baby sucking its thumb and doing flips just played itself over and over.

Vita was sickened from the depths of her gut. When she, her mother, and her grandmother were with Father John yesterday, she had begun to feel at peace with the thought of carrying the baby to full term for adoption. Knowing that baby would have life and be loved by a family sat well with her. But when her father had led her to the car and told her this would all be behind her so that she could move on—well, that felt right at that moment too, she thought. The nauseated feeling in the pit of her stomach however became more intense as the car got closer to its destination. Vita couldn't quell those gut emotions. She could not ignore the child within her. She knew without a shadow of a doubt that taking the life of this baby was wrong . . . inherently wrong. And she didn't know what to do about it.

***

Carmen's trance was broken by the barking and scratching of claws on the back door. Her body was in shutdown mode. She had difficulty in orienting herself and in getting up from the steps. As Carmen let Chaz back into the house, she was digesting what had happened. Processing and organizing her thoughts, she began to contemplate what to do next. She was distracted by a nagging hungry dog. Robotically, she scooped a large cupful of Chaz's dog food from the tub containing the dry dog food and dumped it into his Navajo-designed ceramic dish. Carmen knew her mother would be up by now. She punched the numbers on the phone pad hard and fast, and when Nettie answered, Carmen unloaded the morning's events without taking a breath.

Nettie listened to the sheer panic in her daughter's voice. She advised Carmen to try to calm down by taking a shower and that she would be on her way over. The two of them could then perhaps figure out what to do . . . if anything. Carmen heeded her mother's advice. She was thankful to have her mother's relentless support. Nettie had always been a pillar of strength for Carmen, Brendan, and Vita. She could calmly and systematically deal with emergent situations, no matter what they were. Nettie had a special gift of nurturing and comforting, and it was the comforting that Carmen needed.

Carmen was showered and dressed in time to greet Nettie, who had let herself in the front door. Nettie had Carmen retell the morning's events. As her distressed daughter went through the morning's happenings, Nettie felt the hurt and anger and the sense of betrayal in Carmen's voice. "Honey, I want you to take a deep breath and a step back. Brendan in his mind . . . and I am not sticking up for him here, but in his heart, he is doing what he believes is right. He is fixing, and that is what men do."

"But he went behind my back, Mother!" said Carmen.

"I think he feels," continued Nettie, "that you would come around in time to understand that what he did was ultimately the right decision, but he couldn't take the chance of telling you beforehand."

"What can we do? I'm gonna get the phone books, and maybe we can—"

Nettie interrupted her daughter, "Carmen, you can't stop him now." Nettie knew that she needed to get Carmen's mind occupied. She rethought and suggested that maybe it would be a good idea to get the Yellow Pages out to call the abortion clinics.

Carmen took off up to the second floor and pulled out several thick phone books from a bottom desk drawer in the office. She wrapped her arms around the pile of books, brought them into the kitchen, and plopped them down onto the kitchen table. "These are for four different counties including this one. I am sure Brendan did not choose anything in this vicinity."

The women decided to go through the Yellow Pages to make a list of the abortion clinics and centers. They would start calling the ones that were nearest to them. What would they say to the person answering the phone?

"This is hard for me to conjure up some tale, some lie," said Carmen, thinking aloud.

Carmen and Nettie thought quickly. Carmen would call and tell at least a partial truth that her husband had planned on taking their teenage daughter for an abortion. She would tell them that the daughter was insistent on having the abortion. Carmen planned to say that she observed her daughter eating a cereal bar and milk in the morning, apparently forgetting to fast. Carmen would tell the people that she didn't think the appointment was for today, so she didn't think to mention it when her husband and daughter had left this morning. She would go on to say that her husband knew that she was against the abortion and suspected that he did indeed take their daughter this morning rather than next week when Carmen thought the appointment was scheduled for. She said her daughter would certainly fail to mention that she had eaten as the daughter wanted the abortion done with and would not realize the severity of having eaten. It was a story with a lot of holes, but that is what Nettie and Carmen came up with.

Carmen sighed, "What are the chances of finding them? Brendan has probably used an alias. I suppose I will have to give descriptions of them."

The task of phoning all the abortion clinics within a one-hundred-fifty-mile radius would be daunting. There was not much else they could do but perhaps pray. Nettie knew that at least this proactive busy work was the therapy that Carmen needed for the time being. Maybe if they were very lucky, they would be able to locate Brendan and Vita and get the abortion procedure cancelled.

Carmen wished she'd had an extra phone line in the house so that Nettie could also make calls as time was of the essence. Carmen and Brendan had planned on getting Vita her own phone number and phone for her bedroom for her fourteenth birthday, which was only a couple of months away.

Nettie handed a list with numbers for Carmen to get started. Carmen took the list back up to the office and began the ordeal of making the calls. Nettie in the meantime continued to compile a list of abortion places in the neighboring counties. Carmen tried to stay focused but could not help but think what Vita must be going through at the moment.

***

Pretending to have awoken from her nap, Vita told her father that she was thirsty. "After the procedure, I'll get you whatever you want. Remember, you have to be on an empty stomach for your appointment."

Vita had already known what her dad's response would be. She leaned forward to turn on the radio. "Can I listen?" asked Vita.

"Of course, you can." Vita recognized Madonna's "Papa Don't Preach" with lyrics that spoke about an unwed daughter telling her father that she was going to keep her baby.

Brendan was oblivious to the song and its lyrics. He was intent on getting his daughter to the abortion clinic, and all he thought about was to get this over with. He just wanted to snap his fingers and have life back as it were. His brother also occupied his thoughts.

Tears rolled out of the corner of both of Vita's eyes and landed on her hands that were clasped in her lap. She kept her face turned toward the window so as to keep her father from noticing. She couldn't control her sniffling as tears continued to roll down her cheeks. Vita was too afraid to catch a glimpse of her father. She kept her gaze out the window. Brendan never noticed Vita's tears. Vita wiped away the tears. Her heart was bleeding. She had seen the baby on ultrasound, and now more than ever, she knew she could not bring herself to take the life of this innocent baby. Vita was numb. What could she say to her father? She knew what his response would be. Brendan exited off the Garden State Parkway, which signaled to Vita that they must be near. The impulse came to her to jump out of the car should they stop at a red light, but she disregarded such a thought.

***

Carmen sensed that her attempt to locate Brendan and Vita was futile. She was frustrated with making the calls. Sometimes she was put into an automated voice system or put on hold and hung up on. Apparently, there were a few girls fitting Vita's description; however, none were coupled with a man fitting Brendan's description. There were also the privacy issues to contend with. Carmen set the phone back onto its cradle. "It's useless, Ma . . . It's useless."

"C'mon," Nettie said, "let's go to the church to pray." Nettie extended her hand to her daughter, whose eyes expressed hopelessness. She led Carmen out of the office. They gathered their pocketbooks and left out the front door. Carmen, having never put her makeup on, got in the passenger side of Nettie's car.

***

Vita had her head against the window. The images passed by much slower than before. She contemplated again on how much that represented her life—so much so fast and now everything moving in slow motion.

Brendan tried to decipher the scribbled directions he had written on a piece of scrap paper while keeping the car on the proper side of the road. "This must be it—403 Conway Street," said Brendan.

There was a small nondescript sign next to the door that read "Women's Center." There were however about a dozen people gathered on the sidewalk, which Vita immediately knew to be prolife advocates. They walked quietly, some with signs, some with rosary beads intertwined in their fingers, and others with pamphlets. Vita had been one of those people, having accompanied her mother and grandmother to do the very same thing as these people were here to do. Vita felt like the ultimate hypocrite, as she had been put into the position of having to kill the innocent life within her.

Vita fidgeted as Brendan parked the car about a half a block beyond the clinic. She tried to think of something to say to her father, but she couldn't. She felt as if her body was a lead weight. Not able to move as if paralyzed, she had the sensation of time standing still.

With deep concern in his eyes, Brendan looked over to Vita. "It's time. It'll be okay. In a little while from now, this will all be over with." The words echoed in Vita's mind as if she was in a long dark cave. Brendan's words continued, "I am right here for you. I promise, you will feel better about all of this in a few hours."

Vita's inner voice wanted to scream out, "No! No! My baby wants to live!" What came out instead was a muttered "Daddy, I don't want to walk past all those people."

"Here, sweet pea, I brought a blanket. I'll put it over you like a hooded shawl. You just keep your head down. You don't have to look at anybody."

"They are gonna say mean things, Daddy. I'm afraid. I don't want to . . ." her voice trailed off. Brendan helped Vita out of the car.

Vita huddled close to her father as a baby calf clings to its mother's side. Brendan covered her head with the blanket, but Vita decided she did not want to do that. Brendan rolled the blanket up and tucked it under his arm and wrapped his other arm around the trembling shoulders of his daughter. Together, they headed toward the plain cement building.

Brendan quickened the pace. "Just keep looking down, looking down. Vita, you don't have to look at any of these people."

These people, thought Vita to herself, could be her, her mom, and her grandmom. As Vita and her father approached the peaceful group, Vita could not fight the temptation to glance at "these people." Vita lifted her head and opened her eyes in what turned out to be more than a glance. Her eyes met the eyes of a middle-aged brown-haired woman whose clear soulful blue eyes spoke to Vita. Vita became transfixed on those eyes for what seemed to be more than a few moments. Vita found her hand clasping onto the pamphlet that the woman had placed into her hand while Vita beheld the kind blue eyes. Without looking, Vita tucked the pamphlet into her small handbag that hung by her side. Vita then caught herself and immediately looked down to her own flip-flop-clad feet that seemed to move mechanically along the pavement. Again, she could not resist the temptation to turn her head to peer behind her. And again, her eyes met the gentle sweet blue eyes of the woman who returned a kindly smile back toward Vita.

Brendan coaxed Vita back alongside him as she had lagged a step behind him. When she turned her head forward, they were already about to enter through the entrance of the building. There was a small foyer and then a set of heavy glass doors that opened into a main waiting area. The room's pale green walls and the generic dull grayish industrial linoleum floor held a periphery of wooden missionary-style chairs. The overhead fluorescent lighting seemed so out of place. It made Vita feel as though she was on display. The place had an antiseptic smell to it, even though the place did not appear to be particularly clean. Toward the backside of the room, a woman sat behind a light gray desk with a Formica top. She had the same complexion as the desk. Her dull auburn-tinted hair with noticeable gray roots and her cold steel gray eyes were in par with the unwelcoming atmosphere of the room. The lenses of her large-framed eyeglasses only accentuated the coldness of the gray orbs even more. The wrinkled white scrubs that she wore even had a gray tint to them. Behind her desk were a sliding glass window and a door to enter into the rest of the clinic.

"May I help you?" asked the woman whose magnified gray eyes studied Brendan and Vita as they stood facing her.

Vita looked around the room to check out the others seated while she heard her father say, "My daughter, Vicky, Vicky O'Boyle, has an appointment. She . . ."

Vita held her breath, stunned to hear her father lying. Vita turned back around to face the woman who interrupted Brendan. "Vicky, how old are you?"

Vita answered as she looked up to her father who did not return her look. "I am almost fourteen."

O'Boyle was Brendan's mother's maiden name. Perhaps he chose to use it so that there was some semblance of truth in what he was saying.

"How many months pregnant are you? Do you know?"

Vita looked up once more at Brendan. This time, Brendan returned the look and told the woman, "She is almost halfway through the pregnancy. I believe the doctor said she was eighteen weeks."

The woman looked directly into Vita's eyes. "And where is the boyfriend?" Brendan began to answer. The woman held up her small chubby hand and said, "Vicky, I would like you to answer."

Out of Vita's mouth came the continuation of the lie, "He didn't want to come. His parents don't even know."

The woman, who never introduced herself nor did she wear a name tag, handed Brendan a packet of forms along with information about the abortion procedure. She explained to Brendan that because Vicky was a minor, he would have to sign the consent along with his daughter. "When you are done with these, just bring them back up to me. At that time, I will collect the two-hundred-fifty-dollar fee to be paid in cash or a banker's check. We do not accept personal checks or credit cards," she said as she pointed to a sign on her desk that said just that. "After that, one of our counselors will meet with you to explain the procedure and answer any concerns or questions you might have."

Brendan nodded. He took the packet from the woman's hands as her magnified eyes followed his movements. He thanked her and then placed his arm around Vita to guide her to the periphery of the room that had several empty chairs in a row.

Brendan wanted to read through everything first, which was fine with Vita. She fidgeted as she anxiously observed the others who were doing the same. She saw two other girls who were likely to be in their late teens, one of whom was Hispanic and was accompanied by a young man of the same age. The other young lady was a black girl who had another black woman with her that seemed a few years older, perhaps in the early to midtwenties. Seated in the room were three couples, including a middle-aged white couple wearing wedding bands. There was another woman sitting alone, probably in her late thirties. Off in the opposite corner was a middle-aged man by himself who was obviously waiting for someone. Vita was clearly the youngest in the room. She fretted as a nurse dressed in blue scrubs came through the door from behind the reception lady and called for Maria G. The Hispanic girl got up and followed the nurse back through the door. Vita felt as if she were suffocating. She forced herself to tale deep breaths in and out as the panic set in.

Brendan read line after line on page after page of the endless waivers. Most sentences began with "The Women's Center will not be held responsible for . . ." or "I am aware that . . ." Brendan understood that with any medical procedure, there would be consent forms to sign, but this to him was over the top.

Suddenly, a loud thud was heard and then a scampering of feet. The wheeled swivel chair that the receptionist had sat on had flung against the back wall as the woman disappeared through the door next to the sliding glass window. Much commotion of the staff could be seen through the window. It sounded like furniture was being moved. Excited voices were heard; however, the words were not discernable. The disturbance caught the attention of all those in the waiting room. The receptionist with the faded red hair and the nurse in blue scrubs flew back into the waiting room and walked swiftly to the middle-aged gentleman who had been seated by himself. He stood up as they approached; the magazine fell from his hand unto the floor. The two women hurriedly escorted him back through the door next to the glass window. The image of that man's horrified face stayed with Vita. Everyone could hear him asking over and over in desperation, "What's wrong? Tell me what's wrong. Is she okay?"

Brendan got a sickening feeling in his gut. The waiting room's occupants looked at one another. All wondered what was happening behind those walls. No one dared to get up to look through the window into the back area. It was a good five minutes before one of the receptionists returned to the waiting room. A siren off in the distance sounded louder with each passing second.

The woman with the magnified cold gray eyes motioned all those in the waiting room to her desk. She said in a matter-of-fact sort of way, "The procedures for the rest of the day have been cancelled. The doctor has to attend to an emergency. Please take one of these cards, and you may call to reschedule."

Brendan grabbed Vita by the arm and, with the clipboard with the consents still in the other hand, said, "Come on. Let's get out of here!" He ushered Vita out the front door. What sounded to be an ambulance at the back of the building had silenced its siren. The pro-life people had all gone toward the back of the building to see what they could. Vita broke loose from her father to join them. Several of the women gasped as they clasped their hands over their mouths. The protesters were forbidden to set foot on the private property, so their view was somewhat limited but not limited enough for them to see a woman being wheeled out of the clinic on a stretcher and loaded into the ambulance. Vita recognized the man from the waiting room being helped into the back of the ambulance.

Brendan caught up with Vita just as the ambulance door was closed. The siren resumed full blast. The ambulance was soon out of sight as the sound of the siren waned. Vita studied the faces of the prolifers as she listened to them voicing their concerns over what they had all witnessed.

"Vita, let's go. We need to go," said Brendan firmly but compassionately. He wrapped his arm around his daughter's shoulders, and together, they walked back to the car; neither uttered word.

Vita slung the seatbelt across her upper body and snapped it into place. Brendan pulled out from the curb. "Dad, what happened to that lady? Is she gonna be all right?"

Brendan, visibly shaken, hung his head down for a moment as the car was stopped at a red light. "I don't know, Vita. I don't know what just happened."

Vita wanted to talk about what she had seen. "That man, he just looked so scared, Dad. Do you think that lady is going to die?"

Brendan drove on, concentrating on finding his way back to the Garden State Parkway. "I hope she'll be all right, Vita."

"Well," said Vita, "I'm going to pray for her. That's what Grandma and Mom say to do . . . so we should pray for her, Dad."

"Yes, we should. Let's do that now," agreed Brendan.

Vita looked up at her father. She folded her hands on her lap and waited. A prayer flowed from Brendan's lips. Vita rarely heard her father pray aloud. She gazed back down at her folded hands and closed her eyes. Brendan spoke softly, "Dear Lord, please watch over the woman and the man whom we just witnessed to be in trouble. We pray that you help them both and mend whatever is making her sick. Please bless them, Lord."

Vita blessed herself with the sign of the cross. She looked at her dad. Brendan then blessed himself with the sign of the cross.

"Vita, I am so sorry that I even brought you to a place like this. I had no idea. You have to believe that. I am going to have to make an appointment for you with the hospital and with a doctor that perhaps Dr. Santiago can recommend. This has to be done in the best place possible. I can see that."

Vita asked her father if Dr. Santiago could do it. Brendan told Vita that Dr. Santiago had informed him that she does not perform abortions.

Vita sat in silence for a minute. She knew what she wanted to say, and before she could think about it another second, the words spilled from her mouth. "What if I don't want one?" She didn't think she would ever have the courage to say such a thing to her father, but the words were out before she could stop them.

"Don't want one what . . . a baby?" Brendan asked, somewhat puzzled. "An abortion?" Brendan asked after there was no response from Vita.

Then Vita spoke what was in her heart, "Maybe I don't want this abortion, Dad. Maybe I should just have the baby and then give the baby up for adoption."

"I know you are scared, sweet pea, after what we just saw. But we will make sure to have it done in the safest way possible—in the hospital. I will not let you go through the talking and the questions and the looks from people concerning this pregnancy. You have suffered too much already. And one thing I will tell you is that your uncle will pay for what he has done to you. You don't need any more reminders of—" Brendan stopped midsentence and changed the subject. "Thirsty, right? You must be hungry too?"

"I'm not really hungry, Dad," said Vita.

Brendan sighed, "I hear ya. We'll just stop through a drive-through and pick up something to drink."

Vita's cheeks drew in as her lips tightened around the straw to suck down the thick vanilla milkshake she had ordered. The cold, smooth, creamy texture seemed to coat her insides and calmed her nerves somewhat. She never had any bouts of morning sickness or nausea with the pregnancy. Brendan took a sip of the hot coffee from the little hole at the edge of the lid cover. He placed the Styrofoam cup in the cup holder until they got onto the Garden State Parkway when he could leave the car in fifth gear.

Vita vacuumed the bottom circumference of the large plastic cup in search of the last few drops of the milkshake.

"Done already? Want another one, sweetie? We can stop again," said Brendan with smile.

Vita gazed at the passing greenery along the Parkway. "No, thanks, Dad." She had in her mind to ask about her brother and pondered on how to phrase the question. And once more, words sputtered out of her mouth as if she had no control of them. "Do you ever think of my brother?"

Brendan wasn't sure what he had just heard. "What?"

Vita stared up at her dad as he kept focused on the road. With a sense of courage, she repeated the question, "Do you ever think of my brother . . . your son? Do you, Dad?"

Brendan felt his daughter's eyes upon him. He took his eyes off the road momentarily to meet hers. He turned his head back to the road. "Yes. Yes, Vita. I do. I do think of . . ."—Brendan paused and then added—". . . him. At the time of the . . . the abortion, well . . . to us, it wasn't a baby. We didn't think of it as a baby."

"Him, Dad, you mean him," said Vita firmly.

"Yes . . . him. But, Vita, you have to understand that back then, we were just told it was just a piece of tissue."

Vita questioned her father, "Did you believe that, Dad? Did you? 'Cause I don't think Mom believed he was just a blob of tissue."

"Vita, I don't know what I believe anymore. But what I do know is that I won't let you suffer with this reminder of what was done to you." He continued, "How your brother was conceived and how the fetus in you was conceived are two completely different situations. We will get this procedure done in a hospital setting. You may have to wait another week."

"But Mom's not going to let—" Vita began.

Brendan held his index finger up, abruptly interrupting, "Mom will understand. She will come to understand that this is what has to be done. It's the only way."

Vita stayed silent. A frown came over her face as she thought to herself, *It's not the only way.* However, those words did not manage to escape her mouth.

Chapter 18

THE CAR ROLLED UP THE driveway next to Carmen's car. Brendan was not ready to face his wife. "I'm just going to let you off, Vita. I'll be back in a little while." Brendan watched his daughter walk to the front door.

Vita looked back at her dad still waiting for her to enter the house. She shrugged her shoulders and put her hands up. "Mom's not answering."

Brendan shut off the engine and met Vita at the front door. They heard Chaz barking. Vita was scared. They entered into the foyer.

"Vita, wait here."

Vita could not bear to stand in the foyer. She took off up the stairs as Chaz followed on her heels. "Mom? Mom, where are you?" It was evident that Carmen was not in the house.

"Call Grandma."

Vita had already begun dialing before her father had suggested it. "Grandma?" And then a few seconds later, "Mom?"

Brendan motioned to Vita that he would be back later. Vita told her mother to hang on for a second and held the phone to her chest. "Vita, I have to go someplace. I'll be back later." With that, Brendan was out the door.

Vita brought the phone back to her ear. "Mom?"

She heard how frantic her mother's voice sounded. "Vita! Vita! Dear God! I am coming home right now. Grandma and I will be right there!"

"Mom. Mom . . . wait . . . wait . . ." Vita tried to get a word in edgewise, but Carmen had already hung up.

Vita went into her bedroom. She sat on the edge of the bed and contemplated the events of the morning. Her window was opened just enough for the breeze to billow the light lavender sheers into undulating waves. Chaz beckoned to be picked up. Vita coddled her chubby pooch on her lap with her chin resting on the pug's rounded head. She could not erase the image of the man's face twisted in pain as his loved one was placed into the ambulance at the abortion clinic.

***

Nettie had kept her hand on Carmen's shoulder as Carmen spoke with Vita. When Carmen slammed the phone down, Nettie grabbed her purse. The two women exchanged looks of desperation and then headed out the door.

"I didn't expect them back so soon, did you? I was shocked to hear Vita's voice," said Nettie with both hands firmly gripping the steering wheel.

"Mom, it's strange . . . Vita didn't sound like she was in any distress," commented Carmen. Nettie reasoned that perhaps Vita felt a sense of relief in that the procedure went well. Nettie and Carmen discussed how that feeling of relief would be temporary. "She's feeling numb right now, Mom. I remember feeling like that right after . . ."—Carmen paused—"after my abortion. Seems like so long ago, and sometimes it seems like yesterday."

***

Chaz hopped off Vita's lap when he heard a car pull into the driveway. Vita followed Chaz down the steps into the foyer. The front door exploded open. Carmen and Nettie were shocked to see Vita standing there. Vita was instantly swarmed by two sets of arms.

"Sweetheart, I am so sorry, so sorry . . . You should be lying down."

"Mom! Mom! Listen to me," pleaded Vita. "I didn't have the abortion."

"What?" questioned both women simultaneously as they stepped back to read Vita's face, not sure that they had heard correctly. Carmen repeated Vita's words, "You didn't have the abortion?" Vita shook her head no. Carmen was confused, excited, and somewhat jubilant. "Did Dad change his mind? Brendan changed his mind! Where is Dad?"

"No. Mom, listen to me! Dad had to go back out." Vita proceeded to tell her mother and grandmother everything that had happened at the abortion clinic.

The three of them had managed to meander their way over to sit on the living room couch. Carmen and Nettie were speechless at first, transfixed by Vita's account. Carmen took hold of the small gold crucifix she always wore on a delicate chain around her neck and rubbed it in between her thumb and index finger. Nettie took the rosary beads out of her sweater pocket and held the blue crystalloid beads in her palm. Carmen and Nettie had to console Vita as she described the man she had seen in the waiting room and then saw him again before he got into the ambulance to accompany his wife or his girlfriend. "I wish I could find out how that lady is doing. I hope she will be all right."

"I am so sorry you had to go through this, Vita . . . to have to see this. Your father saw it too. Perhaps he will change his mind."

Vita let her mother and grandmother know that her father would find a hospital where it could be done. She told them that her father was going to ask Dr. Santiago to recommend a good doctor to do it. "I even said to Dad what if I don't want an abortion and that maybe I should have the baby and give the baby up for adoption."

"You said that to Dad?" questioned a surprised but proud Carmen.

"Yeah, but he just insisted that the abortion get done so I don't have to have people see me and ask me questions about being pregnant."

Just then the phone rang. Carmen answered, "Oh, hi, Tony. I'm okay. You, Julie, and the kids? Yeah, Mom's here. Hold on." Carmen handed Nettie the phone. "It's Tony, Ma. He figured you were here."

Carmen asked Vita again if Brendan had mentioned where he was going.

"He didn't say," responded Vita.

Nettie rejoined her daughter and granddaughter. She let them know she took Tony up on his invitation to go out to dinner with him, Julie, and the kids for Mother's Day tomorrow.

"Oh no," muttered Vita. "I completely forgot about Mother's Day."

"Don't worry about it, sweet pea. We have all been dealing with so much," said Carmen.

"I know. I know, but I still have one more day," said Vita.

"That's right, you do," said Nettie.

It was still early in the afternoon. Nettie checked out the contents of Carmen's refrigerator to see what she could put together for a late lunch. She made turkey melt sandwiches and Caesar salad. Vita's appetite had returned, and the feeling of fullness in her stomach was satisfying, which gave her a sense of momentary contentment.

Nettie suggested that they all go to the Saturday vigil Mass. Carmen didn't hesitate to confer with Vita. They agreed with Nettie that they should go as they had much to be thankful for. Vita told them that in church she would pray for that woman and man from the abortion clinic.

***

Brendan entered his quiet, darkened office. No Linda, no aroma of freshly brewed coffee, no Corbin. He was used to this as oftentimes he would go in on a Saturday for a few hours to catch up on some work. It wasn't for this reason that he had come to the office. Brendan not only was not prepared to face Carmen but he was beyond being emotionally and physically spent. The lack of sleep only added to the overwhelming fatigue. The dark leather metal-studded couch in his office invited Brendan's weary body to lie upon it. The cool, smooth firm cushion of the couch caressed Brendan's face as he curled up in a fetal position. Images of the past few days flooded his already-overloaded mind. Fatigue won out as Brendan's eyes closed and a deep breathing with a rhythmic cadence set in.

***

Carmen, Nettie, and Vita were early enough to get their pew. When the opening hymn began, Vita turned to look up the aisle to see which priest would be the celebrant for the Mass. It was Father John. Vita knew her mom would always stop to say a few words to Father John after the Mass. She was already beginning to stress about seeing Father John face-to-face. Vita felt embarrassed and humiliated that the priest knew of the baby inside her and how it got there. She shifted from foot to foot and fidgeted as she watched Father John procession to his place at the altar.

Before Father John began the Mass, he had the ushers pass out a white carnation to all the mothers in the church, asking that all the mothers hold their hands up so that each would receive the flower to celebrate Mother's Day. Vita felt uneasy. Carmen and Nettie felt uneasy for Vita. Vita nudged her mother and grandmother to put their hands up as she could see they were preoccupied, no doubt with the very same thoughts she was having. The three of them always had that kind of connection.

Nettie and Carmen held their white carnations as the Mass was celebrated. When it came time for the readings, Carmen and Nettie looked at each other. Father John was not following the readings that were printed in the missal for that day. Instead, he repeated the ones from the week before, "Before I formed you in the womb, I knew you. Before you were born, I dedicated you . . ."

The words penetrated Carmen and echoed in her mind. Nettie's eyes filled up with tears. Vita did not quite understand what the words meant until Father John gave his homily. "God knows us before we even were. He knew each of us. You and me . . . even before he formed us in our mothers' wombs." The priest's words resonated within Vita. She felt as though he was speaking directly to her. She could sense his eyes upon her.

As predicted, after the Mass ended, Carmen wanted to say hello to Father John, who stood in the church foyer where he shook hands with the exiting parishioners. He joked around with the children as they filed out. Carmen, Nettie, and Vita were toward the end of the line as their pew was near the front.

"Mom, I don't want to talk with Father John. I feel weird about it," whispered Vita.

"Just say a quick hello, and then you can go with Grandma. I'll meet you two by the car," said Carmen as she looked at Nettie to get her nod of agreement. "I just want to talk to Father for a few minutes."

By the time this quick conversation was over, they were a step away from the ruddy-complexioned priest. "Vita, hello! And hello there, Carmen. Hi, Nettie." He patted Vita on the shoulder. "God bless you all."

"Thank you, Father. I enjoyed the homily," said Nettie.

Vita managed a shy smile and uttered a meek, "Hi, Father."

Carmen asked if she could talk with him for a moment. He always made the time for anyone, no matter what. Nettie locked arms with Vita and escorted her out the church door while Carmen remained in the church foyer.

Carmen waited for the last of the parishioners to file through and then motioned the priest over to a corner of the foyer. She gave Father John a brief synopsis of how Brendan had planned the abortion appointment for Vita behind everyone's back and how he had woken Vita up early in the morning and coerced her into going. She told the priest the events at the abortion clinic that resulted in the cancellation of Vita's abortion.

"You know, I thought I saw Nettie's car in the parking lot this morning," commented the priest.

"Yes, Mom and I were here to pray the Rosary."

"You know, Carmen, there is something at work here. I will pray for you and Brendan and Vita. Perhaps Brendan will have an epiphany and a change of heart."

"No, Father. He evidently plans on getting Vita into a hospital for the procedure, thinking now she will be in competent hands."

"Carmen, he believes he is fixing the situation. He cannot bear the reality of what his daughter went through and is going through . . . the fact that Vita is bearing his brother's child . . . conceived by rape . . . that his daughter will give birth to his grandchild, but that child would also be his niece or nephew. Brendan thinks in his own way that somehow ridding this baby will negate the rape or perhaps not negate the rape but sweep it under the carpet so to speak. He does not realize that the violence has already been perpetrated. He does not realize that to inflict yet another act of violence upon the child within Vita and ultimately to Vita herself would be devastating."

Carmen pleaded, "Father, please pray that Brendan will come to understand by tomorrow."

Father John took hold of Carmen's hands, the white carnation still in her grip. "Stay strong, Carmen. Stay strong." He reached over into a nearby basket holding the few leftover white carnations and pulled one out. He handed the long-stemmed flower to her. "Here. Give this to Vita."

Carmen caught up to her mother and daughter in the parking lot. Once in the car, Carmen turned toward the back seat and handed Vita the white carnation. "This one is for you, Vita"—she paused—"from Father John."

Vita daintily took hold of the long stem and tilted the bloom toward her nose. She closed her eyes briefly and contemplated out loud, "Am I a mother? Am I a mother now too?" sounding unsure and curious.

Carmen could not think of how to respond, but Nettie was always ready with words of comfort. She turned to look at Vita seated in the back seat. She reached in between the two bucket seats to place her hand on Vita's knee. In the rearview mirror, Carmen saw her daughter's questioning expression. Nettie told Vita, "Vita, no matter how the baby within you was conceived, you are the mother of that child. The baby didn't ask to be here. You had no control over the awful things that happened to you. But yes . . . right now . . . you are a mother to be."

"So . . . I am a mother though . . . right? I am," said Vita in a defiant yet still questioning manner. Carmen continued to glance periodically at the rearview mirror.

Nettie continued, "Yes, Vita. You are a mother."

Vita looked perplexed as she posed her next question. "What if I have an abortion? Then what? Am I still a mother?" These were challenging questions that even caught Nettie off guard. Carmen's mind was paralyzed. She knew what she wanted to say but could not.

Nettie thought for a moment and said, "Then, Vita, you would still be a mother but a mother who had lost her child."

Vita immediately came back with "You mean I would have lost the baby because I would have caused the baby to die because I had an abortion." There was quiet except for the seemingly apparent sounds of the tires rolling over the uneven pavement.

Carmen felt a flurry of exhilaration that lasted but a moment; the voice inside of her saying, *Dear Lord, I think she's got it . . . She is beginning to understand.*

Vita broke the silence. "But if I have the baby and give the baby up for adoption, I will still be a mother who lost her child, except the child would not really ever be lost. It would have another mother. The baby would have two mothers, right?" A tear that had welled up in Carmen's eye finally cascaded down the side of her face.

Nettie rubbed Vita's knee. "I think you answered your own question."

When they arrived back at the house, Nettie wanted to head back to her home to straighten out her house and select clothes for her Mother's Day outing with her son Tony and his family.

Vita asked her grandmother if she could just stay a bit longer. Nettie agreed. Vita disappeared into her bedroom and reappeared fifteen minutes later in the kitchen where Nettie and Carmen were finishing their tea. "Here, Gram, I made this for you. I wanted to make you an even better one, and I wanted to make you something special . . . a surprise for Mother's Day."

Nettie took hold of the handmade card. It was simple but pretty. The card was made with pink construction paper and a white doily.

"I know it's not much, Gram, but I kinda forgot that Mother's Day was tomorrow."

"Oh, Vita, this is lovely," Nettie said as she opened the card to read it. She kissed Vita on the cheek and placed her hands onto Vita's shoulders to face her. "This is beautiful, Vita. Thank you. You don't have to make me another one. I love this one."

"Okay, Gram, but I'm still gonna make you and Mom a surprise." Nettie and Carmen both sprung a smile. It was a moment of happiness that the three of them relished.

Carmen went into the dining room to the china closet where she had placed the card for her mother. "Happy Mother's Day, Mom. I love you."

Nettie opened the card. After she read it, she held it by her heart. "Thank you, honey. What you wrote . . . it's beautiful."

"And I want you to come out to dinner with us another time," Carmen said. And she added, "And perhaps next week we can go shopping at the nursery. You can pick out a few of those hanging baskets that you love."

Vita chimed in, "Oh yeah, the ones with the purplish flowers and the little balls that hang down."

Nettie smiled. "You mean the fuchsia plant. Thank you so much, honey. I will look forward to that. And what about you, Carmen?"

"What can I say? I have the best mom and the best daughter ever," said Carmen. "I think we will just have a quiet day at home . . . get some takeout, ya know," said Carmen as she felt the awkwardness of this year's Mother's Day.

Carmen accompanied Nettie to the front door. "Have a wonderful time with Tony and Julie and the kids. Thank you, Mom . . . for all that you do for all of us. Call me when you get home from dinner tomorrow."

"Love you, Gram!" shouted Vita who was now back up in her room gathering her craft supplies to work on the Mother's Day presents.

"Love you too, sweetheart!" shouted Nettie.

The two women walked over to Nettie's car. Nettie asked Carmen if she was all right. "You know what would turn this Mother's

Day around, Mom?" Nettie cocked her head. Carmen continued, "If Brendan would have an epiphany. That he would just get it and not pursue this abortion."

Nettie smiled and said, "We'll pray on it." Nettie knew Brendan. She knew in her heart how steadfast he was in protecting his Vita. He would never permit his daughter to go through the trauma of bearing this child.

Carmen reentered the house as Nettie gave a wave out the window as she drove away. Carmen stopped dead in her tracks in the foyer. She paused there for a minute in deep thought and then went into the kitchen. She sat down at the table and sunk her head into her hands. A decision had to be made, and she knew it. Carmen thought that Brendan had most likely retreated to his office and would be there for a while, not wanting to face her. She knew she had to act while he was out of the house.

Desperation, panic, and sadness engulfed Carmen. Her heart raced and pounded. She felt trapped. She knew that there was only one way out. That way out would translate into sacrifices and consequences, but in the end, two lives would be saved. Good can come out of sacrifice. From the deep confines of her soul, Carmen knew that the failed abortion attempt that morning was by the grace of God. She knew that she had one chance and one chance only to get Vita safely away from her father and uncle. Brendan would most certainly pursue attaining an abortion for Vita in a hospital setting. Carmen knew that Brendan wanted this situation fixed as soon as possible and could not bear the pain of knowing that Vita had suffered from repeated rape by his own brother. The brother whom he had loved. The brother who was his lifelong best friend. He could not bear for Vita to go through with this pregnancy and then have to give birth to the product of an incestual rape. Carmen also knew that Corbin would somehow see to it that this baby would not be born for his own selfish reasons. She and Vita had to flee. No question about it.

Carmen was overwhelmed with scattered thoughts. She was unable to focus and became frustrated to the point of tears. Carmen quietly went into her and Brendan's bedroom. She curled up into a fetal position on the bed and cried. A good cry was what she needed to clear her head. She took deep breaths in and out. "Give me clarity and guidance, Lord. You created this child, and if you want this child to have life . . ." Carmen lost her train of thought and then continued, "I hate the way you created this child . . . Please forgive me for saying that, but I do. I will never know why you are putting us through this test. But you need to help me in getting Vita someplace to have this baby."

Carmen realized that the escape plan did not have to be perfect. There was no time to devise such a plan. She had the financial resources and decided that the first thing Monday morning would be to withdraw a sizeable amount of cash from her bank account and then some more from one of the joint accounts she had with Brendan. *I just have to stay one or two steps ahead of them*, Carmen thought to herself. Surely, both Brendan and Corbin would be looking for her and Vita, but she knew that neither would go to the police. And that was her saving grace. Corbin would eventually have to pay for what he had done to Vita, but that would be Vita's decision when and if she wanted to file charges. Such a trial would only cause more trauma for Vita. All of this would have to be decided on in the future. For now, Carmen knew that Brendan would see to it that his brother would never forget the suffering he had inflicted upon Vita. And that would have to be enough for now.

How will I tell Mom? How and when will I tell Vita? It will only be for a few months, Carmen thought to herself. She went into the small office, which also served as a library, and took several legal-sized pads from the desk drawer. She began jotting notes to herself and making lists of what she had to accomplish in the next two days. She would have to come up with something to tell the school. She made sure to add some needed telephone numbers to her telephone book she kept in her pocketbook. Her plan was to leave Tuesday morning after Brendan would leave for work. *Some Mother's Day eve—Mother's Day will never be the same*, she thought to herself.

She kept busy with making lists: of calls she would make on Monday, of places she needed to get to including the bank, and of things she would pack for her and Vita. Carmen thought about going to AAA for maps but then thought again. The AAA office would likely keep a record of the maps she would request. From their many road trips, Carmen and Brendan had accumulated many of their own maps, so she went back into the office to retrieve them.

Selecting a destination was not possible at the moment. Not wanting to go too far south due to the summer heat, which would make for a more uncomfortable pregnancy, but not wanting to limit herself, Carmen pulled the maps for the northeastern and the southeastern United States. She also took a small atlas. With her hands wrapped around the stack of maps, Carmen headed to the kitchen to find a plastic grocery bag to stuff them into. She then went back into her bedroom closet and unzipped one of her empty duffle bags, shoving the bag of maps into it.

Carmen took out her beautiful pale blue linen stationery from her dresser drawer and sat down at the edge of her bed. With closed eyes, she whispered, "This is the hardest letter I have ever had to write. Please help me find the words, dear Lord." Like the plan she was constructing, she knew this letter would be far from perfect but only prayed that Brendan would somehow understand and forgive her. "My dearest Brendan . . ."

***

Brendan lay asleep for nearly four hours. He awoke to the sound of the turning doorknob of his office door. Even the slightest and softest of sounds roused Brendan out of a deep sleep. His skin felt clammy, and the coolness of the leather couch did nothing to keep him from perspiring, although it was more of a cold sweat. Disoriented as to where he was, Brendan slowly moved his weary body. He had been facing the backrest of the couch. As he turned onto his back, he sensed a presence looming over him.

Corbin stood next to the couch and looked down at Brendan. Corbin just stood there with his face that looked like it had seen twelve rounds of brutality in the boxing ring.

Brendan bolted upright in an instant as the flight-or-fright adrenalin rush kicked in. "What do you want? Why are you here, Corbin?" Corbin did not respond immediately. Brendan shook his head so as to clear it. The trip to the abortion center that morning began to register in his mind.

Corbin walked to the back of the couch. Brendan turned his head to follow him. "Ya know, Bren, I could have laid a solid one right to your head while you were lying there in dreamland," said Corbin sarcastically. "After all, you landed all the good punches," he continued. Brendan stared at his brother in disgust. "I missed a few days of work, ya know, 'cause I . . . uh . . . had a little accident," said Corbin in the same sarcastic tone. "So I came in to catch up on a few things. Weren't you supposed to take Vita for the abortion procedure today? How is she?" asked Corbin, only now speaking in a faux caring voice.

Brendan was not in the mood to speak with his brother. He had come to the office for some therapeutic alone time, and the last person he wanted to see stood before him. Brendan sat up. "Why should you care, huh? For your information, I did take Vita, but the clinic had an emergency, and they were forced to close. So if you must know . . . yes . . . she is still in the same condition she was in yesterday," Brendan responded with cynicism.

"And?" asked Corbin.

"And what, bro?" snapped Brendan.

"Are you going to try some other place?" asked Corbin with fake concern.

Guilt seeped into Brendan's mind. "Not there. Not there. I should have researched into how these clinics are run. No, I will make sure she has the procedure done in a hospital where I know she'll be safe." Brendan paused. "Why am I telling you all this . . . Just get out of here. Get out! Get out of my office! You came here to get some work done . . . so just go and do it and get out of my face!"

Corbin put his hand on Brendan's shoulder. "Whatever you want. I know you are going through a trying time." Brendan's body tensed up as his insides shuddered with repulsion, but he did not say another word as Corbin exited his office. Corbin shut the door gingerly until the latch caught. Corbin lumbered into his own office and grimaced as he sat behind his desk. Neat piles of folders and papers had been placed on his desk. Corbin realized his brother had caught him up on most of his work.

Brendan glanced at his watch. He sat awhile to get his bearings and to contemplate what to do next. His body told him to lie back down, but his mind swirled with the images of the morning's travesty. He wanted to hear Vita's voice. He dragged himself over to his desk. Brendan knew how upset Vita was and felt badly that she witnessed what she had. He picked up the phone and dialed his home number in hopes that Vita would answer. Brendan was not ready to face Carmen after whisking their daughter away that morning like he did. He was relieved to hear Vita's voice on the other end of the line, and that was only because Carmen was too immersed in organizing her thoughts for the letter she had begun to write that she asked Vita to answer the phone. "Dad? Where are you?"

Brendan told Vita he was at the office. She listened as her father apologized for having taken her to the abortion clinic without telling her ahead of time. He apologized for taking her to such a place and was sorry that she had to see the crisis at the clinic. "I am so sorry to have taken you there, sweet pea, and I am so sorry for the way I did it. I just want this to be over for you. I want everything to be back to the way it was." He told Vita that he would look into getting her an appointment for an in-hospital abortion.

***

Vita came out of the office and met her mother halfway on the steps. "That was Dad."

"Where is he? What did he want?" asked Carmen, concerned and angry about the stunt he had pulled.

"He's at the office. He just wanted to tell me that he was sorry for taking me to that abortion place today and, you know, sorry that I saw what I saw."

"Is he coming home?" asked Carmen.

Vita told her mom that her father didn't mention when he was coming home and that he would make an appointment at a hospital for the abortion. "Mom, I don't think I want to do that."

"Honey, I will talk with Dad when he comes home. By God's grace for whatever reason, you did not have that abortion today. I have another chance to reason with him."

Vita went back into her room where she had been working on her Mother's Day presents.

Carmen pondered in her mind how she was going to handle Brendan, but she knew she could not waste valuable time. She retreated back into the bedroom.

**

Brendan had a shred of peace within after he spoke with his daughter. He still however was not ready to face Carmen. He knew he had gone behind her back, even though he had felt justified to do so. Brendan, still exhausted, made his way back to the couch. He lay on his back and felt the coolness of the leather through his shirt. With his forearm rested on his forehead, Brendan thought about what he would say to his wife. Perhaps he had gone about it the wrong way. He knew he wanted to apologize to Carmen, but he wanted her to understand why he did what he did. Brendan began to dwell on the what-ifs. What if Vita had undergone the abortion at this subpar facility and something had gone wrong? A chill ran through Brendan's body. He shuttered with the thought of having his daughter so close to undergoing the procedure there. He had honestly never given it much thought, only because he had never realized the vast differences among the outside abortion clinics versus a hospital-performed procedure. Brendan continued to grieve at having put his daughter at risk like that. Carmen had a right to be furious with him as she would certainly know by now what had happened that morning. Such thoughts overloaded Brendan's already-fragile emotional condition, and that made him feel that much more tired. He drifted off to sleep once again.

Almost an hour passed before he stirred. He bolted upright once he realized where he was. He was not happy with himself when he figured he had fallen back to sleep for another hour. He wanted to go home to his family and make amends with Carmen.

Brendan closed the door to his office and entered into the common area where Linda's empty desk was situated. The waiting room was off to the side. He could see the light on in Corbin's office and the door slightly ajar. Brendan had forgotten that Corbin had come in earlier and did not wish to see his face again. He walked to head out of the building and heard Corbin calling his name. "Brendan . . . Hey . . . Bren . . . Come here a sec, okay? Please . . ."

Brendan took a few steps backward. He peered into the office through the slight space. "What do you want?"

Corbin, at his desk, asked, "Are you going to call Mom for Mother's Day?"

Brendan glared at Corbin. Brendan answered Corbin in a matter-of-fact robotic voice, "I sent her a card." Brendan headed back toward the front door and then out of the Law Offices of Malloy and Malloy.

***

The Chaz alarm sounded, which meant that Brendan would be walking through the front door. Carmen quickly gathered her legal pads she had been making her to-do lists on and placed them in the same duffle bag in her closet that held the stash of maps. She hurriedly placed the unfinished letter to Brendan in the envelope and placed that underneath her underwear in her dresser drawer.

Vita opened her bedroom door to let the barking Chaz out. The dog bounded down the steps and danced and pranced in the foyer as he excitedly waited for Brendan to step into the house. Chaz's antics always seemed to break the ice, the timing of which could not have been better. Brendan whisked the overzealous pup into his arms as the pug lavished Brendan's cheeks with wet licks and snorts. Both Carmen and Vita could not help but chuckle. Brendan placed the wriggling Chaz back down on the floor telling the dog that he was such a squirm monkey.

When Brendan's eyes met Carmen's, he immediately felt the need to hug her. She was slow to wrap her tense arms around her husband but eased up and moved closer to him. He whispered to her how sorry he was for having taken Vita without any notice to the abortion clinic that morning. "I never wanted to betray your trust. I am so sorry. I never intended to hurt you or Vita, and I now realize how Vita could have been seriously hurt in such a place. Please, please . . . forgive me."

Vita could hear her father's whispering plea to Carmen. He looked at Vita. "Will you both forgive me? Please? I want this to be over with for you, Vita. I didn't know how dangerous these places truly were."

Carmen thought twice about speaking her mind, but with Vita there, she thought it better to keep the peace for now. Carmen kissed her husband. "I know in your heart you were trying to fix things." She mouthed to Brendan, "We will talk later."

Brendan knelt down next to Vita and hugged her. "Don't worry, sweet pea. We will resolve this very soon." It was apparent that Brendan's intentions were still to rid Vita of his brother's child. Vita glanced at her mother, and Carmen gave Vita a slight shake of the head.

During dinner, the family was in total agreement with having a quiet Mother's Day tomorrow at home and ordering takeout food. Vita retreated back to her bedroom where she resumed her handmade gifts for her mother and grandmother.

With Vita upstairs, Carmen thought about bringing up the subject of allowing Vita to carry the baby to term. She stayed in the kitchen to clean up after dinner. Brendan wanted to avoid a confrontation. He retreated into the family room. He gazed over at his unfinished painting on the color-splashed easel. His mind was as turbulent as the sea on the canvas. Brendan decided against working on his art and read the newspaper instead. Carmen scoured the stainless-steel pots and rubbed the sudsy Brillo pad in forceful small circles throughout the inside of the pot until it shone. Her hands worked mechanically as her mind continued to plan the exodus. Transportation would be an issue. Certainly, she could not take her car as she would be tracked down in no time. Renting a vehicle was also out of the question. She would not be able to obtain a fake driver's license in a day and wouldn't even know how to obtain one even if she could. Any form of public transportation would not do as Vita's condition would become more delicate with time. Besides, they would not be able to lug all their belongings on and off trains, buses, taxis, and planes. Frankie, Carmen's other brother, owned a gas station that also handled car repairs. One of Frankie's hobbies was buying used cars for a steal, get them looking nice and running well, and then flipping the cars for a decent profit. *Maybe Frankie can help me out*, thought Carmen. *Maybe he has a car I can borrow or can get me one for us to use.* Calling Frankie with such a request would likely prompt some questions and require some explanation. Carmen would have to tell her brother most of the circumstances, but she would not reveal to Frankie the nature of Vita's pregnancy nor the identity of the father. She could not make the phone call while Brendan was in the house, and she did not want to bother Frankie tomorrow on Mother's Day. Carmen would have to call him last minute on Monday morning after Brendan left for work in the hopes that Frankie could come through for her on such short notice. She could not think of a backup plan at the moment.

Vita displayed three nearly completed dioramas against the pillow on her bed. She admired her creations. "I think Mom and Grandma and Dad will love these, don't ya think so, Chazzy?" Chaz cocked his head from side to side. "I'm glad ya agree," added Vita. She had constructed three dioramas using shoeboxes, cardboard, construction paper, felt, pipe cleaners, and other miscellaneous craft items. Each diorama displayed a scene from a family vacation that Vita modeled after a photograph. Each had a mother, a father, a grandmother, a young girl, and a dog. She had decided to make one for her father and put it aside for Father's Day. Working on these gifts was therapeutic for Vita in more ways than one, and it helped keep her mind off that morning's events.

She had run out of scotch tape, so she came out of her room to go into the office to get another roll. Extra rolls of tape were usually stashed in one of the desk drawers. "I'll be right back, Chaz. Stay here." The command went in one pug ear and out the other. He just wanted to be with Vita. Chaz jumped off the bed and followed her into the office.

Carmen finished her kitchen cleanup. She decided that maybe now she would approach Brendan. He was still on the couch in the family room reading the paper but now with the television on with the volume set low. Carmen sat down next to her husband. She reached over his lap to take hold of the remote. Carmen turned the television off.

Brendan set the newspaper down on his lap. "I know we need to talk," he said solemnly.

Carmen nodded. "Bren, I don't even know where to start except to tell you how hurt and upset and betrayed I feel."

Brendan put his hand on his wife's knee and turned to face her. "You have every right to be. I . . . I just didn't know how else to handle it. I am upset with myself for bringing Vita to such a place. I placed her in jeopardy, and I can't forgive myself."

Vita had come out of the office from the upstairs hallway and was able to hear her parents' voices coming from the family room. She quickly threw the roll of tape on her bed. "Shhhh," she whispered to Chaz. Vita picked him up and cuddled him close to her chest. She tiptoed down the steps and sat on the bottom step with Chaz on her lap. From here, she was able to discern the conversation in the family room.

"I don't know if I can forgive you, Brendan. I really don't know if I can. I suppose over time I will. I have to, but I will need God's grace in helping me to do so." Brendan remained silent. He just shook his head from side to side. "She doesn't need to be traumatized anymore," said Carmen.

"I know. I know," agreed Brendan in a quiet voice. "That's why the procedure will be done in a hospital with the best of care and the best of medical personnel. I believe Dr. Santiago can recommend a competent doctor."

Carmen pulled back from Brendan. The look of shock on her face was all Brendan needed to see. "I can't believe you are still going to put our daughter through this! You don't see it, do you? Let her carry the baby to term. I will take her somewhere away from here during the summer so she doesn't have to be seen. Let her give the child up for adoption," pleaded Carmen.

"Absolutely not!" exclaimed Brendan. "Are you crazy? I will not have my child carry that . . . that baby and then have to go through the pain of childbirth at this tender age. And then have to know that this kid is walking around somewhere . . . this product of the rape of my daughter by my goddamn brother! That is not happening, Carmen!"

Vita's head sank. She wished she had the courage to stand up to her father. But then she heard her mother do just that. "Brendan, it's what she wants! Did you know that? Vita wants to carry this child to term and give the baby up for adoption. I am telling you . . . you cannot put her through any more trauma."

Brendan waved his hand. "Look . . . that's enough! You and your mom have brainwashed Vita into thinking that way. Your way is far more traumatic than an abortion performed in the appropriate place."

Vita retreated quickly back up into her bedroom with Chaz in her arms when she heard footsteps on the kitchen floor. Carmen knew without a shadow of a doubt that she had to proceed with her plans. She also knew that she would have to tell Vita very soon. She would not do to Vita what Brendan had done to Vita by whisking her away that morning without any prewarning.

Vita moved the three dioramas from the bed onto her dresser. She felt in limbo as she lay on her bed with Chaz curled up next to her. Sometimes Chaz seemed more like a cat than a dog in that way. Vita was numb on the inside. She did not want to think anymore.

Carmen downed a glass of water and came back into the family room. Once again, she sat down next to Brendan and sighed, "Look, I don't want to argue anymore. Can we just have a nice peaceful Mother's Day tomorrow?"

Brendan put his arm around his wife. "I don't want us to be torn apart by all this. I don't want to fight with you, Carmen. You know that."

Carmen didn't say anything. She coaxed a half smile onto her face and leaned her head on Brendan's shoulder. Brendan had turned the Yankee game back on but offered Carmen to change the channel to whatever she wanted to watch. Carmen told Brendan to keep the game on and that she was just content to sit next to him and watch the game with him. Meanwhile, her mind was busy devising more of what had to get done within the next two days.

Chapter 19

NO ALARM CLOCKS WERE SET for Sunday morning. Carmen and Vita had already fulfilled their obligation for Mass. Stress, worry, and sleep deprivation had all taken its toll on the Malloy household. Vita was the first to stir. It was nearly nine o'clock in the morning. Even Chaz had been content to stay in bed with Vita. Vita peered over at her art projects on the dresser. The newness of the day renewed her spirits. She decided to try to finish her handmade gifts but not before she let the fussing Chaz out into the backyard to do his business.

Brendan nudged Carmen. He whispered, "Hey, why don't we go to the Pancake House for breakfast?" Perhaps it was a good night's sleep coupled with the start of another day. Even Brendan's mood was light.

Carmen, although half asleep, heard Brendan's suggestion. "Breakfast? Mmmm." She thought for a moment. The family was in need of time to just be with one another.

"C'mon, Carmen. It's Mother's Day. Let's just put aside all of this for a little while and—" Brendan began to say.

"Yes. You know, Bren . . . I like that idea," interjected Carmen.

Brendan sprung out of bed and was in and out of the shower in no time. He pulled on a pair of jeans and a T-shirt. "I'll be right back," he said and gave Carmen a kiss. Before she could ask where he was going, Brendan was out the bedroom door. He knocked on Vita's door, which was slightly ajar, and began to push it open. "Vita?"

"Dad . . . no . . . no . . . don't open it yet. I'm working on something." Vita came to the door.

"Get ready, sweet pea. We're going to the Pancake House for breakfast. I'll be back in a few minutes. I want to pick up some flowers for your mother."

Vita loved to go to the Pancake House. A stack of chocolate chip pancakes resonated well with her. "Okay!" Vita put the finishing touches on her gift for her mother and wrapped it carefully in lavender tissue paper. She gathered the edges and tied it off with a bright yellow curling ribbon.

When Brendan returned, Vita was already showered and ready to go. She worked on the final handiwork on Nettie's gift. Brendan heard the shower water running. His arms tightly hugged two glass vases, each full of a dozen roses. He managed to set the vases down onto the kitchen table, as one of the vases was ready to slip from the grasp of his arms. Brendan pushed the vase with the pink roses into the center of the kitchen table and brought the other vase with the red roses up to the bedroom. He placed them on the dresser on top of a saucer he had brought with him from the kitchen. He stepped back to admire the freshness and the beauty of the blooms. Brendan had a knack for picking out flowers. This was a perfect dozen, he thought to himself. One-third of the roses were fully blossomed; one-third was in varying stages of bloom, and one-third of the bouquet was still in the bud stage. It would surely be the first thing Carmen would see when she came out of the bathroom.

Brendan returned to the kitchen where he set the envelope with the card he chose for Carmen up against the vase that held another perfect dozen roses. Chaz scratched at the back door. As soon as Brendan let him in, the pug beckoned to be fed.

The running water from their bedroom shower ceased. He awaited Carmen's response. It wasn't but a minute later that there was squeal of delight followed by "Oh, how beautiful! Oh, they smell sooo good." Brendan met his wife in the bedroom. Carmen stood there barefoot in her short red terry-cloth robe, with wet hair in a turbaned towel. She held the vase of red roses up to her nose.

"I want you to have some joy today. You are the most wonderful mother to our daughter. Please try to—" said Brendan.

Carmen set the flowers down and wrapped her arms around his neck. "Thank you, Bren. Thank you. They are beautiful."

"As are you," added Brendan. They kissed.

"I will try, Bren," said Carmen.

***

The hostess at the Pancake House seated the family. The conversation on the car ride over had steered clear of the issue at hand. Brendan, Carmen, and Vita each intended to avoid the issue during breakfast. Vita waited until the waitress took their orders. Then she handed her mother the gift bag containing the gift wrapped in the lavender tissue paper. Brendan sat across from his wife and daughter in the booth and watched as Carmen lifted the wrapped gift out of the bag. "I was wondering what was in that bag," she said jokingly. "What a lovely job you did wrapping this, Vita." Vita nodded and gave her mother a look to prod her on to open the present. "I know. I know. I'm opening it." Carmen cooed as she gently unraveled the present. Brendan leaned over the table to get a glimpse of what was inside of all that tissue paper.

Inside was the diorama made out of half of a shoebox. Carmen immediately recognized what it was of. "Oh my gosh! This is amazing! It is us on our vacation when we went to the Portland Lighthouse in Maine!" There stood the Portland Lighthouse made out of construction paper that sat atop of a rocky coast, with the ocean made up of felt, in the background. There were four figures and a dog in the scene, each colorfully painted with the likenesses of Carmen, Brendan, Nettie, Vita, and Chaz. Although Chaz was not along on these vacations, Vita included him in the dioramas anyway. Vita had glued pieces of seashells onto the rocks. She even sprayed the diorama with some of her perfume that smelled like fresh water. Carmen held it up to her eyes and admired it. She turned it so Brendan could see it. Overwhelmed that her daughter could even think of making her something like this during such a trying time in her life, Carmen couldn't help but praise Vita. "This is so beautiful, Vita. I mean I just . . . I just love it! I remember you and Dad had a great time climbing those rocks. Thank you, sweetheart. I just love this!"

Carmen handed Brendan the diorama. "Wow, Vita! How long did it take you to do this? I remember almost taking a dive on those rocks . . . stepped on a slippery one. That was what . . . three years ago, right?"

"Yup, 'cause I was still ten, and when we came home, I had my birthday party the next week when I turned eleven."

They were reminiscing about their vacation that summer in Maine when the pancakes were served. Vita had her usual chocolate chip mini pancakes. She separated them into two stacks, one of which she drizzled maple syrup on and the other she sprinkled with powdered sugar. Carmen and Brendan both took such satisfaction in watching their daughter enjoy that breakfast. Carmen thought to herself that these precious moments were surely a Mother's Day blessing.

Outside the restaurant window, the sun shone brightly. The street that the Pancake House sat on was lined with flowering pear trees in full bloom. All the talk of that summer in Maine spurred an idea in Brendan's head about a taking a drive to spend the afternoon down the shore. Days in May didn't get better than this one. "Listen, why don't we take a ride to Point Pleasant and walk the boardwalk, go on the beach for a bit, maybe dip our feet in the ocean?" Although Carmen had much on her mind, there would be little she could accomplish at home. And this drive down the shore could be more of what they all really needed.

Vita did not hesitate to agree. "Yeah, Mom! Wouldn't that be fun to do for Mother's Day? Chazzy can come, can't he? And we can get pizza on the boardwalk too, Mom! Wouldn't that be great? The pizza at that place on the boardwalk is the best!" exclaimed Vita.

Carmen saw how exuberant Vita was about the idea. "Do you think the boardwalk is open?" asked Carmen.

"As far as I know, mostly everything on the boardwalk including the amusements and rides are open on the weekends starting in early

May and sometimes even in late April," responded Brendan. Brendan and Vita anxiously awaited Carmen's thoughts on the suggestion.

Carmen smiled and cocked her head. "Sounds like a plan."

"Oh goody! Chaz can come too . . . can't he?" repeated Vita.

"Last year, dogs were allowed on the beach before the season opened Memorial Day weekend. Plus, I know dogs are allowed during the season early in the morning and in the afternoon after five o'clock in the afternoon," recalled Brendan. Then he added, "Of course, he can come. Why don't we take him?"

"He doesn't like the water. Remember how funny he was when he barked at it?" Vita laughed. "I can't wait to look for shells," she said excitedly as she shoveled the pancakes into her mouth by the forkful.

Carmen reached over the table to momentarily hold Brendan's hand. Their eyes met. They both relished these simple moments of contentment and happiness.

Back at the house, Vita packed two dog bowls for Chaz, a baggy with dried dog food kibbles, a baggy with three biscuits, and a thirty-two-ounce bottle of water.

Carmen admired the pretty pink roses on the kitchen table and quipped, "What did I ever do to deserve not one but two beautiful bouquets? I'm going to open my card, okay, Bren?"

"Please do," he answered. It was a lovely and dainty-looking card with bright sunflowers on it.

Carmen read the words to herself and then the words that Brendan had written: "I thank God for you, Carmen, every day. I am the happiest and luckiest man in the world to have you as my wife and as the mother of our beautiful daughter. You are the glue of our family. I love you. Brendan."

Carmen's eyes filled with tears. She felt the saliva build up in her mouth. She swallowed. "Thank you, Brendan. This is beautiful . . . and means so much to me." They hugged. It was a long and hard embrace. Seeing her parents together like this helped Vita forget the tumultuous events of recent days.

***

Brendan scanned both sides of Ocean Avenue for a parking spot. "I guess others had the same idea, huh?" he commented. Brendan parked the Bimmer half a block from the boardwalk, which was still considered to be a prime spot. It was close to one thirty in the afternoon when the Malloy clan set foot on the boardwalk. There was not a cloud to be had in the sky. The warmth of the sun's rays felt marvelous. The light ocean breeze carried the fresh saltwater air to their noses. The leashed Chaz pranced alongside Vita, with his nose in the air, as he took in all the marine scents that were not so familiar to him.

Vita was excited to run barefoot on the beach with her pup. She was the first to toss off her sneakers. The feel of the silky soft fine sand seeping in between her toes with each step felt glorious to Vita. She ran toward the calm ocean waters, leash in hand, as Chaz bounded alongside her. Fragments of broken seashells with sharp edges poked through the sand and forced Vita to slow her gait. She let go of the leash to see how Chaz would react to the gently rolling waves and to the coolness of the wet hardened sand by the water's edge.

Her parents, hand in hand, strolled along on the sand in their bare feet. They watched Vita coax Chaz closer to the water. It gave them both such joy to hear Vita squeal with laughter as the cold water swiftly swept over her feet. Her laugh became louder as Chaz barked as the water crept up toward him. He would back up away from it, barking continuously, turn in circles, and then follow the receding water, getting as close to it as he dared. This cycle would repeat itself over and over again, amusing any and everyone in the near vicinity. Vita's shiny straight brown hair with its natural chestnut highlights glistened in the sun.

Brendan squeezed Carmen's hand. "This is what Vita's life should be about right now. It shouldn't be about having to deal with what's on her plate. In a few days, things will be somewhat better for her. Some of that plate will be cleared. She'll be able to be a thirteen-year-old again. Look at her."

Carmen said nothing. It would be futile for Carmen to attempt to contradict Brendan. She felt sourness in her stomach, knowing the course of action she would be embarking on in a few hours.

Carmen was only able to respond to Brendan's comments by returning a squeeze of his hand. Brendan smiled as he thought to himself that Carmen was finally understanding and accepting why Vita had to have this abortion.

"Mom! Dad!" yelled Vita. She pointed to the obvious show that Chaz was performing. "He really thinks he can scare those waves away. You're such a big bully, Chaz!"

Brendan's comments went onto the back burner. Carmen knew Brendan didn't intend to start an argument. He was just talking aloud. And Carmen did not want to destroy the fine time they were all having together on this Mother's Day.

Vita took hold of Chaz's leash. The family walked along the water's edge. "Hey, Dad, could you hold Chazzy's leash? I want to find some cool shells," said Vita. Vita was upset with herself for forgetting to bring a pail to stash any shells.

Carmen always kept a few plastic grocery bags tucked inside her large tote beach bag that was slung over her shoulder. "Here ya go, Veet. You know I always come prepared," said Carmen as she handed the bag to Vita.

"Wow! Look! A pretty one!" exclaimed Vita as she spotted a lion's paw shell in the shallows of the clear water. She scooped up the shell as the water receded. "Look," said Vita as she proudly displayed the orangey pink scalloped lion's paw shell on the open palm of her hand. They all admired the shell with the pretty pattern of orange and pinks before Vita placed it into the bag.

Vita ardently searched the sand by the water's edge as that was where the mother lode of shells could usually be found. After an hour or so of walking on the beach, the salt air brought on their appetites. The family headed for the boardwalk, first to their favorite eatery called Jenkinson's located on the pier by the same name. Leashed dogs were allowed on the outside patio area with the umbrella-covered circular iron mesh tables. The Malloys were fortunate in only having to wait ten minutes for one of the tables to vacate.

Vita gave Chaz one of his Milk-Bones before they put their order in. The pizza was a must-have along with the buttery corn on the cob. Vita added an order of fries to her meal, and Brendan added the sausage and pepper on a long roll. When the food was brought out, Vita unpacked Chaz's two dishes and set them down by her feet. She unloaded the baggy with the kibbles into one bowl and poured water into the other. Still, Chaz could not resist begging for something more delectable from the table. His large dark brown orbs followed the food from plate to mouth of each of his human companions.

"Okay, here ya go, Champ," said Brendan as he tossed a piece of sausage to the ground.

Chaz vacuumed it up as if he was playing shortstop. He licked his chops and tilted his head as if to say, "Next." Vita hand-fed her pooch a fry or two, and Carmen saved a piece of pizza crust for the dog.

"Don't give him too much, or one of us will be waking up during the night to take him out," warned Brendan. They all chuckled, knowing full well that could be the case.

"Why don't we walk around the boardwalk so we can make room for Kohrs," suggested Carmen. The Jersey shore boardwalk was full of sweets that could only be had down the shore especially the Kohr's soft custard ice cream, the saltwater taffy, and the fudge. There was one particular game that Vita played every time they did the boardwalk. One had to shoot a stream of water from a high-powered water pistol into the mouth of a clown's head that turned from side to side. The water would fill up a balloon, and the first person to pop the balloon would win. Brendan held the leash as Carmen and Vita played. Then Carmen did likewise so Vita and her dad could play. They tried to wait for other players; the more players, the better the prize.

After several rounds, Brendan nailed the big one. "What will it be, sweet pea?"

Vita chose a huge furry lavender teddy bear, which she proudly lugged. They decided to walk back to the car to drop off the new addition along with the bag of shells before they returned to the boardwalk for dessert.

The soft custard ice cream at Kohr's was like none other. Vita had her favorite chocolate peanut butter ripple. Carmen and Brendan both went for the butterscotch ripple. Even Chaz got a sample-size cup of soft vanilla ice cream. Carmen appreciated these moments. She savored them. Here there were, the three of them with Chaz, walking the boardwalk, enjoying one another's company, while the sun—now low in the sky—still beamed its glorious rays with the light ocean breeze becoming somewhat cooler. Before they left the boardwalk, they bought fudge and saltwater taffy from one of the many sweetshops.

"Grandma loves the vanilla-flavored fudge," Vita reminded her parents. This gift of a day would be one they would each treasure forever.

The Malloys were on their way back home before sundown. Vita fell asleep in the back seat in between Chaz and the large lavender teddy. The sun was setting as the car motored northbound on the Garden State Parkway. It was a quiet ride.

Carmen wanted to talk with Brendan but couldn't think of anything to say other than "Thanks, Bren . . . what a wonderful day. Thank you for everything. I think we all needed this." She smiled and placed her hand on Brendan's lap. Brendan smiled back. Carmen leaned her head against the window and soon was fast asleep.

Why is it that sleeping kids in cars always seem to wake up within a few miles of reaching home? Perhaps it was the change in speed from the highway to the side roads, but nonetheless, Vita woke up. "What time is it Dad?"

"Did you have a good snooze? It's almost seven thirty," responded Brendan.

"Can we visit Grandma if it's not too late?" asked Vita.

Carmen was coming to. "What time is it?"

"Seven thirty," repeated Brendan. "Would you like to go and visit your mom? I'm sure she is back from dinner by now," he added.

"Maybe we should call first. And Vita . . . you have school tomorrow," said Carmen.

Vita persuaded her mother, "C'mon, Mom. We can give Grandma her fudge and her taffy, and if we stop home first to call her, I can get my present for Grandma and give it to her while it is still Mother's Day."

"It's your call, Car," said Brendan.

The Malloys parked in their driveway and unloaded the car. Vita went up to her room and wrapped the diorama for Nettie in much the same way she had done her mother's. Carmen called Nettie who had been home for the past hour.

"Okay!" Carmen yelled from the kitchen phone. "Mom says to come on over!"

It was at first decided to leave Chaz home. The salt air, the food, and all the walking had exhausted the pooch.

Vita expressed her nervousness about leaving Chaz behind. "Can't we take him? He'll be safe with us." Her worrisome voice brought reality to the surface once more.

"Sure, he can come, but it looks like you will have to carry him," said Brendan, not wanting to put any damper on the day. With the gift bag dangling from her wrist and the pug coddled in her arms, Vita got back into the back seat of the Bimmer.

Nettie had a pot of decaf brewing when the Malloys walked in. Carmen admired the lovely Mother's Day flower arrangement Frankie had sent.

"What can I get you to drink, Vita?" asked Nettie. Vita opted for some nice ice tea. Nettie went on about the wonderful time she had at dinner with Tony and his family and how tall the kids were getting. Vita said how much she missed her cousins.

"Hey, Gram, we got you some fudge and saltwater taffy, and um, this is for you too," said Vita as she handed her grandmother a gift bag with something wrapped in lavender tissue paper.

"What's all this for?" said Nettie.

"Gram, that's your fav flavor, right?"

Nettie opened the box of fudge. She couldn't resist but to break off a piece and pop it into her mouth. "Yes, indeed . . . Vanilla . . . my favorite!" exclaimed Nettie. She went into the kitchen to get a knife and proceeded to cut a few cubes of the fudge. "Thank you! Ohhh . . . this is too good!" She passed the box around; but Brendan, Carmen, and Vita had eaten enough.

"That's yours, Gram."

All eyes were on Nettie as she unraveled the tissue paper. Nettie carefully held the diorama up to her face. "Vita, this is absolutely lovely! The cherry blossoms! From when we went to DC! Oh, look . . . this must be me! How did you ever do this?" Nettie passed the diorama to Carmen who then passed it to Brendan.

"Vita gave me one this morning. It was of our trip to Maine, the Portland Lighthouse," said Carmen.

Brendan jokingly asked, "Hey, where is mine?"

Vita returned her answer in a singsong tone, "You'll see . . . You just gotta wait."

Nettie talked some more about her Mother's Day dinner with Tony and his family. The Malloys shared with Nettie their day down the shore.

Vita told Nettie of Chaz's antics and how he bullied the water. From her pocket, she handed her grandmother one of the orangey pink scalloped shells. "I found lots of these ones with this color. This one is for you."

"Only God can make these colors . . . so pretty . . . Thank you, Vita. I'll set it up right here on the mantle."

"Mom, I'm so glad we got here to see you for Mother's Day, even if it was for a little while. It's almost nine o'clock, and Vita has school tomorrow," said Carmen.

"I know you've got to go, and I appreciate you coming by," said Nettie.

Brendan decided to take Chaz out for a quick walk before leaving for home while Carmen and Nettie collected the coffee mugs and glass. Vita remained in the living room and watched television as the two women stood in the kitchen.

"It sounds as though you had a wonderful day today. You know you all needed that," said Nettie with her hand on Carmen's shoulder.

Carmen reached up to lay her hand upon her mother's. "I know. And I will always cherish it," said Carmen softly. Then she suddenly turned to face her mother, their hands joined. "Mom, that is what makes my decision even harder." Nettie read her daughter's eyes. She knew what Carmen was thinking. "Mom, Brendan will likely make the appointment this week for Vita. He is going to call tomorrow, so it could be as early as Tuesday or Wednesday," whispered Carmen. "After the day we had today, it tears me up inside, but . . . but . . . I have to . . ."

Nettie finished Carmen's sentence, "Do what you need to do." Nettie nodded as she rubbed Carmen's hand. "I know. I know, Carmen, what you feel you have to do. I know your back is up against a wall. You know I support you and will help you in whatever way I can. I also know how heartsick and broken Brendan will feel; but we are thinking of two lives here—Vita and that baby's."

"And we'll be back by the fall," said Carmen. "Oh my god, how we will miss you and Brendan desperately," Carmen sadly added. "I didn't tell Vita yet, Ma. Can't tell her tonight. We had such a good day," said Carmen.

"When do you plan on leaving?" asked Nettie.

"Tuesday morning," responded Carmen. Nettie figured it would be soon and was saddened it had to come to this. "You have to let her know tomorrow. You can't do what Brendan did to her. Promise me you will tell her tomorrow."

Carmen nodded. "I know. I have to. It will devastate her, but it is only temporary."

Nettie queried Carmen on her transportation plans. And that was when Carmen told Nettie of her idea to talk with Frankie about getting a car from him. "Look, honey, if you would like, I could speak with your brother tomorrow morning. It would be one less thing you would have to concern yourself with."

"You'll talk to Frankie for me? Okay, Mom, but I will call you first in the morning because I have to figure out what you are going to tell him."

Just then, they heard Brendan reenter the house. Chaz bounded through the living room and then into the kitchen and back into the living room with renewed energy.

Nettie watched as the dog ran out of the kitchen. "What about Chaz? That will devastate Vita even more if she has to leave him behind." Carmen did not have time to respond as Brendan called for everyone to gather their things. Carmen had not given thought to taking Chaz, but if it would make this whole ordeal smoother for

Vita, it was something to think about. Carmen, Brendan, and Vita each kissed and hugged Nettie goodbye.

Vita was tired. As soon as she entered the foyer of their house, she declared that she was changing into her PJs and going to bed. Chaz, whose renewed energy was short-lived, followed Vita into her bedroom. Carmen yelled upstairs for Vita to at least wash her face, hands, and brush her teeth.

Brendan too reached the point of not being able to stay awake. He had done all the driving. "Why don't we just get into bed and get a solid night's sleep. I have got a lot to do in the office and . . ."—Brendan paused—"and I don't know what I'll be facing tomorrow with my brother." Reality had returned for Brendan too.

Carmen and Brendan went into Vita's darkened room to kiss her good night. Carmen thanked her daughter again for the beautiful gift she had made. Chaz shared the bed with Vita as usual. The large lavender teddy bear was propped up in a corner of the room.

Carmen and Brendan retired to their bedroom. Carmen turned off the small lamp on the night table. She whispered to Brendan, "Thank you for such a beautiful day . . . all of it. And I am thankful we got through the day without having to deal with anything else than just us all being together." They kissed good night. Brendan was asleep in a matter of minutes. Carmen, as tired as she was, just lay there staring at the ceiling. Her mind was overwhelmed with what she had to accomplish by tomorrow, not to mention the disheartening task of telling Vita. She daintily slipped out from beneath the covers, tiptoed out of the bedroom, down the stairs, and then into the kitchen. She sipped on a glass of merlot and then went back upstairs to try to get some sleep. She would need it. Carmen gingerly climbed back into bed. She lay on her back and eventually succumbed to the luxury of sleep. By ten thirty in the evening, the Malloy household was in a deep slumber.

Chapter 20

A SICKENING GUTTURAL FEELING, CARMEN WAS engulfed by it. Reality had reared her face once again at the front lines, and Carmen was not ready to do battle with her. She watched as Brendan and Vita ate their breakfast. Carmen leaned against the kitchen counter, her coffee mug in between her hands. Her appetite was gone. She had left it down the shore. Brendan and Vita thought nothing of Carmen not eating breakfast with them as that was the norm on the weekdays. It was a cup of coffee while her husband and daughter ate breakfast, and then Carmen would eat by herself after Brendan and Vita had left for work and school respectively. This was a scene she would perhaps get to experience one more time tomorrow. Then it would be months and months of breakfasts in an unknown place.

Brendan glanced at the clock and said he wanted to leave to get to his office. He knew he had to deal with Corbin, plus he had to be in court by ten thirty in the morning. He expressed his hope to Vita and Carmen about being able to make some calls to set up the hospital-based abortion. "I will try to get Dr. Santiago this morning. Hopefully, her office is open by nine and that she can recommend a physician for us," said Brendan. Carmen and Vita made quick eye contact with each other that went unnoticed by Brendan. They did not respond to his comments. "Sweet pea, would you mind catching the bus today? I have to get going," said Brendan as he brought his cereal bowl to the sink. He took one last swig out of his coffee mug and then kissed Vita and Carmen each goodbye.

"That's okay, Dad," said Vita.

Carmen chimed in, "I can drop her off at school today. I have to get moving myself."

Carmen was relieved that Brendan had left. She now had this small window of time to speak with Vita. Carmen thought about delaying confronting Vita with the plan until after school. It would be impossible for Vita to stay focused in class, but Carmen really had no choice other than to deal with it now, time being the commodity that it was.

Vita also had something on her mind that she wanted to say to her mother as soon as her father had left the house. "Mom, I'm scared. I don't want to have an abortion." And so the moment presented itself.

"I know. I know you are. Vita, we need to talk. Let's go in your room. We can sit on your bed." The two went upstairs to Vita's room and sat side by side on Vita's bed. Chaz had followed them upstairs and parked himself at their feet. Carmen held Vita's right hand in between her palms. "You know I have tried to talk your father out of the abortion. He won't budge. Sweetheart, in his mind, he is trying to fix all of this for you. He just wants everything to be all right." Vita listened intently but did not look up at her mother. "But this is a complicated issue. Life is a complicated issue. You know what we talked about with Father John."

Vita nodded. "I wish I could just hide, Mom. I wish I could just hide somewhere," mumbled Vita.

And that was when Carmen came right out with it. "Listen to me, Vita. That is exactly what we have to do. You and I have to go away someplace. We have to hide, in a way."

Vita lifted her gaze to meet her mother's eyes. "Where?" asked Vita.

"We need to go somewhere where you can safely give birth to this baby. There are special places that help girls in your situation. We need to go, and we cannot let your dad know where," said Carmen.

"Or Uncle Corbin," echoed Vita.

"Especially Uncle Corbin," repeated Carmen. Carmen continued, "We will only be gone as long as we have to, five months or so, and we will be back the middle of October, in time for you to catch up on the first month of school.

Reality now took its turn and caught up with Vita. She tried to absorb all her mother had told her. How her grandmother would obtain the necessary schoolwork for these last three weeks of school and the first few weeks of schoolwork in fall for the start of ninth grade. She listened as her mother explained to her that the school would be told that there was a family emergency out of state that had to be attended to.

"What about Dad? And Grandma? Is Grandma coming?" questioned Vita.

"No, sweetheart. Grandma has the rest of her family here, and besides, what would Grandma do being away from her house for so long? And Dad . . . yes, Dad will be hurt. And Dad will be angry at first, but I think he will come around to realize . . . one day perhaps," answered Carmen.

"No, Mom! I don't want to leave Dad and Grandma." And then the thought of Chaz who sat before her came to her mind. "And Chazzy! I am not leaving him! I can't leave him!" cried Vita.

"Grandma can take care of Chaz," suggested Carmen. Carmen had up her sleeve the bargaining power of the offer to take Chaz with them.

"He still won't be safe, Mom. I don't trust Uncle Corbin. And Chaz would be so sad. He would think that I abandoned him," Vita reasoned. And hence came the opportune moment to lay down the bargaining chip.

"Okay, Vita. We can take Chaz with us. It may not be easy to find a place to stay, but I promise that he can come with us." Vita picked up her pug who by now had done the head tilt several times upon hearing his name mentioned. "Vita, do you think this is easy for me? Do you think I like doing this? Leaving here is tearing me apart. But it is temporary. I even suggested to Dad to let me take you someplace away from here for the summer and part of the fall so you could have the baby to put up for adoption. He would not allow it," said Carmen.

Vita held on to Chaz even tighter. Her chin rested on his head. "When? When would we leave?" asked Vita in a melancholy tone.

Carmen did not answer right away. Vita looked up once more into her mother's eyes and knew the answer before the word came out of her mother's mouth, "Tomorrow."

"Then I don't want to go to school today," said Vita.

"You have to go to school today, sweetheart. You have to go, and you will go, and you will somehow get through the day," urged Carmen.

"I want to see Dad and Grandma. Does Grandma know?"

"Yes, she does. Grandma knows, and Grandma will help Dad understand why we are doing this." Carmen wrapped her arms around her daughter who still had her arms wrapped around Chaz. Carmen held Vita. "I will miss Dad, and I will miss Grandma very, very much too. But we will get through this, Vita. We will do the right thing, and we will return. And we will try to keep in touch with Dad and Grandma, but we will have to be careful about it." Carmen could feel Vita nodding her head in affirmation. "Sweet pea, you try to get through school today. I have a lot to do. And yes, we will see Grandma before we leave tomorrow."

Vita was in a state of disbelief. Everything would be different tomorrow. Carmen helped Vita get her backpack and lunch together. "Mom, I'm supposed to have twirling practice today," she said as she held her baton up. "Can I still go?"

"Sure, you can go."

After Carmen dropped Vita off at school, she headed over to Nettie's house. She had remembered to tell Vita to bring all her books home as Vita exited the car.

Raindrops began to fall to a steady light rain. The cadence of the windshield wipers and the pitter-patter of the rain mesmerized Carmen as the car seemingly drove itself to Nettie's house. With so much to do, Carmen's mind was elsewhere. Overwhelmingness can become paralyzing; when there are a hundred things to do, the brain cannot even begin to know where to start on a one.

Nettie was expecting her phone to ring around seven thirty in the morning, not her doorbell. Nonetheless, the early riser and organized lady wasn't surprised to see her daughter at the front door. "Come in, sweetheart. I'll put on a nice fresh pot of coffee," said Nettie as she placed her arm around Carmen's waist and guided her in.

"I'm going to have to live on caffeine today," said Carmen.

Nettie read the lost expression on Carmen's face. "You tell me what I can do for you." They sat at the kitchen table after Nettie set up the coffee maker.

Carmen spoke, "I told Vita this morning."

"And?" questioned Nettie. Carmen filled Nettie in on the conversation she had with Vita before dropping her off at school. "That dog is a godsend in more ways than one," said Nettie as she poured them each a mug of the fully caffeinated java.

"What are your plans today?" asked Nettie.

Carmen's mind seemed to kick back into gear. She asked Nettie to call her brother Frankie for her and instructed her mother to tell him the basic reason for the escape and not to reveal that Vita had conceived through rape nor mention the identity of the father. "That may come out in due time, but for now, Mom, all Frankie needs to know is that Vita is pregnant and that I am taking Vita away to an undisclosed place to have the baby for adoption placement. He knows my stance on abortion. Just tell him that Brendan was insistent on putting Vita through the abortion procedure." Carmen paused and then added, "I hate putting you in that spot, Ma."

"I'll handle it, honey. You have enough to do," said Nettie. "What else can I do for you?" asked Nettie.

Carmen requested that Nettie go to the school to collect the assignments Vita would need to finish the school year. "I'm going to give you the textbooks this afternoon, and if you could just make copies of what Vita needs, I will have you send them to me when I know where we will be going." Carmen explained to Nettie that she would go to the school tomorrow morning and request an emergency meeting with the principal to explain why Vita had to leave with her for an out-of-state family emergency. "I have the letter ready to give the school requesting Vita's teachers to list the assignments that have to be completed and that you, Vita's grandmother, would be getting those assignments and sending them to us. And this way too, Mom, you could bring the textbooks back to the school on the last day of school, which I believe is June 7."

"I can do that," said Nettie.

They spoke of how diligent they had to be in taking precaution in not giving any opportunity for Brendan and Corbin to snoop. "I don't trust Corbin, Mom. I would not put it past him to hire someone to go through your garbage or even the mail in your mailbox just to get any iota of information as to our location . . . ya know, phone bills and such."

"And Brendan? What do you want me to say to him? You know I will be the first person he will come to when he finds out. You are leaving him a letter, yes?" asked Nettie.

"Hardest thing I have ever had to write. I haven't finished it yet," Carmen sighed with sadness in her voice. "I am sick inside with the hurt he will feel. Mom, you have always been there for him as if you were his own mother. You are more a mother to him than his mother ever was. He will need your comfort and your shoulder to lean on."

Nettie nodded. She held Carmen's face between her small weathered hands. "I will miss you and Vita dearly, but I know you need to do this. I will try to be there for Brendan, but you know he will pressure me as to your whereabouts, and God forgive me, I will not be able to say anything to him. I will do that for you."

Carmen took hold of her mother's arms as Nettie's small hands still held her face. It was their eyes that did the talking.

They finished their coffee. Carmen's plan was to go back home and pack. "I can get some packing done, and as soon as the banks open at nine o'clock, I will head over there."

Nettie kissed Carmen as she walked out the front door. "I am going to call your brother and see what he can do. I will call you as soon as I know something." With that, they parted.

***

Brendan had counted on being solo in the office so as to organize his thoughts and plan his morning. He didn't bother with putting on a pot of coffee. He knew Linda would do that as soon as she would arrive in an hour, at eight thirty. Besides, he had already had two cups during breakfast, so the need for more caffeine was not necessary. Brendan barely had all the lights turned on in the place before he heard the front door open and close. Corbin decided to get an early start that day too.

The brothers exchanged glances. Brendan did a quick about-face and walked back into his office with disgust. His temples pulsated as the blood rushed to his head. There were things he had wanted to say to Corbin. He decided he would vent some of his thoughts. By this time, Corbin had gone into his own office.

Brendan now stood in the doorway of Corbin's office. "C'mon in, Bren," said Corbin matter-of-factly, as if there was nothing between them.

Brendan entered Corbin's office just enough so that he had room to close the door behind him. Corbin eyed Brendan intently. He wondered if his brother was going to assault him again. Brendan spoke, "Linda is going to pick up that there is a problem here. Somehow, we are going to keep it under wraps. I suggest we stagger our time here so that we are not here together. And eventually, I want us to split our practice. I can't stand to be in the same room with you anymore, but for the time being, we are going to have to make this work for appearance sake."

Corbin listened. He responded with "So you still believe I did what you, oh . . . excuse me, what Vita is accusing me of?"

Brendan's face was red with anger. "Don't push me, Corbin! Don't do it! Look, I've got to be in court by ten thirty, and I've got some calls I've got to make before I leave. So if you need to talk to me about business, then we will deal with it. Anything else . . . don't even look my way. Oh, and all I told Linda was that you had taken a fall and had to have some minor surgery. So you fill in the blanks," said Brendan before vacating Corbin's office. Brendan slammed the door shut upon exiting Corbin's office.

Corbin stared ahead and mouthed the words to himself, "Whatever you want, bro. Whatever you want."

When Linda walked into the Law Offices of Malloy and Malloy, the first thing she did was to ask Corbin how was he feeling and what did he do to himself. "'Cause you still look pretty well bruised up there, Corbin," commented Linda. Corbin attributed his injuries to a fall he had taken when he took an evening run the past Thursday, after having stepped off a curb that he did not see. He told Linda he hit his head and gashed his leg for which he needed stitches.

The second thing Linda did was to put on the morning pot of coffee. She poked her head into Brendan's office. "Good morning, Brendan."

"Hi there, Linda. Did you have a good weekend and a good Mother's Day?" asked Brendan.

"Oh yeah," replied Linda. "The usual schlepping the boys to Little League practice and games. Do you believe they actually had a game scheduled on Mother's Day! I just put on the coffee. Would you like a cup?"

"That will be great, Linda, but just a half a cup. Thanks." Brendan smiled.

Linda briefed Brendan on the calendar for the day, which meant being in court by ten thirty and then meeting with three separate clients in the afternoon. She then popped into Corbin's office to review his appointments for the day. Before she returned to her desk, she brought both men a mug of coffee, with Brendan's half full as he had requested.

Brendan hoped to get a call into Dr. Santiago's office before he had to leave for court. As soon as nine o'clock rolled around, he thought about phoning the good doctor's office but figured the staff would be busy retrieving calls left on the answering machine during the weekend. He decided to wait until nine fifteen before dialing the number for Dr. Martina Santiago. Brendan recognized the voice on the other end of the line. It was the nurse Mindy who had answered.

"Dr. Santiago is due in any minute," the nurse told Brendan. Mindy remembered Brendan, his wife Carmen, and their daughter Vita. Brendan asked Mindy to have the doctor call him as soon as possible and that he would be in his office for another half hour or so. He gave her the telephone number for the law office and thanked her. Disappointed and anxious, he had hoped to get the ball rolling on resolving Vita's present condition.

The first phone call of the morning came into the Law Offices of Malloy and Malloy a few minutes past nine thirty. "Law Offices of Malloy and Malloy, Linda speaking. How can I help you?" said Linda to the caller.

"Oh yes, Doctor . . . Hold on one second, and I will transfer you," said Linda.

Perhaps Dr. Santiago did not hear the "Malloy and Malloy" as she requested to speak to Mr. Malloy. Linda was always in the habit of asking which Malloy whenever someone called asking to speak with a Mr. Malloy or an Attorney Malloy. This time, however, when the caller identified herself as Dr. Santiago returning Mr. Malloy's call, Linda assumed the call was for Corbin, who had just spoken to Linda of his injuries and stitches.

Corbin answered the phone on the first ring, "Good morning. Attorney Malloy speaking."

"Yes, how are you Mr. Malloy? This is Dr. Santiago. I was going to call your home phone later today, but you got to me first. The test results are in for Vita" came the voice on the other end.

"Hold on one moment. I believe you are looking for my brother Brendan," said Corbin as he pressed the button to put the caller on hold. Corbin's interest in the call was instantly peaked. He sauntered over to Brendan's office and rapped on the slightly ajar door before pushing it open. "I have a Dr. Santiago on my line. I believe it is you she is looking for," said Corbin with a twist of sarcasm in his voice. Brendan jumped up out of his chair as Corbin exited Brendan's office. "I'll transfer the doctor to your line."

Brendan stared down at his phone. It rang. He snatched up the receiver faster than a cowboy could draw his Smith & Wesson from a holster. "Dr. Santiago? I'm sorry you were connected to my brother's line instead." Dr. Santiago explained that she had asked to speak with Mr. Malloy and assumed it was Brendan to whom she was speaking with. "I apologize. Our secretary must have made a mistake."

Dr. Santiago told Brendan what she had already mentioned to his brother. "The test results are in, so we can go over them when Vita comes in for her appointment."

"Actually, Dr. Santiago, I need to talk to you about something first. Excuse me, hold on one moment." He placed the phone down on the desk and went over to his office door to shut it. Brendan sat back on the edge of his desk and brought the phone back up to his ear. "Dr. Santiago, what I wanted to speak with you about was getting a recommendation of a physician who performs the abortion procedure in a hospital setting. We have decided this will be the best option for Vita."

"Mr. Malloy," said Dr. Santiago, "as you know, I do not perform abortions because I do not believe in taking a life. Therefore, I cannot even point you to someone who would be willing to do just that. I hope you can understand where I am coming from."

Brendan did not respond. He thought for a moment and then told the doctor that he did not want to risk taking Vita to some makeshift clinic where her health would be jeopardized. "You can understand that I want this procedure to be done in the safest environment with the best medical personnel."

Dr. Santiago could hear the desperation in Brendan's voice. "I understand that fully, Mr. Malloy. Let me say though that even an abortion done under the best of circumstances can go awry, not to mention the possibility of damage to the reproductive organs." She continued, "Usually, most hospitals have a physician referral service. If you and your wife and Vita really see fit to have this abortion done, I can only suggest getting a recommendation or reference from the hospital you choose to get the procedure done in. If you call the general hospital number, just request the physician referral service and take it from there."

"Thank you for getting back to me. I will do what you suggest," said Brendan.

"Did you still want to keep Vita's appointment here with us?" inquired the doctor.

"Uh . . . you know, just keep her on for that appointment. Either I or my wife will call your office tomorrow to let you know for sure."

"Did you want to go over Vita's test results?" queried the doctor.

Brendan had forgotten that the doctor had mentioned that at the beginning of their conversation. He knew he did not have time to talk much longer. "Is everything all right? I . . . I have to run out of the office to get to court. Can I call you back later, or is it something you can tell me quickly?" said Brendan hurriedly.

"There is nothing to worry about. Why don't we just speak tomorrow when you call about whether or not you will be keeping the appointment for your daughter," said the good doctor.

"Okay. That will work. Thank you, thank you, Dr. Santiago." Brendan placed the phone gently onto its cradle and immediately went to place the necessary folders with the papers he needed for court into his attaché case.

Brendan heard a light knock on his door. Before Brendan could say come in, Linda had opened the door enough to poke her head in. "I am so sorry, Brendan. I assumed the call was for Corbin. When the caller said she was a doctor returning Mr. Malloy's call, I just assumed it had to do with Corbin's injuries. I apologize," said Linda with sincerity. "I usually do ask which Malloy, ya know."

"Don't worry about it," said Brendan. "But what I have to do now is make a few quick phone calls before I leave for court." Linda closed the door quietly as she exited Brendan's office. Brendan glanced at his watch and figured he had about fifteen minutes before he had to leave. Brendan reached down to pull the bottom drawer of his desk that held the Yellow Pages for the county. He thumbed his way to the Hs and then ran his index finger down the page to locate the heading for "Hospitals." He had no idea which hospital would be best for his daughter. Brendan thought that he would select the larger medical centers that he had heard of first. He jotted down the names and numbers of four different hospitals onto a yellow legal pad. He then dialed the first number on the list and asked for the physician referral service as Dr. Santiago had suggested. Fortunately, the hospital did indeed have such a service to which Brendan was immediately connected to. He gave the referral service representative the necessary information and stated that he needed the names and numbers of ob-gyn physicians, preferably female, who regularly perform the abortion procedure in the hospital. Brendan was put on hold for several minutes. He flicked his wrist over to check the time on his watch.

Before he had a chance to contemplate whether or not to hang up, the voice on the other end of the line returned, "Do you have a paper and pen ready?" Brendan scribbled the name, number, and location of the physicians that were referred to him, two of whom were females.

"Thank you. I appreciate your help." He hung up the phone and hastily shoved the phone book back into the drawer it had come from. Brendan then proceeded to reopen his attaché case, tucked the yellow legal pad into one of the compartments, yanked his suit jacket off the back of his chair, and slung the jacket over his arm. He rushed out of his office into the main reception area, attaché case in one hand, car keys in the other, and suit jacket over his right forearm. As he passed Linda's desk, he told her that he shouldn't take long and would be back around one o'clock in the afternoon or so, in time to see the clients.

"Okay, Bren, we will see you then," said Linda.

Brendan never acknowledged Corbin as he walked past Corbin's office whose door was open enough to see Corbin at his desk. Linda did think it unusual for Brendan not to say something to Corbin but shrugged it off, thinking that Brendan was in a hurry.

Brendan ran briskly through the drizzle to his car. Corbin's instinct was to follow his brother out to the parking lot to inquire about the doctor's call as his curiosity was getting the best of him. He remained, however, seated at his desk. He tapped his pencil, unable to focus on his work. Corbin thought about his lavish lifestyle. Could that telephone call affect that life of luxury that was his? Could that call be anything to do with the DNA of the baby in Vita's womb? Was Vita going to have the abortion as Brendan had said? He was determined to find the answers to his questions. Corbin was well used to his abundant way of living, having indulged in cars, boats, travel, and women. Relationships with women were almost always short-lived, and any suggestion of commitment on the woman's part meant that she was history. Corbin was a player, and that's the way he liked it. Brendan and Carmen figured that one day, Corbin would get tired of that kind of an empty life. There was however never any indication of that happening. And Corbin was not about to let anything or anyone come in the way for what he had worked for. From time to time, Brendan would try to talk to Corbin about his priorities, asking him many a time about the possibility of having a family of his own. Corbin's response to that was "Why . . . I already have one right here," as he was a frequent visitor to Brendan's home.

***

Carmen felt uncomfortable holding that exorbitant amount of cash in her pocketbook, which sat on the passenger seat as she drove home. She had managed to pack most of the clothes that she and Vita would need before she had left for the bank. She knew she would have to purchase looser-fitting clothes and even maternity clothes as Vita progressed through her pregnancy. Carmen had run into a snag at the bank when the teller informed Carmen that for the large amount of cash Carmen was planning on withdrawing, the bank's policy was to be notified at least one day in advance. Carmen explained nicely that she really needed to withdraw that amount of cash due to a family emergency. The vice president of the bank ended up accommodating Carmen as best he could. He had told her to return to the bank in one hour and that the money would be ready for her then. She spent that hour at the church speaking with Father John. Carmen was fortunate that he was still in his office.

Carmen explained to the priest how her back was up against the wall with Brendan's decision to still pursue the abortion and that he would most likely secure an appointment for a hospital-based abortion as soon as possible. Carmen's hope was that the pastor could recommend a place or home that dealt with pregnant teens and young single mothers to be. She told the priest she was looking to get far enough away where she and Vita could hide out and where Vita could get good prenatal care and have the baby in a hospital associated with such a program. Father John had told Carmen that he had some resources available to him. He went in that same file cabinet where he had retrieved the study regarding women who decided to give birth to their baby conceived by rape. Father John had found the folder he was searching for and, after shuffling through its contents, pulled out several pages.

As Carmen drove through the rain, she continued to replay in her head the visit with the priest. "Let me copy these for you, Carmen. These are organizations that run homes for young single pregnant women who have nowhere to go to have their babies. They are listed by state. Most of these organizations have connections to adoption agencies," Father John had said. The papers sat folded under her pocketbook on the car seat. Carmen had perused the list and noted several places in Maryland, Virginia, and the Carolinas, thinking that she may be headed that way. She had asked the Father if she was doing the right thing and had told him how horrible she felt about leaving Brendan like this. The priest had told her, "You are saving two lives here. The right way isn't always the easy way. As a matter of fact, the right way usually is the more difficult course of action. I will pray for you and Vita and Brendan too. You call me whenever you have to." He had also asked if Nettie would be going, and Carmen had informed him that her mother was staying home. Carmen could still hear his final words to her. "You are courageous. You and Vita will be all right. God bless you both."

Carmen pulled into her driveway, the pavement wet from the steady drizzle. She heard the barking pug as she exited the car. It wasn't quite noon yet. There were no messages on the answering machine. Carmen wondered how her mother was progressing with the transportation issue. She decided to plow ahead with the packing operation and worked on readying the supplies for Chaz along with medications, vitamins, first-aid supplies, toiletries, list of necessary phone numbers, and the like.

Time passed quickly. The next time Carmen glanced up at the clock, it was after one o'clock in the afternoon. Perhaps it was a good sign that she had not yet heard from Nettie. She took a few deep breaths to refocus her thoughts and energies now to finishing her letter to Brendan.

As Carmen reread what she had written so far in her letter, tears spilled out of the corner of her eyes and glided down her face much the same way the raindrops slid down the panes of the bedroom windows. It all seemed so surreal. Was this really happening? She tried to imagine an almost-normal scene one year from now as her mantra to regain her concentration on the letter. Chaz stayed curled on the bedroom floor rug as Carmen sat on the bed with her legs stretched out in front of her, two propped pillows behind her back, and a writing tablet on her lap. She never imagined she would have to write such a letter. As the words took form on the blue-lined paper, the heaviness in Carmen's heart became more burdensome.

Carmen set the pen down and placed the pad alongside her. She rested her head back on the pillows and closed her eyes. The letter was completed. Carmen could not rid her mind of the images of what Brendan's reactions might when he read it. The ringing phone broke her reverie. Startled, Carmen sat straight up and lunged to answer the phone on the night table. "Mom?" Carmen listened as Nettie gave her the news that Frankie would be able to help his sister out. It was an '85 Corolla with high mileage but in good condition. That was the best vehicle of the six that Frankie had at his gas station/car repair shop. He kept the cars until he could resell them after getting the vehicles in good running condition and sprucing them up. The car was registered under Frankie's business of DiAngelo's Garage. Nettie relayed to her daughter how upset Frankie was to learn of Vita's circumstances. He had only been told that Vita was pregnant and nothing else.

According to Nettie, Frankie was anxious to speak with Carmen. "You may see Frankie tomorrow morning when he brings the car over here. I will drive him back to his work afterward," said Nettie. They discussed more of the details on the phone. Carmen and Nettie were both somewhat relieved to know that at least Carmen and Vita would have a decent car to travel in that would hopefully remain untraceable for several months.

"Ma, I have to pick up Vita after baton practice. We want to stop by. Would that be okay? And we can go over the rest of the finalities. Okay, Mom, see you then. I love you and . . . thank you. Ba bye." Carmen placed the phone back on its cradle. Chaz paced back and forth. He was antsy. "You know something is going on, don't you, Chaz? I know. I know, good boy," said Carmen as she pat the pooch on his head. "C'mon, you want to go out for a quick walk? I think that would do us both some good, don't you?" And with a tilt of his head accompanied by a resounding short bark, Carmen and Chaz went downstairs to get ready for their stroll in the light rain.

***

Linda had just told Brendan's first client to have a seat as Brendan came in through the front door of Malloy and Malloy. She noticed his raindrop-stained suit jacket and damp hair with no evidence whatsoever of an umbrella in hand. "How are you today, Mr. Novak? I'll be with you shortly. Just give me a few minutes," said Brendan as he headed into his office. Linda followed him in. "Would you like a towel?" she asked Brendan. Before he had time to answer, she had gone back out of his office only to return from the kitchen in less than a minute with a handful of paper towels.

"Do I look that bad?" said Brendan half jokingly. "Thanks, Linda." Brendan patted his face with the paper towel. He then blotted his hair with another paper towel and then ran his fingers through his short-cropped hair, which somehow managed to fall into place.

"Much better," commented Linda.

Brendan opened the folder that was on his desk. "Give me two minutes and then send him in," said Brendan.

"How was court this morning?" queried Linda. Brendan told her how pleased he was that things had moved along smoothly in court without any holdups. "Glad that happens once in a while," said Linda as she exited Brendan's office.

Brendan hoped to have a slice of free time when he could make his calls. His first client was about to walk in, plus he had two more scheduled to follow. *Maybe I'll have a few moments in between appointments*, Brendan thought to himself just as Linda escorted Mr. Novak into his office.

Between client number 2 and client number 3, Brendan had the opportunity to call the second hospital on the list to obtain additional recommendations. Linda buzzed Brendan to let him know client number 3 was here. "Linda, can you do me a favor?" Brendan had not eaten lunch yet. "Would you mind picking me up a sub? Surprise me," said Brendan. He handed her a twenty-dollar bill as she let the last client in. "Get a bite for yourself."

"I'm good. Thanks," said Linda.

Corbin hadn't said a word to his brother since Brendan had returned from court. He could see that Brendan was busy, plus Corbin had his own work to attend to. He was getting more and more anxious but knew he had to wait for the right moment to approach his brother.

***

Halfway through the walk, Carmen was able to put her umbrella down. The sky, however, remained overcast with low-lying gray clouds. By the time they returned home, Chaz was almost dry. Carmen still towel dried the pooch, even though the dog had proceeded in assisting with the drying efforts by giving his coat a robust shimmy. "Stay still there, Chazzy," coaxed Carmen as the pug squirmed his way through the towel hold Carmen had on him. "C'mon, Chazzy. Let's go pick our girl up."

Chaz sat atop another dry towel Carmen had placed on the passenger seat of the Bimmer. She hoped Vita remembered to take all her books with her. As Carmen pulled up to the curb near the school gymnasium door, Vita was exiting the building. She struggled with the open backpack that was bursting from its seams. Carmen parked and quickly got out to assist her daughter. Chaz jumped back and forth from front seat to back seat.

"Just about everyone has left. I went back to my locker just before you got here 'cause I didn't want anyone to see me with all these books," said Vita as she huffed and puffed while walking toward the car. Her load was lightened now that Carmen had relieved her of the heavy backpack. Vita still toted a duffle bag and her baton as her small pocketbook dangled off her shoulder. Both the front and back passenger side windows of the car were majorly smudged. An excited high-pitched bark came from inside the car.

"We going to Grandma's now?" asked Vita as she was being greeted by her overzealous pooch as she sat in the front seat of the car.

Carmen nodded. Carmen was at a loss for words knowing they both would have their lives turned upside down in a matter of hours. "How was school and twirling practice?" was what finally came out. Having Chaz on her lap kept Vita from sinking totally into a melancholy hole. She felt as if a part of her life was slipping away from her: the hanging out with her girlfriends, the last few weeks of school when all the students were giddy with anticipation of what summer would hold.

"It was weird" was all Vita could say. Inside, she felt alienated: alienated from her friends, from her school life, from her dad, and from her grandmother.

"I know," responded Carmen. She understood Vita's pain but didn't know how to comfort her daughter at the moment. Only Chaz could do that. Carmen saw from the corner of her eye as Vita's hand stroked the top of the dog's head.

The image of the unfinished gift for her father popped into Vita's head. She thought to herself that when she got back to their house, the very first thing she would do was to finish the diorama for her father. She envisioned that she would leave the gift in a special hiding place. She thought too about making a card for her father with a message of some sort, and also in that card, she would disclose the location of the present that was to be opened on Father's Day. Vita's heart sank with the thought of her dad spending Father's Day alone. She consoled herself with the thought that her grandmother would help him get through the day.

Once at Nettie's house, they gathered at the kitchen table. On the table were pretty blue-and-white gingham cloth placemats, each with a tall glass of Nettie's nice ice tea. A plate of homemade oatmeal-raisin cookies sat in the middle of the table. Usually, Vita would take her drink and cookies and sit in the living room to watch TV. Today, she sat in the kitchen with her mother and grandmother, wanting to spend as much time with Nettie as possible.

Vita listened as Carmen and Nettie made the plans for the next morning. Her uncle Frank would have the car that she, her mother, and

Chaz would be using for the next few months. Chaz eventually parked himself on the kitchen floor after he had investigated Nettie's house for any new and interesting scents. "You want a cookie too, Chazzy?" Vita went to the kitchen cabinet where Nettie kept a box of Milk-Bones. "Here ya go, Chazzy," said Vita as she held the edge of the dog biscuit. "Do nice." Chaz gently took the treat out from Vita's fingers.

Vita didn't partake of the conversation but only listened as her mom and grandmother continued to work out as much of a plan as they could brainstorm. When they got on the subject of Brendan, Vita became concerned. "What about Dad? Grandma, please make sure Daddy is okay. I am worried that Uncle Corbin will do something bad. And I am worried about Daddy in the house all alone."

"Sweetheart, I will make sure your dad comes over here to eat and whenever he wants to. And I will try my darndest to help him understand why you and your mom are giving this baby his or her right to be born," said Nettie.

"And we will talk to Dad by phone," added Carmen. "We just have to be careful that the calls are not traced to our location."

"Mom, where are we going again?" asked Vita. She had heard her mother and grandmother throwing around the names of places while they were discussing such things earlier. "I think we are going to head south, toward Maryland. I don't know where we will end up, perhaps Virginia or the Carolinas."

Vita nodded. She then searched her pocketbook, rooting around for several seconds before extracting a crumbled pamphlet. "Here, Mom. Maybe this will help you," said Vita. "It's something that some lady who was praying outside the abortion place gave me."

"Oh?" said Carmen as she unraveled the wrinkled paper. Carmen perused the pamphlet and then smoothed it out. She folded it neatly before tucking it away in her own handbag. "I'll hold on to this. Thank you, Vita."

***

Four thirty in the afternoon—quitting time for Linda. She poked her head into Brendan's office and then into Corbin's office to tell each of them to have a good evening. After Linda left, Brendan got up from his desk and closed the door completely as Linda had left it slightly ajar. Corbin was restless and more than anxious to approach Brendan. He noticed that Brendan's phone extension was still busy as indicated by the red light next to Brendan's extension number. Corbin thought about picking up the phone to listen in on the conversation as he had a hunch it concerned Vita. That was too risky. Instead, Corbin quietly stepped out of his office and positioned himself outside Brendan's office door. He cupped his hand around his ear and leaned his ear against the door. Corbin concentrated as he tried to hear Brendan's side of the conversation. Several key words such as "abortion procedure" and "my daughter is a minor" caused Corbin to press his ear right up against the door. When he still could not pick up the continuity of Brendan's conversation, Corbin quickly ran off to the kitchen to obtain a small drinking glass. He then locked the front door of the office. Back at Brendan's door, he carefully placed the open end of the glass on the door. With a firm grip on the glass, Corbin pressed his ear to the bottom of the glass. Corbin now heard Brendan's words with clarity and listened intently as Brendan made apparent arrangements for Vita to see a physician tomorrow afternoon. Corbin ascertained that this doctor's visit would be a prelude to a possible abortion procedure by the end of the week. He could feel his anxiety level drop down a few notches, but he still did not have the answer to the question he had pertaining to Vita's test results that Dr. Santiago had mentioned. Could one of those tests possibly be a DNA profile on the baby in Vita's womb? Corbin decided not to press his luck and returned back to his own office. He unlocked the front door before he did so.

Corbin began to review the two files he would need for the two cases he had in court for the next day. When he was done checking all the paperwork, Corbin noticed that Brendan's phone extension was still in use. Two weeks ago, he would have encouraged his brother to wrap things up so that they could unwind at their favorite watering hole before they would each head home. Now, that was all in the past. Corbin placed the files into his attaché case and readied himself to leave. He had found out enough of what he needed to know for the time being. He also decided it was best not to approach Brendan at all. He thought about knocking on Brendan's door to say good-bye, but on second thought, it would be better just to leave without doing so. After all, Brendan wanted the least amount of contact with Corbin. The last thing Corbin did before he left the office was to call one of his female friends for a last-minute date.

***

Nettie got up from the kitchen table to answer the phone. She motioned to Carmen that it was Brendan. "Hi, Bren. What's up?"

Brendan answered, "You weren't home, so I figured you and Vita stopped by your mom's. Listen, I was able to get Vita an appoint-ment with a female gynecologist associated with one of the medical centers. The doctor can see her tomorrow at four o'clock in the after-noon. I have been on the phone for the past hour and was also able to speak with someone from Dr. Santiago's office. They will leave a copy of Vita's test results for me in their mailbox. Dr. Santiago had left for the day when I called. Oh, I did tell the receptionist to cancel the appointment for Wednesday with Dr. Santiago. I'm on my way over to Dr. Santiago's office now to pick up the results, and then I will head home. Are you there?"

Carmen had been listening to Brendan spew off his plan. Although she had expected something like this to happen, she was still taken aback by it. "I heard you," said Carmen. She did not know what else to say.

Brendan continued, "All right. Look, we can talk when I get home. There is a good chance that if all goes right tomorrow, Vita could be set up for an abortion by Friday." Again, there was silence from Carmen's end. "Look, I know how you feel, but trust me . . . this is the best decision for all of us right now" came Brendan's voice through the phone.

Nettie could tell by Carmen's expression exactly what was hap-pening. "We will be leaving here in a little while. Oh, how did it go with Corbin today?" asked Carmen.

Brendan told Carmen that they hadn't seen much of each other and that he had suggested to Corbin that they stagger their hours at the office. He told Carmen that Corbin had told Linda he had fallen off a curb while running and had hit his head and cut his leg, which needed stitches.

After Carmen hung up the phone, Vita did not hesitate to ask, "What did Dad want?"

Carmen sighed. Nettie placed her hand on her daughter's shoulder as Carmen sat back down at the table. "Dad has already made an appointment for you tomorrow afternoon to see a female doctor at one of the medical centers. And he said that there was a possibility that the abortion could be set up for the end of the week."

"What does that mean, Mom?" questioned Vita. She knew the response.

"It means that we will absolutely have to be ready to go tomorrow morning as soon as Dad leaves for work—no ifs, ands, or buts about it," said Carmen with sadness.

"Then I want to get home and be with Dad tonight. Besides, I was making Dad a Father's Day present, and I want to finish it so he has something for Father's Day," said Vita.

"I know how hard all of this is for you, sweet pea—how hard it will be for all of us, but in a few months, we will all be together again. And I will be seeing you and your mom tomorrow morning too," said Nettie as she tried to hold back her own tears.

Nettie took out from the refrigerator a defrosted eggplant parmesan casserole she had made. "Here, dear. Just have to heat this up. You are going to need all the time you have left to get everything else together." Carmen thanked her mother. Nettie was always a step ahead, anticipating the need of others. Carmen and Vita said their goodbyes to Nettie for the day. The plan was for Nettie to pick up Carmen, Vita, and Chaz in the morning after Carmen would be back from Vita's school.

As they drove home, Vita in the passenger seat with Chaz on her lap, she wanted to know what her mother had packed for her. "I hope you packed clothes I like," said Vita.

"If there is anything you see that I did not pack, just put it on your bed, but keep in mind we are limited in what we can take. And besides, you won't be fitting in most of your clothes much longer," said Carmen. That thought had not crossed Vita's mind. She looked over at her mother. Carmen added, "We'll just buy you what you need when you need it."

When they arrived home, Vita took off to her bedroom to put the finishing touches on the gift for her father. She also worked on a Father's Day card for him. Carmen put Chaz out in the backyard and then placed the eggplant parmesan in the oven. She knew she would have some time before Brendan came home. Carmen went up to the bedroom closet to organize everything in one place. Brendan had a walk-in cedar closet made for Carmen when they first had moved into their home. She piled several duffle bags in the back corner of the closet, covering the pile with a blanket. All of this was concealed by a rack of long dresses. Emotion seemed to have taken a back burner for the moment. Carmen was on autopilot—getting done what needed to be done.

She rapped on Vita's door. "Veet, did you find anything you want to take?"

Vita opened the door. What caught Carmen's eye was the giant furry lavender teddy bear on top of her daughter's bed. That sight jolted her momentarily out of the autopilot mode. "Here, Mom, just this jacket and these sneakers too." Then she opened a drawer of her dresser. "And these shorts too." They were lavender terry cloth shorts with an elastic waistband that would certainly fit for the duration of the pregnancy. "I can sleep in these with a T-shirt," added Vita.

At the dinner table, Brendan laid out the plan to see the doctor at the medical center. "I'll have Linda move up my last appointment so that I can get back home here by three o'clock to pick you up."

"I, uh, will send Vita with a note to school tomorrow to excuse her at two thirty," said Carmen. She hated lying. Vita said nothing. There was not much in the way of additional conversation after Brendan spoke about the plans for tomorrow afternoon. Brendan assumed Carmen and Vita were quiet as they were adjusting to the fact that definite plans had been made. He knew Carmen would have difficulty in accepting the final decision, and so he expected the awkward silence.

Vita too felt sickened by the sense of betraying her father. She looked over at Chaz, who had finished his bowl of dog food.

"Can I give him some of this?" Brendan laughed.

"I don't think that would be a good idea. He may think that he likes eggplant parmesan, but I have a feeling eggplant parmesan won't like him." And as had happened the past couple of weeks, Chaz had managed to lighten the atmosphere for a few moments.

After dinner, Vita cuddled up next to her father on the couch to watch the Yankee game. He wrapped his arm around his daughter as she leaned her head upon his shoulder. Carmen joined them after she had cleaned up after dinner. As she walked into the living room, she held two opened bottles of beer in between the fingers of her right hand. "Here, Bren."

"Oh, thank you, honey!" said Brendan.

Carmen sat on the other side of Vita and placed her beer bottle on the coffee table. "I thought I could do with one of these too."

Chapter 21

VITA SAT AT THE BREAKFAST table and told her parents how Bebe chirped so early this morning that it woke her up way before her alarm had been set to go off. "It sounded like she was right outside my window, but I was too tired to get up and look." Vita had not gotten much in the way of sleep. It was the message in the card that she wrote that had kept her up. She had lain awake and had pondered on what to write. She finally had gathered her thoughts to say what she wanted to say in her card to her dad.

As usual, Vita and Brendan ate their breakfast at the table while Carmen stood leaning on the kitchen counter, coffee mug engulfed by both hands. Chaz had been out in the backyard already for his morning obligation. He nervously pranced back and forth and in and out of the kitchen. "Why such a nervous Nellie this morning, boy?" asked Brendan half jokingly.

Vita picked at the strawberries on the cereal. "I don't think I can eat this cereal right now. I just want some of the strawberries," said Vita. "I think the milk in the cereal is making me feel crummy."

"Are you nauseous?" asked her father.

Vita nodded. "A little, I guess."

Brendan suggested that maybe the morning sickness had kicked in. Carmen did not mention to Brendan that morning sickness generally occurs during the first trimester of pregnancy and that Vita was already well into her second trimester.

Brendan put his arm around his daughter. "You won't have to be dealing with all of this anymore. You're going to be all right, sweet pea," he said gently. Brendan reminded Carmen and Vita that he would be by the house at three o'clock in the afternoon to pick them up. "We'll just take my Z there. I have the copy of the test results. The doctor can go over everything with us. From what I could read, there weren't any concerns."

Vita excused herself from the table. "My stomach is queasy" was all she said. She went into the upstairs bathroom, shut the door, sat on the lid of the toilet seat, and buried her face into her hands. She couldn't hide her emotions any longer. She knew that she would have to do everything in her power to try not to lose it when it came time to kiss her dad goodbye as she did every morning before he left for work. She would have to wait months to kiss and hug him again. The realization that this would be the last time she would be seeing her dad was all too much for Vita to bear. She sobbed for several minutes. She then talked herself into calming down, threw some cold water on her face, and went back downstairs to find Chaz. As usual, Chaz was a comfort as well as a great distraction.

"Vita, are you okay? Maybe you should stay home today, sweet pea," suggested Brendan as he looked over at his wife for approval. "Carm, maybe it would be best if she did."

Carmen agreed. "I'll drive her in later if she feels better, but maybe you are right, Brendan, as we have to get her out of school around two to two thirty anyway." Carmen looked over at her daughter. She knew how Vita's heart ached. "Vita, it's up to you. If you are not feeling well, it may be just a good idea for you to stay home from school today," echoed Carmen.

Brendan shoved the last morsel of the cream cheese bagel into his mouth and washed it down with what was left of his coffee. "I've got to get to the office early again." Brendan was feeling better about life today. He had gotten a good night sleep knowing that he had taken the necessary steps to fix Vita's problem. He had even taken a quick jog earlier in the morning despite the chafed skin around the ankle bones. A run was how Brendan preferred to start his day. "Okay, girls, I will see you at three o'clock. I'll call later to see how you are feeling, Vita." He hugged Carmen and kissed her goodbye. Carmen wished she could hold Brendan tighter. She wished she did not have to unwrap her arms from him. Carmen kissed him lovingly on the lips and then straightened his tie. Did he sense the sadness in her eyes? And if he did, in his mind, it had to do with Vita's impending abortion.

Brendan went over to where Vita sat in the living room with Chaz on her lap. Vita placed her dog on the floor. She wrapped her arms around her father and pressed her face against his chest as he stroked her silky, shiny brown hair. Vita tilted her head up toward Brendan's face as he stooped down to kiss his daughter.

Mother and daughter stood silently at the front door as they heard the Z's engine turn over. Their eyes followed Brendan's car until it was out of sight. They immediately embraced each other and sobbed. Chaz laid his head upon his paws while his eyes rolled upward toward his people as mother and daughter rocked each other in their embrace. Carmen slowly loosened her hold from Vita. She placed her hands on her daughter's shoulders and then gathered Vita's hair to sweep it behind Vita's neck. Carmen spoke softly, "We will both miss Dad so very much, but we have work to do now, and we have very little time to do it. I want you to come upstairs with me." Vita followed her mother into the master bedroom. Carmen showed Vita the pile under the blanket in the back of Carmen's closet. "I'll need you to bring these bags into the garage while I drop off the note to your school and hopefully meet with the principal." Carmen had already showered. "I am going to get dressed now and get some makeup on. You can help by getting Chaz's bowl, food, and leash and putting them in with the rest of his supplies." The chores helped distract Vita from the burning in her heart.

The plan was for Nettie to pick up Carmen and Vita. She was to pull into the garage. The attached garage had a door that opened into the main foyer. Before Carmen left to go to Vita's school, she phoned Nettie. "Mom, we are ready for you." Carmen let her mother know that she would be back to the house within a half hour or so. "Vita will be moving the duffle bags and backpacks to the garage." Carmen had chosen to pack everything this way as these were easier to handle and easier to pack in a car trunk.

The timing couldn't have been better. Carmen had only been gone for twenty-five minutes. She was fortunate to catch the principal for an impromptu meeting and was able to accomplish all that she had hoped to at the school. As she drove up the street to the house, she observed the garage door descending.

Carmen entered through the front door of her home, the last time she would be doing so for a long while. The door in the foyer to the garage was open. Nettie and Vita were standing in front of Nettie's car. The garage, which rarely housed Carmen and Brendan's vehicles, was one for the *Better Homes and Gardens* magazine. A painted gray cement floor with a sheen, light blue-gray painted drywall with shelving on the far wall and back wall of the garage, and a workbench/tool area with everything in its place, made this garage picture-perfect. Carmen kissed her mother. "The principal knows that you will be getting Vita's assignments. She was very understanding. She never pried."

"Yeah, Mrs. Brickell is a pretty nice lady," chimed in Vita.

Duffle bags and backpacks and a few shopping bags were stacked in front of Nettie's car. "Thank you, Vita. It looks like you have gotten all of it. Let's do a quick check and a run-through before we pack it into the trunk," said Carmen.

A full hour had not passed before Vita with her dog, her mother, and grandmother were on their way to Nettie's house. Carmen's BMW was left in its usual spot in the Malloy driveway. They stopped at a phone booth so Nettie could let Frank know to meet them at her house. The women did not want to have a trace to Frank's telephone number on neither the Malloy house phone nor Nettie's home phone.

Nettie felt like an accomplice aiding fugitives, and both Carmen and Vita felt like fugitives aided by their unlikely accomplice.

Vita wanted to know what her uncle Frank knew. "Do my cousins know? I don't want anyone to know!"

Nettie assured her granddaughter that her uncle Frank knew only that Vita was pregnant and that they were leaving to have the child for adoption purposes and how Brendan was opposed to it. Nettie let Vita know that Uncle Frank felt it only right to tell his wife and that it would not go any further than that.

"They probably think I am a slut now!" exclaimed Vita. Both Nettie and Carmen reiterated to Vita that that was not the case.

Carmen lamented how devastated she felt when she had placed the envelope that held the letter to Brendan against the bed pillow.

Vita mentioned to her grandmother that she had a card that she wanted Nettie to give to Brendan on Father's Day. "Grandma, I want to give it to you as soon as we get to your house. I made Dad a diorama too, and in the card, I wrote where he will be able to find it. It's in a special hiding place," said Vita.

"That will mean so much to him, Vita." Nettie smiled as she kept her eye on the road.

"Yes," agreed Carmen, "I am so glad you thought of doing that for Dad."

Nettie pulled her car to the top of her driveway. "Frank should be here within a half hour. Let's go inside," said Nettie.

Vita carried Chaz into the house and then set him down on the floor. "Here, Gram," said Vita as she handed the envelope from her pocketbook to her grandmother.

Nettie placed her hand on the side of Vita's head and gently guided the side of Vita's face to her bosom. "Don't worry, honey. I will look after your daddy, and I will make sure he gets this on Father's Day. I promise."

Vita wrapped her arms around the petite woman. Nettie detected a tremor that emanated from Vita's body. "Gram, I am going to miss you so much. I wish you could come with us."

Nettie stroked Vita's hair. "I will miss you and your mom more than you will ever know. And I am so proud of you . . . more than you will ever know . . . for your courage, Vita." She paused and then added, "You know I would come along with you, but someone's got to hold down the fort. Besides, I need to be here for your dad." Nettie and Vita tightened their hug.

Nettie, Vita, and Carmen savored these final personal moments before Frankie was to arrive. Carmen thanked her mother for always being there for her, Vita, and Brendan. "I love you, Mom. We'll be all right. I know you will be praying for us."

Chaz was the first to sense the vibration of a car pulling into the driveway. Nettie opened the front door as Vita held on to Chaz. Frank kissed his mother. "Hey, Mom." He went over to his sister to hug her. Frank whispered into Carmen's ear, "I am here for you. You need anything . . . and I mean anything . . . you call me."

Carmen could barely look into Frank's eyes, knowing that he believed that Vita had engaged in sexual relations at such a tender age. And that perhaps he thought that Carmen and Brendan had not done their job as parents.

There was awkwardness in the room. Carmen motioned Vita over to where she stood with Frank. "We want to thank you, Frankie, for going out of your way to help us and at the last minute."

Vita could not look up at her uncle. "Thank you, Uncle Frankie," Vita uttered meekly.

Frank delicately placed his hand under Vita's chin and tilted her chin up so that their eyes met as much as Vita tried in earnest to look downward. "Vita, honey, you will be all right. I told your mom if there is anything at all that you need, you call me. Okay? You know that I love you." And with that, he kissed Vita on the forehead.

One can never truly fathom what it is like when those moments we dread most are upon us. It was time to depart. The time was near nine thirty in the morning, and Carmen knew there was no lingering to be afforded. "Okay. Let's do it." Nettie and Vita remained in the house while Frank and Carmen transferred all of Carmen's and Vita's belongings into the trunk of the Toyota. Brother and sister were back in Nettie's living room in a matter of minutes. Frank and Carmen had engaged in a brief conversation. Carmen was thankful that Frank knew not to push the boundaries. He had reemphasized to her that whatever help she needed, he would be there for her. He also mentioned to Vita that only his wife knew and that it would not go any further, not even to their other brother Tony. Carmen certainly understood Frank not wanting to keep any secrets from his wife.

Carmen started to say, "There is no good time to say our good-byes, but now we—"

Nettie finished the sentence for Carmen, "Have to get on the road. So go now, you two," said Nettie as she embraced Carmen and

Vita. "I love you both so much. You are strong girls. You will be all right, and I will be talking to you. Please let me know tonight that you are okay."

"We will, Mom. We will. Love you," said Carmen soberly. Vita clung to her grandmother after Carmen had gone over to Frank to hug him and to thank him once more.

The four of them walked outside to the silver Corolla sedan. Vita took Chaz onto the lawn so that he could do his last-minute business. Nettie opened the passenger side of the Toyota. Vita managed to get in with Chaz in her arms. Frank stood at the driver's side and closed the car door for Carmen. As she adjusted the seat and mirrors, Frank told her, "This is a good running car."

Nettie and her son stood in the driveway, their arms around each other's waist, as the silver car backed out of the driveway. Nettie's frame appeared smaller and smaller as the car traveled down the road. The well of emotions was too much for Vita to bear. Tears sprung from her eyes. "You'll be okay. We'll be okay," said Carmen as tears crept out of the corner of her own eyes and tracked down the sides of her face.

***

"Damn it!" Brendan slammed the phone down onto its cradle. He slid his attaché case off his desk and marched out of his office, a purposeful expression on his face. "Thank you, Linda, for getting me out early today. I'll see you tomorrow morning."

Linda smiled and waved her hand. "Have a good evening, Brendan. See you in the morning."

Brendan was anxious to get home. The Z seemed to be winning the red-light lottery this afternoon. Brendan tapped his fingers on the steering wheel impatiently as he waited for the light to turn green. *What is Carmen doing? Running errands all day?* he thought to himself. He had tried calling home at noon but did not leave a message. He attempted to call once more just before he left his office, but again, the answering machine had picked up. And again, Brendan left no message. The light turned green. Brendan pulled out from the stop as if racing a dragster. *Vita probably felt better and went to school. Carmen is probably picking her up now*, Brendan reassured himself.

The digital clock on the Z's dash read two forty-three in the afternoon. Brendan was relieved to see Carmen's car in its usual spot in their driveway. Brendan exited his car. He did not hear the dog. Brendan had already put his key ring back into his pant pocket as he had expected the front door to open as he approached it. The front door remained closed. He opened the screen door and placed his hand on the knob of the solid oak door. He turned the doorknob, figuring it was unlocked and that Carmen and Vita were ready to go. The knob turned only an eighth of a turn and no farther. He lightly rapped on the door with his left hand while he retrieved his keys from his pocket with his right hand. *Still don't hear Chaz. That's odd*, thought Brendan to himself as he unlocked the door and entered into the foyer. Not a sound could be heard from anywhere in the house. "I'm home! Ready to go? Hello? Anybody home?" Brendan repeated these words like a mantra as he walked through the first floor of their home. When he returned back to the foyer, he noticed Chaz's leash missing from where it normally hung. Thinking Carmen and Vita took Chaz out for a last-minute walk, Brendan stepped outside and onto his front lawn. He took in a deep breath and sighed. He glanced at his watch and grew increasingly irate. *Where are they? They know we have to be on our way by three o'clock.* Brendan walked out to the sidewalk and scanned the distance up and down the street. No sign of his wife and daughter. He stormed back into the house. "I don't understand this!" he muttered angrily. The thought then crossed his mind that perhaps this was a ploy on Carmen's part to be late so that the appointment would have to be rescheduled.

The kitchen clock read two fifty. Brendan spun around and raced out of the house and back into his car. He drove around the block. "Where are they?" he yelled in disbelief. He decided to drive to the park a few blocks down the road. He pulled into the parking area at the entrance of the park. Brendan stood at the hood of his car and did a three-hundred-sixty-degree scan of the area. "Jesus . . . What is going on?" He slid back into the Z and started the engine. By the time he reentered the house, it was two minutes after three o'clock. "Damn!" Brendan ran up the steps, two at a time, to the second floor. He peered into Vita's room, and the only thing that peered back was the large lavender teddy bear propped on Vita's bed. He then walked into the master bedroom. His eyes caught sight of the envelope leaning upright against the bed pillows. Brendan's legs grew weak. The pit in his gut became heavier as he hesitantly walked over to the king-sized bed.

Chapter 22

The Letter

My dearest Brendan—the love of my life,

You must believe that, my love—always and no matter what. I hope and pray you will understand why I had to do this. Perhaps one day you will. You have no idea how my heart is weeping as I write this letter. Vita and I have to leave for our safety, for the safety of the baby, and for the preservation of our hearts and souls.

I know that you were planning on setting up an abortion for Vita as a hospital procedure. I know in your heart that you believe one hundred percent that this is the right decision for our daughter, unlike your brother who wants this baby "wiped out" for his own reasons. But my dearest Brendan, you must know that the horrendous acts of violence have already been done to Vita. None of us can undo this damage that Corbin has inflicted on our precious daughter. As much as you and I pray to be able to bear her suffering, that won't happen. The damage to Vita has been done, and to have her kill the child inside of her, that life inside of her . . . will surely kill Vita's soul . . . and it is a slow kill—I assure you.

I know you say this situation is different from ours. Yes, it is. I agree with that. However, the bottom line is *a life is still a life*. This child was not conceived through love but was the product of vicious, violent, and horrendous acts done to our daughter. This child just "is" and is a total innocent. We will never understand why God permitted such a thing. But the fact is that there is a baby four and a half months old in Vita's womb. I saw it. Vita saw it. You saw the pictures. He or she was sucking on his or her thumb.

Abortion is just a word, Brendan. The truth of abortion is that it is a violent torture and dismemberment of a little person . . . and that little person *will* feel every bit of it. Do you think your daughter can bear and live with the fact that she permitted the child inside of her to be killed, and in such a horrific manner? It would haunt her for the rest of her life. Trust me. Please understand that as difficult as it is for her to have to carry the baby four and a half more months and then to birth the baby, it does not even come close to the suffering she would bear permanently from killing the child. She already bears the suffering of being raped multiple times, but please do not force her to have to bear the additional suffering and guilt of the taking of an innocent life.

This child will be given up for adoption. He or she will have a chance at life, which is what God had intended for that baby . . . or He never would have created it. Vita and I have talked with Father John O'Brien. Vita actually asked Father John if the child was part of the devil, a demon seed, so to speak. Father John told her that only God can create life, and God has allowed this child to be conceived for reasons that we cannot understand. That God allows us humans to have free will and that in our imperfect world, imperfect things happen . . . even as awful as what happened to Vita.

After Vita gives birth, that baby will immediately be taken for adoption. We will then return home. Our lives will never be the same anymore, but we will try our best to regain some "normalcy." Please do not come looking for us. I will try to contact you; however, I fear that Corbin will likely hire a private investigator to try and track us down. You and I both know that Corbin does not want any evidence of this child . . . anywhere . . . ever . . . and I suspect he will do whatever it takes to rid Vita of this baby. I also know that you want to rid Vita of this baby, thinking that it would be best for her, so I fear that even though I have spelled out the reasons for having her go through the birth, you will still seek us out in order to have the baby aborted.

Brendan, I love you. Always have and always will. I can't imagine ever being away from you, but I feel I have no choice right now. I know you and Corbin can't even go to the police as you both want this kept under wraps, each for your own reasons. It will be up to Vita to decide if she wants to press charges against Corbin. That is another matter. I can't imagine her wanting to deal with the thought of that right now.

As far as the school knows, they were informed that Vita left due to an out-of-state family emergency. They are aware that she will be out for the rest of the school year of which there is less than four weeks left. We will deal with the school and the makeup work.

Please, Brendan, find it in your heart to understand. I pray for that every moment, every day. I too want us to be whole again. Right now, we are like a fragile piece of fine china that has been broken, but I believe one day we will mend, and we will be whole again, and one day we will still be that beautiful piece of china.

I love you, my dearest Brendan.

—Carmen

Chapter 23

THE EMPTINESS WAS OVERWHELMING. THE abandonment was too much to bear, yet there was an undercurrent of anger and confusion. Brendan felt as if a tornado had come and leveled his home, having taken the dearest and most precious to him—his family. Brendan lay on the bed, paralyzed with a thousand swirling emotions that he could not feel any one of them at any given time—only numbness. Just numbness.

The loud ringing of the phone next to the bed jarred Brendan from the state of shock he was in. He answered it, never looking at the caller ID. He hoped to hear Carmen's voice at the other end. "Hello?"

"Am I speaking with Mr. Malloy? I am calling from County OB Gynecological Associates. You had an appointment for Vita Malloy to be here at four o'clock to see Dr. Lisa Chen," said the female voice over the phone.

Caught off guard, Brendan did not know what else to say except that he was sorry. He told the woman that his wife had just called him from a phone booth as she was stuck in traffic and that he was just going to call the doctor's office to let them know. She asked Brendan when they would like to reschedule. "I'll have to get back to you on that, and again, I sincerely apologize," said Brendan.

Still in shell shock, he descended the steps and wandered into the kitchen. Mechanical-like, he reached into the cabinet that housed his Dewar's. Brendan gripped the bottle of comfort and continued in a robotic gait to the living room couch. He threw his head back and took a swig of the whiskey. Then he took another. And then another. Brendan placed the bottle next to his feet rather than putting it on the coffee table in front of him. With hands clasped and elbows on his knees, he brought his forehead to lean upon his knuckles. "Nettie must know where they went," murmured Brendan. He was going to call Nettie. *Who knows though, maybe she is with Carmen and Vita,* he thought. He decided he would drive over to Nettie's house.

When Brendan turned the corner onto Nettie's block, he saw Nettie's car in the driveway. He pulled the black Z behind her car. Brendan jogged up the walkway and rang the bell. Nettie was expecting to hear from Brendan one way or the other. She could see Brendan's car in the driveway as she glanced out the living room window on her way to the front door.

The heaviness now weighed upon Nettie's heart. Brendan was like a true son to her. Somehow, she had to be his support, yet she would have to stay mum on the whereabouts of her daughter and granddaughter. She had not heard from them as of yet, so at least for now she could tell Brendan truthfully that she did not know where his family had gone to. These thoughts transpired as Nettie opened the door to reveal Brendan's figure that stood before her. Nettie held the screen door open. "Come in, Brendan." It was a silent and awkward moment. Each surmised what the other one likely knew.

Brendan spoke first, "Mom, you know why I am here."

"Yes, Brendan. Yes. Yes, I do," said Nettie. "Come into the kitchen and have a seat." Brendan looked like the life had been drained out of him. He shuffled into the kitchen. Nettie followed him. "Can I get you something to drink?"

"Can I just have a glass of water, Mom?" Nettie put some ice cubes in a glass, knowing that Brendan liked his water that way. She filled the glass with water from the tap and set it before him. "Thanks," said Brendan solemnly as he ran his open palm along the side of the cold glass. Nettie sat down across the table from Brendan. Brendan stared past the tall glass of ice water as his fingers continued to caress the cold glass with its beads of condensation meandering downward. Brendan picked up the glass and touched it to his forehead before taking a few sips. "I don't understand," he finally said.

"Why?" Brendan felt Nettie's hand upon his wrist. "Brendan, what I can tell you is that Carmen felt she had no other choice. She did not plan to leave. It was only after the failed attempt on Saturday that she began thinking about it. She hoped to be able to talk you out of having Vita go through an abortion." Brendan listened as Nettie continued to speak. "But when you insisted on having Vita go through the abortion with plans on scheduling it in a hospital, that's when she made the decision to go."

Brendan shook his head. "Mom, you know I was trying to do what is best here. I know how Carmen feels about abortion, but this . . . this is . . . different . . . different circumstances." Nettie did not respond to Brendan's comments. There was a long uncomfortable silence lasting half a minute or so. "Do you know where they are? Are they on a bus or something? Where are they going?" Brendan asked hesitantly. He knew full well that Nettie would never disclose such information.

Nettie, her hand still on Brendan's wrist, told Brendan that she had not heard from them since the morning. "Brendan, you know, first of all, that I love you as my own son. And I think you know that I support Carmen in allowing Vita to have the baby to be put up for adoption. To have Vita go through a second trauma . . . an abortion . . . is never going to change the fact that she was repeatedly raped." Nettie could feel the tendons in Brendan's wrist tighten as he balled his hand into a fist upon hearing the words—repeatedly raped. "She is carrying a child within her. That is all I am going to say on that," said Nettie. Nettie avoided answering the question as to Carmen and Vita's whereabouts.

Brendan inquired about his family once more. Nettie tilted her head and looked directly into Brendan's blue eyes. Before she could say anything, he answered for his mother-in-law. "Mom, I am not going to push you into telling me anything. I'm not going to do that to you. I know you have to do what you have to do." Brendan opened his fist and gently flipped his hand over to hold the hand Nettie had on his wrist. "But, Mom, I want you to understand that I have to do what I have to do."

Nettie could sense the void in Brendan's heart. As the nurturer that she was, she wanted to come to his aid, but the help he wanted, she could not give him.

"Mom," said Brendan, "one thing that I will ask of you is to at least let me know that they are safe. That is the only thing that I will ask of you."

Nettie squeezed Brendan's hand. "Of course, I will."

Brendan stood up, letting out a loud sigh. "I'd better be heading back." Nettie offered to make Brendan something to eat, even though she anticipated that he likely had no appetite. "Thanks, Mom. Maybe I'll grab something later, but right now, I'm just not hungry." Brendan got up, kissed his mother-in law, and proceeded out the front door. Nettie watched from her front door as Brendan walked like an old man to his car. He seemed so feeble and weak.

Hopelessness has a way of taking hold of one's heart and soul and then plunging them into the depths of despair. He considered driving over to Quinlan's to drown his sorrows, but Corbin was likely to be there as that was their primary after-work watering hole.

Brendan pulled his car up next to Carmen's sedan. Her car in the driveway at that time of day signified that Carmen was busy preparing dinner. He imagined her standing at the kitchen counter whipping up one of her creations. As he entered the foyer, there was no aroma emanating from the kitchen. There was no prancing pug at his feet. No one to greet him with a kiss.

Brendan never bothered to flip a light switch on. He shuffled into the kitchen and opened the refrigerator door and stared blankly at its contents. He finally reached in for a quart bottle of beer. Brendan popped the cap and flung it onto the kitchen table. He shuffled into the living room and plunked himself down onto the couch. The bottle of Dewar's still sat on the floor in front of the couch. It did not take him long to empty the bottle of beer.

He pulled off his shoes and socks, loosened his belt, pulled the shirt out of his pants, and undid most of the buttons. The emotional shock to his system fatigued Brendan greatly. Before laying his body down across the couch, he took hold of the Dewar's and finished that off. Then he lay his weary body down upon the couch and let hopelessness pull his heart and his soul farther down into the abyss.

***

Vita surfed the channels of the television with its grainy picture as she sat on the bottom edge of the bed, three feet away from the TV set. "It's all different here," she muttered aloud. "The channels are all messed up." Chaz restlessly roamed around their hotel room. It was a combination of the unfamiliar surroundings and the new scents that kept him from settling down. It had been a long day of driving with several stops along the way to eat, gas up, and walk the dog. Carmen and Vita had stopped at two other hotels that permitted pets before ending up at the one they decided to stay in. The other two hotels were subpar. Carmen and Vita were prepared to spend the night in the car, but this third hotel, although not the charm, was deemed acceptable. The main concern was that it appeared to be clean.

Carmen sat on the king-sized bed with Vita. She positioned herself next to the night table with the phone on it. Carmen dialed Nettie's number. The two women spoke. Carmen told Nettie of the difficulty in finding a suitable hotel that would allow dogs but that they were now finally settled into their room. She told her mother that they ended up in the middle of Virginia. Carmen had thought about western Maryland, but after perusing the list of the locations of these centers for unwed young mothers to be that Father John had given her, she decided to pick the most centrally located spot.

Nettie told Carmen that Brendan had been over after finding the letter and that he had left about an hour ago. "He looked like such an old man the way he was walking back to his car," she told her daughter. Carmen's heart flooded with sadness. She did not know what to say.

"Can I talk to Grandma?" blurted Vita. Carmen handed the phone to Vita. "Hi, Gram. It's okay I guess. I'm bored. There's nothing to do," Carmen heard her daughter tell Nettie. Nettie encouraged Vita to hang in there and stay strong.

Carmen got back on the phone with her mother. "I'll call you in a few days. By then, I hope to have some sort of an idea of where we will be. And, Mom, thank you for being there for Bren. I want you to know that I am able to find comfort in that."

"Love you too, Mom. Goodbye."

Chapter 24

F LICKERS OF SUNLIGHT DANCED THROUGH the narrow gaps of the drapes as Carmen woke up as Vita slept next to her with Chaz at the foot of the bed in between them. Carmen watched as the sun's rays waxed and waned as the tree branches outside swayed in the breeze. Chaz picked his head up as soon as he was aware that one of his people was awake. Carmen gingerly slipped the covers off herself without disturbing Vita. Chaz hopped off the bed, anxious to relieve himself. Vita stirred. Carmen laid her hand on Vita's shoulder and whispered, "I'm just going to take Chaz outside. He has to go. I'll be right back." Carmen had gone to sleep in a pair of sweatpants and a T-shirt. She slipped on her flip-flops and attached Chaz's leash to his collar. Vita cracked open her eyes just enough to ascertain the familiar-unfamiliar surroundings. She closed her eyes and slipped back into a light sleep.

The hotel was a three-story remodeled Holiday Inn with outside corridors from which to enter one's room. Their room was on the second floor. Carmen grabbed the room key before quietly exiting the room with Chaz in her arms. She carried Chaz down the flight of the cement steps as the steps had such large spaces between them. Carmen spotted a small wooded area by the parking lot. "Darn. Forgot the baggy," she said to herself. Fortunately, Chaz only had to empty his bladder. The warmth of the sun bathing Carmen's face felt glorious. It made her feel good inside, even if it was only for a fleeting moment. She pondered on what she hoped to accomplish today. First thing she would do was to call Father John to let him know where she was and to see if he could make some calls on her behalf to try to get Vita into one of these programs.

The pup needed some exercise. Carmen decided to give him a quick walk up the block and back and then one block in the other direction and back. There were new scents to be had, so a quick walk turned into a stop-and-go stroll. Once back into the room, Carmen poured the dog food into Chaz's Navajo bowl and placed it on the bathroom floor next to his water dish. She then drew open the heavy generic hotel drapes, leaving the sheers in place to get some natural illumination into the room.

The hotel offered a free breakfast with the last seating at ten o'clock. As it was only eight thirty in the morning, Carmen thought it best to let Vita sleep with plans to wake her at nine fifteen if she hadn't woken up by then. She took out Vita's prenatal vitamins from the bag packed with medical supplies and placed them on the night table.

Thank goodness for the instant coffee maker in the room, thought Carmen. It wasn't quite the same with the powdered instant creamer, but it did just fine. Carmen sat at a small round table sipping from her generic hotel coffee cup as she perused the list of centers. Her idea was to drive to two of the centers that were within a thirty-mile radius rather than to call them. She thought it a good idea to have Father John telephone the ones that were farther away to see if he could obtain information concerning their programs and availability. Plus, a priest placing a call would certainly carry more weight than a layperson. *The sooner we can get into one of these places, the better. Then I can find us a small apartment to rent and get us into some kind of a routine*, thought Carmen. It wasn't even twenty-four hours that they had been gone and already Carmen was fidgety. She could just imagine how Vita was feeling.

Carmen gently nudged Vita's shoulder. "Sweet pea . . . time to get up. Come on . . . we have about forty-five minutes to get breakfast."

Vita turned onto her back and squinted from the sunlight that poured into the room. Chaz, who had gone back up on the bed after his meal, snorted in Vita's face as he licked her cheeks. She sat up and hugged her amorous pup. "I guess I have to take a shower," said a weary Vita.

"I guess yes," responded Carmen.

While Vita was in the bathroom, Carmen phoned Father John. Fortunately, he was in his office and available to speak. He was more than happy to assist Carmen in any way he could. He took down her number at the hotel. "I'll call you tonight and let you know how I made out. Good luck with your day today. You have your work cut out for you."

"Thank you, Father. Pray for us," said Carmen.

"I haven't stopped. God bless you both."

After breakfast, Carmen, Vita, and Chaz hit the highway once more in hopes of accomplishing what was on the agenda. They took along snacks for them and the dog along with bottled water and Chaz's water bowl. As Carmen drove, she silently prayed, "Have mercy on us, Lord, as we put our trust in you."

**

Brendan's arm slid off his stomach as he shifted his body. His hand connected with the empty whiskey bottle, toppling it over. Groggy and disoriented, he struggled to push himself up into a sitting position. His head was pounding. His breath and body reeked of whiskey. The living room was amply illuminated by the moonlight that filtered through the window sheers. Brendan rubbed his forehead all the while trying to keep his eyes open. He brought his wrist in front of his eyes to peer at his watch but was unsuccessful in reading the time. He shuffled over to the bay window where the moonlight was more plentiful and moved the curtains enough so that the light fell upon his watch. "Almost five o'clock in the morning," he told himself. Brendan parted the curtains and leaned on the windowsill with the palms of his hands. He stared out into the front yard and driveway and saw the silhouettes of his car and Carmen's car. *Right now, Carmen and Vita should be asleep in their beds upstairs. Where did I go wrong?* he thought.

Brendan decided it best to get showered and head over to the office. He had to be in court by ten o'clock in the morning and knew he had to be in the right frame of mind. It would be unfair to his client if he was anything less than his usual professional and prepared self.

Brendan made an art out of driving his five-speed Z while juggling a cup of coffee and a bagel with cream cheese he had picked up at the local Dunkin' Donuts. It was too awkward for him to sit at the kitchen table solo for breakfast. Brendan knew Nettie was an early riser. First on his list was to give his mother-in-law a call in hopes of learning that his wife and daughter were safe . . . somewhere.

Brendan was seated at his desk by six thirty in the morning. It would be a good two hours before Corbin or Linda would show up. He decided to wait to the more respectable time of six forty-five to call Nettie. Nettie answered on the second ring, making Brendan feel somewhat relieved in not having called too her early. "Mom, I'm sorry to bother you, but please tell me that you have heard from Carmen and Vita and that they are all right." Nettie confirmed to Brendan that she had indeed heard from Carmen last night and that their travel had been uneventful. "Thank you, Mom. That's all I wanted to know," said Brendan gratefully before saying goodbye.

Brendan got a fresh pot of coffee going. Another cup of coffee was in order before reviewing the cases for today's court work. With his mind at ease for the time being, he was able to focus on the task at hand.

It was close to nine thirty in the morning when Brendan set foot into the county courthouse. His mind was not ready to contemplate family affairs right now, and the distraction of having to concentrate on his work was welcoming to him. The awkwardness at the office that morning made going to court all the more appealing. Linda had sensed a rift between the brothers, and Brendan could sense her tenseness. Linda was not her usual talkative self. She had gone about her work and kept conversation limited to business. It was clear she was uncomfortable. When Corbin had come into the office, he never bothered to poke his head into Brendan's office to say hello. Brendan had closed the door to his office, which was something he did when seeing a client. When Corbin inquired as to whether Brendan had a client, Linda responded with a negative. Linda was surprised with Corbin's reaction. Rather than go into Brendan's office to razz him a bit, he raised his eyebrows and replied with a simple "Oh?" before he had retreated into his own office.

Curiosity had been eating at Corbin. He had noticed that Brendan had cleared his appointment book for yesterday afternoon. Corbin had surmised that this was the allotted time for the abortion procedure or at least a consultation for the procedure.

The long day in court had been beneficial to Brendan. His mind had been forced to be occupied with legal matters. On the drive back to the office however, his thoughts reverted back to his family. Brendan parked his car next to the lone car that belonged to his brother in the Malloy and Malloy parking lot. It was a few minutes after five o'clock in the afternoon. Linda had already left for the day. Brendan was hesitant to go inside the office and contemplated taking the files home with him rather than dropping them off inside and then having to deal with Corbin. And that was exactly what Brendan did.

With the keys still in the ignition, he started the engine, depressed the gas pedal all the way down, and revved the motor loud enough so that Corbin would hear it. Corbin had heard the familiar sound of the Z pulling into the parking lot. He anticipated that Brendan would be walking into the office at any moment. Corbin was set to play the concerned brother and uncle and planned on inquiring about Vita's health. Then he had heard the loud vroom of Brendan's car followed by the sound of the Z's motor waning as it drove away.

Daylight was still to be had for several more hours. Brendan turned into his driveway and parked next to the Bimmer. "A run would do me good," he muttered. Brendan had not taken his jog that morning. He entered the house. It was as lifeless as he had left it early that morning. He set his briefcase down in the foyer by the front door so as to remember to take it into the office the next day.

As Brendan changed into his running attire, a calm settled over him. There comes a wave of consolation with thoughts of hope.

Brendan began to ponder the ideas that came into his mind. He took those thoughts with him as he pounded the pavement, step by step. "I am going to find my girls. I am going to find my girls,'" he repeated to himself as a mantra. By the time he returned to the front door of his home, with the perspiration dripping from the tip of his nose and droplets of sweat running down his neck, he was convinced that he would locate his wife and daughter. He was confident that he could sway Vita and even Carmen into his way of thinking.

So quenching was the cold tap water. Brendan placed the glass mug into the sink and gazed out the kitchen window before he headed upstairs to shower. When Brendan returned downstairs, he felt refreshed and recharged. He made himself a turkey and cheese sandwich and took that along with a beer into the family room. Brendan took a gaping bite out of his sandwich and followed that with a guzzle of beer. He began to dial a number on the phone while still chewing on a wad of food. The recipient of the call answered sooner than Brendan had intended. "Hey, Mike . . . Hey, it's Brendan . . . Hold on a sec . . . Sorry, I had a mouthful."

Mike Greene, a retired Newark police sergeant who now worked as a private investigator, owned the middle name of Integrity. Brendan had known him for several years via various county court proceedings. Brendan and Corbin had developed a friendship with Mike. Brendan had such admiration for this man, a good and honest cop, who was ten years his senior. "Bren . . . How are ya? What's cookin'?" came the jovial voice on the phone.

"Listen, Mike . . ." Brendan began and then paused.

"Wha . . . What's the matter, bud? Sounds like something serious goin' on."

"Yeah, Mike," responded Brendan. "I have some issues. Some family issues . . . and I may need your help."

His concerned friend answered, "Sure. Sure. Anything you need. You know that! Carmen and Vita all right?"

Brendan answered, "Uh . . . yes, they are. They are fine. Listen, can we—"

A still concerned Mike interrupted with "Corbin? Is Corbin okay?"

"Mike, they are all in good health. Can we meet, or I can come over by your place . . . or you can come here . . . whatever and wherever is convenient for you. I just need to talk with you person to person," said Brendan. Even though they had not seen each other socially for a while, Mike did not hesitate to offer to come over to see Brendan now. "You sure? You don't mind?" asked Brendan. He wanted to do the courteous thing, which was to tell Mike that it could wait until tomorrow or another day that was convenient, but Brendan had to get moving on locating his family.

"Bren, no problem, I'll be there in an hour, okay, bud?"

"Thanks, thanks a lot, Mike," Brendan said graciously. "I'll make some sandwiches, and I've got plenty of beer." Brendan had learned over the years from Nettie and Carmen the tradition of Italian hospitality, which was always to have something to eat for any and every one that came to the house.

And as a man true to his word, Mike was at Brendan's front door within an hour. The two men hugged. Brendan led Mike into the family room, grabbing two beers on the way. It didn't take long for Mike to register the vibes of the empty house. He had been divorced for eight years and knew all too well the feeling one gets when entering into such an environment. Mike had been living in a condo since the divorce. His wife and their two sons remained in the house where they had reared the boys. He recently became a dog owner so that he would have someone waiting for him. "Bren, they're gone, aren't they?"

Brendan was surprised by Mike's remark, but then again, he realized that Mike was a keen observer with a sixth sense. Brendan nodded.

Mike looked around. "Where's your dog?"

"He's gone too," said Brendan.

"I'm sorry, buddy," said Mike as he looked into his friend's lonesome eyes. "What happened?"

Brendan twisted the top off his beer bottle and took a swig. Mike did the same. Brendan then took a deep breath. "I don't know where to start." He paused for a few moments to gather his thoughts.

"Well, I guess I'll come right out and start with telling you that my daughter, Vita, is pregnant."

Mike closed his eyes and shook his head. He listened intently as Brendan relayed to him most of the story, leaving out the identity of the baby's father. He felt horrible about lying to his friend, but he could never let the truth be known. He told Mike that Vita was obstinate in not revealing the boy's name with whom she had been having relations with.

Naturally, Mike's sixth sense kicked in. "Don't be upset with me, but I have to ask you something."

"Go ahead," said Brendan.

"Could it be that Vita was pressured into having sex by someone older?"

Brendan, afraid that Mike would pursue that line of questioning pooh-poohed the notion. He told another lie. This time about Vita. "Uh, no, no, no . . . I know she was . . . uh . . . seeing a boy. I had heard her on the phone with a girlfriend. I just thought it was a kind of first-boyfriend innocent kind of thing, you know." Brendan felt disgusted at himself for perpetrating the lie, but he could not bring himself to tell the truth. He was still having a difficult time accepting the truth himself.

Brendan held up his hand as a traffic cop would. "And of course I know that the father of the baby has rights, but, Mike, this is my thirteen-year-old daughter"—Brendan paused—"and I do not want her going through with the pregnancy." Mike let Brendan talk. "You know Carmen's stance on abortion."

"Yeah, I do," responded Mike. Brendan told Mike how he had set up an appointment for Vita to initiate the workup for a hospital-based abortion after the tragic incident at an abortion clinic that he and Vita had witnessed. "I went about it the wrong way, Mike. I knew that Carmen was dead set against an abortion, so I basically blindsided Carmen and Vita that morning by whisking Vita off to that clinic. When I returned home with Vita after that fiasco at the clinic, Carmen took that as a sign that her prayers were answered. She tried again to talk me out of Vita having an abortion. She knew I wouldn't budge . . . and so they left . . . so that Vita could give birth and put the baby up for adoption."

Mike was curious as to how far along in her pregnancy Vita was. He wanted to know how Vita felt about all of this.

"She is sixteen to eighteen weeks pregnant. I don't think Vita knows what she wants, except to wish that this whole ordeal never happened. She just wants to be a normal thirteen-year-old again. She wants the baby to go away. Naturally, she is afraid of the abortion procedure, but I think that is what has to be done. Then she will do a turnaround and say she doesn't want to go through an abortion and would rather give the baby up for adoption. She is just parroting her mother and grandmother."

Mike put his hand on Brendan's shoulder. "You want me to locate them."

Brendan's desperate eyes met Mike's consoling eyes. "Can you? Will you? I need you to find them, Mike. I need you to do that for me."

"You know I want to help you, Bren. What is your intention should we locate them?"

"I still think I can convince Carmen to see things my way," insisted Brendan.

Mike tightened his hand on Brendan's shoulder, giving it a firm squeeze. "Brendan, you know I love you and Carmen and Vita, and I want to help you." A few seconds later, he added, "I'll do my best in finding them for you." Brendan hugged his pal.

"There is just one request I have," said Brendan. "I believe Carmen's mother, Nettie, knows where they are. You have to promise me that you will not go to her for any information. I don't want her hassled." Mike raised his eyebrows but then nodded that he understood. "She is my mom too. More of a mother than my own mother ever was to me and Corbin. I don't want her bothered," said Brendan.

"How is Corbin? Does Corbin know what's going on?" questioned Mike.

Brendan relayed to Mike that Corbin knew of Vita's pregnancy but did not know that Carmen and Vita had left. "I will probably tell him tomorrow."

Brendan then assembled two Italian hoagies at the kitchen counter while Mike leaned against the counter and nursed his second beer. He listened as Brendan gave him useful information. Mike had an unbelievable memory and the ability to retain whatever was told to him, a talent that he had honed to perfection over the years as a policeman. He would take his mental notes now and likely jot them down later when he got home. Each of the two men carried their plate, holding the hoagie and chips in one hand and a bottle of beer in the other, to the kitchen table.

"Ya know, buddy, if you press kidnapping charges, we could find them a hell of a lot faster. I would be able to subpoena telephone records and such. Once we find them, you could drop the charges. It's going to be difficult otherwise."

Brendan looked solemnly at Mike. "I am not doing that. That is off the table. This all has to be done under the radar." Mike had questions, and Brendan gave him the answers, many of which were filtered and spun in keeping with the situation.

***

Nettie tried to busy herself with cooking for most of the day. She had made all sorts of things and then froze them with plans on bringing most of what she had made to Brendan. Nettie fidgeted on her couch while attempting to focus on what was on television. It was already nine thirty-five in the evening, and she had hoped to hear from Carmen. This was only the second day that Carmen and Vita were gone. Nettie was feeling extremely anxious from the void. She got up to collect her tote bag of yarn and crocheting needles that also held the completed squares for a navy-and-green afghan she was working on to donate to the church bazaar. As she sat back down on the couch, she glanced over at the phone on the end table as if she could will it to ring. Nettie had no sooner gotten the yarn and the crochet needle out of the bag when the phone did indeed ring. It jarred her nonetheless. "Carmen? You and Vita have been on my mind all day. I am so glad you called! How are you?" Carmen heard the relief in Nettie's voice.

Carmen sounded tired. She couldn't hide her disappointment from her mother. Nettie listened as Carmen spoke to her about the two places she and Vita had visited. One of the homes for single pregnant teens had a waiting list, and the other place did not feel like a good fit. "Mom, they were so disorganized there, plus the house looked in disarray. I don't know . . . I suppose if we can't find anything else, that will have to do." Then Carmen added with an ounce of encouragement in her voice, "I just got off the phone with Father John, and he has some real possibilities for us." Nettie felt a wave of assurance when Carmen mentioned this. It was as if God was saying to Nettie that He was going to provide the perfect place for her granddaughter and daughter. "The only thing is that we have a long drive ahead of us. Father wants us to go to the farthest one first. He said he had a good feeling about this place after getting off the phone with the director. It's in Mississippi." Carmen awaited Nettie's reaction.

"Mississippi? Well, if Father has a good feeling about it, then we should too," said Nettie. Nettie asked where the other places were located. Carmen told her that one was in North Carolina and the other was in Georgia. Nettie and Carmen spoke with each other a few more minutes. Nettie told Carmen she had planned to bring Brendan meals that he could store in his freezer.

Vita then got on the phone with her grandmother. Nettie could have predicted the first few sentences out of Vita. "I miss you, Gram. I am so bored. Even Chaz doesn't know what to do."

Nettie kidded with Vita that she would soon have her full of schoolwork to do as she reminded Vita that as soon as they were settled in one place, she would mail the schoolwork. Nettie had a thought and took the chance of mentioning it to Vita. "Listen, sweet pea. Why don't you write down your experiences in a journal or a diary? You can get another one."

Vita's response was somewhat of a surprise to Nettie. "Well, actually, Gram, I was thinking of doing that. Mom has my old one here, and I was going to try to continue in that one."

Nettie told her granddaughter how proud she was of her and how much she loved her. When Carmen got back on the phone with her mother, Nettie let Carmen know of her plans to go to the school the beginning of the next week to collect the assignments. She wished them safe travels. "I love you both, and if you are able to . . . *please* call me tomorrow."

As soon as Carmen was off the phone, she asked Vita, "'Mom has my old' . . . what?" Vita looked quizzically at her mother. "You told Grandma, 'Mom has my old'—"

"Oh yeah," said Vita, "I told Gram that you had my old diary. You do have my diary, don't you?"

Carmen nodded. "Yes, I have it."

"Well, Mom, I was thinking that I want to start writing in it again."

Chapter 25

CORBIN STARED BLANKLY OUT THE solo window in his office as he tapped his pen incessantly on the desk. It was a rainy Thursday morning, and Corbin felt as dismal as the weather. The digital clock on the desk read seven twenty-two in the morning. He had gotten there early before Linda was due in with the hopes of confronting Brendan with his concerns for Vita. According to Brendan's appointment book, Corbin had noticed that Brendan was expecting to see two clients in the morning. He knew his brother came in early most days to prepare for the morning appointments and court cases.

Corbin had one thing on his mind. He never bothered to put on a pot of coffee and could not even fathom tackling his work. All Corbin managed to do was to gaze out the window and nervously tap his pen on the desk. He wasn't at all concerned about having to be in court by nine thirty. In his mind, he was plenty prepared. After all, he was a pro at performing on the spot.

Finally, the familiar purr of the Z's engine could be heard outside. As it was only seven thirty-seven in the morning, Corbin had ample time to engage in conversation with his brother. Brendan had seen Corbin's Vette sitting in the parking lot. He preferred to avoid his brother but knew eventually Corbin would figure out that Carmen and Vita had left town. Still, Brendan figured he would not volunteer that information but would not withhold it either, should Corbin inquire.

Corbin remained in his own office as Brendan entered the main area of the law office where Linda's desk sat. He laid his briefcase on her desk, unclasped the latches, and took out the folders from yesterday's court proceedings. Brendan placed the folders neatly in the center of Linda's desk and closed and latched the briefcase. Corbin watched as Brendan slid the briefcase off Linda's desk by the handle. Brendan sensed Corbin's eyes on him as he made his way toward his own office.

Brendan sat at his desk and rooted through his tie drawer to decide which one to put on. He missed his wife's final tie adjustments she would do before he would leave the house. Today, he had left the house without a tie.

"I'd go with the dark gray" came a voice all too familiar to Brendan. Corbin stood at Brendan's door as he leaned on the door frame.

Brendan lifted his head. Their eyes met. Brendan noticed that Corbin's eyes were still inflamed from their encounter one week ago. Brendan had the gray tie in his hand but quickly placed it back in the drawer and drew up a burgundy one, which he placed on his desk. "I think I will go with this one today," said Brendan sternly. Corbin took three steps into Brendan's office as if Simon said, "Simon says to take three steps forward." "If you need to say something to me, Corbin, please say it and then get out of my way!" exclaimed Brendan.

Corbin walked over to where Brendan sat. "Look, Bren, I come in peace, okay? I just wanted to ask you how Vita was feeling." There was no response from Brendan. Corbin took another few steps closer to Brendan. "She must have been so afraid to have the abortion. I know it must have been frightening for her to go through the procedure. But I bet she feels better now that it is done with, huh?"

Brendan looked down as he fiddled with the latches on his briefcase. Still, he did not respond. Brendan picked up the burgundy tie and walked over to one of his framed watercolors displayed on the wall and used the reflection in the glass. He knotted his tie. Corbin watched. Brendan then walked to where Corbin stood and went face-to-face with him, their eyes no more than a foot apart from each other's. Brendan glared into his brother's eyes. Corbin felt the penetrating disdain that emanated from Brendan's hateful stare. Then Brendan walked past Corbin and sat back down at his desk. He looked up at Corbin and, with a matter-of-fact tone to his voice, said, "Corbin, I will tell you this once. You would have found out eventually. Carmen and Vita are gone. That's right. Gone. They've left town. They've been gone since Tuesday. When I got to the house Tuesday afternoon to take them to see another physician about setting up an abortion in a hospital, the house was empty. I don't know where they are. Now . . . please leave."

Corbin closed his eyes momentarily, not for concern for what his brother was going through but for concern for himself and what this could mean for him. Yet Corbin played the role of the caring older sibling. He had the nerve to place his hand on Brendan's shoulder, which aroused an instant expression of repulsion on Brendan's face. "What can I do to help? I want to help you find them. Bren, what you think of me is not what's important here. You will find out that you are wrong about me. That aside, I want to help you in any way I can," said Corbin in his faux sincere voice.

Brendan slowly turned his head toward Corbin's hand that still sat on his shoulder. "Haven't you done enough already? Just leave me be."

Corbin removed his hand off Brendan. Before he walked out of Brendan's office, he turned one last time to his brother. "Bren, the offer still stands. I am here if you need me." Brendan waited for Corbin to exit before he got up to close the door.

Brendan needed to clear his head. He was expecting two clients, plus he wanted to get some information that Mike Greene needed from him, which included activity in his and Carmen's bank accounts. He would have to wait until nine o'clock in the morning to call the banks.

Corbin sat in his office with his door open. Linda would be in within the hour. He got up and walked toward the window and peered out while his mind worked on a plan to locate his sister-in-law and niece. Somehow, he would make sure that that baby would not be born. "I'm going to have to find them," he murmured to himself over and over again. Now that Corbin knew of Vita's status, he could formulate a plan. That would have to wait as he had to turn his efforts toward gathering his documents for his morning in court.

Brendan reopened his door as soon as he saw Linda pulling into the parking lot. Brendan knew that Linda had detected that something was amiss between he and Corbin. He wanted to keep the uncomfortable atmosphere to a minimum if possible. A few minutes later, Linda cheerfully greeted the brothers after she unloaded her purse onto her desk. She poked her head into their respective offices and asked each of them if they would like a cup of coffee. Corbin declined. Brendan accepted Linda's offer. With a mug securely in each hand, Linda walked into Brendan's office and gently placed a mug atop a coaster on Brendan's desk.

"Thank you, Linda."

"No problem, Brendan. Your first client should be here in about half an hour," said Linda.

"I have everything ready to go right here," said Brendan as he patted the small pile of clipped paperwork on his desk. "Oh, Linda . . . I left the folders from yesterday's court cases on your desk," said Brendan.

"Oh yes—couldn't miss them sitting right smack in the middle of my desk," said Linda jokingly.

The rest of the day in the office went smoothly for Brendan. Corbin had left shortly before nine o'clock in the morning for court and spent most of his day there. By the time Corbin returned to the law office near five o'clock in the afternoon, Brendan had left for the day, and Linda was on her way out. Brendan was able to get to the bank before closing to pick up statements on the recent activity in the family's bank accounts. And because he was listed on Carmen's account as a co-owner, he had access to that information. It only took a quick glance at the account activity to notice the sizeable cash withdrawal on two accounts made the week before. He placed the statements down on the passenger seat of the car and drove back to his empty house.

As he entered into the foyer, he felt his heart sink. Part of him wanted to repeat his performance on Tuesday of drinking himself into oblivion. The grayness of the day with the intermittent drizzle played into his mood. A bold orange-colored sticky note on the kitchen table caught Brendan's eye. It read: "Dear Brendan, I hope you don't mind, but I stopped over briefly this afternoon to put something for you in the refrigerator and in the freezer. Love, Mom." A half smile appeared on Brendan's face. He opened the freezer and refrigerator doors to see the array of prepared food Nettie had left for him. He immediately recognized the eggplant parmesan and the aroma of the lemon-garlic chicken on the top shelf of the fridge. Each of the opaque containers in the freezer had a layer of the heavy-duty aluminum foil over the top. Brendan peeled back the edge on one of the containers to peek in. "My favorite." He chuckled to himself. It was a dish Nettie made with rice mixed with her tomato sauce and peas, layered with meat sauce and mozzarella cheese. On the kitchen counter was a loaf of fresh Italian bread from the bakery near Nettie's house.

Brendan knew it would be difficult to engage in conversation with Nettie, given the situation. Nevertheless, he picked up the phone to thank her for her thoughtfulness and generosity toward him.

"Hello," answered the spry voice.

"Hello, Mom . . . Listen, you didn't have to go through all this trouble."

"No trouble at all, dear," responded Nettie.

"Thank you, thank you, Mom . . . for all of . . . You made me so much. I . . . I . . . do appreciate it. I want you to know that. You are too good to me." Brendan paused. He did not know what else to say. He felt awkward.

But Nettie always knew how to ease out of such a moment. "Brendan, dear . . . you are a son to me. I think you know that. I know the difficult and painful situation you are in and how awkward things may get between you and me, but know that I am here for you."

Again, a half smile instinctively crept up on Brendan's face. He did know in his heart how deeply his mother-in-law cared for him. And he had those reciprocal feelings toward her. "Thank you, Mom" was all he could muster. It was on the tip of Brendan's tongue to ask about Carmen and Vita. He did not. Nettie knew that Brendan needed to hear some reassuring words concerning his family. She voluntarily told him that she had not heard from them today and did not expect to hear from them every day; however, as of last night, his wife and daughter were safe and sound.

Two minutes had not gone by from when Brendan had gotten off the phone with Nettie that it rang. Brendan anxiously grabbed the phone. "Hello?"

"Bren, Mike here. I thought you might be interested in knowing that I got a call from Corbin today asking me to locate Carmen and Vita. He said he wanted to help you out in any way he could." Both Brendan and Corbin had been tight with Mike. The last time all three of them had been together was three months before, in February. Brendan and Corbin had met Mike at Quinlan's. They had known he would be drinking heavily that night and had known where to find him. It had been the fifth anniversary of the death of Mike's partner. John (Krieg) Krieger and Mike had been partners on the force for fifteen years with the last ten years working as police sergeant detectives. Krieg had died in Mike's arms after the two of them responded to a robbery and had given chase to the perpetrators. Krieg took a bullet to his chest that pierced his aorta. He had not put on the bulletproof vest that night. Mike and Krieg were like brothers, the way Brendan and Corbin used to be. Krieg's last words to Mike as he had struggled with his last few breaths were "Tell my wife and my girls that I love them. And you, bud . . . you know I love . . ." Those words played in Mike's head like a broken record. The image of his bloodied arms cradling Krieg's lifeless body was seared into his mind. And it was on the anniversary date that Mike would drink most heavily as his only way to cope with those images and the loss of his best friend.

Brendan did not know how to respond at first to what Mike had just told him. After a few seconds, he told Mike that he had only told Corbin that Carmen and Vita had left town and the manner in which they had left. "I didn't get a chance to go further into detail about having already spoken with you. I had clients, and he was in court all day," said Brendan. Brendan continued, "You know Corbin will always be the big brother . . . always looking out for me. Did you tell him I got to you first?"

"Yeah, I did. That okay?" replied Mike as he knew the closeness of the brothers and never gave it a second thought.

Brendan tried to sound nonchalant, "Not a problem."

"So how you doing today, buddy?" Mike asked between cigarette drags.

"Well, I've got the bank info for you. I can drop it off, or better yet, if you want some good cooking, come on over," suggested Brendan.

"You grillin'?" asked Mike. He knew Brendan grilled a mean steak.

"No, no . . . you would not believe it, but Nettie surprised me and stocked my refrigerator and freezer with my favorite dishes. I just got off the phone to thank her."

Mike replied, "You don't have to ask me twice, buddy. I'll be over in a bit. We can go over some things, plus I will need some additional info from you." With that, they got off the phone. It was a good thing as both men happened to be in need of each other's company.

Chapter 26

DROPLETS OF PERSPIRATION ROLLED DOWN Vita's forehead, her neck already soaked in sweat. Although the car was parked under the shade of a large cypress tree, the dense, humid air of a mid-May Mississippi morning was already unbearable. Vita and her panting pup had been alone in the car with the windows rolled down for less than five minutes when a short, rather-rotund black woman in a brightly colored dress with a robust walk came to the passenger side of the car where Vita sat. "Well, hello there. You must be Vita," said the friendly round face with the thickest of southern drawls. "My name is Seraphina. I work right here at the Bryce Center. Your mom is inside speaking to one of our people and filling out some paperwork. C'mon, I'll get you out of this heat. Let's go inside."

Vita gave a hesitant smile. She was taught not to talk with strangers, but somehow, she felt she had already met this woman somewhere before. Indeed, Seraphina had a familiar comforting manner about her, a quality shared with Vita's grandmother. Seraphina noticed the dog on the girl's lap. Before Vita could utter a word, Seraphina added, "And yes, of course, you can take your doggie with you. What's his name, assumin' that he is a he?" Seraphina laughed.

Vita smiled again as she clipped the leash onto Chaz's collar. "His name is Chaz."

"That short for Charlie or something?" queried Seraphina, still chuckling.

"Oh . . . I don't know," responded Vita.

"Make sure you lock up now and grab those keys. C'mon, let's get something nice and cold for you both to drink. I believe you and your mom are going to be staying with us awhile," said Seraphina to Vita as they walked across the parking lot and into a side entrance of what looked to be one of two large Victorian homes that appeared to be connected to each other.

Carmen was seated in one of the counselor's offices, busy filling out forms. Seraphina appeared in the doorway with Vita and Chaz to let Carmen and the counselor know that she would be right back. She was going to take Vita and the dog to the kitchen for something cold to drink. "Can I bring y'all anything?" she asked the two women at the desk.

"Two sweet teas would be wonderful, Seraphina. Thank you," said the counselor, a woman in her midfifties by the name of Mary Graham. As the girl and the rotund woman left the office, Mary commented to Carmen, "I'll introduce you to Seraphina when they come back. She does a bit of everything around here. She is one of our LPNs, licensed practical nurses. She looks after everyone, she does."

Apparently, the Bryce Center accepted Vita into the program after hearing of Vita's plight from a phone call Father John had made. Mary gave Carmen the option of having Vita as one of the residents or having Vita stay wherever Carmen planned to live. "Unfortunately, we cannot allow the dog to live here. It would be unfair to the others if we made an exception," apologized Mary Graham.

"I fully understand. The dog will stay with me, and I will leave it up to Vita if she would like to be a resident or a commuter. She is attached to Chaz, our dog. He has been her rock. I am thinking that she will opt to stay with me."

Carmen was feeling both overwhelmed and relieved at the same time. The counselor promised her guidance in finding a suitable place to live. Carmen and Vita already had a room in a local hotel whose owner was charmed by Chaz, which had been another round of good luck. "I want to find the right place, so I don't need it by tomorrow," said Carmen.

Carmen shuffled the papers to make sure that everything that needed to be filled in was filled in. She came to the page that required the medical insurance information. Carmen was concerned about showing coverage for medical expenses. "I unfortunately do not want to use the medical plan we have. My husband will easily trace us here."

Mary, fully aware of the situation, was willing to speak to the director of the facility. "I am sure something can be worked out. You are not the first one in this situation." Mary explained that the biggest expense would be the delivery in the hospital and that the insurance info for that would not be needed until that day. "We have two wonderful women doctors who work with us and are very flexible. Vita will receive the utmost in prenatal care here. You pay what you can, and we can deal with the rest later. I will speak to our director— not to worry."

Mary told Carmen that the only people who knew of the circumstances concerning Vita's pregnancy were the director, the three counselors including herself, Seraphina, and the other two LPNs, and the two female physicians. "That will stay confidential among us. We leave it up to Vita to tell whomever she wants to tell. She may decide to talk with some of the others in the program. The girls get close here. They form bonds and share experiences that run deep. Don't be surprised if Vita is able to open up to one of these girls or young women."

"That would be a godsend if that would happen. It would be such a huge step for her . . . for all of us really," responded Carmen.

Mary then said, "I need to say this to you. In any case of a rape of a minor, we are required to report it . . . eventually . . . if you get my drift. What were you planning on doing about this person, her uncle?"

Carmen sighed. "Vita is not ready. There would be no way that she could deal with testifying about . . . you know . . . the incest. We will eventually have to report it, I know." Mary took hold of Carmen's hand and rubbed the top of it with her thumb. Carmen continued, "My husband has taken matters into his own hands for the time being. That's all I can say for now."

The two women spoke some more and were just touching upon the subject of the process of adoption when Seraphina, Vita, and Chaz returned. Vita was already on her third glass of sweet tea that she held in one hand and Chaz's leash in the other. Seraphina brought two tall cold glasses of sweet tea toward the coffee table that was in between two small couches. "Mary, honey, would you just reach into my pocket and grab those coasters," she said as she jutted her hip out toward Mary. Mary placed the coasters on the table. "I'll just set these right here for y'all," said Seraphina with a broad grin.

Mary stood up and put her hand around Vita's shoulder. "Hello, Vita. My name is Mary, and I have been having a nice conversation with your mom. I am one of the counselors here, and I am here for you and to help you get through this difficult time. I see you already know Seraphina.

"Carmen, I'd like to introduce you to one of our licensed practical nurses, Seraphina. Seraphina, this is Carmen Malloy, Vita's mother," said Mary with a hand on each of the woman's shoulders as the two women faced each other.

Seraphina picked up both of Carmen's hands and held them. Carmen took notice of Seraphina's strong and confident grip. Seraphina with her radiant smile said, "It is such a pleasure to meet you. We will take excellent care of your daughter. I promise you that."

Carmen, her hands still within the grasp of Seraphina, returned a smile and, with sincerity, told Seraphina, "Thank you. You are wonderful people here. You can't imagine how relieved and thankful I feel that we are here."

"Seraphina is the glue of this place. She really is!" exclaimed Mary.

"Now, Ms. Mary, don't you get me blushin'," joked Seraphina.

"It's true. Seraphina, you will see, is the heart and soul of this place." Seraphina shrugged her shoulders and tilted her head, and if there was an ounce of shyness in her being, perhaps a bit of it shown through.

Seraphina took the leash gently from Vita and walked Chaz over to Mary. "And have you met Master Chaz?"

Mary stooped down to allow the amiable snorting pooch to smell her hand before giving him a pat on the head. "How old is he, Vita? He is such a cutie pie."

Vita answered Mary, "I think, let me see . . . I think he is three, right, Mom?"

Carmen nodded. "Yes, he is a three-year-old puppy." Chaz soaked up the attention for but a few moments. There were too many scents to be had. His snorting and sneezing as he poked his head into wherever he could drew laughs from all in the room.

The choice of where to live was presented to Vita. And as her mother predicted, Vita did not want to be without her Chaz. Mary recommended that Vita come nine o'clock in the morning to six o'clock in the evening daily from Monday through Friday so that she could at least have lunch and dinner with the residents, which was the recommendation for the commuters so as to promote cohesiveness among the girls and young women. It was also suggested that Vita attend on some Saturdays from noon till early evening to be part of the leisure activities. Mary and Seraphina spoke about the program that Vita would take part in. She was grouped with other girls who were also planning on giving their child up for adoption rather than the girls/young women who were planning on raising their child. Those girls would be learning primarily parenting skills. There would be several overlapping classes and skills for both groups.

Mary spoke, "What I'd like to do after we finish this paperwork is to have you and your mom . . . and Chaz too . . . take a tour of our facility with Seraphina and me. And then, Vita, I would like to have a chat with you . . . and Chaz too." Mary smiled.

When Mary inquired about Vita's schooling, she was glad to hear that Carmen had arranged for Vita to complete the remaining three and a half weeks of schoolwork.

"Would it be all right if I have my mother mail the packet here, or I can just get a PO box if—"

Mary interjected, "You can have her send it here and just have your mother put it to my attention." Mary handed Carmen a business card from her desk.

"Oh, wonderful. Thank you. I will call her today and have her send that ASAP so Vita can get started on that," said Carmen.

Vita smirked and rolled her eyes. "Oh yeah, I forgot about that."

Mary guided Carmen over to her desk chair and moved the phone close to her. "In fact, why don't you give her a call right now? And you know that we have tutors available too."

Mary thought it best for Seraphina to take Vita around and introduce her to some of the staff and residents while she and Carmen worked on completing the registration process. "We will catch up with you in a little while for the tour," said Mary. Seraphina and Vita with Chaz in her arms left Mary's office as Carmen began to dial Nettie's telephone number.

Chaz, as usual, turned out to be the icebreaker and the first topic of conversation as Seraphina introduced Vita to more of the staff and some of the program's participants. Having Chaz took the edge off the discomfort Vita was feeling as she met girls and young women in varying stages of pregnancy. The first five girls Vita met were somewhere in their late teens. She felt so much younger than they were. Then Seraphina brought her over to a group of three girls who were in a classroom. Seraphina asked permission to introduce Vita to the girls, one of whom appeared near in age to Vita. As the introductions began, Vita felt a small wave of ease. She learned the one girl was fourteen, and the other two were fifteen years of age. Vita sensed a connection to the girls even through the awkwardness of the whole situation. The three girls and the instructor descended upon Chaz having been charmed by his cuteness, and that shot the awkwardness right out of the room. It would be with these three girls that Vita would grow closest with. The stories behind the pregnancies varied; however, all three of these young teens were planning on giving their babies up for adoption.

Chapter 27

THE BRIGHT ORANGE AND YELLOW flowers seemed to pop from the kitchen wallpaper. The blooms on the wallpaper were asking to be picked. Seraphina's kitchen was as cheerful as the owner of the house itself. Vita liked to sit at the kitchen table. The busyness of the décor did not distract Vita from her homework. She had been working on the packet Nettie had sent for almost a week now. Vita had class time at the center and some additional time in the evening once back at her new temporary home.

Seeing that Carmen was not having success finding an apartment that would allow a dog, Seraphina with her generous heart had offered Carmen and Vita to stay with her. Besides, for whatever reason, she felt an extra special nurturing toward the girl and her mother. Carmen at first had graciously declined; however, the persistence of the short, round, robust woman prevailed. Carmen insisted on paying rent to Seraphina; however, Seraphina would only agree to a small amount to go toward the utilities.

The kitchen felt cozy to Vita, especially now that it had a plastic placemat on the floor upon which sat Chaz's Navajo ceramic food bowl. Vita had most of the assigned work done. The tutors at the center had been guiding Vita through her schoolwork. She hoped to finish the packet in a day or two so her mother could send it back to Nettie who would drop it off at her school. Vita closed her books for the evening and sat for a moment. *Things seemed to be going okay for the past week*, she thought. Mary was so kind, patient, and understanding. She really kept the counseling sessions confidential as promised. Vita trusted Mary, and she trusted and loved Seraphina. Vita pondered lots of things. She thought of her father. *What must he be feeling?* She wondered if he felt abandoned, angry, lonely, confused, or maybe all these things. In a few weeks, it would be Father's Day. Vita hoped that her card with the directions for her father to find her handmade gift she had hidden would bring him a glimmer of happiness. She knew her grandmother would get that card to him on Father's Day. And she thought of Nettie. How she missed her fun and comforting grandma. *I can always count on Grandma*, she thought. Perhaps that was the something that Seraphina had that made Vita feel as though she had known her before.

Vita got up from the table and walked into the parlor. It too looked as a spring garden in full bloom. Carmen and Seraphina sat on one of the floral print couches and perused a photo album while Chaz was curled up at Seraphina's feet. Chaz had made a new best friend as dog biscuits seemed to grow in Seraphina's dress pockets.

"Oh, you must be so proud of him," said Carmen, pointing to the photos of Seraphina's son, Willie, who had played college basketball. Willie had graduated college eight years ago. Large framed graduation portrait photos adorned the parlor walls—one from the high school graduation and the other from the college graduation. It was obvious from the pictures that Willie did not share the same body type as his mother.

"Can I look too?" asked Vita. "I'm done with my stuff for tonight."

"Sure can, honey," said Seraphina.

Chaz picked his head up and shook his little curled tail as Vita sat between her mother and Seraphina. "How old is Willie now?" asked Vita.

"He is twenty-nine years old. Lives in Georgia. Got himself a good job there too," said the proud Seraphina.

"What does he do?" queried Carmen.

"He's an accountant for a big company in Atlanta," replied Seraphina.

"Oh, that's wonderful. Is he married?" asked Carmen.

"Not yet. Nothing serious yet," said Seraphina.

Carmen turned to Vita. "Seraphina looks way too young to have a twenty-nine-year-old son, doesn't she?"

Vita smiled and looked upon Seraphina. "Yeah."

Seraphina laughed. "Well, thank you, honey, but to tell you the truth, I had Willie when I was only a few years older than you are now, Vita. I had just turned seventeen when Willie came into this world."

"Where's his dad?" blurted Vita.

"Vita!" exclaimed Carmen, who was taken aback.

Seraphina quickly responded, "Not to worry. That's quite all right. It's just a natural question." Vita looked confused, not at all aware that what she had asked might be a tad personal.

Carmen, still embarrassed by Vita's question, said, "I'm sorry about that."

Seraphina patted Vita's leg. "Well, Vita, I don't know where Willie's father is . . . That's the truth. When I was sixteen, I began to see this boy. He was seventeen. You see, we was in the same class, and we took quite a liking to each other. One thing lead to another. When I became pregnant, my grandmother and mother confronted him and his parents only after I told them about how me and Ernie snuck around to meet each other. My father was angry, and there was no tellin' what he truly wanted to do. So my mother and grandmother said they would handle it . . . and he let 'em. Ernie denied ever having been with me, and his family believed him. They had plans for that boy." Seraphina paused as Carmen and Vita listened. "And then they managed to move away before Willie was born."

Carmen, not knowing what else to say, whispered, "I'm so sorry."

"Oh, don't be," said Seraphina. "Willie was and will always be the love of my life. That boy is everything to me." Vita continued to listen as Carmen commented how hard it must have been for Seraphina. "It was hard on Mama and Granny. We all raised Willie." Carmen could feel the pangs of guilt as she thought of the child she had aborted.

The three of them spent the rest of the evening looking at the photo albums. This was followed by some hot tea and shortbread cookies before retiring to bed.

The next morning, Vita and Carmen had a light breakfast before they drove to the Bryce Center. Seraphina had left a few hours earlier as she usually started her shift at eight o'clock in the morning. Carmen decided to go into the center with Vita instead of dropping her off. Carmen wanted to speak to someone about volunteering there a few days a week. *An idle mind just breeds more worry, and worrying won't help a darn thing*, she told herself. This advice was something Nettie had said many a time. Carmen also wanted to pitch in with helping Seraphina with the housework, cooking, and food shopping. Being in a routine and keeping occupied was not only essential to Vita but also to Carmen.

Once in the center, Vita and Carmen parted ways. Carmen went into the main office while Vita entered one of the classrooms. This class was attended by both commuters and residents, regardless of whether they were giving the baby up for adoption or choosing to raise the baby themselves. The class was on maternal health and the importance of maintaining good health for the sake of both mother and child. Also discussed were the changes the body would be going through, physically and emotionally, during the different stages of pregnancy.

The next class was a parenting class meant for the girls who planned on keeping their baby. Once in a while, the instructors would have the girls who planned on giving their child up for adoption sit in on this class. They learned the responsibility of rearing a child and with having to now deal with adult situations, expenses, no sleep, school, job, and not being able to hang out with one's friends.

The morning had gone by in a flash. Vita sat in the large dining room with the three girls that were closest in age to her who were also giving their babies up for adoption. Their names were easy to remember—all Js—Jody, Jackie, and Jolene. Jolene was fourteen and only in her first trimester of pregnancy while the other two girls were fifteen years old. Jody was roughly at the same stage of pregnancy as Vita, approximately twenty-one weeks, while Jackie was already in her third trimester. All three girls were residents there.

From their conversations, Vita had gleaned that all three girls had become pregnant from their boyfriends. The girls assumed that

Vita's pregnancy was likewise. Vita did not share information on her situation as it never really came up.

"Look at me!" exclaimed Jackie. "I'm about to burst! This is freakin' crazy. I have to pee all the time, especially at night."

"Yeah, I know. I have to get up now at night too . . . more than once," said Jody.

"Not me. Not yet," chimed in Vita as they ate their lunch. "But my regular pants are so tight now. That's why I have these on today," said Vita as she revealed her elastic waistband of her shorts under her T-shirt.

Jolene lifted up her shirt to reveal her tight-fitting jeans. "I ain't there yet," she said as she wiggled her hips from side to side.

"Hey, why don't we share our big momma clothes?" suggested Jody. "And then we can give them all to Jolene 'cause by the time we're done with them, she'll just be needing them."

"I ain't wearin' those. You'll see. I won't get so big," said Jolene with her sassy tone.

Jackie responded, "I bet you're gonna be bigger than a house like Monica over there." Monica was a seventeen-year-old who was planning on keeping her baby. She apparently was a big girl to begin with, and the extra poundage seemed to be added all over her body. The poor girl was asked all the time if she was having twins.

Jolene equipped, "No way. You won't ever see me like that. She waddles when she walks . . . Watch. No way. Uh-ah . . . not me!" The girls chuckled. Vita felt bad about the poking fun at Monica, but nonetheless, she laughed so as to fit in.

Vita spent the rest of the afternoon in counseling sessions with Mary and then worked with one of the tutors on her school packet. Seraphina's day included assisting one of the female gynecologists in the morning with examining all the girls in their third trimester, which had included Jackie. Seraphina taught the Lamaze class and the infant care class in the afternoon.

When Seraphina had gotten home, Carmen had dinner ready for her and Seraphina. Vita ate her dinners from Monday through Friday at the center. "Ooooh—that do smell good. Looks Italian. I don't get to eat much real Italian, but I sure do like it." Seraphina chuckled as she tilted her head back, her nose pointed in the air to inhale the aromas of Carmen's savory dish.

"That's linguini carbonara," said Carmen.

"Linguini . . . who?" said Seraphina.

"Let's see. It has ham in it with garlic and olive oil and eggs," said Carmen as she tossed the linguini.

"Well, thank you, Carmen. You don't have to do this. But I'm sure glad you did."

Chaz didn't know who to watch as the two women dined. His gaze targeted on Seraphina and then onto Carmen, back and forth. Chaz's large bulging dark brown eyes followed the dangling linguini on the fork and into the diner's mouth.

"Got some news for ya," said Carmen.

"Oh, do tell," said Seraphina.

Carmen told Seraphina how she would be volunteering at the Bryce Center a few days a week with whatever needed to be done. "It helps me to function if I just keep busy by helping out with what you wonderful people do there at the center."

The two women cleaned up after dinner with Carmen washing the dishes and Seraphina drying them and putting them away. "Oh, that sure do hit the spot," said Seraphina as she rubbed her round abdomen. "But we're gonna have to make some room for dessert. I picked up some fried peach pies."

"A fried pie? I don't believe I know what one even looks like," Carmen said quizzically.

"You'll see. After you pick Vita up, we all gonna have some," said Seraphina.

"Okay then!" said Carmen. Carmen took Chaz with her to pick Vita up from the center. Vita's friends got a kick out of seeing Chaz when Carmen came to get Vita at the end of the day.

The fried peach pie was a hit with all, and that included Chaz, who managed to snag a morsel. After dessert, Vita surprised her mom and Seraphina by handing her schoolwork packet over to Carmen. "I'm all done!" exclaimed the jubilant girl. "I finished it this afternoon. Can you make sure it's all there, Mom?"

"That's wonderful, Vita! I'm so proud of you to be able to focus on getting that done. I will leave it right here on the coffee table, and I will go over it later so I can send it off to Grandma tomorrow morning," said Carmen as she kissed Vita.

Seraphina chimed in, "I knew you could do it. Now let Seraphina give you one of her big bear hugs!"

"Oh, Mom . . . not this weekend, but next weekend, can I stay overnight with the girls at the center . . . you know . . . with Jackie, Jody, and Jolene? Mary said I would have to ask you first. It would be overnight on Saturday, and then I could hang out with them for a bit on Sunday . . . before we go to church." Vita figured the mention of "church" would score points with her mother.

Carmen realized that was the weekend of Father's Day and thought that perhaps this would be a blessing in disguise with the best place for Vita being busy with her new friends. "That's very nice of them. Yes, of course, you can," Carmen answered.

"Now you know that you ain't gonna get a lick of sleep. You will have yourself some fun though. I sure like those girls . . . all good kids . . . all of them," said Seraphina.

Vita had another request. "Mom, you said that maybe we could call Dad. Can we talk to him? Please, Mom," pleaded Vita.

"I know I did. We just have to be very careful that the calls are not traced. We'll find a way. I know that Dad needs to hear from us."

"Oh, and, Mom . . . um . . . would it be okay if I bring in my diary for Mary? She said it would be up to me if I wanted her to read it." Vita's thoughts were certainly being verbalized one right after the other. It came as a surprise to Carmen that Vita would want to share her diary. This meant progress to Carmen. She told Vita to do whatever she felt she was ready and comfortable with doing. Vita responded with a concern, "But, Mom, there's stuff in there about my brother. Things I wrote after you and Dad had read it."

A serious expression came over Carmen's face. Vita's comment and the immediate effect on Carmen did not go unnoticed by Seraphina. After a deep breath, Carmen placed her hand upon her daughter's knee and, with a smile, said, "That's all right. You go ahead and share your diary with Mary. The truth can't hide forever."

Vita nodded and looked over at Seraphina. Both Vita and Carmen saw the curious look on Seraphina's face. Seraphina felt it was not her place to inquire. She arose from the chair. "Let me wrap up the rest of those fried pies," she said in trying to diffuse the discomfort.

"Seraphina, please come and sit back down. I do want you to know. You should know. I trust you. You have been so good to us," said Carmen as her eyes watered up. Carmen took hold of Seraphina's hands as she sat back down next to Carmen on the floral couch. "This is not easy for me," began Carmen. She could feel Seraphina tighten the hold on her hands. "When I was a senior in college and Vita's father, Brendan, was in law school, I became pregnant." Carmen paused and sighed. "I cannot make excuses. You know back then we were told it was just a blob of tissue. But a part of me knew it was more than that. And it just wasn't the right time, you know . . . for Brendan and me to have a baby. It was inconvenient. I hate that word now—'inconvenient.'" Carmen could no longer hold back her tears. Vita picked Chaz up onto her lap and proceeded to bury her face in his fur. Carmen continued, "I had the abortion. I took the life of my son. And then I see the picture of your Willie and how you somehow managed to plow through and raise your son regardless of how difficult it must have been for you." Seraphina wrapped her short plump arms around Carmen and rocked her. Carmen muttered, "I knew back then . . . I knew inside . . . I just knew . . . that it was wrong."

Vita felt guilty about bringing up the subject of her brother. "Mommy, I don't have to show my diary."

Carmen patted Seraphina on her shoulder in graciousness and turned to Vita. "Sweet pea, you absolutely go through with sharing your diary with Mary. This is part of the healing process for all of us."

Seraphina suggested that Carmen would do well in getting counseling from Mary. Carmen knew how Mary had brought her daughter along in such a short time. She agreed that perhaps counseling with Mary would be a good idea.

Vita and Carmen and Chaz shared a full-sized bed in one bedroom in Seraphina's small two-bedroom ranch-style home. That night, they all lay awake rehashing the emotions of the evening, each in their own way before falling asleep.

Chapter 28

BRENDAN'S FINAL CLIENT FOR THE day left his office. The June sun was still high in the sky in the late afternoon. The opened windows allowed the warm breezes to circulate about the office. Corbin had been out of the office all day with court obligations. Brendan had purposely arranged his schedule so that he would be in the office when Corbin was either in court or taking the day off. This rearranging and coordination of appointments made Linda crazy. She knew something was not kosher between the two brothers for several weeks but did not want to pry. The aloofness between the two men was obvious to her despite their attempt at faking their usual ways. Although Carmen phoned the office infrequently, Linda was quite aware that Carmen had not phoned the office in over a month. Brendan was looking gaunt and tired to her the past few days, along with a sadness she picked up on. His appearance wasn't unkempt, but it had lost its finished and polished look. Still, Linda felt it was none of her business to ask and figured that if either brother wanted to confide in her, they would have done so.

Linda was rinsing out the coffee pot when the phone rang. She hurried back out to her desk. "Malloy and Malloy Law Office, this is Linda. How may I help you?

"Sure, Mike. Hold on one second," said Linda. She poked her head into Brendan's office. "Bren, it's Mike Greene. Can I put him through?"

Brendan put a smile on his weary face. "Oh, Mike . . . yes, Linda . . . thanks . . . You can put him through."

"Listen, bud, why don't you come over tonight. I want to go over a few things with you" came the roaring voice on the other end of the line. "Got the grill on my patio. I'll cook us up some burgers."

Brendan obliged and told Mike that he would like that. They agreed that six thirty would be a good time.

Brendan arrived at the condo Mike had been living in since his divorce. Brendan was greeted by puffs of smoke that billowed out from the cigarette that hung out of the corner of Mike's mouth. Brendan was also greeted by Mike's amorous black lab mix. "Sorry about that," said Mike. Brendan was not sure if he meant the dog or the smoke. Lady's long sturdy wagging tail thumped against the door as Brendan stepped into Mike's abode. "Lady . . . c'mon, girl . . . let Brendan in. C'm' 'ere, girl. How about a beer?" Before Brendan could respond, Mike was already reaching into the refrigerator.

"Sure," said Brendan.

The melancholy tone in his friend's one-word response and the noticeable weariness of Brendan's face concerned Mike.

Mike placed his arm around Brendan as he handed him the bottle. "I'm workin' on it, buddy."

"Thanks, Mike. I know you are, and I know I'm not making it easy on you," said Brendan. Mike knew that Brendan was referring to Brendan's refusal in charging Carmen with kidnapping and then dropping the charges afterward and in also not permitting Mike to interfere with Nettie.

"Let me get the burgers off the grill and then we can sit, eat, and talk," suggested Mike. Lady followed her master as he stepped outside onto the fenced-in patio, her tail swung from side to side as her nose aimed upward.

Mike returned holding a platter with four cheeseburgers and one plain burger and placed it on the kitchen table. "Hold on, girl . . . it's comin'," said Mike. Mike took a large tub of unopened potato salad from the refrigerator. "This stuff is the best. I get it from a deli down the block. Have a seat, Bren," said Mike. Before Mike joined Brendan at the table, he broke the plain burger up into chunks and placed them into Lady's bowl. "Go for it, girl!"

"No calls from Carmen yet, huh." Mike had put a phone tap on Brendan's home phone. He had instructed Brendan on how to operate the equipment should a call from Carmen come through and that the call would have to be of a certain length in time if it were to be successfully traced. Mike filled Brendan in with what else he had been working on. He told Brendan that he had gone to the Church of Our Lady to speak with Father John O'Brien. "He knows where they are, Bren. The good Father made a promise to Carmen not to reveal their whereabouts." Mike told Brendan that he had asked for the names, locations, and telephone numbers of pregnancy centers and homes for unwed young women in the eastern United States. Father John complied by giving Mike an envelope later that day with the information Mike had requested. "I also went to another Catholic church and made the same request. So now I am gonna compare the lists and see if the good Father left out a place or two," said Mike.

Brendan listened as Mike continued, "Haven't been able to determine their mode of transportation yet. I'd like to pay a visit to Carmen's brother Frank. He's got that gas station/auto repair place. You think he's privy to what's going on?" asked Mike.

"They are a close family, Mike. It's my feeling that Nettie has let her sons know something. She wouldn't keep Carmen and Vita's leaving from them," answered Brendan.

"I'm gonna go up to his station," said Mike. "I'm sure he'll remember me from one of your barbecues. He probably has a few cars that he buys, repairs, and then sells, right?" asked Mike.

"He might, Mike. I didn't think of that. But you know he will never give you any information Nettie has given him," said Brendan.

"I'm gonna give it a shot, Bren. I'll say I'm lookin' for a used car. I'll say that you sent me. I won't even mention a thing about Carmen or Vita," said Mike.

"Sounds like a plan. Good luck," said Brendan in a doubting tone for which he quickly apologized for. "I'm sorry, Mike. I just miss my family."

Brendan told Mike he had not received any credit card or bank statements that recorded any activity since Carmen and Vita had left other than the initial cash withdrawals.

"Any medical insurance claims or bills?" inquired Mike.

"Nope," responded Brendan as he reached for a second burger.

"What is this? Your first meal in a week? You're looking thin," said Mike with concern.

"Just don't have much of an appetite at times. But tonight, I do," said Brendan jokingly. He realized how much Mike was doing for him. He didn't want to seem like an ungrateful guest.

"Another beer there, buddy?" asked Mike.

"Yeah. Sure," responded Brendan.

Mike informed Brendan on how he was collecting the church trash and Nettie's trash in hopes of finding some kind of evidence. "It's a messy job, Bren. And your mother-in-law is meticulous. I'm finding lots of shredded paper. The other day, I went out early to Nettie's to make my, ya know, garbage pickup, and lo and behold . . . did Corbin tell you he beat me to it? He's tryin' too, huh."

Brendan tried not to appear surprised at this information. "Uh, no . . . no . . . he hasn't mentioned it to me, but then again, I haven't seen him for a few days. He never had mentioned to me that he was planning on rummaging through Nettie's trash. He probably doesn't want to tell me anything that he is trying to do to help so that I don't get my hopes up. I know he would feel like he was disappointing me if he was not able to turn up any information."

"I don't think the garbage thing is worth it anymore, Bren. Like I said . . . it's messy and so far not a clue. Would you mind if I ditched the rummaging?" asked Mike.

"You're the boss, Mike. Whatever you think," said Brendan. And playing it nonchalantly, he added, "And besides, Corbin seems like he has that job locked down."

Brendan decided to hang out with Mike the rest of the evening. Mike had put some more burgers on the grill, determined to put some meat on his friend. They got off the subject of the investigation and watched a Yankee game while downing a few more burgers and beer. It felt good to both of them to be in each other's company.

Before Brendan left, Mike invited Brendan to join him and his two sons for Father's Day, which was three days away. One son had graduated college the year before, and the other son had just completed his sophomore year. "Yeah, they are planning on taking me fishing on our favorite charter boat down the shore. Would love if you could join us."

Brendan declined, "Thanks, man. Hey, that's really very nice of your sons. But believe it or not, Nettie is making me some of her lasagna. See, she's trying to fatten me up too. We plan on going to the cemetery to visit her husband's grave, my father-in-law, and also my father's grave."

"You're good people, Bren. I love ya. Hang in there. We will find your family," said Mike as he hugged Brendan.

"Thanks, Mike, for this . . . for everything. I needed this. You enjoy your day with your boys." Brendan reached down to pet Lady. "And, Ms. Lady, you take care of your master, you hear?" said Brendan.

Chapter 29

THE COOL AIR THAT EMANATED from air conditioner and the ceiling fan circulating it felt ultrarefreshing to the girls. Vita, the three J girls—Jody, Jolene, and Jackie—and four others were congregated in the bedroom that Jody and Jackie shared. Vita would occasionally spend Saturdays at the center and would usually leave the center after dinner. A movie was always shown on Saturday evenings for the residents who wanted to view it. Vita had not had the opportunity to see one before this night. She had felt comfortable and part of the crowd in the center's living room while they had watched the movie *Kindergarten Cop*. As the girls sat in the bedroom, they all seemed to be in a good-spirited mood following the comedic film. Jolene's roommate, Tina, was one of the girls who decided to keep her baby. Two of the three other girls there were also residents who also planned on keeping their child. The other girl in the room, like Vita, was a fellow commuter who was giving her baby up for adoption.

The eight young women decided to change into their pajamas before getting into a game of charades. Vita changed into her lavender nightshirt. The girls rearranged the beds. The center of the room was cleared out with the two twin beds lined up back to front one behind the other against the wall. This arrangement, which was not new, had been perfect for charades with room for a stage and an audience.

Vita was the new kid on the block but no stranger to the game of charades. She was the only non-Southerner. The girls got a kick out of Vita's New Jersey accent. "Keep talking! I love your accent!" said Tina, who was Vita's teammate in the game. After charades, each of the girls got to model her maternity nightwear as Jolene provided the commentary on the various fashions. Jolene certainly was the spunkiest of the bunch, even though she was the only one of the girls there who was having a time with all-day morning sickness.

Vita felt a kinship with these young women. She felt as if they had been her friends for a good while. They were all in their teens, with Vita being the youngest. The oldest girl in the room, Miranda, a seventeen-and-a-half-year-old, was one of the residents there who planned on keeping her baby. Miranda went downstairs with Jody to the kitchen to bring up two pitchers of sweet tea, a stack of paper cups, and a package of cookies. The chaperones in the house saw to it that the girls did not abuse the junk food.

The eight girls sat in a circle. Five of them sat on the floor while the three girls who were nearing their due date, including Jackie and Miranda, sat on the edge of one of the beds. "I'm gonna miss y'all after I have this baby," said Miranda.

"Oh no, you won't. It's not like you're goin' far. We'll be visiting you all the time," said Jody.

The girls that were keeping their child to rear would move into new quarters once their baby was born. The new quarters happened to be right next door in the other large Victorian house that was connected to the one they were in. Once there, these young women were provided with resources to help them get on their feet so that they could either return to their home or survive on their own with their newborn.

Miranda planned on returning home. She had just graduated high school and had finished her coursework while at the center. Her mother was a single parent. Miranda's father had never been a part of her life. Her plan was to live back home with her working mother, who was willing to help her Miranda rear the baby. Miranda's hope was to get a part-time job while continuing with her education part-time with the help of the counselors at the center. She could help her mother pay the bills, and her mom would help with babysitting duties during her off time. "My ex-boyfriend . . . and I ain't sayin' his name 'cause he ain't worth it, just up and left me. I'm just scared, ya know," said Miranda.

Tina added, "I know. Me too. And isn't that why we are all here? Our so-called boyfriends . . . they are all nothin' but pieces of shit."

One of the others chimed in, "And so are their parents. They don't even want to know about it."

Jody, who was closest in age to Vita, said, "Well, I think you girls are brave. Sometimes I think I am taking the easy way out, you know, by like giving the baby up for adoption. I feel guilty sometimes about that."

Jolene voiced her opinion, "No way! You shouldn't feel like that. Hey, my baby is gonna have a good home somewhere. A home I cannot give him or her. Be proud. Don't be guilty. You can't think that way. I don't feel guilty. Look at me, Jackie, and Vita . . . We're not killing our babies by having an abortion. Now that is the easy way out—not adoption."

"You're just a kid yourself, Jody. Don't ever feel because some of us are keeping our baby that you're a bad person. You're giving your kid a chance, and that makes you a good person," said Miranda.

Jackie had a question for Vita. "Can I ask you why you came so far, all the way down here to Mississippi to this place? Why didn't you go someplace in NJ?"

Vita tensed up. "My mom found this place. I don't know why she picked here. I think because there was no room at the places in Jersey."

"But why all the way here in Mississippi? Must be some closer places," persisted Jackie.

Vita just shrugged her shoulders. "I don't know. You'll have to ask my mom."

The other commuter, a sixteen-year-old, who was also planning on giving her baby up for adoption, never volunteered much information about her situation. She and Vita were similar in that respect. She had been at the center a month before Vita had come. Her name was Stacy.

Jolene asked curiously, "So what is your story, Vita? And yours too, Stacy? We haven't heard much from you two. You got the same good-for-nothings that got you pregnant?"

"Yeah, I guess you can say that," replied Stacy.

Jackie, just as curious, spoke next, "You've been here two months, and we don't know what your story is. You can talk to us. We all are here in this together you know. Who are we going to tell?"

"Stacy will tell us when she is ready. What's the rush?" said Miranda.

Stacy felt compelled to volunteer some information. She sighed. "He was older, and well, he . . . I mean we . . . well, it just happened. I should have not let it get that far, but you know I thought I guess I was cool and all. You know—'cause he was older."

"How old was he?" asked Jolene.

"I don't know . . . like maybe twenty-five, I guess," said Stacy hesitantly.

"And? Did he just dump you after he found out you were pregnant?" asked Jackie.

Stacy didn't answer right away. Vita sensed Stacy's reluctance to answer and wondered why. Stacy finally responded, "He didn't even wait that long. We were together a few weeks, was all. My parents didn't even know that I was with him. I never told my parents who the father was. They know him. I couldn't say anything. I just told my parents that if they kept pushing me, that I would kill myself. It would be big trouble is all if they knew he was the one."

Miranda saw that Stacy did not want to continue explaining her situation. "Honey, you don't have to tell us anymore. I'm proud of you for telling us what you did. Feel all right?" said Miranda as she rubbed Stacy's shoulder.

Stacy nodded. "I'm okay."

Vita nervously began to chew on her already-short nails. Jody was the one who posed the question to Vita. "You too, Vita? I guess you had one of those boys that hit and run."

Vita took her hand away from her mouth and shifted her cross-legged position on the floor. "Yeah."

Jackie chimed in again, "You can tell us, Vita. It's okay."

Vita felt that she had to relinquish some information, "Like Stacy . . . he was older too."

Miranda added, "Sometimes the older ones are worse and less responsible and all. How old?"

Now was when Vita had to veer from the truth. "He was twenty."

Miranda, as the older "sister" of the group, again commented, "A twenty-year-old man should know better than to mess with a thirteen-year-old."

The others agreed. Vita's response was the same as Stacy's. "I just thought, like Stacy, that I was cool. He was cute, and he liked me. My parents didn't know what was going on. He was an older brother of one of my girlfriends, and it was while he was home from college during his winter break. I only started getting my period a year ago, so when I didn't get it, I didn't really think anything about it 'cause it never came on time anyway. Then my clothes got tight, and I got boobs. My mom noticed. I had to tell her what happened, and then she had me take one of those pregnancy tests. And then she made me tell my father." Vita looked over at Stacy as she continued to weave her web of lies, something she had become accustomed to.

"So what happened with the guy? Did your parents speak to him and his parents?" asked the normally quiet Stacy.

Vita thought for what seemed like an eternity and said, "Oh yeah. My mom and dad went over to their house, but he had already been back at college for a while by then. It was a mess. His parents insisted I get an abortion. They said they would pay for it. Well, my mom . . . we . . . don't believe in abortion. We talked to our priest. I think that's how my mom found this place. My parents thought it would be a good idea to be far from home."

"Good for you! You are giving this child a chance!" cheered Jolene.

Vita looked down and, wanting to put an end to her fabricated tale, said, "Sooo, that's it."

Miranda knew Vita was uncomfortable and said, "We should all be proud of ourselves for having the courage to do what is right. We are strong. We are sister strong, and we don't take the easy way out!" The girls erupted in support of one another like cheerleaders.

Jolene stood up and said, "This calls for some more cookies and sweet tea. Who wants to go down to the kitchen with me?"

It wasn't until two thirty in the morning that the girls decided to get some sleep. Jackie had already fallen asleep on one of the twin beds. Miranda gently eased into the twin bed alongside Jackie. Two others slept in the other twin bed while the other four girls, including Vita and Stacy, slept in sleeping bags supplied by the center. Vita and Stacy, the two commuters, had brought their pillows from home. The four sleeping bags were lined up on the floor that had served as the charades stage. Vita and Stacy were positioned next to each other. A night-light was left on as most of the girls were in the habit of having to use the bathroom once or twice during the night. The only other light emitted was the red glow of the numbers from the digital alarm clock.

"Vita. Vita." Vita thought she heard someone whispering her name into her ear. "Vita. Vita? Are you awake?" came the voice.

Vita awoke to Stacy's eyes inches from her own. "Stacy? What time is it?"

"Oh, good, you're awake," said Stacy.

Vita looked up at the red glow on the nightstand—five thirty-seven. "Are you okay?" Vita asked Stacy.

"Yeah. Can we talk? I just want to ask you something. Okay?" whispered Stacy.

Vita was still trying to get her bearings. "Uh, I guess. What is it?" Vita whispered back with her eyes locking onto Stacy's wide-awake gaze.

"What really happened with you?" asked Stacy.

Vita seemed puzzled. "What do you mean?"

Stacy continued, "I think there is more to your story." Vita did not reply. She felt her heart pounding. Stacy went on in a low but deliberate whisper, "I think you and me . . . I think we are alike . . . you know . . . in some ways. I don't know, but I feel like . . . connected to you or something." Vita was still speechless. Stacy continued, "I feel like I can talk with you. I think something happened to us. Something very bad happened to you and to me."

Vita whispered back, "What? Like what?" The anxiety mounted within Vita. Stacy's wide eyes stared into Vita's wide eyes. The tears welling up in Stacy's eyes triggered a sudden wave of sorrow in Vita.

Stacy then blurted her secret. "He raped me. My father's friend, whom I called 'uncle' . . . he raped me, Vita," sobbed Stacy. The two girls whose eyes had been locked onto each other's now locked arms. Vita began to cry with Stacy.

Stacy's story was eerily similar to Vita's. As Vita listened to Stacy and cried with Stacy, something happened inside of Vita. As she tried to console Stacy, she began to tell Stacy the truth of what had happened to her. The words seemed to flow out from her mouth naturally. It was an immense cleansing for both Vita and for Stacy. An instant bond, one that runs deep and one of insurmountable strength, was formed. As both girls bared their souls to each other, a unique sisterhood was born.

The muffled sobs awoke Jackie, which in turn awoke Miranda who was next to her. Miranda, the self-appointed nurturer, eased out of bed to see what the disturbance was about. Jackie followed. It was only a matter of minutes before the rest of the girls were gathered around Vita and Stacy. And it was soon after that when both Vita and Stacy recanted their horrible truths to their new sisters. The girls huddled and hugged Vita and Stacy as the two spoke. All those in that room promised not to share what was said. Vita and Stacy knew they could trust these girls with whom a definite kinship had developed.

Chapter 30

BRENDAN WAS ALERTED TO NETTIE's arrival by the doorbell as there was no Chaz to detect the familiar sound of Nettie's car. Brendan opened the front door to a pair of thin outstretched arms upon which sat one large tray of homemade lasagna. "Happy Father's Day, Brendan! We will make today work," said the owner of the skinny limbs.

"Oh! Thank you, Mom. Hey, let me take this from you," said Brendan. He ran to the kitchen to drop off the mother lode of lasagna and then returned to Nettie. With their arms extended to embrace each other, they proceeded to engage in a long, hard hug. No words were spoken. Nettie cupped her hands to hold Brendan's face and gently kissed his cheek. She stepped back to make a spot-check evaluation of Brendan. Despite looking dapper in his khaki shorts and royal blue polo shirt that enhanced the blueness of his eyes, it was obvious Brendan had lost more than a few pounds.

"Well, dear, I have more in the car. Looks like you need just the meal I have in mind and then some," said Nettie. Brendan and Nettie went back out to her car to lug in the rest of the cuisine. There were Nettie's meatballs, her gravy, and a nice salad with the fixings for her special dressing. There was also a bag that held a loaf of warm Italian bread and a pastry box that held the cannolis, both with "Vito's Italian Bakery" inscribed on them.

"Here are some reserves for you, dear." Nettie revealed a tray of eggplant parmesan and a tray of chicken parmesan, both of which she placed in the freezer.

"Mom, I don't know what to say . . . other than thank you." And with that, Brendan gave his mother-in-law another hug. He wouldn't let go. Unexpectedly overcome with emotion, he sobbed into Nettie's shoulders. "I'm sorry, Mom. I miss my family. I missed you. You're my family." Brendan, somewhat embarrassed, collected himself and sat down.

Nettie placed her hand onto his shoulder. "I know you do, Brendan. I know you do. I miss them awful myself. But we must be patient, son. It will work out . . . We have to allow things to do so. Our girls will be home." Before Brendan could make any inquiries, Nettie was handing Brendan a cold bottle of beer from his refrigerator. "You relax, and I will get things warmed up and on the table."

Nettie suggested eating in the dining room, but Brendan preferred the kitchen table. Familiarity was his friend. They made small talk during dinner, each skirting the topic of their dear ones. Nettie spoke of how she was keeping busy with volunteering at church, visiting her friends, and knitting. Brendan told Nettie that he still took his daily run and tried to keep busy with some landscaping and with working on his painting but that most of the time he chilled watching baseball on the television.

After Nettie cleared the table, she said to Brendan, "I have something for you." She pulled out a white envelope from her pocketbook. It was adorned with drawings of little sailboats and pugs with "Happy Father's Day!" written on it in bright magic marker colors. Nettie handed the envelope to Brendan.

As he reached for it, his eyes came alive. He stared at the drawings. "Pugs and sailboats," he said with a big smile. Brendan opened the envelope to find a lovely handmade card from Vita with a folded note inside. The outside of the card was a drawing of a marina at sunset filled with sailboats. Inside, the card simply stated, "Happy Father's Day, Daddy. I love you. Love, Vita." On the left panel of the card was a message: "I made a present for you. You have to go in my closet. In the back of the closet, there are a stack of shoeboxes. In the second box from the bottom, a surprise awaits you."

Nettie stood over Brendan as he reread the instructions. He put the unopened note inside the card and set it down. "Come with me,

Mom." With the enthusiasm of a young boy, Brendan bounded up the stairs and into Vita's room. He waited for Nettie. She was happy to see some life sprung back into her son-in-law. Brendan got on his hands and knees and crawled to the back of Vita's closet. Nettie heard Brendan mutter, "Second from the bottom. Here we are." He backed his way out of the closet and emerged with the shoebox with "Handle with Care" written on the lid.

Brendan sat on Vita's bed and motioned with his head for Nettie to join him. The shoebox sat upon his lap. He placed his hands on either side of the top of the shoebox and slowly lifted the lid off. The inside of the box revealed a diorama of a special moment in Vita's life. Both Brendan and Nettie let out an excitable gasp. "Would you look at that!" exclaimed Brendan. It was a scene from the day Vita picked out the Navajo bowl for her Chaz while on vacation to Arizona a couple of years before. There was an Indian village made up of Navajo hogans against a background of a beautiful southwestern sunset. There were the likenesses of Vita, Carmen, Brendan, and Nettie. In the hands of the Vita figurine was the Navajo dog bowl. Brendan chuckled. "Oh God. I remember that shirt. How did she remember that shirt . . . Guess it was obvious it was a favorite." Brendan continued, "I will treasure this. You don't know how good I feel right now." Brendan stared into the shoebox. His grin went from ear to ear.

"It's really something, isn't it?" said Nettie.

"I am going to put it right on my night table, right next to the bed so I can see it just before I go to sleep and then first thing in the morning," said Brendan.

Nettie accompanied Brendan into his and Carmen's bedroom. He set the diorama up on the nightstand next to his side of the bed. Nettie noticed the contraption set up next to the telephone on Carmen's nightstand. Brendan noticed that Nettie had noticed it. She had never seen it there before and knew it was not an answering machine. Nettie surmised to herself what the get-up might be and opted not to inquire about it. Brendan felt awkward. He was compelled to say something, but he too opted not to comment. Neither wanted to diminish the positivity of the day. Nettie quickly suggested that they visit the cemetery where Anthony DiAngelo and Corbin

Michael Malloy Sr. rested. Nettie's plan was to go and spend time at the cemetery and then come back for dessert. Brendan agreed with the plan. He didn't forget about the folded note inside of Vita's card and decided to read it later. "I'll drive, Mom. Thanks for suggesting this," said Brendan.

"Oh, Brendan, dear, I have two potted plants for the graves in the back seat of my car," said Nettie.

Brendan, touched by the thoughtfulness of his mother-in-law, hugged her and said, "Mom, what don't you think of?"

So fragrant were the lilies that Brendan had to keep a finger on the side of his nose to keep from sneezing while he held the large potted plant with his other arm. Nettie carried the other potted white lily plant with both hands as they walked to the glistening green marble tombstone on the grave of Anthony DiAngelo. Nettie had chosen the Italian green marble stone and had a beautiful silhouette of the Virgin Mary engraved onto it. She slowly bent at the knees and lowered herself to place the plant upon his grave. Then she knelt down. Brendan placed the plant he held on the ground and proceeded to kneel down next to Nettie. Nettie prayed silently. Brendan bowed his head. With hands clasped, he immersed himself in the peace of the moment and then said a silent prayer for his late father-in-law. Brendan took the cue from Nettie as he helped her back to her feet when she was done praying. "Our Vita has his eyes you know," said Nettie with a smile.

"Yes, she does," agreed Brendan.

"Oh, how I miss him. Drove me crazy sometimes, but how I do miss him," continued Nettie.

Brendan placed his arm around his mother-in-law's shoulder. "I know you do. He was a good man. A wonderful father, grandfather, and husband," said Brendan. It wasn't often that he had the opportunity to comfort Nettie.

They spent another few minutes at the grave and then decided to walk where Brendan's father was buried. It was a warm June day, but the humidity was lower than usual. Corbin Michael Malloy Sr.'s grave was on the other side of the large Catholic cemetery. As they walked the paths that led to the west side of the cemetery, the question of how his wife and daughter were doing gnawed at Brendan's heart. "Mom, may I ask you . . . How are Carmen and Vita doing? I just need to know if they are safe and all right."

Nettie responded, "Last I heard from them, they were doing well. Vita finished her schoolwork for the year."

Brendan told Nettie he was relieved to hear that they were okay. "Listen, Mom, I won't ever ask information of you other than my concern for their safety. I don't ever want to destroy our relationship. But I know you know that I have to do what I have to do . . . and that is to continue to look for them."

Nettie fully understood where Brendan was coming from. "I appreciate your concern for my feelings and your value on our relationship. You know you are as a son to me," said Nettie lovingly.

As they approached the grave of Brendan's father, Brendan noticed a familiar car in the cemetery's west end parking lot that was still a distance away. He also recognized the sound of the engine. As the car left the lot, Brendan muttered, "I am not going to let him ruin my day."

Nettie was quick to realize what Brendan was referring to. "That was Corbin leaving, wasn't it?"

Brendan nodded. It appeared that Corbin had not seen them. "I wonder what Dad would do if he knew what Corbin had done." Both Brendan and Nettie pondered their own answers to that question in silence. "I try to avoid Corbin these days as much as possible," commented Brendan. Nettie patted Brendan's arm as they walked arm and arm toward the grave.

Brendan placed the potted lily he had been carrying in front of the classic dark gray-silver granite tombstone of Corbin Michael Malloy Sr. He made sure that the best blooms faced outward. Also on the grave was a newly placed small wreath. "My dad missed so much. I wish to God that he had gotten to meet Carmen and Vita and you and Tony. You would have liked him." Brendan knelt down directly in front of the tombstone. Out of the side of his eyes, he saw that Nettie wanted to kneel down. Brendan assisted Nettie to her knees.

"I wish Tony and I had the chance to meet your father. From the stories you have told me, I could tell he was your mentor," she said.

Brendan held Nettie's hand. "He was always there for me and Corbin. Even though his work schedule was crazy busy in setting up his law practice, he would always make time for us. He came to our Little League games and even was the assistant coach one year for my team and another year for Corbin's team. Taught us how to play tennis and how to sail. We had those *Sunfish* starter sailboats as kids, you know." Brendan stopped reminiscing as soon as he realized good memories of Corbin made him uncomfortable. So hurtful and conflicting were his emotions that he just became silent. Nettie did not comment but gave Brendan's hand a caring squeeze.

When they returned back to the house, Nettie put on a pot of coffee. She took out the box with "Vito's Italian Bakery" on it from the refrigerator. Brendan picked up Vita's card he had left on the kitchen table. He remembered the note inside. He unfolded the lavender-and-pink embellished stationery and oriented it for reading.

Dear Daddy,

I feel sad. I am writing this knowing that I won't be there with you on Father's Day. Part of me doesn't want to leave, but part of me knows I have to. When I saw the baby moving inside of me and when I saw that it looked like a little person, well, I don't have to love it because I don't love it, but I can't kill it. I just can't. I hate Uncle Corbin. I hate him. Sometimes I hate this baby. Sometimes I don't hate this baby though, and I don't think I can live with myself if I allow the baby to be killed. I see the pain Mom is in and maybe you are in too. I wonder about how life would be if my older brother were here. Like Father John said, "Only God can create life." I am trying to believe that. So I have to give this baby its chance to have a life with some family. Maybe someday, I will wonder what kind of life that child has. And that is better than wondering how I would deal with killing the baby by having

an abortion. I love you, Daddy. We will be back.
I can't wait to see you again.

Love,
Vita

Nettie placed the two mugs of coffee on the table along with two cake plates for the cannolis. She noticed Brendan's pained face as he read and reread Vita's letter. Nettie rubbed Brendan's shoulder. Brendan handed the note up to Nettie where she stood behind him. "I want to share this with you, Mom."

Nettie sat down and read Vita's words. She was somewhat surprised at Vita's thoughts—how Vita was surer of her feelings and more determined not to have the abortion. Brendan sipped his coffee and nibbled on a cannoli as Nettie read the letter again. Nettie hoped that this letter would persuade Brendan to let things be. The long awkward silent moment was broken by the ringing of the phone.

Brendan answered the phone. His eyes widened as his two-handed grip on the receiver tightened. "Vita? Vita!" The voice on the other end was rushed and to the point.

Vita had been instructed by her mother to keep the phone call less than thirty seconds. "Daddy! Daddy! I love you! Happy Father's Day! I miss you! Did you get my present?"

Brendan was paralyzed in his tracks, but then his body leaned as if he was going out of the kitchen. He knew this was his chance to engage the tracking device upstairs. But he did not move. "Sweet pea! Yes! Yes! Grandma gave me your beautiful card. She's here now. And I found the present. I love it!"

"Daddy, I have to go. I have to go now. I love you."

A pause and then Carmen's voice, "I love you, Brendan." And that was it.

Brendan stood with the phone receiver in his hand and then placed it against the left side of his chest. With his head bent, he said in a soft voice, "Thank you, God."

Brendan hung up the phone and turned to give Nettie a long hug. "God knows what you need when you need it," said Nettie while she gave him a reassuring hug. Nettie had seen that Brendan did not attempt to trace the call by going upstairs.

"You know, Mom, I didn't quite know how I would get through this Father's Day, but to tell you the truth, it was better than I would have ever hoped it to be. I thank you for what you have done for me." He paused a moment and added, "Did you know Vita and Carmen were going to call me?"

Nettie responded, "I was as surprised as you were, and I am so glad that they did. Did you hear from Carmen too?"

Brendan told her, "Yes, but only at the very end of the call."

***

Vita and Carmen shared their joy and their sadness. "Dad sounded so happy to hear from us. And Grandma was there with him," said Vita.

"Grandma was there?" asked Carmen.

They both smiled as Vita responded affirmatively. Seraphina had given Vita and Carmen privacy while they sat in the parlor to make the special phone call that Vita had been pressuring Carmen about.

It had been an eventful day for Carmen and Vita too. After Carmen picked Vita up from the center to go to noon Mass, Carmen and Vita had gone out to lunch. Vita could not wait to tell her mother all that had happened during the sleepover with the girls. When they had gotten back to Seraphina's house, Vita and Carmen had recanted Vita's giant breakthrough to Seraphina. The three of them celebrated Vita's coming forth with some sweet tea and fried peach pies. Vita told her mom and Seraphina what she had said to the girls, "I told the girls that I pray to God to please at least make the baby beautiful."

Chapter 31

"STAY, LADY! I'LL BE BACK in a few minutes, girl," said Mike as he closed the driver's side door. The car windows were left open. The black lab mix sat straight like a soldier in the passenger seat. Her eyes followed her master as he walked toward the large gray cement building with multiple garages with the signage "DiAngelo's Garage" in bold red letters outlined in black.

Mike lit up a cigarette and strolled toward the building where he noticed cars with "For Sale" signs. Mike was greeted by a young man in his early thirties who wore mechanic overalls. "How can I help you sir?"

Mike pointed over to the row of cars on the side of the building. "Yeah—I'm looking for a car for my son. I see you have some vehicles over there for sale."

The man in the overalls held out his hand to shake Mike's hand. "Sure. My name is Alan. Let me show you what we have. Come on, and we'll see what is ready to go. I don't keep tabs on what is coming and going." As they got closer to the cars, Alan continued, "These five here are ready to go, and you know we had a nice older Toyota Corolla in great shape . . . I don't know . . . Frank might have sold it. I would have to check."

As soon as Alan mentioned the Corolla that had been there, bells and whistles went off in Mike's head. "Good cars, Toyotas. Hold their value. Yeah, can you find out about that one for me?" asked Mike.

"Sure thing, sir," said the polite man.

"Oh, I'm sorry, I'm Mike. Frank in?"

"Yes, he is," said Alan.

"I'm a friend of his sister's husband," said Mike.

"Well, Mike, come and follow me. Let's see where the boss is," said Alan with a smile.

As the two men walked back toward the front of the building, a bark emanated from Mike's car as Lady's black head hung out the window. "Hold on a sec," Mike told Alan. He went back to his car and put out what was left of his cigarette. He patted Lady on the head. "Few more minutes, girl. Okay." Lady was always up for a car ride, so Mike had decided to take her for the forty-five-minute drive to Bergen County where Carmen's brother's business was located.

While Mike tended to his dog, Alan had found Frank. The two men met as Mike was walking back from his car. Frank had met Mike at the Malloy house on multiple occasions, mostly for barbecues. Mike and Frank embraced. "Hey, Mike . . . good to see you! How've you been? What brings you here?" asked Frank.

"It's good to see you too, Frank. I remember Brendan saying you usually have some used cars for sale. I'm here to check out some cars . . . for my son," said Mike.

Alan, sensing that his obligation was done, shook hands with Mike. "Nice to meet you Mike."

"Same here. Thanks, Alan," responded Mike.

Frank put his arm around Mike. "First things first. That pup of yours . . . He? She?"

Mike interjected, "She . . . Her name is Lady."

Frank continued, "Looks like Lady would like out of the car."

"You don't mind?" asked Mike. With that, Mike returned to the car and snapped the leash onto Lady's collar. She bounded out of the car enthusiastically, thrilled to be a participant.

"Nice-looking dog . . . Lab mix?" commented Frank.

"Yeah . . . that's exactly what she is, aren't ya, girl?" said Mike as he patted Lady's side.

The two men and the dog strolled back to where the cars were. Mike told Frank that one of his sons had graduated college, and the other one was starting his junior year in college. "I'm looking for a decent car for my younger son now that he is a junior and allowed to have a car on campus. Alan said something about a late-model Corolla in great shape."

"Oh, that car is gone," said Frank. "I have these two Ford Escorts and this late-model Honda Civic here, all in good shape."

Mike asked to test drive those three cars plus two others so that he could get a feel for the cars. Frank, an obvious animal lover, was more than happy to dog sit Lady while Mike test drove each car. Frank placed a metal bowl full of cold water down on the floor for Lady, which she readily lapped up.

When Mike returned to Frank's office, he pointed to Lady and said jokingly, "I see she has made herself at home." Mike told Frank that he was interested in three of the cars but would like the info on all five vehicles, including the VINs so he could check on the history of each vehicle and talk to his son about the cars.

Frank wondered if Mike had known that Carmen had left Brendan. "Have you seen Brendan and Carmen lately?" asked Frank.

Mike, not wanting Frank to suspect why he was there, was quick to answer. "It's been a couple of months, I hate to say. I gotta give 'em a call. Summertime, ya know? Time for the Malloy barbecues."

"I hear ya. No one can grill like Brendan." Frank chuckled.

Mike joked back, trying to dispel any suspicion, "Wait a minute. I'm not half bad. I betcha a six-pack I could outgrill that Brendan!"

"Deal! The next time, we're gonna have a cook-off between you two," said Frank, laughing. The two men spoke with each other while Frank made copies of the information on the cars that Mike had requested. Lady was content to hang out in the office with the two men. Mike inquired how Frank's wife and children were doing, having met the family previously.

He told Mike that everyone was well and that the kids were thrilled that school was out for the summer. "We're going down the shore in a couple of weeks for vacation. Let me know which car you and your son are interested in . . . No rush," said Frank.

"Will do. It can wait till you return from the shore. My son won't need it until the third week of August when he starts back to school, although I'm sure he wouldn't mind getting the car sooner.

We'll see, but I will keep in touch," said Mike. With that, the two men embraced and shook hands.

Lady eagerly pranced by her master's side as they walked back to the car. Mike opened the passenger side, and Lady took her familiar spot in the copilot's seat. Her tongue hung out the side of her mouth as she panted. As Mike drove south on the Garden State Parkway, he thought about his next step. His plan was to run the VINs through Motor Vehicle to see what would turn up.

***

"Malloy and Malloy Law Offices. This is Linda. How may I help you? Sure, Mike, I'll send you through to Brendan," said Linda. "Hold on." Linda pressed the button on her desk phone to connect to Brendan's line. "Brendan, it's Mike Greene. I'll put him through."

It was a few minutes after three o'clock in the afternoon. Brendan was done with his clients for the day, and Corbin who had been in court most of the day was due back to the office. Brendan picked up the phone. "Hey, Mike! What's going on?"

Mike informed Brendan he had been at Frank DiAngelo's garage and about what had transpired. "I'm going to run the VINs with the DMV and see if I can find any info on the Toyota that was there. I'll keep you posted."

After Brendan got off the phone with Mike, he came out of his office into the main area where Linda sat. He looked lost. "Are you okay, Brendan?" queried Linda.

"Oh, you know, Linda . . . I guess I forgot why I came out here . . . Long day." Brendan smiled, embarrassed by his absentmindedness. His mind was on Vita and Carmen, with hopes that Mike was onto something.

"Brendan, would you mind if I asked you a personal question?" asked Linda.

Brendan came back to his senses. "Sure, Linda. What is it?"

Linda continued, "You can tell me if it's none of my business . . . but you and Corbin seem . . . well . . . as if things are not the same between you two. Is everything okay? I noticed too when I asked how your Father's Day was two days ago, your reaction was not what I expected."

Brendan looked down and then had Linda come into his office. She sat down, concerned with what her boss was telling her. "Linda, I'm sorry. Yes, there are a few things going on right now. First thing . . . yes . . . Father's Day was not the same this year. I haven't mentioned to you that Carmen and Vita have been gone for almost a month now. Carmen had to help care for an ailing aunt who lives in Maine."

"Oh, I am so sorry to hear that," said Linda.

"That is probably why I seem in a funk sometimes. And the answer to your other question . . . well . . . yes . . . Corbin and I have had a personal disagreement. I am sorry. We didn't mean for it to interfere with work, but I suppose it has spilled over and has been obvious, hasn't it?" said Brendan.

Linda commented not only was it obvious but that she thought that both he and Corbin did not look well. She mentioned how tired and thin they both appeared.

Brendan thanked Linda for her concern. He told her that both he and Corbin had been going through some stressful times. "I am going to have a talk with him. Maybe he and I need to try harder about not bringing our personal issues to work."

Linda was satisfied with what Brendan had told her. She knew better than to pry any further. She was not the type to have to know the internal goings-on. She had just wanted to confirm her suspicions that things were not quite right between the brothers.

Linda left for the day at four thirty. Corbin had not as yet returned from court. Brendan waited another hour and still no Corbin. As much as he did not want to speak face-to-face with his brother, Brendan still decided that he would take a ride to Quinlan's Bar first to see if Corbin was there.

"Hey, Bren . . . looking for Corbin?" asked the bartender.

"Hey, Jack, yeah . . . Has he been here today?" asked Brendan.

"Not yet. Saw him yesterday. Haven't seen you much here, Bren," answered the bald-headed muscular man.

"I know. I know. Been busy with . . . you know . . . just stuff. Thanks, Jack," said Brendan as he patted the bar.

Brendan drove into Corbin's complex, parking next to the shiny black Corvette. He placed his hand on the hood. The engine was still warm. Even though it was after six in the evening, the sun's rays were strong. The hum of the central air-conditioning units occupied the still and humid air. As Brendan approached the steps to Corbin's home, he noticed the front door ajar. He rang the doorbell. He waited and rang the doorbell once more. Brendan opened the outside screen door and knocked on the large wooden door that was ajar. "Corbin? Corbin? You here?" Clothing and shoes of both the male and female variety were strewn across the living room floor. The distinct rancid odor of the mix of sex, alcohol, perfume, and cologne hung in the room.

Corbin, his sandy blond hair tousled, appeared wearing only sweat shorts. A female voice with a familiarity to it sounded, "Who is it?" It didn't take but a second for Brendan to match the voice as belonging to a recent client of Corbin's.

"What are you doing here? Hold on . . ." said Corbin as he rushed back to his bedroom and then reappeared. Corbin combed his fingers through his hair in an attempt to neaten up his appearance. He repeated his question to Brendan, "What are you doing here?" Corbin reeked of the same sickening odor that permeated the living room.

"I waited for you in the office. I know you had a long day in court. I have some things I needed to talk to you about."

"Got done early," replied Corbin.

Brendan looked around the room and said, "I see you're busy. I'll make this quick."

Corbin responded in the most sarcastic tone, "Never too busy for my little brother. Shoot."

"Listen, Linda said something to me today about how obvious the riff is between us. I know we try not to be in the office together, but when we are . . . we have to at least make a better effort in creating an atmosphere that is less awkward. I don't care how much we have to fake it . . . whatever it takes. Aren't you due for a vacation?"

said Brendan, looking at his brother with disgust. He knew full well that Corbin would not be going anywhere, lest he miss a clue to Vita and Carmen's whereabouts.

"No problem, Bren. I can do that. Fake it I mean. Vacation . . . hmmm—not planning one yet. Anything else?" asked Corbin flatly.

Brendan wasn't going to comment, but he could not help himself. "You're getting a little sloppy. Your expertise seems to be slipping. Do you really need to be sleeping with your clients? C'mon, Corbin!"

And with that, Brendan left as an inebriated Corbin yelled out after him, "Just livin' life, bro . . . just livin' life!"

Chapter 32

A WET SNORT FROM THE PRECOCIOUS pug awoke Vita on this stormy Saturday. It was late morning. Carmen had already been up for a few hours. Saturdays and Sundays were Vita's days to sleep late, and she took full advantage of that. In her twenty-sixth week of pregnancy, Vita's pubescent body needed the rest. It was a good day to sleep in anyway with the constant pelting of the raindrops heard against the window panes. Every now and then, a gust of wind would intensify the force with which the raindrops hit the glass. Vita slept most often on her left side. She pulled Chaz in closer to her. "Okay, Chazzy. Okay, Chazzy. That's plenty of kisses," said Vita as she wiped her mouth with the backside of her wrist.

The aroma of Seraphina's freshly baked biscuits permeated the house and was just the incentive Vita needed to get herself out of bed. Vita sat on the edge of the bed. Chaz stood on the floor. His eyes told Vita to get a move on. She thought about how amazing the past week at the center had been. She and Stacy had become incredibly close. They were soul sisters. They were each other's confidants, and for both of them, it was truly a liberation of sorts. Vita planned on asking her mother if she could stay overnight again at the center. Miranda and Jackie would be having their babies soon, and Vita wanted to spend more time with those girls before they would move on to the other house at the center. Vita thought of her best friend Chelsea as she did from time to time. What was Chelsea thinking about her? What was the story she may have heard? Vita missed her friends at home. She decided to ask Carmen at breakfast if she could write Chelsea a letter.

Chaz arrived in the kitchen ahead of Vita. "Well, a good morning to you there, Miss Vita," said Seraphina in her ruffled bright yellow apron tied around her waist over an equally bright sleeveless dress adorned with sunflowers.

Carmen, her mug of coffee in hand, kissed her daughter on the cheek. "Good morning, Vita."

"Morning," said Vita. "Oh, these are my favorite!" exclaimed Vita as she placed two of the biscuits onto her plate.

"I know that," said Seraphina with a chuckle.

Vita helped herself to some grits and scrambled eggs as Chaz paid close attention.

"He's already had enough, Vita. He was in here earlier this morning," said Carmen.

"Oh, c'mon, Mom. Look how cute he is. Can't I just give him one little itty-bitty piece of a biscuit," pleaded Vita.

Carmen gave in, "All right—one, and I mean one itty-bitty piece."

Seraphina laughed and said, "He's going to end up looking like a sausage is what's going to happen." Chaz watched intently as Vita broke off a small piece of the biscuit and flipped the morsel onto the floor. Chaz tried to catch it in midair but missed. As soon as it hit the floor, it was vacuumed up instantaneously. All three laughed as Chaz picked up his head, his tongue smacking his lips as he anticipated more goodies to come his way. When he realized there were no further offerings, he waddled over to the placemat and lapped the rest of the water out of his Navajo water bowl.

"Mom, can I stay overnight at the center tonight? Some of the girls are due with their babies any day, and I don't know if I'll get the chance to hang out with them again," asked Vita. Before Carmen could answer, Vita came forth with her next request. "And, oh, Mom . . . can I write Chelsea a letter? I really miss her."

"Anything else?" mused Carmen. Carmen gave an affirmative to both requests. She told Vita not to put a return address.

"I will put it in another envelope and mail it to Grandma, and then she can mail it to Chelsea. Now I don't know what Chelsea has been told, but the school believes we are in Maine caring for an ailing aunt. I don't expect you to lie. I don't want you to lie, but try and keep it . . . you know . . . light and short. Okay?" responded Carmen.

"Okay, Mom. I think Chelsea will just be happy to hear from me," said Vita.

"Just let me read it before we send it if that's okay," said Carmen.

Vita responded, "I know, Mom. I understand. Mom . . . guess what? A lot of the girls said you were really, really good!" exclaimed Vita as she bit into her second biscuit.

Seraphina added, "Yes, indeedy! I heard the same thing. I am so proud of you, Carmen!"

Carmen had given talks the past week dealing with living with the regret of abortion. She told the girls how brave and unselfish they each were in what they were doing. She spoke to them of the permanent scar on her heart and of the guilt with the knowledge that she had taken a life. She also spoke of some peace in the forgiveness of Christ and how she prayed daily not only for peace of mind and soul but for the child she aborted. She prayed that he was among the angels in heaven and was cared for by the Blessed Virgin Mother Mary.

Carmen said to Vita and Seraphina, "Believe it or not, it helps me too to talk about it. I hope I am giving the girls some insight with what abortion does, and I really want them to know that God will always bless them for bringing forth the life he has created." Seraphina reached up and placed her arm around Carmen's shoulder and gave her a squeeze of encouragement.

"I hope Dad understands what I wrote in the note I put in his Father's Day card," said Vita while on the subject of abortion.

"You wrote Dad something about abortion?" asked Carmen with surprise.

"Yeah. In the note, I put that I would rather deal with wondering what kind of life the child was having rather than having to deal with taking the life of the child," said Vita.

"You really said that to Dad?" asked Carmen, shocked that Vita was able to write such a thing six weeks ago.

Vita continued, "I wrote that I saw the pain you were in . . . you know about the abortion."

Carmen hugged her daughter. "You've come a long way . . . a long way . . . I am so proud of you." The passage of time suddenly kicked in with Carmen. "Goodness, your birthday is in two weeks, Vita! Think of what you want to do."

"Is it really?" Seraphina asked with a broad smile. Vita nodded. "Fourteen, right?" asked Seraphina even though she already knew.

Vita nodded again and, with a bit of pride, said, "Yup . . . fourteen."

***

Brendan returned from his run. It was almost noon on this humid Saturday. Unlike the storms in Mississippi where his wife and daughter were, the sun shone through the haze in this part of New Jersey. Brendan, drenched in perspiration with his T-shirt melded onto him like a second skin, wanted to shower up before Mike came over. Before he went into the bathroom, Brendan picked up the diorama off the night table for the umpteenth time that day to gaze upon it. He also reread the artistic card with the marina on it. The note was kept in the top drawer of his night table along with the envelope covered with drawings of pugs and sailboats. Carmen's letter also was stored in that same drawer. It was as if Brendan got a dose of happy juice when he held the diorama and Vita's handmade card.

Brendan's timing was spot on. The doorbell rang as he came down the stairs. He was anxious to hear the update from Mike. "Jesus Christ . . . It's a sauna out there . . . That AC feels great!" said Mike as he wiped his brow. Mike had on a white T-shirt with the Yankees logo, a pair of long denim shorts, and flip-flops.

"Tell me about it. I just ran in it," commented Brendan.

"That's why you look like that, and I look like this. Don't know how you do that . . . but then again, you are a hell of a lot younger than I am," quipped Mike.

"Beer?" asked Brendan.

"Ya know what, Bren . . . how about some good ol' ice water . . . for now," said Mike, again as he wiped his forehead.

Brendan suggested defrosting Nettie's eggplant parmesan and heating it up in the oven to which Mike responded, "What are you, fuckin' nuts? Heat this kitchen up? No way. And don't think about reheating it in the microwave. Not the same. Let's go out and grab a bite after we go over some things." Brendan agreed with Mike's logic.

Brendan asked Mike about his Father's Day fishing trip with his boys. "It was super! Actually caught some good-sized blues and this sunburn," joked Mike as he pointed to his peeling face.

Brendan told Mike about his surprisingly pleasant Father's Day. He had Mike wait as he ran upstairs to retrieve the diorama Vita had made.

"She made this? It's so . . . so detailed," commented Mike.

"I treasure this, Mike. I treasure this. She left it for me to find. And I have to tell you that Vita and Carmen called," said Brendan. Mike jumped out of his chair as if to go upstairs. Brendan put his hand up like a traffic cop and told Mike that Nettie had been over when the call came, and he did not have the heart to run upstairs to engage the tracing equipment. "Besides, the call was barely half a minute long, if that," said Brendan.

"Yeah. Nowhere long enough anyway," said Mike. Mike hugged Brendan. "I am happy for you, buddy."

They sat in the family room where Mike informed Brendan that he had run the VINs with the DMV on the five cars Frank had for sale. "Found out the titles are in the name of DiAngelo's Garage. Did some cross-checking and found all the vehicles currently owned by DiAngelo's Garage included those cars for sale and his work trucks and tow trucks and one late-model Toyota Corolla. Ya know, the car I told ya Frank's mechanic had previously seen. Yup, a 1985 silver Toyota Corolla sedan with Jersey plates JCD72. Bingo, my man . . . got an APB out for that vehicle as we speak." Mike detected a glimmer of hope in Brendan's eyes.

"Wow! That's a big piece of the puzzle," said Brendan. He added, "Listen, Mike, just keep this in between you and me. This is my immediate family's business. Let me be the one to fill Corbin in."

"Sure, Bren . . . whatever ya want. I understand the delicate nature of the situation," responded Mike.

"I gotta say, Carmen knows what she is doing. Still nada on bank statements, credit cards, and any medical bills, huh?" asked Mike.

"Nothing there. That's my wife. You know Carmen. She's a planner . . . an organizer," Brendan said with a half smile. "What about the name of those centers that you had gotten from Father John and the other churches?" asked Brendan.

Mike answered, "There are a lot of places in the eastern half of the US . . . and let's hope Carmen didn't go farther . . . but that is where I am focusing. Anyway, Father John's list is the same exact list supplied by the diocese. There are a lot of these places. Well, nice that the good Father apparently is an honest and nondeceitful good Father."

Brendan and Mike spent the rest of the afternoon and early evening at Spike's Sports Bar and Restaurant, which was in walking distance from Mike's condo. Brendan had taken his own car and left it parked in the lot of the condo complex before they headed to the bar. They returned to Mike's condo and ended up watching baseball, eating, and drinking the rest of the evening. Brendan decided it best to crash on Mike's couch for the night. Lady kept tabs on the visitor, making sure to check every now and then as she would make the rounds from Mike's bedroom, out into the living room, and back to Mike's bedroom during the night.

Chapter 33

Seraphina, Carmen, and Mary sat having coffee in Mary's office. It was a Monday morning, two days before Vita's fourteenth birthday. Her birthday was July 10. They had been discussing the advances Vita had made since her short time at the center. Carmen commented on how right Mary was in that the bond that these girls made with one another oftentimes would be the impetus for a breakthrough. They were also looking forward to celebrating Vita's birthday during lunch on Wednesday. As was custom for birthdays there, the center would provide pizza and make the cake. The center also gave the birthday celebrant a twenty-five-dollar Wal-Mart gift certificate so that the young woman could pick something out for herself. She would also get a huge birthday card signed by the staff and the residents.

After they finished their coffee, each of the women went about their respective morning obligations. Mary was having one of the residents come in for a counseling session. Seraphina was doing physical exams that morning, and Carmen was setting up a classroom for infant care instruction after which she was headed to the kitchen and dining area for work to be done there.

***

Back home in New Jersey, Nettie had just returned from the early morning daily Mass. The phone rang. It was Brendan. He had a request for Nettie. "Mom, would you mind doing me a favor? I have a birthday card for Vita and a small package. Would you send those to her? I know it's last minute. I was hesitant to ask, but I want Vita to know that I would never miss her birthday no matter what and that she is always in my heart and on my mind."

Nettie told Brendan she would be more than happy to do that for him. "I mailed her a card on Saturday, but you know I found something I thought she would like while I was at the mall yesterday. I'll mail it all out together," said Nettie into the phone. Brendan asked her if it would be all right if he dropped the card and the small package off to Nettie in a half hour or so as he had to be in court in an hour and could swing by her house.

Mike watched from his car as Brendan pulled into Nettie's driveway. He wondered why Brendan was paying Nettie a visit. Mike kept Nettie under surveillance from time to time, with his car at a distance and never in the same spot.

Once inside, Nettie and Brendan embraced. Nettie offered him a cup of coffee, but Brendan reminded her that he had to be in court shortly. He handed Nettie the lavender envelope with the card inside. Then he took something wrapped in tissue paper out of a small gift bag. He unwrapped it.

"You picked this out, Brendan?" asked Nettie as she took the small article of clothing from Brendan's hands. It was a neon-green T-shirt meant for a dog Chaz's size with the words "Superhero" on the back.

"They didn't have lavender, and I don't know how Chaz, being a boy, would have appreciated lavender anyway," joked Brendan. Both Nettie and Brendan laughed aloud and agreed that Vita would love it.

"I picked this up for Vita yesterday," said Nettie as she revealed a small lavender leather pocketbook with fringe. It was flat with a shoulder strap and measured four inches by six inches. "I found it at one of the kiosks at the mall."

"She is going to like that . . . and we know it's all about lavender," said Brendan.

Nettie promised she would get everything into a package and that she would mail it special delivery within the hour. Brendan thanked Nettie and gave her a peck on the cheek.

As Brendan pulled his car out of Nettie's driveway, he saw Mike drive by. He followed Mike to the exit/entrance of the over-fifty-five development. Once out of the development, Mike pulled over to the curb, and Brendan pulled behind him.

Mike got out of his car and approached Brendan's car on the driver's side. "What's up? Anything I should know?" queried Mike.

Brendan exclaimed, "You amaze me, Mike! You're good! I just dropped off a birthday card and a small present for Vita on my way to court. Nettie said she would mail them for me today. Vita's birthday is Wednesday."

"All right then. Gives me an idea. I need stamps," said Mike. The two men locked hands and said they would speak with each other later.

Mike proceeded to drive to the only post office in the vicinity. He parked his car across the street from the post office and waited. Surveillance required the patience of a saint with long periods of time of "nothing happening." Mike had with him the usual paraphernalia to pass the time, which included a newspaper, a crossword puzzle book, and his smokes. He was somehow able to comprehend what he read with only quick intermittent glances at the newspaper, lest he miss what there was to see outside his vehicle. This was one of the many skills he had honed over the years. Mike was also a regular listener to the multitude of talking heads on talk radio.

As it turned out, Mike did not have a long wait. He hadn't even been there forty-five minutes when he recognized Nettie's car pulling into the post office parking lot. He timed it so he would enter the post office behind Nettie to be sure to get in line behind her.

"Hello there, Mrs. D'Angelo. How have you been?" said Mike in a friendly voice.

Nettie turned around and, not one to forget a face, said amicably, "Oh, Mike, right? Hello! How are you?" They certainly had met at the many barbecues and get-togethers at the Malloy house. Mike was in luck as there were a half-dozen people in front of them. This gave him an opportunity to attempt to decipher the address on the package Nettie held. Unfortunately, the way Nettie held the package prevented Mike from reading the address. "It's good to see you. What are you doing these days?" continued Nettie.

"Just trying to enjoy retirement. Out today doing some errands and then going to see the boys," answered Mike. Mike hoped Nettie would adjust the package in her hand. He also hoped that she would turn her head forward so he could get a glance over her shoulder, but she kept her head turned toward him.

"You have two sons, right? Are they still in college?" inquired Nettie. Nettie then turned her head forward to move up in line, and this gave Mike a chance to peer over the short woman's shoulder. He was able to make out the first letter of the state's abbreviation—M. Yes, it definitely was the capital letter M.

"You remember well. One boy is done with college, and the other has two more years left," said Mike as Nettie turned back around to listen to Mike's response. "I'm sorry about Carmen's aunt. I heard she and Vita had to go up someplace in New England to care for her," said Mike.

Nettie, quick to realize that this was the excuse Carmen had written in her letter to Brendan as to what she had told the school, said, "Actually, she is my late husband's sister. I plan to go up and relieve them in a few weeks." Nettie said a quick prayer silently to herself as she hated the idea of telling lies.

"Yeah, I had called Brendan to ask him why no barbecues yet, or did he forget to invite me or something? That's when he told me that Carmen and Vita would be gone for a while," said Mike. Nettie never suspected anything of Mike, even though she was aware of his previous profession. As she turned once again to move up in line, Mike tried hard to zero in on the address. He could not make out the letter next to the M. Nettie's thumb still covered it. However, above her thumb, he could read the last part of the street name—Cypress Street.

"Next in line," said the middle clerk to which Nettie turned to Mike before she proceeded forward.

"So good to see you again, Mike."

"Same here, Mrs. D," said Mike.

"Next," said another postal clerk.

Mike stepped up to the counter. "I'll take three books of stamps please."

As soon as he got in the car, Mike flipped open the pad he had resting on the passenger seat and wrote "Cypress Street" and then "Massachusetts, Maine, Maryland, Minnesota, Michigan, Missouri, Mississippi, and Montana." Mike had his work cut out for himself for the rest of the day.

Mike called Brendan close to nine o'clock in the evening and related to him having scored big at the post office that morning. Brendan was excited to hear all that Mike had accomplished. Mike now had the APB on the Toyota concentrated on those eight states. "The lists with the centers don't all have street addresses. Only about half of them do. The rest have a city, state, and telephone number. No hits on the ones with the streets listed . . . so guess what I've been doing." Mike had taken a break from calling the facilities with no listed street address to inquire of the street address. "Offices are closed in most of them. Some have answering machines that have the address info. There are a lot of these places . . . a lot . . . especially in the more heavily populated states." Mike also told Brendan he would go back to the church tomorrow and obtain a list of those women centers in the states beginning with the letter M, which were not in the eastern half of the United States.

Brendan thanked Mike over and over again. He was hopeful that more pieces of the puzzle would come together.

"Listen, Bren, I got more work to do tonight. I'll call ya tomorrow," said Mike.

Brendan tried his best to suppress his emotions after getting off the phone with Mike. He got out his calendar and calculated that Vita was in her twenty-eighth week of pregnancy. *There's still enough time*, he thought.

Chapter 34

T HE HUSH PUPPIES DISAPPEARED QUICKLY from the plastic weave basket lined with wax paper. "Vita, I know you are eating for two, but leave room for everything else." Carmen chuckled.

Carmen, Seraphina, and Vita sat in a roomy booth in the Log Cabin, Vita's choice for her birthday dinner. Carmen and Vita had been to the restaurant with Seraphina a few weeks before. The Log Cabin had become an instant hit. Vita had been officially fourteen years of age for almost twelve hours, having been born at six in the morning on July 10, 1977, according to her mother.

"Are you having a great b-day, dear heart?" asked Seraphina as she cut into her fried catfish.

"I just love this stuff!" exclaimed Vita as she popped yet another hush puppy into her mouth and downed it with a swig from an ice-cold mug of Barq's root beer.

"That was great that Jackie and Miranda were there today for pizza and my birthday cake," recalled Vita. Miranda had given birth the week before and had moved next door into the house for new mothers. She would stay there another few months before making a go of it at home with her mom. Jackie gave birth just three days before Vita's birthday and gave her child up for adoption. She had gotten back from the hospital the day before and wanted more than anything to stay to the end of the week at the center before heading back home to resume life in Alabama. Vita and Jackie made sure to exchange addresses and phone numbers. "I'm gonna miss Jackie. At least, I will still be able to see Miranda," said Vita.

Seraphina chimed in, "They nice girls . . . they all nice girls . . . and they all eat pizza and birthday cake like it goin' out a style. Not a single drop of that pizza or cake left." They all laughed.

"And that is one gigantic birthday card, Vita! Where did you put it?" asked Carmen, referring to the huge card signed by all at the center.

"For now, I put it up on the dresser right next to the card from Grandma." Nettie's card had arrived at the center that day. Vita, Carmen, and Seraphina had left the center around five o'clock in the afternoon and had stopped briefly at Seraphina's house before taking Carmen's car to the Log Cabin. An ice cream cake sat in the freezer that Carmen had picked up the day before.

"Mom, you like your . . . What's that called again?" asked Vita.

"Country fried steak," Seraphina informed Vita.

"Yeah, do you like your country fried steak, Mom?" Vita asked again.

"It is absolutely delicious, and with the gravy and the biscuits, I'd say it is heaven. Better than pasta I dare say!" exclaimed Carmen.

"I know. I don't know what my favorite is—the hush puppies or the biscuits with gravy or the mac and cheese or the barbecue," said Vita.

"See what you people up north have been missing out on," chided Seraphina.

The plan after the dinner was to go to the mall. Carmen and Seraphina wanted Vita to pick out something for her birthday. "So what do you think you would like for yourself?" asked Seraphina as she sipped on her sweet tea.

"I think maybe some sandals. Oh. And I may need a new diary soon. I really wrote a lot of stuff in it the other day and some more early this morning," replied Vita.

"Have a surprise for you," said Carmen as they drove home from the mall.

"What? What is it?" begged Vita.

Carmen had hidden the package that had arrived via Express Mail to the center that day into her pocketbook and had placed it for safekeeping under Vita's pillow when they had made the brief stop to Seraphina's house before the trip to the restaurant and the mall. "You'll just have to wait till we get home," teased Carmen.

Chaz was there to greet the three as they walked through the front door. "Oh, it felt good to do some walkin' in the mall," commented Seraphina. "Now I am only full up to here," said Seraphina, pointing to just below her breastbone.

"But I bet we all have room for some birthday ice cream cake," said Carmen.

"Yay!" exclaimed Vita. Vita carried in a small bag while her mother had the large shopping bag. Carmen went into the kitchen and took the ice cream cake out from the freezer for softening. Vita was anxious to take her new sandals out of the box to model them. "Thanks so much, Mom. I really like these. Aren't they cute?" Then she pulled a small light brown leather diary adorned with a little red leather rose from the small bag. "And thank you, Seraphina, so much for the diary. I know I'm going to need it soon. It's so pretty, and it smells so good," Vita said.

"You are quite welcome, young lady. Happy birthday," said Seraphina.

Carmen and Seraphina sang *Happy Birthday* as Carmen carried the cake to set it onto the kitchen table. The ice cream cake was aglow with fifteen candles, the fourteen plus one for good luck. "Quick, make a wish before we have ice cream soup," joked Carmen.

Vita closed her eyes wishing silently that her dad could be there. "Okay," said Vita, indicating a wish had been made and then proceeded to blow out the candles.

"Good girl! Got them all!" Seraphina laughed.

Chaz was quite pleased to lick the leftover melted ice cream left on the plates.

"Vita, take a look under your pillow," said Carmen.

"For real! I thought the cake was my surprise," said Vita. She rushed into the bedroom and was back out in a flash. She held a medium-sized padded orange envelope.

"This came to the center today," said Carmen as her daughter tore open the package. Inside were two presents with a lavender envelope taped onto the present that was wrapped in white tissue paper. Vita decided to open the other present first that was wrapped in lavender-and-pink birthday paper.

"Mmmm . . . it smells like the diary does," noted Vita. She peeled back the wrapping paper to reveal a lovely leather pocketbook with a small card resting on it that said, "Love, Grandma." "Look! It's so pretty! Where did Grandma find a lavender pocketbook?" Vita hung the shoulder strap from her wrist and displayed her new gift as she played with the fringe on the bottom of the handbag.

Then she pulled the card off the gift wrapped in the tissue paper. It was addressed "To My Sweet Pea." Inside the envelope was a card titled "Happy Birthday, Daughter." The front of the card was covered in flower-power type flowers in bold colors. Inside it was signed "Happy birthday, princess. I love you, and I miss you dearly. Love, Daddy." Vita covered her mouth with her hand. "Daddy," she whispered. She was breathless. Vita peeled back the white tissue paper to reveal the gift. "Oh my god . . . it's so cute! Look! It's a shirt for Chazzy! That's wild!" exclaimed Vita. "C'm' 'ere, Chazzy. Let's try it on! You are my *superhero*!"

Chaz pranced in circles seemingly proud to show off his bright new neon-green attire. "Superhero . . . huh." Seraphina laughed.

Vita picked up her pup, hugged him, and smooshed her face into his head. "He is my Superman, aren't ya, Chazzy! Guess what? My wish kinda came true. I wished Daddy was here. And well, he sort of is here in a way." Vita smiled.

***

Brendan found it difficult to leave the office. He decided to stay late instead of going to an empty home on the night of his daughter's birthday. There would usually be a dinner at a restaurant of Vita's choice followed by birthday cake at home with Nettie and Corbin there. There would also be a birthday party with her friends on one of the weekends near her birthday. Last year for her thirteenth birthday party, Brendan and Carmen allowed Vita to have her first sleepover party with nine of her girlfriends. Brendan sat in his office and wondered if Vita had received his card and gift today. He tried to imagine her expression when she would lay eyes on the T-shirt for Chaz.

Brendan knew Corbin was still in his office. He had been there for the past three hours. It was already just past six o'clock in the evening. Brendan hoped Corbin would leave soon. In Brendan's mind, the choice not to go home tonight was the better one, and he had made up his mind to spend the night at the office.

A loud, hard, and hurried knock suddenly rattled the front door of the Law Offices of Malloy and Malloy. Linda had locked the door at four thirty in the afternoon when she had left. "It's me, Mike" came the voice from the other side of the door. Corbin, whose office was closest to the main room, got to the door seconds before Brendan.

Mike had seen the brothers' cars still in the lot. He was more than anxious to bring them good news. As soon as Corbin opened the door, Mike stepped in and blurted, "Bingo . . . found the girls . . . Lookin' for an old silver Corolla with Jersey plates . . . McCauley, Mississippi at a place called the Bryce Center 182-184 Cypress Street." Brendan didn't have a chance to signal Mike to silence him. Mike had figured this was the news Brendan and his brother had been waiting for.

Brendan stood stunned as a deer caught in headlights. He had the news he had been praying for. He just hadn't counted on Corbin hearing it. His momentary paralysis was broken by hugs from both Corbin and Mike.

Naturally, Corbin had the mental imprint of the address secured in his head. Corbin, putting on a show for Mike, pulled Brendan close to him and hugged him tightly again. He placed his hand behind Brendan's head and coaxed Brendan's face close to his until their cheeks came in contact with each other. "I am so happy for you, brother . . . so happy," continued Corbin with his charade. Brendan felt the instant disdain that filled his being, but he did not pull away from Corbin. Corbin let go of Brendan and then hugged Mike. He shook Mike's hand and said, "Thank you. Thank you, Mike. You've given Brendan the hope he needed." With that, Corbin went back into his office, shut the lights, and, before he left, said, "I'll leave you two to discuss things. Listen, Bren, you let me know what you need. Call me with whatever you need me to do. I'm here for you."

Mike put his arm around Brendan. "You okay?"

Brendan's mind was spun with all sorts of concerns, but he just turned to Mike and hugged him again. "Thank you. Thank you. I'm just overwhelmed . . . What do we do? What's the next step?" asked Brendan. He contemplated telling Mike the whole truth. Brendan knew that Corbin would be on his way to locate Vita.

Mike broke Brendan's train of thought. "I'm gonna book you a flight to Jackson, Mississippi. From there, it is about a one-and-a-half-hour drive to McCauley. Do you want me to come?" asked Mike.

Brendan, still confused as of what to do, said, "Yeah, Mike . . . I'm . . . I'm just trying to gather myself here, but yes . . . I would like you to come. Can you book the flights and the rental car? See if there are any flights tonight. I'll pay whatever." Brendan reached for his wallet and pulled out a credit card and handed it to Mike.

"I'll do that right now, Bren. Which phone can I use?"

Meanwhile, Corbin, who had friends in the right places, managed to get a hold of one of his rich pals who owed Corbin a favor. This guy happened to own and pilot a private jet. Corbin informed this acquaintance only that he had to be in Mississippi tonight and that it was an emergent situation that he was not at liberty to discuss. His friend assumed it had to do with a legal case and confidentiality that surrounded such an issue and did not question it. Besides, Corbin had the cash upfront to pay for the fuel and the pilot's time. The pilot told Corbin to meet him in one hour at Morristown Airport, a small airport in northern Jersey, where the private jet was kept.

Mike got off the phone. "Flight leaves outta Newark at nine fifty-five in the evening. It's not a direct, but it's the best we can do. That leaves us about two hours to get our stuff together and get there."

Brendan was frantic as he shut the lights and began to lock up. He realized that he would have to call Linda. He figured that neither he nor Corbin would be back in the office until Monday or Tuesday.

Mike told Brendan he would meet him back at Brendan's house. "I'm gonna run home and throw a few things in a duffle bag and call my older boy to see if he could stay in my condo and take care of Lady. We can take my car to the airport." Brendan was good with that plan.

As soon as Brendan got through the front door of his house, he went to the phone in the kitchen. He had taken Linda's home number with him from the office. "Hi, Linda . . . this is Brendan. I need your help. I really need your help."

Linda could sense the urgency in Brendan's voice. "What is it, Brendan? Are you okay? Tell me what I can do for you," she said with concern.

"Has Corbin called you?" Brendan asked.

Linda replied, "No."

"There has been an emergency. I can't go into it right now, but neither I nor Corbin will be in the office until at least Monday. Can you cancel and move our appointments and cases that are on for tomorrow and Friday? I am so sorry to have to ask you to do this."

Linda knew Brendan never made any demands. He sounded so desperate. She replied, "Brendan, I will go in early, and I will take care of everything. Please don't worry. You and Corbin do whatever it is that you have to do."

"Linda, I don't know how to thank you. Please give our apologies to all we have inconvenienced."

Linda told Brendan once more that she would handle it. "Be safe. Please, you and Corbin, be safe," pleaded Linda.

Chapter 35

BY THE TIME MIKE HAD pulled into Brendan's driveway, Brendan was ready with a packed duffle bag, which he threw in the back seat of the car alongside Mike's.

"We're doin' good on time. We should be at the airport in a half hour, which still gives us an hour before the flight leaves," said Mike.

Brendan wondered if Corbin would be on the same flight. But then again, he knew that Corbin had a friend who owned and piloted a Lear jet. He knew there was a good chance Corbin, with his persuasive powers, had gotten this person to fly him to Mississippi.

Mike informed Brendan he had reserved a room at a hotel on the highway a few miles from McCauley. Brendan's mind was apparently elsewhere as there was no response to Mike's comment. "Bren, did you hear what I just said?" asked Mike with concern.

"Uh . . . no, Mike . . . I'm sorry. I don't mean to be rude, man, but I guess I'm just anxious, ya know," said Brendan. Mike repeated to Brendan that he had booked them a hotel.

The early evening sky still had some light at this time of year. Not much was said for the next ten minutes or so. As Mike drove, he sensed the nervousness in Brendan. This was not the normal nervousness that would perhaps accompany the excitement of seeing his family but a disturbed and worrisome nervousness. "Bren, what's up with you? Something goin' on? You're not right . . . I'm just sayin'."

It was then that Brendan made the decision to let Mike in on the whole truth. "Mike, there is probably not going to be a good time and place to tell you this." And then Brendan proceeded to spill the horrid truth of Vita's pregnancy.

Mike had to pull the car over to the shoulder of the highway. He was visibly shaken. "I don't know what to say. I am so sorry. Why didn't you tell me?" said a teary-eyed Mike as he placed his hand on his friend's shoulder.

"How could I, Mike? What would you do if you were in my shoes?" asked Brendan.

Mike understood. He pulled back onto the highway as they were only minutes from the airport. "I don't know what to say. I can't believe it, ya know? Corbin? How could it be?" said Mike, thinking aloud. Mike continued, "They are your flesh. How could he?"

"Mike, I'm all cried out. It's been nothing short of hell. I'm numb. I've just been numb," said Brendan. There was a pause before Brendan added the fact that he had roughed Corbin up a bit and on more than one occasion. Brendan promised to fill in the details once they were checked in and at the gate.

Sure enough, there was no sign of Corbin at the gate. This was the only flight out of Newark this evening to Jackson, Mississippi. "He's already in the air. I am sure of it. He has an acquaintance who owns and pilots a small jet out of Morristown Airport," said a down-trodden Brendan.

"Listen, buddy, we'll get there. What could Corbin do even if he arrives there by ten tonight," commented Mike.

"God, I hope you are right, Mike. I hope you're right," lamented Brendan. Brendan then went on to fill in whatever detail Mike wanted to know about.

The nine fifty-five-in-the-evening flight left on time. Once in the air, Mike ordered three shots of Jack Daniels. "Drink up, buddy. You're gonna need a few of these to take some edge off," said Mike. Brendan said nothing as he downed the two shots Mike placed in front of him while Mike took care of the third shot.

No sooner had Brendan fallen asleep when he heard Mike's voice awakening him to inform him that they had landed in Charlotte, North Carolina, and had to change planes for the connecting flight to Jackson. The two men each pulled their duffle bags down from the overhead bin. The connecting flight would leave in one hour from the next gate over from where their plane had pulled in.

Brendan's agitation was obvious. He kept shifting in his seat and then getting up to walk around the waiting area, only to sit back down and repeat the whole process a few minutes later. "I'm going to the restroom to throw some cold water on my face," Brendan told Mike. Mike felt for his friend. He could not imagine the internal strife that Brendan had been enduring.

As Brendan returned from the restroom, a crackling of the public announcement system was followed by the announcement that the flight to Jackson, Mississippi, would begin the boarding process momentarily. The plane, a 737, was half empty. It was already midnight, but it would still be midnight by the time they would land in Jackson with the time change.

Something about taxiing down the runway on this flight that would connect him to his family triggered an emotional upheaval within Brendan. Brendan tried his best to quell his overwhelming emotions, but his attempt was unsuccessful. Mike heard the muffled sobs as his friend's shoulders shook. Brendan buried his face in his hands. He felt Mike's hand rest upon his back. "I didn't want to do this. Not here," sobbed Brendan.

"It's okay, buddy. It's okay to let it out. You've been holding all this in for all of this time. Just let it out, bud. You're gonna be with your family shortly, and everything will turn out all right," said Mike as he rubbed Brendan's shoulder.

Brendan wiped his eyes of any evidence of his upset. Mike pushed the call button to summon the stewardess over. "Can we get two beers please?"

***

As the two men exited the airport to await the shuttle bus to the car rental facility, they were met with a wall of dense, moist, and stagnant hot air. Brendan wondered how Carmen and Vita tolerated the unbearable humidity, especially Vita.

The cool air on the shuttle bus was a welcome relief. Once into the rental car, Mike, who was driving, cranked up the air-conditioning to high. "Full blast, baby . . . Let's go!" The only illumination on the desolate highway came from the headlights of their car. Once in a while, a tractor trailer would pass them going in the opposite direction. "Listen, buddy, just lean your head back and try to relax. We should be at the hotel in an hour or so. We can try to get a few hours shut-eye once we get in, ya know. I think the best thing is to plan on getting to the Bryce Center in McCauley by six o'clock in the morning and drive around the place to look for that Toyota . . . if that is where they are staying."

Brendan, his head leaning back on the headrest, turned his head toward Mike. "Don't know if I can fall asleep. My mind is in a thousand places . . . Just don't know what in God's name to expect."

"I know, buddy. I know. Just try . . . just try," said Mike.

"Mike, I can't help but wonder where Corbin is now. What does he think he is going to do? I can't let him get to Vita," said Brendan.

"You think he would try to harm Vita?" asked Mike.

"Mike, I don't know . . . I just don't know anymore, but I can't trust that he won't."

***

Streams of beads of sweat ran down Corbin's face, neck, and back even though the car's air-conditioning was on the coldest setting possible. Corbin picked up one of the two towels he had taken from the airport hotel to wipe his brow. The other towel was used to cover the small revolver that rested on the passenger seat. The tip of the gun's barrel peeked out and pointed toward the passenger door. Having driven around the Bryce Center earlier to see that the Toyota in question was not in the parking lot, he had become increasingly frustrated as he drove up and down the nearby streets looking for the silver Corolla with the Jersey plates. He decided to park on the same side of the street as the center but a half a block away. From here, Corbin was able to see the front entrance of both houses of the center and also the entrance to the parking lot on the side street. It was almost six o'clock in the morning and already bright. Corbin opened the newspaper and made as if he was reading. He touched the bottom part of his water bottle to his forehead. The bottle was still cool enough to give momentary relief. Corbin was prepared to wait for as long as it took. He assumed that Carmen was not living at the center but that perhaps Vita would be. He was however counting on the fact that Vita would never want to be apart from her dog so that it was very possible Vita was staying with Carmen, in which case they would be showing up at the center. Corbin was also on the lookout for his brother. Certainly, Brendan would have taken the next available flight, but it was Corbin's hope that there hadn't been any flight until the morning.

***

Amazingly enough, both Brendan and Mike managed to get an hour of sleep. They had talked for a good hour once they were in the hotel room. Brendan was able to let loose with the tumultuous emotions, and Mike was there to lend an ear to his friend. Mike reassured Brendan that they would find Vita before Corbin would. Perhaps that was what allowed Brendan to relax enough to get some sleep.

Brendan sat shotgun with a local map on his lap that they had gotten from the hotel lobby. They too had driven into the Bryce Center parking lot, but there was no evidence of a silver Toyota Corolla with Jersey plates. Mike had traversed as many streets as possible with still no sighting of the car. They even had unknowingly driven past Seraphina's house, but her driveway was narrow, and Carmen's car was parked in front of Seraphina's car. Mike peered at his watch. "Bren, let's head back to Bryce. It's almost six fifteen." Brendan agreed.

Mike parked on the corner across the street from the Bryce Center. Brendan's heart pounded. From here, they could also see the driveway and the back parking lot on the side street. Both men simultaneously had the hunch that the car a half block ahead and across the street was occupied by Corbin. "That's got to be him," said Brendan, leaning forward, his head close to the windshield.

"Affirmative," said Mike.

"What should we do?" asked Brendan. Before Mike could respond, Brendan answered his own question. "I should go talk with him. He and I want the same thing . . . for Vita not to have this baby. He needs to let me handle this," said Brendan.

Mike rested his hand upon Brendan's shoulder. "Hold up, buddy. Are you sure you want to do that? Why don't we sit here and wait a bit . . . Think it over. We're not even sure it's him," advised Mike.

Brendan, getting anxious by the moment, said, "Oh . . . it's Corbin. I can feel it." He paused and then agreed with Mike to sit and watch for a short time. "Not too long, Mike. I just don't trust him!"

Mike pointed out the fact that they were in close proximity to the front of the center and that the car Corbin was suspected to be in was equidistant to the back parking lot as they were. Mike suggested waiting until Carmen and Vita showed. Mike's plan would be to intercept Corbin so that Brendan could get to Vita and Carmen first.

Corbin, immediately aware of the compact white Ford parked across the street from the center, lowered the newspaper enough to peer over it. He could make out the silhouette of two persons and knew in his gut that Brendan was one of them. He wondered how Brendan was able to find a flight to get here within such a short span of time. Corbin glanced down at the passenger seat and covered the exposed tip of the gun's barrel with the towel.

It was obvious that there was a shift change as the time approached seven o'clock in the morning. Several cars pulled into the center's parking lot, however none fitting the description desired by the Malloy brothers. Four cars left the lot between seven five and seven fifteen. Anxiety and impatience tugged away at Brendan. "Listen, Mike, I have got to talk with Corbin. No telling what he might do if we wait for Vita and Carmen to show."

"Okay, buddy. You know your brother. You do what you feel you have to do. Just be careful, huh. I got your back," said Mike.

"Thanks and thanks," said Brendan as he exited the car.

Brendan tried to squash the uneasy feeling as he approached the car in which Corbin sat. Brendan heard the motor running, and he knew Corbin's eyes were upon him. Corbin grabbed the pistol, wrapped it in the towel, and quickly stashed it under the seat. Seconds later, there was a knock on the driver's side window.

Corbin lowered the window. "I was expecting you," he said in a cynical tone.

Brendan spoke firmly, "Door unlocked? Let me in." He went around the front of the car as Corbin reached across the passenger seat to thrust open the door for his brother. Meanwhile, Mike kept an eye on the car with the two men.

Corbin's and Brendan's eyes met in an apprehensive cold stare. Brendan spoke first, "Look, I'm going to cut to the chase. We both want the same thing. Bottom line . . . Vita cannot have that baby." Corbin said nothing. He turned his head away from Brendan and looked straight ahead at the Bryce Center. Brendan continued, "I will handle this. You have no business here. I don't want you around my family. I don't want you in our lives. Leave now! I will handle this!"

Corbin, with his hands rested on the steering wheel, gazed ahead. He finally responded, "Why should I? You failed twice at getting your daughter to have the abortion."

"I said I will take care of it!" replied Brendan emphatically. "And I want to know what your plans were here today!"

Corbin wore a smug look accompanied by a half grin and said in a most sadistic tone, "I was just going to put a scare into your daughter and your wife. I was not going to hurt them if that is what you were thinking. I was only going to talk with them. You know I can be very convincing. That's what I do best . . . better than you could ever do."

Brendan felt his blood boil. "You disgust me, Corbin. You disgust me. I'm not done with you," said Brendan.

Corbin acted as if he hadn't heard a word. Corbin turned off the ignition to give the air-conditioning a break and then put down the windows. "I could never live down here. Seven thirty in the morning and it already feels like a sauna," said Corbin nonchalantly. He took a swig from his water bottle and then held it in front of Brendan's face. "Thirsty?" Brendan turned his head away. Corbin continued to speak, "How about Mike? He thirsty? I got a case of water in the trunk." Brendan did not know this dark and cruel stranger next to him. "So you have Mike with you to hold your hand, huh? Or is he here to arrest me?" prodded Corbin.

Brendan could not bear being in his brother's presence another moment. He opened the car door and got out. Lowering his head to the level of the open passenger window, Brendan spoke one more time to his brother, "Leave! Leave now!" Corbin simply ignored Brendan. Mike observed Brendan crossing back to his side of the street to head back toward their car.

***

Carmen left for the center when Seraphina had. She was asked to come in earlier to help set up for a guest speaker. The silver Toyota Corolla turned onto Cypress Street. Vita couldn't wait to show her friends the pretty lavender leather pocketbook from her grandmother. She ran her fingers over the soft leather. "So soft and smells so good," commented Vita to her mother.

"You know Grandma . . . only the best for her granddaughter," said Carmen, smiling.

"Mom, can you let me off in the usual?' asked Vita.

Most of the time, Carmen would drop Vita off on Cypress Street before making the right-hand turn on the side street to park in the parking lot, and Vita would cross the side street and go into the front entrance of the Bryce Center, which sat on a corner. Carmen could see Seraphina's car make the right-hand turn two blocks ahead of her. "I'll pull over here, just after that car," said Carmen as she approached the corner. It was the car in which Corbin sat. What happened in the next few minutes was something only Mike would be able to recall.

Corbin immediately homed in on the silver Corolla that had pulled in front of him. It had the familiar pale-yellow New Jersey plates with the black lettering. Brendan was already on the other side of the street with his back to Corbin's car. He continued to walk toward the car where Mike sat. In one swift move, Corbin grabbed the edge of the towel underneath his seat, which allowed the gun to roll out of it and into his hand as he exited the car.

Mike flung open his car door and screamed out to Brendan at the same time Corbin yelled out to Vita. Vita turned around in total shock to see her uncle coming toward her. She could see the partially concealed gun in his hand. "I'm not going to hurt you. Just listen and follow," said Corbin. Carmen was out of the car in an instant and ran to where Vita stood frozen.

"He has a gun, Mommy! He has a gun!" screamed Vita.

Carmen quickly shielded Vita and then pushed her toward the center. "Run! Run and get inside!" Vita ran across the side street toward the center. Brendan and Mike ran down Cypress Street but were unable to cross due to the passing cars. They had no idea Corbin was wielding a gun. Brendan yelled for Vita. Carmen could see and hear Brendan and Mike just as Corbin grabbed her wrist to hold her captive. Carmen twisted violently and managed to free herself. Her quick movements threw her off balance and caused her to step backward onto Cypress Street. It appeared to Brendan and Mike that Corbin may have pushed her; however, that was not the case.

There was a screeching of brakes and the awful sound of the loud thump of the impact of a body on a car grill. Carmen's limp body lay motionless in the street, her limbs contorted in an unnatural manner. She felt nothing. She saw nothing. She only heard ringing and buzzing sounds and voices.

Brendan got to his daughter.

"Mommy! Mommy! Mommy!" screamed Vita. Brendan held Vita tightly and tried to prevent Vita from seeing her mother lying and bleeding in the street. Mike attempted to tackle Corbin but not before Corbin was able to aim the gun to his own torso and pull the trigger. Mike caught Corbin as he fell to the ground and then lowered him onto the sidewalk.

Seraphina heard the commotion as she got out of her car in the parking lot. She ran to the corner. Mary and a few others had come out from the center. Seraphina yelled to them to call for several ambulances. She saw Carmen's broken body lying in the street. And then there was Vita crying hysterically while in the arms of a man. There was also a man knelt down on the sidewalk, who held another man who was covered in blood.

Seraphina ran over to Carmen as Mary took Vita from Brendan. Seraphina and Brendan knelt over Carmen. Brendan cried as he stroked Carmen. "My Carmen . . . please . . . please, Lord, please save my Carmen."

Seraphina held Carmen's hand. She placed her other hand on Brendan's shoulder. "Ambulances are on the way. You are Vita's father. My name is Seraphina. Carmen and Vita have been living with me. I'm one of the nurses here. I love Carmen and Vita too."

As Brendan wept, he heard Mike desperately calling his name. Mike was kneeling on the sidewalk, cradling a dying Corbin. Flashbacks flooded into Mike's head of how he held his dying partner in his arms. Corbin was in and out of consciousness. He barely got out a whisper, "Brendan, Brendan, please . . ." Corbin's shirt was soaked in blood. Blood trickled from the corner of his mouth. Brendan got over to Mike. Mike gently moved Corbin's heavy body onto Brendan. "Brendan, is that you?" whispered Corbin, struggling to get his words out.

Brendan held his brother. "Yes. Yes. I'm here. I'm here, Corbin." His brother was dying. His wife was dying. He wanted to tell Corbin that he loved him. He wanted to be by his wife. He wanted to comfort his daughter. The three people closest to him were failing.

Corbin managed a few more words. He whispered each word between his labored breaths. Brendan placed his ear near Corbin's bloodied mouth. "I'm sorry . . . so sorry . . . so sorry, my brother. I didn't . . . want . . . to do it . . . Couldn't help myself . . . In my drawer . . . look in my drawer . . . I love . . ." With that, Corbin's body went limp in Brendan's arms with the last exhaled breath.

More tears flooded to Brendan's eyes as he mouthed the words, "I did love you." And he then added, "I do love you." Mike placed two fingers onto Corbin's bloodstained neck to feel for a carotid pulse.

"He's gone," said Mike.

"We need help here! We need help!" came Mary's voice. Vita was doubled over in pain.

As Seraphina left Carmen's side, Brendan returned to kneel alongside his wife. He held her hand and stroked her hair. "I'm right here, honey. Vita's right here. You are going to be all right. You are going to be all right," Brendan cried. He desperately wanted to believe his words.

Seraphina went over to where Mary was huddled over Vita, who was sat hunched over on the center's steps. "She's in labor," said Seraphina.

Two ambulances and two police cars emerged onto the scene. Mike showed his badge to the four police officers. "Look, I am with him," Mike pointed to Brendan. "He needs to go with his wife. She may not make it. I saw the whole thing. I know the background of the situation. I will give you a statement. Just one moment." Mike went over to where Brendan stood as the EMTs put a backboard under Carmen and a neck brace. The EMTs worked quickly to stabilize her.

Seraphina came down from the center steps and walked over to Brendan. "I will meet you at the hospital. Vita appears to be in labor. I will be with Vita in the other ambulance."

Mike put his arm around Brendan. He walked Brendan over to the center's steps.

Brendan saw Vita grimacing with pain as she held her abdomen. He hugged her and kissed her. "I will be with Mommy. I have to go with her in the ambulance. Seraphina is going to be with you in the other ambulance. Daddy will see you at the hospital. Okay, sweet pea. I love you more than anything. You know that. I need you to be brave." He hugged and kissed his daughter and then hugged Seraphina.

Mike then escorted Brendan into the ambulance as Carmen was being loaded into the back of the ambulance. Brendan rode in the front seat with the driver as the medics worked to keep Carmen alive. A stretcher was brought to where Vita sat. The two EMTs helped Vita to her feet and had her sit onto the stretcher before they assisted her in lying down. She was strapped in but asked if she could keep her knees bent up. That position afforded her some relief. "Where's Mom? Where's my mom?" she cried.

Seraphina held Vita's hand as she was being wheeled to the waiting ambulance. "Your mommy is on her way to the hospital. Your daddy is with her. She will get the help she needs." Seraphina got into the back of the ambulance with Vita so as to assist in the delivery should the baby be born on the way.

"I'm scared! I'm scared!" Vita repeated before another contraction forced her to scream in pain.

"I'm right here. I am right here. I will be with you. I am not leaving you. You squeeze my hand as tight as you have to . . . You hear me?" said Seraphina.

As the second ambulance left, a coroner's wagon pulled up to remove the body of Corbin Malloy. Mike and several other witnesses, which included the distraught driver of the vehicle that hit Carmen, stayed with the police to give their accounts. Mike's plan was then to go to where Corbin's body was to be taken.

Chapter 36

"Now listen to me, dear heart," said Seraphina as the ambulance sped to the hospital, "you remember what we went over in class. Now you push when you feel the urge to push, and you push as hard as you can, you hear?"

"Okay! Okay! I will! But it hurts!" cried Vita as another contraction came.

Seraphina informed the medics that the baby was only twenty-eight weeks gestation. She persuaded the EMTs to allow her to deliver the baby as she had plenty of experience should they not get to the delivery room in time. Seraphina gloved up to check how far Vita was dilated as she urged Vita to breathe like the girls in the class were taught. "Now, dear heart, you are going to feel my hands down by your private parts just like when the doctor checks you."

"Okay," Vita said meekly.

"Yes, indeed. She is dilated to seven centimeters!"

The ambulance arrived at the hospital emergency room in eight minutes. No baby yet. Seraphina raced alongside Vita's stretcher as they were ushered into labor and delivery. There, Vita was made comfortable as she was given an epidural to ease the pain. She heard one of the nurses claim, "Nine centimeters! We are off to the delivery room."

Vita had been brought to a special delivery room equipped for difficult births. She heard the doctor say, "This baby is almost three months premature." It was the voice of a male doctor, but Vita did not concern herself with that.

Seraphina remained by Vita's side. She held her hand and coached and reassured her. "You can do this. I know you can. You are a strong young lady. Push, honey . . . push like you've never pushed before! I want to tell your mom and dad how strong you are! C'mon, baby, you can do it!"

"Okay, one more push," said the doctor. It did not take much of a push. Vita felt something warm move through her private area. And then the doctor said, "Here she is!" The doctor held up the tiny baby. It didn't even look like a baby. It was so small, wet, bloody, and even hairy. "We will clean her up, give her a good checkup, and bring her over to you in a little while. She is very tiny, so she will need a special bassinet," said the doctor. The staff whisked the tiny newborn away. She needed immediate attention.

"You did wonderfully. Would you like to see the baby? That is up to you," said Seraphina to Vita as she gently brushed wisps of Vita's hair away from her face.

"Yes. I do. I do want to see her," said Vita courageously. Seraphina let the staff know that this was an adoption situation but that Vita did want to see the baby.

Within a half an hour, a nurse rolled the incubator that held the tiny neonate. The baby girl was so small Vita thought she could fit into one of her shoes. It was hard to see the little newborn as she had wires taped to her to monitor her vital signs.

"Why is she in this thing?" questioned Vita.

"It's called an incubator. She is very small and was born earlier than expected, so this incubator keeps her warm and safe from germs until she can get bigger and stronger. We can keep a close eye on her heart and breathing. She will have to be fed in a special way too," explained the nurse. One of the other nurses brought the back of Vita's stretcher up so she could peer into the incubator.

"Can I touch her?" asked Vita.

"Yes, we can do that. First, I need to wash your hands and forearms and then put this gown and then gloves on you."

As the nurse prepared Vita with the necessary precautions, Vita stared at the little face. "Her eyes are so big and dark blue. And what is that purple thing on the side of her face?" asked Vita.

"Well, Vita, that is a birthmark. They are called port-wine stains, but it is a type of beauty mark, is all," replied Seraphina.

"Oh," said Vita. Then she added, "But doesn't it look like a little angel? Look, Seraphina, it has the shape of an angel! See, there are the wings."

Seraphina agreed, "Yes. I see what you see. God has placed a little angel on this angel's face."

"And God made her beautiful just like I had prayed," said Vita.

"Yes, he did. And God made you brave just like I and your mom prayed," said Seraphina.

"Where is Mom now? Is she going to be all right?" asked Vita with urgency. Just then, the nurse told Vita she could put her hand through one of the holes in the incubator. She was quickly distracted as the tiny hand of the baby girl gripped one of Vita's gloved fingers. Astonished, Vita exclaimed, "Look, Seraphina! She is holding my finger! She has my finger! Wow!"

"She looks like she has a good grip too. She's gonna be a fighter. You know it!" said Seraphina with a smile.

The nurse who had brought the incubator over then told Vita that she had to take the baby to a special unit called the NICU—neonatal intensive care unit—so that the newborn, almost twelve weeks premature, could be properly cared for. Vita wanted to know if she could see the baby again. The nurse let her know that once Vita was settled in her room, she would be able to go and see the baby in the NICU.

Vita's mind quickly reverted back to her mother. "Where is my mom? Please tell me she is going to be all right! I want to see her!" exclaimed Vita.

"Your mom is in the operating room right here in this hospital. The doctors are helping her right now as we speak," said one of the doctors who was aware that the motor vehicle victim just brought in was Vita's mother.

"I pray that God can get my mom better. That is all I want now." Seraphina kissed the top of Vita's head. "I want my mom to see the baby." Seraphina reassured Vita that she would try to make that happen. She explained to Vita how the baby would have to remain in the hospital for some time in the special neonate unit until she was healthy enough to be with her new family. She told Vita it was possible that the baby would have to be transferred to another hospital that had more specialized neonatal care for a baby this premature. Given her young age, Vita was brought to a private room on the maternity floor.

Brendan sat in a waiting room outside the operating room suite. He was summoned by one of the female resident doctors. Carmen had been in the operating room for over two hours. "Why don't you come with me. Your wife will be in surgery for several more hours. She not only sustained internal injuries but also a broken back and head trauma. The doctors are making progress. Your daughter is resting in a room on our maternity floor. I can take you to her." Brendan, still numb with shock, began to connect the dots of what the young doctor had said to him—that his daughter was on the maternity floor. *Had the baby survived?* he wondered.

He followed the young lady in scrubs to another floor in the hospital. When they stepped off the elevator, she pointed down the hall. "Your daughter is in a private room, room 20, which is at the end of the hallway on the right." Brendan thanked the doctor. She promised him that someone would come up to give him the information concerning Carmen's condition. Brendan thanked the resident once more.

Vita smiled when her father walked in. No words were said. They hugged each other tightly and sobbed. He then hugged Seraphina. Brendan sat down on Vita's bed facing her. He held her hand. "Mommy is still in the operating room. It's going to be a few more hours. She was hurt badly."

"Please, Daddy, tell me . . . is she going to be all right?"

Brendan's eyes were red and swollen. "She is a fighter, Vita . . . like you are. She will make it." He kept his daughter's dainty hands in his hands. He turned toward Seraphina. "The baby?"

Before Brendan could say anything else, Seraphina told Brendan that Vita had indeed given birth to a girl as soon as they had arrived at the hospital. "You have a strong and courageous daughter and a strong and courageous wife. They are two of the most amazing people I know." Brendan was not sure if Seraphina knew the whole story of Vita's pregnancy but assumed she did.

"Do you want to see the baby?" asked Vita. Brendan was shocked his daughter would ask him such a question and with such a tone of pride in her voice. He searched for an answer. Vita added, "She has to stay in the hospital for a while because she is so tiny. I want to see her again. And I want Mommy to see her before she goes with her new family."

Brendan thought if his daughter was strong enough to see the baby, then he would have to muster the strength and nerve to see the child. "Okay, sweet pea." For Brendan knew how difficult it would be to look upon this infant. This infant that was his grandchild, his niece, his brother's daughter, his daughter's child . . . How could this be? The complicated relations swirled in his head.

Seraphina knew that the adoptive parents would need to be notified and that the final paperwork would have to be drawn up. She knew how essential it was for the adoptive parents to bond with the baby as soon as possible. Seraphina excused herself to make the phone call to the Bryce Center to let them know of the status of Vita and Carmen and to get the adoption process moving. The prospective parents would have to be told that the child was very early and that there were likely to be issues associated with the child's development. Seraphina also went to the gift shop to purchase a disposable camera. She thought she would take pictures of the baby, knowing that Carmen, should she survive, would not be well enough to see the baby in time.

"I'm scared, I'm scared about Mommy," Vita cried to her father.

Brendan, still holding Vita's hands said, "I know. I know you are. I am too. But like you heard Seraphina say . . . your mom is a fighter . . . strong. You take after her, you know? We will pray."

Vita closed her eyes when she saw her father do so. Together, they prayed for Carmen. Praying is something that Brendan did often these days—something Vita had not seen her father do.

After they prayed, Vita said, "I'm afraid Uncle Corbin is going to come here and hurt the baby, and then he is going to find Chaz and hurt him too."

Brendan realized that Vita was unaware of what had happened to Corbin. Brendan did his best to hold back his tears. "Vita, you didn't see what happened to Uncle Corbin, did you?" Vita shook her head. Brendan continued, "Uncle Corbin took his own life. He is dead. He will never hurt you again."

"What? How?" Vita wanted to know. It was evident that with the shock of seeing her mother's crumbled body lying in the street and the sudden onset of the excruciating labor pains, Vita had not been aware of the sound of the gunshot nor had she seen Corbin's bloodied body.

"Let's leave that for now, Vita." Brendan quickly changed the subject. "And Chaz? Where is Chaz?"

Vita told her father that Chaz was at Seraphina's house and how Seraphina had invited her, her mom, and Chaz to stay with her. Vita spoke of Seraphina's kindness, generosity, and good heart. "She reminds me of Grandma. I miss Grandma." Vita immediately sat up. "Did you call Grandma? Does Grandma know about Mommy?"

"No. Not yet, Vita. Everything happened so fast. I did not want to alarm your grandmother. I will call her as soon as Seraphina comes back. I was hoping to hear first from one of the doctors how the surgery is going," said Brendan.

These were awkward moments. Much had transpired in the two months since Carmen and Vita had left New Jersey. There were long moments of silence as both Vita and Brendan, still numb with shock, did not know what else to say to each other. Brendan turned on the television in Vita's room out of habit. He flicked through the channels with the remote. He landed on a cable network that showed reruns of some sitcom from the mid-eighties. He lowered the volume so that it was just background noise and barely audible.

Vita eventually spoke again, "Dad, how did you find us?"

Brendan responded, "Vita, that is a long story I do not want to get into now except that Mike . . . Uncle Mike . . . was the one that located you and Mom. I had asked him for his help. I missed you and Mom and, yes, even Chaz every minute of every one of those days."

Vita smiled and said softly, "And we missed you too." Vita and Brendan stared up at and through the television. Vita, exhausted from the childbirth and the emotional upheaval of the tragic events, finally succumbed to sleep. Brendan was just as exhausted. He sat on the lounge chair next to the bed, rested his head back, and dozed off.

Mike had run into Seraphina in the hospital lobby. Seraphina recognized Mike and offered to take him up to Vita's room where Brendan was. They spoke on the way up to the room. Mike had taken care of what needed to be done regarding Corbin's body and the police report. Brendan would have to sign the appropriate papers to have Corbin's body released and flown back north to a funeral home in New Jersey. Seraphina told Mike that the baby had been born. She relayed to Mike what she had been informed. The baby girl would have to be transported to a specialized neonatal unit in the large medical center located in Jackson, which was better equipped to administer care for such a preemie. The adoptive parents would be flying to the medical center to finalize adoption and to bond with their new daughter. It was likely that the baby would have to stay in that NICU for six to eight weeks. "I know how Vita wanted her mother to see this baby, but I'm afraid I'm going to have to let Vita know that's just not goin' to happen," lamented Seraphina. She held the disposable camera that she had purchased in the hospital gift shop. "I already took some pictures of the baby in the unit. Just spoke with one of the nurses, and she told me Carmen is still in surgery and that when she comes out of surgery, she will be heavily sedated for several days. There ain't a chance that she will see this child," said Seraphina.

"I know. I know," said Mike.

Seraphina shook her head. "Brendan hasn't seen the baby yet as far as I know. I've been gone a couple of hours taking care of things, you know."

They stood in the hallway a few doors away from Vita's room. "Brendan is a good person. He's been through a lot . . . well, you know. He loves his wife and daughter more than anything else. And he was close to his brother . . ."—Mike paused—"before all this sh . . . I mean complicated stuff happened," said Mike, catching himself in mid-profanity. "Now his only sibling is gone. C'mon," said Mike as he put his arm around Seraphina as they walked toward Vita's room.

Both Vita and Brendan were awakened as Mike and Seraphina entered the room. Seraphina gently broke the news to Vita that the baby girl Malloy would have to be flown shortly to a large medical center in Jackson, Mississippi, where she would receive the best care for a baby born so early and be able to bond with her new parents.

"But I want Mommy to see her! I want Mommy to see her! Please, Daddy! Please, Seraphina!" exclaimed Vita.

Seraphina held up the camera. "I took lots of pictures, sweetie. Your mommy will get to see her. Don't you worry." Seraphina kissed Vita on her head.

"I want to see her then. I want to see her one last time. Please," pleaded Vita.

Seraphina, who was a known face on the maternity ward and NICU having been there with other young ladies, told Vita she would see what she could do about bringing the incubator into the room. "If not, then we can take a walk and have a look at her in the special nursery where she is."

Brendan held his daughter's hand. "Are you sure you want to do this?"

Vita nodded yes and replied, "And I want you to see her too." Seraphina left the room on her mission.

Brendan sat on the side of Vita's bed while Mike took residence in the lounge chair next to the bed. "Sweet pea, the doctors are doing everything to help Mommy. When she comes out of surgery, she will need a lot of rest," said Brendan as he wondered to himself if Carmen would pull through.

"And she will be given special medicine so that she stays asleep for several days," said Mike.

"Why, Uncle Mike? asked Vita.

"To keep her still so she can begin to heal," answered Mike. There was quiet for several moments before Mike took hold of Vita's and Brendan's hand. "Let's pray." It was Mike who then led them in a decade of the Rosary.

When they were done, Vita added, "Dear God, please, please save my mom." All three had tears in their eyes.

Seraphina had used her charm and familiarity as evidenced by the appearance of the incubator that rolled into Vita's room. "This is the head nurse on the floor, Val, who was so kind to help us out." Seraphina smiled.

"Hello, Val," said Brendan. He stood up and extended a hand to greet the nurse. "Thank you." He looked over at Seraphina and mouthed the same two words to her. Inside the incubator lie a very small person connected to all kinds of contraptions. The heart monitor pulsed with the cadence of the rapid heartbeat. Brendan felt each of those beats in the pit of his stomach. He stared at the baby. Brendan's emotions were numbed by the conflicting thoughts that spun in his head.

"I will tell you that she has a strong heart for one born so prematurely," said Val. Vita sat up and placed her face close to the incubator. The tiny person with her wrinkled purplish skin had a perfectly round head. She weighed in at one pound and fifteen ounces and measured twelve and a half inches in length.

"Can I touch her again like they let me do when I had her?" asked Vita.

Val nodded yes. "So you know the drill, Vita. I am going to ask you to wash your hands with this soap, and then you can put these sterile long gloves on. I will help you," said Val as she held up the packet that contained the gloves. Vita bounded out of bed, apparently forgetting about the condition of her own body.

"Easy there, child . . . Here, grab onto me," said Seraphina. Seraphina steadied Vita as she walked to the bathroom sink and handed her the soap to wash her hands. Seraphina told Vita not to touch anything. Val then demonstrated to Vita how to hold up her hands, like a doctor going into the operating room, and placed the gloves onto her hands and over her forearms. Seraphina guided Vita back to the incubator and reminded her once more, "Now don't touch a thing 'cause these hands of yours are going right into the incubator." Val placed her own hands carefully above each of Vita's elbows and gently assisted Vita with inserting her hands through the holes in the incubator.

"She looks like an alien, and oh . . . that is the tiniest diaper I have ever seen," commented Vita as she brought her hands to the little body. "I can touch her?"

"Very, very gently. Why don't you put your finger by her hand, and with the other hand, you can caress her leg lightly. Babies need touch," said Nurse Val.

Brendan and Mike looked on. Mike sensed the conflicting emotions of his good friend.

Vita's eyes grew to the size of quarters. "Oh my god! She's doing it again! She is holding my finger! Look! Look! She is squeezing it!"

"She got some grip," said Seraphina.

"Yes," giggled Vita. Vita and Seraphina smiled at each other. "Daddy . . . look!" exclaimed Vita.

Brendan stood up and placed his hand atop Vita's shoulder. He kissed her head. He was unable to utter a word. He suddenly felt ill and got up to go into the hallway. Mike followed Brendan. As Mike embraced Brendan outside of Vita's room, Brendan collapsed into Mike's arms. He wept uncontrollably. An alert nurse rushed over to assist Mike in getting Brendan to a nearby vacant room for privacy. After they got Brendan seated onto the bed, Mike quietly thanked the nurse.

She whispered to him, "Call me if you need me," as she pointed to the call button on the bed.

Mike kept his arms around his friend. Brendan leaned heavily into Mike's chest. "It's okay, Bren. You need to let it out. I'm right here for you. Just let it out," said a consoling Mike.

Meanwhile, three rooms away, Vita's daughter held tight on to her mother's finger as Seraphina and Val looked on. Vita matured greatly in these moments with the realization of this life brought forth and with hopes for this little girl to have a blessed future with her new family.

Chapter 37

Two New York Giants plates with oodles of maple syrup on them in one hand and a white blue-edged Corelle plate with barely any syrup on it in the other hand, Vita lowered the dishes into the kitchen sink. One of the New York Giant plates still had a half-eaten waffle stuck to it. She paused at the refrigerator to admire the pictures of her twin five-year-old boys. The photos had been placed in magnetic picture frames with the New York Giants logo. The pictures taken earlier in the school year looked like the same child, except that one of the boys was missing his top two front teeth. Brendan Joseph, called BJ, was the one in the photo with the missing teeth. Anthony Michael, called Tony, had not lost even one of the two front teeth yet. BJ had collected two dollars in January, one dollar per tooth. BJ relentlessly teased his brother that because he lost his teeth first, he was the older one. Tony even tried to wiggle his front teeth loose so he could catch up, but his parents discouraged him from doing so. Vita told him that perhaps the fairy godmother would pay him interest because the teeth remained in his mouth longer. Tony had asked his mother what interest was. Vita explained to him that when a person saved their money in a bank account for a certain amount of time, the bank would pay that person interest, which was more money. This confused Tony somewhat until Vita said it just meant that because Tony kept his teeth longer, maybe the fairy godmother would put a little bit more money under his pillow. So Tony had stopped trying to loosen his top front teeth. And BJ had stopped teasing his brother. BJ was not thrilled with the prospect of his brother receiving this interest for his teeth.

"C'mon, boys! Brush your teeth and don't forget to go pee-pee," said Vita as she returned to the kitchen table. Both blond-headed boys, whose large dark brown eyes that seemed to occupy half their faces, pushed their chairs away from the table. They raced each other to the bathroom. "And wash your hands . . . with soap!" added Vita. Vita and Joe laughed.

Vita's husband, Joseph Daro, could have passed for a New York Giant linebacker himself. The boys had inherited their big brown orbs from their father. Joe carried his coffee mug to the sink. "Listen, honey, Mother's Day is this weekend. Have you thought about something special that you would like to do?" asked Joe as he bent his large six-feet-five-inches frame over to kiss Vita.

"Oh, I don't know. You know I like surprises. Surprise me. How's that?" said Vita whimsically.

Joe let out a devilish laugh accompanied by a devilish grin. "Oh, so you are gonna make it tough on me. Okay . . . I'll ask the boys to come up with a plan." They both laughed as the twins came bounding down the stairs from the bathroom.

Vita took two identical lunch boxes out of the refrigerator, each covered with logos of every NFL team and placed them into the two blue-and-red New York Giants backpacks. Both BJ and Tony were seasoned Giants fans like their dad. The two boys were in the habit of watching ESPN with their father every evening. The twins were fully capable of holding their own in a conversation with any adult sports fanatic. They were quite adept at memorizing the scores of the various sports teams that were reported on ESPN. It happened to be baseball season, so Joe, BJ, and Tony were in the mode of watching the Yankees. Sometimes Grandpa Brendan would come over to catch a game with the Daro clan. Joe even coached his sons' T-ball team.

"Okay, boys! What do you say? Let's go!" said Joe like a drill sergeant.

"Mom, can't we say goodbye to Buster first?" begged Tony.

"Oh gee, whiz. I forgot about Buster, didn't I?" said Vita. She walked over to the sliding glass door in the neighboring family room to let their pet dog in from his romp in the fenced-in backyard. The boys immediately huddled over the pug. Vita had insisted on getting another pug when it had come time to get a family dog. Chaz had lived to the ripe old age of seventeen and had passed away a few months before Vita and Joe were married. "Easy, guys—give Buster a chance to breathe," cautioned Vita. She kissed the two boys after she handed each their backpack. Joe kissed his wife again as he and the boys exited the house. "Have a good day, Joe. Love you! Love you, Tony and Beej!" Vita called out.

"Okay, fellows, let's march out and into the truck," commanded Joe.

"Bye, Mommy!" squealed the boys. Joe would drop the twins off to school each morning in his big work van on his way to his morning plumbing job. Joe had helped his father on plumbing jobs as a teenager and decided that he wanted to carry on the tradition. Yes, it could be a dirty job, but he enjoyed meeting and talking to his customers and found contentment in helping them out. Joe had been part of his father's team for fifteen years. They were a trusted family business. This Wednesday morning like most school mornings, BJ and Tony hopped into the van's front seat. Joe would strap them both in with the one passenger seat belt. The boys felt they were hot stuff getting out of the big white van that read "Daro & Daro Plumbing."

With the house to herself and Buster, Vita turned on the small TV on the kitchen counter as she continued with the post-breakfast cleaning. She opened the window above the kitchen sink and took in the cool fresh air of the sunlit morning. The lavender sheers rippled with the spring breeze. She was sipping from her mug of coffee when a promo came on the television about an upcoming segment on the morning show. "We will return to tell you all about a bright young lady with a most promising future. She is this year's valedictorian of Princeton University and is preparing to graduate Saturday. She is a budding scientist whose research work in her senior year gained her worldwide attention in the area of neuroscience and spinal cord injuries." Vita's interest peaked the instant she saw the image of the young lady wearing a lab coat and working in what appeared to be some sort of a research lab. The image was fleeting but left Vita stunned.

A commercial followed. Vita tried to digest the possibility of seeing what she thought she had seen. The girl in the lab coat with the long brown hair pulled back in a ponytail had what looked like a small port-wine birthmark on the right side of her face.

With her stomach in her throat, Vita dared not take her eyes off the TV as she excitedly waited for the show to return. Vita began to feel faint as the show resumed with a close-up of the two hosts. The one host began the introduction to the segment. "We visited Princeton University last week to speak with the valedictorian of Princeton's 2013 graduating class. Commencement ceremonies will be taking place in three days on Saturday when Angelica Henner will give her speech. Angelica, at age twenty-two, has garnered worldwide attention and commendations for her research work in neuroscience, specifically in the healing of spinal cord injuries. She will be continuing her graduate work at John Hopkins University in the fall. We spoke with Angelica about her work and her achievements. Take a look. I think you will find this fascinating young lady to be quite inspirational." The show segued to the taped interview, first showing the petite young woman in the lab coat looking into a microscope. As the camera panned to a close-up of the young woman's face, Vita felt her body go limp, but she dared not take her focus off the TV. There it was—as clear as clear could be—a port-wine stain in the shape on an angel on the girl's right cheek. And the eyes . . . those eyes were the same shape and color as her own eyes and the same as those of her late grandfather, Anthony. Vita was literally in shock for the next few minutes and missed the details of Angelica Henner's research. Vita recovered enough to hear the important information of where and when the graduation ceremony was to take place.

After the segment ended, Vita sat down at the kitchen table to catch her breath. She stared ahead as if in a deep trance but was in deep thought. Buster, who had been in the kitchen, sensed something in his human companion. He came over to where she sat, stood up on his hindquarters, and placed his two front paws on Vita's lap. Vita flinched as she was awakened from her thoughts. She patted Buster. "Buster, could it be? Buster, I think I know what I want to do for Mother's Day weekend."

Vita tried in earnest to plow through her morning housework but was distracted by her thoughts. She could not wait to tell Joe what she had seen and heard on the television. Like most days, she took Buster for a walk at noontime before running her errands. Vita was on automatic pilot as her mind was focused on the one thing. Vita was driven. She knew by the warm feeling she had in her heart that this petite young woman, Angelica Henner, was the very soul she had carried in her womb almost twenty-three years ago.

***

For the hundredth time, Vita read the twins their favorite bedtime story, *The Cat in the Hat*, as the boys joined in the rhyme that they knew by heart. Vita and Joe kissed their children good night. In the sport-themed blue-and-red bedroom they shared, BJ and Tony curled up, each in their own twin bed. They faced each other. Vita knew the ritual the two boys had nightly of having to have their own chat before drifting into dreamland. She closed the door partly as she and Joe walked out of their room.

Vita had done all she could do to suppress her excitement that afternoon and evening. The twins naturally had kept her occupied once she had picked them up from school. During dinner, she had been bursting at the seams to tell her husband of what she had seen on the television that morning. Now it was time to let out her exuberance. She grasped her husband's hand and led him into their bedroom. Vita faced him as she held both his hands. Her smile was brilliant, and her face glowed.

Joe wasn't quite sure what to think. In a half-excited tone, he asked, "Pregnant?"

Vita, still with a smile as wide as a mile said, "Well, not exactly, but I know what I want to do for Mother's Day." She proceeded to tell Joe about the young woman named Angelica Henner who had appeared on one of the morning shows. Vita told Joe of the port-wine angel-shaped birthmark on the girl's face.

Vita had not thought often of the baby girl she had given birth to and had put up for adoption almost twenty-three years ago. The way she dealt with the past was to sweep that period of her life under the carpet. That was how Vita was able to function even after years of counseling and therapy. What she had though was the peace in her heart and her soul in knowing that she gave life to this child that God had created. Vita had come to understand and witness the agony and emotional suffering those women went through after their abortions. She continued to attend prolife events and spoke with women who were a part of the Silent No More campaign. These were women who had aborted their children ten, twenty, thirty, even forty years earlier and wanted now to voice their message of the internal pain they have endured. Many of the women had been quiet about their abortions but were now speaking out about the guilt, the depression, and the anguish they felt in having taken the life of their own flesh. Vita was pain free in that respect and was thankful that her mother and grandmother had done everything possible for her so that she was spared this sorrow and the baby was spared a tortuous death.

Now that Vita had seen this young accomplished woman on the television, she felt a deep yearning in her heart to see the daughter she had given birth to. She knew that this was the very person that came from her womb. Her heart swelled with goodness and love, which surprised Vita. "You know, Joe, it's strange, but I feel a love for this person. I don't know why I should, but I just do."

Joe could see the wonderment in Vita's eyes. He told his wife he would support her in any way he could. Vita wanted nothing more than to be at the Princeton University graduation on Saturday. Joe immediately called his parents to make babysitting arrangements for Saturday but did not elaborate to his parents as to what their plans were. He would leave that up to Vita for some time in the future.

"Tomorrow, I will call the university and make it my mission, no matter what it takes to get two tickets to that graduation," said a most determined Vita.

"Honey, even if you can get one ticket, that would be more than fortunate. I will take you there and wait in the car for you," said Joe.

Vita, thinking ahead, said, "Joe, do we have some SD cards for the camcorder? Oh, and the camera with the really good zoom . . .

can you show me how to use that? And—" Joe kissed his wife on the cheek.

"Honey, relax and take a few breaths. I will take care of everything for you. I will make sure the batteries are charged and that we take the SD cards with plenty of memory. Tomorrow, I will show you how to use the good camera. Okay?"

Vita exclaimed, "Deal! Deal, honey! I know I will get those tickets! I know I will! I have to!"

"And I know you will too," said Joe. "How about I get us a couple of glasses of wine? I'll be back in a jiff," said Joe.

Joe returned to the bedroom with two glasses of Chilean Merlot. Vita did not hear Joe come back into the room. He could see she was preoccupied, her focus on the worn lined paper she held in her hands. It was obvious the paper had been torn out of a spiral-type notebook. "Whatcha got there, hon?" queried Joe as he set the two wineglasses down onto the night table.

Chapter 38

V ITA'S THUMBS LIGHTLY CARESSED THE top sheet of the limp and somewhat-tattered notebook paper she held in her hands. Her previous jubilant mood turned serious. "I want you to read this, Joe. I have never shown this to you or anyone else for that matter," said Vita earnestly. She handed the papers over to Joe. The notebook papers were frayed and yellowed by age. They bore the deep creases from the many foldings and unfoldings over the past five decades. As an elderly soul, whose furrowed face told the trials of a rough life endured, so these wrinkled pages with the faded blue ink spoke of a story of tragedy.

"My father gave me this after I had graduated college. He waited till then because he did not want me distracted from my studies. That and his hope that I had reached a certain level of maturity and emotional stability by then." Vita took a deep breath. "I don't take this letter out so much anymore. It is something my father's brother, Corbin . . . you know . . . the one who—"

"I know. I know. I know," Joe interrupted as Vita's voice had trailed off.

Vita continued, "My uncle wrote this when he was twelve years old. It's very upsetting and very sad. My father said it had helped him in working toward forgiveness toward his brother. I told you of the day of what happened to my mother and Corbin. As Corbin was dying on the sidewalk with my dad next to him, his last few words were something about 'looking in his dresser drawer.' When my father went through the drawers in the dresser in my uncle's bedroom, he found this note. My dad gave it to me with the hope that I may be able to find some peace through the process of forgiveness."

Joe felt the delicateness of the paper with his fingertips that were toughened by his profession. "Forgiving my uncle Corbin is still an ongoing process, but I have come a long way in part because I know of the tragedy of the sexual abuse my uncle went through. I want you to read this. Go ahead."

Vita sat in silence, her head bent and her hands clasped as if in prayer while Joe spent the next several minutes reading the words written long ago of a troubled twelve-year-old boy. She heard Joe quietly utter, "Oh my god. Oh no. How awful!" as he poured over the letter. Joe solemnly looked up. His teary eyes met Vita's. "I am so sorry. So sorry with what had happened to you and so sorry to know what happened to your uncle Corbin. What happened here snowballed and scarred all your lives," said Joe as he took his time and carefully folded the letter. The limp paper easily fell into the comfort of its worn crevices.

"Did he ever get any help in dealing with this?" asked Joe.

"No. Not that we know of. His own mother, my grandmother, never knew what had happened, but then again from what my dad had told me, she was quite selfish and known to cheat on more than one occasion on my grandfather."

The letter told of Corbin being forced into having sex by a man who was having an affair with Corbin and Brendan's mother. Corbin was eleven years old when the abuse started, and apparently, it went on for several months. He was a frightened and tormented child. This person had threatened to do the same to his younger brother should he mention it to anyone, so Corbin had kept this ugly secret hidden his whole life. What happened to Corbin certainly explained much of his behavior and frequent distantness over the years. "You know, Joe, strange how some of the words that Corbin used to describe his feelings were the very words I had written in my diary," said Vita.

Joe kissed Vita on her cheek. They sat there and hugged each other. "How about that wine now," suggested Vita, so as to break the somberness. Joe picked up the two wineglasses and handed one over to his wife. They held their wine glasses up as Vita toasted, "Here is to scoring two tickets to the graduation at Princeton University." They tapped their glasses together before bringing the wine glasses to their lips.

The wine had done its magic. Vita had a sound and solid night's sleep in her husband's arms. Joe always cherished those times when Vita would sleep cuddled up next to him, his muscular arms encompassing her. It had taken Vita many years of counseling to be able to lie down next to her husband, let alone to feel secure and truly loved. She still dealt with ambiguous feelings when making love with Joe, but Joe understood her anguish as best he could and gave her the space she needed.

Chapter 39

BJ AND TONY WERE RELENTLESS in asking their grandparents, "What are we doing today?" Joe's parents, the Daros, always had some adventure planned for when their twin grandsons came over to spend the day. Joe's parents only knew that their son was taking his wife out as part of her Mother's Day weekend and that Joe would explain later when they would return in the early evening. Ann Daro, Joe's mother, had a delectable breakfast buffet ready to go when Joe, Vita, and the boys arrived in the early morning on that Saturday.

Vita ate very little. "I ate a big dinner last night, Mom, so I'm just going to nibble," said Vita to her mother-in-law who tried to get Vita to *mangia*. Joe and the boys, with their usual hardy appetites, ate till their stomachs were pleasingly full.

"Thought we would take you boys to Newark Airport," said Joe Sr.

"Yay! Goodie! Can we ride the train?" asked the boys simultaneously. The twins often came out with the same response at the same time.

"Of course! You mean the monorail!" responded their grandfather.

"Yeah, the 'norail'!" exclaimed Tony.

"And can we go to McDonald's?" queried BJ.

"Of course," said Grandpa Joe. There was a McDonald's in one of the terminals where the boys had gone before with their grandparents.

BJ and Tony had one more request. Together, they exclaimed, "And the moving sidewalk!"

"We will do it all, right, Grandma?" said Grandpa Joe to which his wife emphatically replied, "Okay!"

BJ and Tony stood with their grandparents on the front walk. They waved and blew kisses to their mom and dad as the car pulled out the driveway. Joe stopped and yelled out the window, "And, Ma, you gotta decide where we are goin' for dinner tonight. Okay? Love you." Joe and Vita were planning on taking his mom and dad, along with the boys, for her Mother's Day dinner.

Ann had two favorite Italian restaurants that she could not make up her mind about. She nodded. "Don't worry. You have a good time! We will see you later." Joe planned on picking up his mom's favorite flowers, yellow tulips, on the way back.

As Joe drove onto the ramp of the interstate to head to Princeton University, Vita opened the sunroof as Joe opened all the windows so that the refreshing air of that beautiful May morning circulated throughout the car. The ponytail that was classic Vita whipped around in circles as the currents of air swept through their SUV. It did not bother Joe or Vita to have to near yell at each other to be heard above the wind tunnel.

"Camcorder, camera, lenses, binoculars—check, check, check, and check!" exclaimed Vita. "I want you to see the angel on her face, Joe. Do you suppose her parents named her Angelica for a reason? What power are those binoculars?" Vita had much to say.

"Don't worry, honey. They have great magnification," replied Joe.

Vita then excitedly repeated the story of the angel-like birthmark on the face of the baby girl she gave birth to almost twenty-three years ago and how she happened to have the television on that channel at that moment when she glanced at the screen to catch that particular feature on that show. Even though Joe had heard about the incredible coincidence several times the past few days, he gladly listened so to share in his wife's excitement.

They arrived an hour later onto the elite campus of Princeton University and drove past the majestic buildings where generations of scholars had honed their intellects. Joe followed the line of cars guided by the campus police into one of the large parking areas. A neon-yellow-clad parking attendant waved and pointed Joe into a parking space.

Vita was visibly nervous as she exited the car. She thought about this child, now a young woman, the product of horrid memories, the very person in her teenage womb, whom she once hated but grew to love after she had seen the baby. How could it be that now she had even more feelings of—call it love—than she did on the day the infant girl was born? Vita knew this young woman, Angelica Henner, was still a part of her no matter what the beginnings were. She wrestled with these feelings as she and Joe followed the crowd toward the seating area on Cannon Green. As they walked, she quietly gave thanks to God for being able to acquire the two tickets. Vita had called the television station and eventually was put in touch with someone who after hearing her story was able to contact the university. Two tickets were mailed special delivery, having arrived the day before.

Joe carried the camera bag with the camcorder while the camera hung around his neck. The binoculars hung from Vita's neck and swayed as she walked hand in hand with her husband. Joe squeezed Vita's hand. He smiled and kissed her as they headed toward Cannon Green.

They settled into their seats. Vita gazed upon the lawn where the graduates would be seated. The rows and rows of folding chairs were neatly arranged in perfectly straight lines. A large crisp orange cloth bow edged with black trim adorned the ends of each row. Joe took the camcorder out and tucked the camera bag under the seat. Vita thumbed through the commencement program, eager to spot the name Angelica Henner. Members of the Princeton University marching band clad in orange plaid tailored blazers and black pants filed into a seating area to the right of the stage. "Here she is! Look, Joe!" Just above Vita's french-manicured fingernail was the name of the valedictorian in a lovely ornate font. Angelica Henner was to give her valedictory address once all the graduating class had received their diplomas.

Vita tried to soak in the reality of where she was and what she was going to witness. She felt as if in a parallel universe. The anticipation was overwhelming but glorious. Part of her felt like an outsider, as if she did not belong there, but another part of her felt a sense of pride and gratitude. She was basking in the euphoria of the moment when the announcement came that the commencement ceremony was about to begin.

Trumpets blared, and then the marching band broke into *Pomp and Circumstance*. The base drum resonated within Vita. She grabbed Joe's hand. Heads turned to see the senior class walking in pairs behind the college dignitaries as they kept in perfect step with the beat of the *Pomp and Circumstance* graduation march. The black gowns with the two vertical bright orange stripes, rippled as flags, as the students processed. The wide black sleeves of the gowns, looking as angel wings, each had three horizontal brilliant orange stripes.

Leading the students was a petite young lady who seemed as a doll in her gown and a very tall young man whose frame did justice to the flowing robe. They each wore a sash that commemorated their status as valedictorian and salutatorian. "Oh my god, Joe! Oh my god! That's her! That's her!" Vita brought the binoculars to her eyes as Joe's steady hands held the camcorder. Vita tried to keep focus on the young woman with the long shiny dark hair exiting out the graduation cap. The brown tresses undulated in the breeze. It was difficult to keep the petite valedictorian in view, but Vita managed to get a close-up of her face. "Oh my, she is beautiful, and see . . . there is the angel. I can see it! Here, Joe, look!"

Joe quickly replied, "Honey, you keep looking. I can see her as I zoom in. Yup, I can see the angel."

Vita basked in those joyous moments as they listened to the keynote speaker. Joe assured his wife that he would see to recording the video. He wanted her to relish in the experience and to take in as much of it as her senses would allow. Vita took several pictures with the camera. Joe would intermittently take the camera from Vita to get some good close-up photos during the time he was not using the camcorder.

It was fun to watch each of the graduates cross the stage as each name was announced. Each was handed a diploma and congratulated by the president and the dean of the university before proceeding on to shake the hands of the other deans and dignitaries on the stage. Some of the girls walked precariously on four-inch stilettos while others had mastered the art of the stride in such high heels. Most of the young men had their unique saunter and strut. One thing for certain was that every one of the young adults maintained decent posture as they crossed the stage, something that must have been emphasized during rehearsal for the ceremony. Cheers and applause rose up from the crowd as proud family members let those around them know who their graduate was. Vita wondered if she should give a loud cheer when Angelica's name was called.

Vita had her binoculars focused on the back of Angelica who sat in the front row of the student body. "All right. Here we go. They are starting the Hs," whispered Vita. Vita was ready. The name Angelica Marie Henner, bachelor of science and the valedictorian of Princeton University's class of 2013, was announced. People applauded loudly. Happy hoots and hollering came from not only the student body but from a group of people seated only a few rows in front of Joe and Vita. A teen boy yelled, "You go, Ange!" Four adults yelled, "Yay, Angie!" Another teenager, a girl, yelled, "Go, sis!"

The binoculars were focused enough to see the wide and beaming smile as Angelica glided gracefully across the stage. Her angel mark was hidden as only the left side of her face was visible. She turned toward the crowd and held the diploma in one hand over her head as she waved to where she heard her family cheering her on. She seemed to exude such confidence. The thought occurred to both Joe and Vita, unbeknownst to each other, that Angelica bore a striking resemblance to Vita, except that Angelica was quite petite, more so than Vita. If they were to stand side by side, surely the connection would be undeniable. Once Angelica returned to her seat, Vita peered over at the group a few rows in front of her. A good feeling—one of warmth, peace, and true satisfaction—swept over Vita. "She grew up with a loving and nice family," surmised Vita. She wondered if the two younger siblings were also adopted or if the Henners adopted Angelica because they were unable to conceive. And as oftentimes happens after adopting a child, a couple suddenly becomes fertile. It's as if the adopted child was meant to be in that family. It took a solid hour for the class of 2013 to receive their diplomas.

According to the lineup in the program, Vita would be giving the valedictory speech shortly. Joe and Vita were geared up and prepared. Joe assured Vita that he had plenty of memory in the camcorder's SD card and the battery life was good. Vita was ready with the binoculars and the thirty-five-millimeter camera with the good lens, both of which hung from her neck.

The president of the university, clad in full regalia, looking every bit a monarch, took his place at the podium. "As president of Princeton University, I—along with our vice president, deans, and distinguished faculty—am honored to introduce to you the valedictorian of Princeton University's class of 2013. She is an incredible young woman with a bright future ahead of her. She will continue with her postgraduate studies in neuroscience at John Hopkins University this fall. She has garnered attention for her research done here on spinal cord injuries, which will be her focus at John Hopkins. I now proudly present to you the valedictorian of Princeton University, Miss Angelica Marie Henner of Norwalk, Connecticut." Joe glanced at his wife. She was beaming with pride. Joe gave her a quick hug and peck on the cheek so he could get back to the business of filming the speech. Cheers and applause ensued along with a loud whistle that emanated from the rows in front of Vita and Joe. Apparently, Angelica's brother was quite adept at producing such a sound with his two fingers stretching out his mouth. Vita knew the happiness, joy, and pride that Angelica's family was experiencing. She thought to herself if only they knew that her proud birth mother was here to experience the same emotions.

The young woman graciously thanked the president before assuming her spot behind the podium. Angelica nodded to the president to let him know that the position he lowered the microphone for her was fine. She confidently surveyed her class and then the crowd. Angelica waited for the applause to silence. Her wide smile was genuine. Angelica brushed away the wisps of hair that had blown across her face. And then Angelica, with a voice sweet and crystal clear, addressed the audience. Her words were spoken with such clarity and enunciation. The crowd listened intently. Vita felt as if in a dream. It was all too surreal—like being transported into some other dimension. A dimension where she hoped that time would stand still.

"This is really happening," Vita whispered to herself as she basked in the glory of these moments. Vita could still see the tiny newborn in the incubator as she listened to Angelica's valedictory speech. The speech drew countless cheers from the graduates as she recounted their four years spent at Princeton University. Suspended in these precious moments, Vita was enveloped with a warmness and sense of fulfillment in her heart.

Chapter 40

Tony and BJ dashed up the walkway and then darted up the ramp seeing who could ring the doorbell first. From the car, Joe unloaded two shopping bags full of takeout food from DelGiorno's Restaurante. Vita struggled with the pocketbook strap while she held a vase containing a brilliant arrangement of Gerber daisies and a shopping bag with two sturdy tulip plants, one bright pink and the other red. "Slow down, boys!" Vita yelled to her sons. Much to their chagrin, the boys were each dressed in navy trousers, dress shoes, a white button-down dress shirt, with a navy-and-dark-red striped tie. It was hard to tell who reached the doorbell first, as they each laid claim to it and were busy pounding on the doorbell with their thumbs.

"Easy, guys! Take it easy! Give Grandpa a chance!" reprimanded Joe.

"I call I get to ride on Grandma's chair first!" exclaimed Tony.

"Aw," retorted BJ, somewhat disappointed.

Vita was right on top of it. "BJ, you went first last time. It's Tony's turn to go first, honey."

"Yeah!" responded Tony victoriously.

One could hear the door being unlocked on the other side. Tony pulled open the screen door as the solid oak door opened. "Hi, Seraphina!" said the boys in unison as they scooted past her rotund figure.

"Hey, you two little tigers. Come back here and give ol' Seraphina a hug and a kiss." Seraphina chuckled. Twenty-two years

366

later and Seraphina, at seventy-two, still looked like Seraphina, with not a wrinkle to be had on her round jovial face. There were a few more pounds to be had; and her hair, which was pulled back tightly into a neat bun, was graying at the temples and along the crown of her hairline.

"Oh yeah," said BJ, and the twins ran back over to Seraphina.

She wrapped her short plump arms around the boys as they threw their arms around her. "You know Seraphina got to give her boys a nice big bear hug." She kissed the top of each of their heads before releasing them.

Seraphina returned to the front door to hold the screen door open for Vita and Joe. "Happy Mother's Day, sweetheart! Oh, let me help you with these," said Seraphina as she kissed Vita on the cheek.

"Well, happy Mother's Day to you too, Seraphina! These pink tulips are for you. And see how they match the pink flowers on your beautiful dress," said Vita.

"Oh, thank you, sweetie! They are gorgeous! You didn't have to do that. I think I'll set them right here for now. You go ahead into the family room where your mom and grandmom are," said Seraphina.

Joe set the two shopping bags down on the floor of the foyer. He hugged Seraphina, "Happy Mother's Day, Seraphina!"

"Oh, thank you Joe, and thank you for the lovely tulips. Something smell real good in those bags."

Just then, Brendan emerged from the family room after he had received an overexuberant greeting from his grandsons. Brendan still retained a youthful, athletic appearance. At age sixty-two, his once sandy blond hair had become interspersed with light gray. He had a few shallow furrows on his forehead along with crow's feet but wore it well, despite the difficulty of the past twenty-three years. He continued to go on his daily jog but now accompanied by his companion golden retriever named Dublin. He presently worked at his law firm three days a week, with his two younger partners holding down the fort. Malloy, Cohen, and Pagliaro, an Irishman, a Jew, and an Italian were quite the United Nations of law offices. Brendan had taken on one partner twenty years ago and the second partner ten years ago. Brendan gave Joe a hardy handshake and pulled him in for a man hug. "How are you, Joe? Here, let me bring these in the kitchen. Mmmm . . . smells Italian."

Joe and Seraphina followed Brendan into the kitchen. "I'm good, Dad. How about you?" asked Joe.

"I'll feel better if the Yanks win today. Three games in a row lost and each by one run. We're leaving a lot of men on base," said Brendan.

"I hear ya," said Joe.

"You boys go into the family room. I'm going to unpack the food and set it up on the counter," said Seraphina.

Joe stood in front of Seraphina so as to block her way to the kitchen counter. "It's Mother's Day. Your turn to relax. I got it," said Joe.

"Well, thank you, honey. I got the dining room table all set and ready to go," said Seraphina.

Brendan and Seraphina entered the family room from the kitchen. After Vita had graduated from college, Brendan and Carmen had downsized to a three-bedroom ranch home with a small fenced-in yard with a lovely patio. Carmen's injuries had been so severe and debilitating that it had taken five months of hospitalization before she was transferred to a rehabilitation facility back in New Jersey. There, she had spent the next six months as an inpatient and had received intensive physical therapy. Brendan had asked Seraphina if she would consider working for him as a live-in nurse after Carmen's release from the facility. After much thought, Seraphina had joined the Malloys after Carmen was discharged from the Jersey facility. Brendan had a construction company recommended by Mike make their previous home wheelchair accessible with two bedrooms on the first floor, one for Carmen and the other for Seraphina. She had been with the Malloys for twenty-one years already. Seraphina had initially rented out her home in Mississippi but eventually sold it. Her son Willie, married for the past twelve years, had taken a job in New York City as a certified public accountant for a large financial firm ten years ago. He and his wife had decided to remain childless. Their true love was to travel to far and away places every opportunity they had. In fact, Willie and his wife were presently on a Mediterranean cruise. It was nice for Seraphina that Willie's condo was less than an hour away and she was able to see him often.

"Look at my three girls here! All lookin' so purty," said Seraphina proudly.

A delicate-looking older woman with a pixie haircut and recently colored dark auburn hair sat slightly hunched in a wheelchair. Her soulful brown eyes spoke volumes as her capacity to articulate was limited as a result of the accident. Dublin, a four-year-old male golden retriever, was lying next to the wheelchair. Carmen, now fifty-nine, was paralyzed from the waist down, but with physical therapy, she had developed enough upper arm strength to be able to transfer herself with assistance from the wheelchair to a bed or couch. Carmen looked very springy in her floral boat-neck chiffon top of yellow, pink, purple, and green on a white background. She wore loose-fitting white Capri pants and light tan Aerosole flats on her feet.

Vita stood stooped over her mother as she held the vase with the boldly colored Gerber daisies. She slowly rotated the vase as Carmen appreciated the beauty of her favorite flowers. Vita wore her form-fitting white Capri pants and a flowing sleeveless yellow tunic top. She had already removed the high heels and stood comfortably barefoot.

Next to Carmen sat her spry eighty-four-year-old mother. Nettie still looked the same all these years later and with the same unbelievable energy. One wondered if it were not for Carmen's accident, would she have the genetic disposition for good health in her later years as did her mother. Nettie kept her short wavy hair a light brown color. She had tried letting herself go all gray but decided that she liked the look of color in her hair—and that did not include being a light-blue-haired elderly church lady. Even as an octogenarian, Nettie was quite self-sufficient and continued to live in the same home in the adult community. She still drove and came over often to visit and help care for her daughter. Once a month, Nettie and Seraphina would take Carmen for a ladies' night out at the church for bingo.

"Grandpa! Grandpa! Look at what Great-grandmom-mom gave us!" exclaimed BJ. Tony and BJ waved their coloring books in the air to show off their new acquisitions along with a sixty-four-count box of new Crayola crayons for each.

"Oh, very nice. Did you boys thank Great-grandmom-mom?" said Brendan.

"Yes, they did," chimed in Nettie.

And out of the mouth of babes, Tony added, "Mommy already told us too."

"Oh, I remember when I was a kid, how excited I was to get that giant box of new Crayola crayons . . . Remember, Mom? It had a sharpener in the back of the box," commented Vita. Carmen nodded. Vita continued, "Nothing like looking at a box of all those brand-new colorful crayons with the perfect points looking back at you ready for their first coloring job."

The boys were lying on their bellies busy coloring next to their grandmother's wheelchair and Dublin the dog. "Look, Dubby likes to watch us color," said BJ.

"And Dublin likes to watch your grandpa color too," added Nettie, referring to Brendan's many paintings.

"Hey, Dad, did you finish the lighthouse painting yet?" queried Vita.

"Still putting the finishing touches on it," answered her father. Brendan's artwork hung throughout the house and also in Joe and Vita's home. In addition, there were family vacation pictures displayed here and there. Every other year, Brendan, Carmen, Nettie, the Daros, and Seraphina would do a family cruise.

"Grandma, when can we get to ride with you on the wheelchair?" asked Tony, also speaking for BJ.

In a slow but deliberate voice, Carmen responded with a smile, "I promise we will go, but after we eat. I smell something good in the kitchen."

"Goody! And I go first!" Tony reminded BJ.

"I better check on Joe in the kitchen. He probably started digging in," said Vita.

"I'll go. You relax, sweet pea. It's Mother's Day," said Brendan.

"Okay with me, Dad."

Brendan went back into the kitchen and saw that Joe had everything just about set up on the counter. He noticed that Joe hadn't sampled anything yet or at least it was not apparent if he had. "Looks like you have everything under control, Joe," commented Brendan.

"Hey, Dad, do you think the ladies will let us catch some of the Yankee game later? Comes on at four o'clock."

Brendan placed his hand on his son-in-law's shoulder. "I'll see what I can do."

Brendan and Joe returned to the family room. "Joe has got everything set up on the counter, buffet style—so everyone helps themselves. Plates are on the dining room table," announced Brendan.

"Thank you, Joe," said Carmen as she formed her lips in an exaggerated way before getting each syllable out.

Brendan backed up Carmen's wheelchair and wheeled her into the kitchen. "The matriarchs go first. Go on ahead, Nettie," said Brendan.

"Are you implying that I am the elderly queen mother?" Nettie chuckled.

"And, my queen, you tell me what you would like, your majesty," said Brendan to his wife as Nettie handed him a plate for Carmen.

"A little of everything," said Carmen in her hesitant manner of speaking.

"That's my girl!" said Brendan. There was Caesar salad, garlic knots, vodka penne pasta, chicken picatta, manicotti, eggplant parmesan, two loaves of Italian bread, and olives and freshly grated Romano cheese.

Vita made the plates for the twins. It was no surprise that they asked for the same thing—the penne pasta with bread and butter. Seraphina took Carmen's plate from Brendan to place on the dining room table while Joe wheeled Carmen into the dining room. "You get yours, Dad. I'll help Mom onto her chair," said Joe. Carmen had a special thick-cushioned chair at the table that was set up high and had a footrest with the back and arms of the chair fitted so that she would be supported.

"Oh, that floral centerpiece is stunning!" said Vita of the arrangement of spring flowers bursting with color. It sat in the middle of the dining room table, which was covered with a pastel mint green linen tablecloth.

"My Willie sent those for Mother's Day. He thought of his mama even from overseas. Beautiful, aren't they?" said Seraphina proudly.

"Good boy," said Carmen. Also on the table was some nice Italian Chianti that Nettie had brought over.

Once they were all seated, Carmen nodded to Brendan. "Let's say grace. Who would like to say grace?" asked Brendan.

Vita turned her eyes to the twins. "The boys know how to say grace—right guys?"

BJ and Tony looked at each other. BJ shyly said, "I guess so." Vita started and then the boys immediately joined in, saying the whole prayer on their own. "Bless us, oh Lord, for these thy gifts, for which we are about to receive from thy bounty through Christ our Lord. Amen."

"Thank you, BJ and Tony," said Brendan. Carmen blew the boys a kiss.

"That was wonderful!" said Seraphina.

"Beautiful job," said Nettie. The two boys beamed with pride.

They dined and chatted, and Dublin, who was well trained, knew his place, which was not to beg at the table. Dublin was content to lie behind Carmen's chair, just glad to be with his people.

Vita was excited to tell her parents, grandmother, and Seraphina of the surprise she had for them. She waited for the right moment, which was after BJ and Tony left the table. They were itching to get back to their coloring books after they had eaten. "I have a wonderful surprise to share with all of you after," announced Vita as she took hold of Joe's hand. Joe's and Vita's eyes met. Both were smiling.

Carmen raised her eyebrows. "Pregnant?" "Well . . . no. I have a video that we can all watch later. I did not want the boys to hear about me making a big deal of this surprise, and I think you will learn why," said Vita.

"Can you give us a hint?" asked Seraphina.

"Well, if I did that, I think that would blow my surprise. And I want it to be as special as it truly is," said Vita. Joe nodded in agreement.

"I will clean up. It is Mother's Day after all, ladies. So you all go and relax," said Joe.

Brendan went to help Joe, but Joe insisted he had it covered. Brendan guided Carmen back into her other wheelchair—a motorized one. "Who wants to ride with Grandma?" Brendan asked.

Brendan, Carmen, Nettie, Seraphina, the boys, and Dublin gathered in the driveway. Brendan had Dublin on a leash. He had already set out two lawn chairs on the front lawn for Nettie and Seraphina so they could sit and watch and chat. Carmen had maneuvered her motorized wheelchair to the foot of the driveway. Tony was already positioned on Carmen's lap. The cul-de-sac where Brendan and Carmen lived was a perfect place for such wheelchair rides. Vita and BJ walked along one side of Carmen while Brendan with Dublin walked on the other side.

Joe joined the family as the boys were on their fourth excursion with Grandma Carmen. Joe joined his hand with Tony's hand. Vita and Joe, with Tony in the middle, kept pace on one side of Carmen with BJ upon her lap while Brendan with Dublin walked briskly on the other side. The buff-colored golden retriever's tail was in a perpetual wag the whole time.

Afterward, they all gathered again in the family room. Joe had brought the necessary paraphernalia to be able to play the video on the large-screen smart TV. Nettie and Seraphina had enough of relaxation and slipped back into their more comfortable mode of the hospitable hosts. Nettie made the coffee as Seraphina placed the cannolis the Daros had brought on a decorative platter with a round lacey doily. The folding tables were set up so that the dessert could be had while they watched the video. Nettie placed two glasses of milk on the coffee table for BJ and Tony. "Yay—nolis! I love nolis!" exclaimed BJ.

Brendan had managed to get permission to watch the Yankee game later to which Joe gave a thumbs-up. That usually was never an issue. Carmen, Nettie, and even Seraphina actually enjoyed watching Yankee baseball.

Vita stood up in front of the large flat-screen television. "Yesterday, Joe and I attended the graduation ceremony at Princeton University. And I will fill you all in later how that came to be. I think perhaps the best thing is to play the video and the amazing blessing will reveal itself. Enough said." With that, Vita sat next to her mother and took hold of Carmen's hand. "Okay, Joe," said Vita.

The adults were riveted to the television. The trumpet introduction to *Pomp and Circumstance* grabbed the twins' attention. Then came the close-up of the petite young lady with the flowing dark hair and the obvious purplish mark on her face. Vita tightened her grip on her mother's hand and kissed Carmen on the cheek.

BJ asked, "Mommy, is that you?" Even the five-year-old was able to detect the resemblance.

"No, honey. That is not me. She is someone special that we know—a very smart young lady," answered Vita.

"What's that on her face?" asked Tony.

Vita asked Joe to replay that part of the video and to freeze on one of the close-up images of the young woman's face. Vita asked her sons, "What does it look like to you?"

Both boys simultaneously blurted out the same response, "An angel!"

"Yes, it does, doesn't it? Her name is Angelica Henner," said Vita with pride. Nettie pulled up a chair on the other side of Carmen and took hold of her other hand.

Joe clicked on the remote to resume the video. Brendan stood up and stood behind Vita with his hands on her shoulders. She reached up with her right hand to hold her father's hand. Seraphina's eyes filled with tears of joy.

The grown-ups sat enthralled with what was on the large screen. BJ and Tony, no longer interested, were busy with their coloring. Joe fast-forwarded to Angelica receiving her diploma and then to her valedictory speech.

***

The Speech

"You must be the change you wish to see in the world," Mahatma Gandhi.

Good morning to President, Provost, Chancellor, the trustees, dais guests, faculty, parents, families, and, of course, my fellow classmates. My name is Angelica Henner. It is with great honor that I stand before you in representing the 2013 graduating class of Princeton University. We chose Princeton University for a reason. The tradition of having the highest standard in education, with the emphasis on the responsibility toward our fellowman and our planet Earth. We have been afforded excellence in the opportunities and experiences here these past four years to give us the tools to get out into the world and to be the change we wish to see in the world.

Once more—everyone—join with me in "The Locomotive." Here we go:

> Hip hip rah rah rah
> Tiger tiger tiger
> Sis sis sis
> Boom boom boom ah!
> Princeton! Princeton! Princeton!

That feels good, doesn't it?

How can we ever forget as incoming freshman the prerade four years ago—our initiation into Princeton by our upperclassmen. Or our tradition of the Cane Spree. And the bonfire that we had right here on Cannon Green last year when our Tigers beat Harvard and Yale. These are part of our tradition here at Princeton that will be engrained in our memories forever with pride.

As I walked through our campus this past week, I truly realized and perhaps finally appreciated the jewels we are so fortunate to have here: our art museum with over seventy thousand objects from ancient to contemporary art worldwide, our beautiful gothic-style university chapel, our Firestone Library, which is one of Princeton University's many libraries and happens to be one of the largest university libraries in the world. I think of former alumni who have walked these halls: presidents James Madison and Woodrow Wilson, Apollo 12 astronaut Pete Conrad who was the third man to walk on the moon. They are the pride of Princeton University. *We are* the pride of Princeton University. We thank our professors and all the staff in maintaining the valued culture we have here at Princeton. And with our educators help, we have all been committed and diligent in maintaining this Princeton work ethic or we would not be sitting here today. We have had our days of elation and our days of struggles, disappointments and tears, and all the in-between that goes along with life. It's the mountains and the valleys and the plains . . . just the natural terrain we all had to journey through. And Princeton University has equipped us to continue on our journey through the terrain of life as we now enter the next phase of our lives. We thank our families who are here today that have in many cases been our stronghold and our foundation.

So today we celebrate our accomplishments, and it is with a full heart and excitement that we begin the next chapter—a new life outside of Princeton University. Some of us have jobs waiting. Some of us are still exploring opportunities. Some of us are continuing our education, and some of us will join our military to uphold the freedom and honor that our founding fathers fought for. Yes—it is the next adventure if you will. Adventure . . . yes . . . but again, a new expedition and one that I pray we will have the courage to find courage. I have another quote. This from Mark Twain. "Courage is the resistance to fear, mastery of fear—not absence of fear."

Here I would like to interject a very personal story of courage. Please allow me these few moments to tell you about the courage of my parents who adopted me, a high-risk preemie born two and a half months early. Let me tell you there were multiple health issues and concerns, especially the first few years, but my parents gave me their all—their heart and soul. With the love and nurturing, I eventually emerged a healthy child. But now I want to say something that I have kept to myself. I also want to speak of the courage of my birth mother. She became pregnant at age thirteen and gave birth at age fourteen. I am the result of a rape. Yes, my birth mother was thirteen when she was raped by a family member. I stand here before you, a graduate of Princeton University who plans on continuing my studies in neurological science at John Hopkins because this young teenage girl had the courage to give me life. She could have taken the easy way out. Somehow, this amazing human being resisted the fear and mastered the fear . . . so I will always be indebted to this incredible person, my birth mother, for her undeniable courage in bringing forth my life. I will always thank God for her from the very bottom of my heart.

So it is with courage, a very necessary ingredient that I pray we can embrace as we leave the comforts and security of our great university. Let us use the lessons and skills learned here. Let us succeed in using our abilities and creativity to make a difference from macrocosm to microcosm. So much work to be done—yes. Feed the hungry, clothe the poor, peace among the nations and peace between the peoples within each nation, peace in our own communities. We need to work in cleaning up and preserving our planet so that she will sustain the future generations. That is our responsibility. To give back to our planet rather than continuously take from her. Explore new worlds and new dimensions.

And so as we give thanks to God and pray to God to give us the courage to work and try our darndest in meeting the needs of our fellow brothers and sisters and Mother Earth, so as Gandhi said, we may be the change we wish to see in the world! Congratulations and God bless and Godspeed. Thank you.

Epilogue

THE NOONTIME SUN SHONE BRILLIANTLY this first Friday of June in the city of Norwalk, Connecticut. A United States Postal truck pulled up in front of a well-kept cornflower blue Victorian gingerbread-style home with white trim and a white-railed porch. The doorbell rang. Mrs. Henner, who was nearby in the kitchen, answered the door. "Special delivery for a Ms. Angelica Henner. Can you please sign for the parcel, ma'am," requested the woman postal worker.

"Oh yes. Angelica is my daughter. Please wait one minute, and I will get her," said the polite woman.

Within a minute, Angelica, with her long hair pulled back into a ponytail looking as Vita did in her younger years, came to the door. She signed for the parcel and handed the clipboard back as she was handed the package. "Thank you," said Angelica.

The box was a medium-sized express mail USPS box. Inside was another box, a decorative floral cardboard box. Mrs. Henner stood over her daughter. Angelica sat on the couch with the box on her lap. She slowly lifted the lid off and gently peeled back the white-and-lavender tissue paper. Staring up at Angelica was a lavender leather diary with a broken strap and an envelope. Mrs. Henner then sat next to her daughter to get a closer look. Inside the envelope was a picture of Angelica from the commencement, a note, and a picture of a woman in her thirties with long dark hair and blue eyes.

The End

About the Author

MARIANNE KANE (NÉE ALONZO) GREW up in an Italian-American family in Linden, New Jersey, a part of the New York City Metropolitan Area and graduated Douglass College of Rutgers University in 1981. She has worked as a vascular sonographer for over thirty years. Marianne currently resides in the Pocono Mountains of Pennsylvania with her husband, Howard Jenkinson, and their two cats. She is also the proud mom of son, Michael Kane, and daughter-in-law, Jenny, who live nearby. Besides spending time with family and friends, Marianne enjoys reading, traveling, the outdoors, and indulging in an extreme sport or two once in a while.

"As a teenager of the tumultuous seventies, when *Roe v Wade* gave women the legal right to abortion, I was taught in school that the fetus was just a blob of tissue. With the passage of time, I have learned otherwise."

CPSIA information can be obtained
at www.ICGtesting.com
Printed in the USA
BVHW031542180219
540524BV00002B/109/P

9 781640 039629